The Elder Scrolls:

Žaneta's Chronicles

By

A. L. Zuniga

CONTENTS

Žaneta's Chronicles

Part One: Vvardenfell

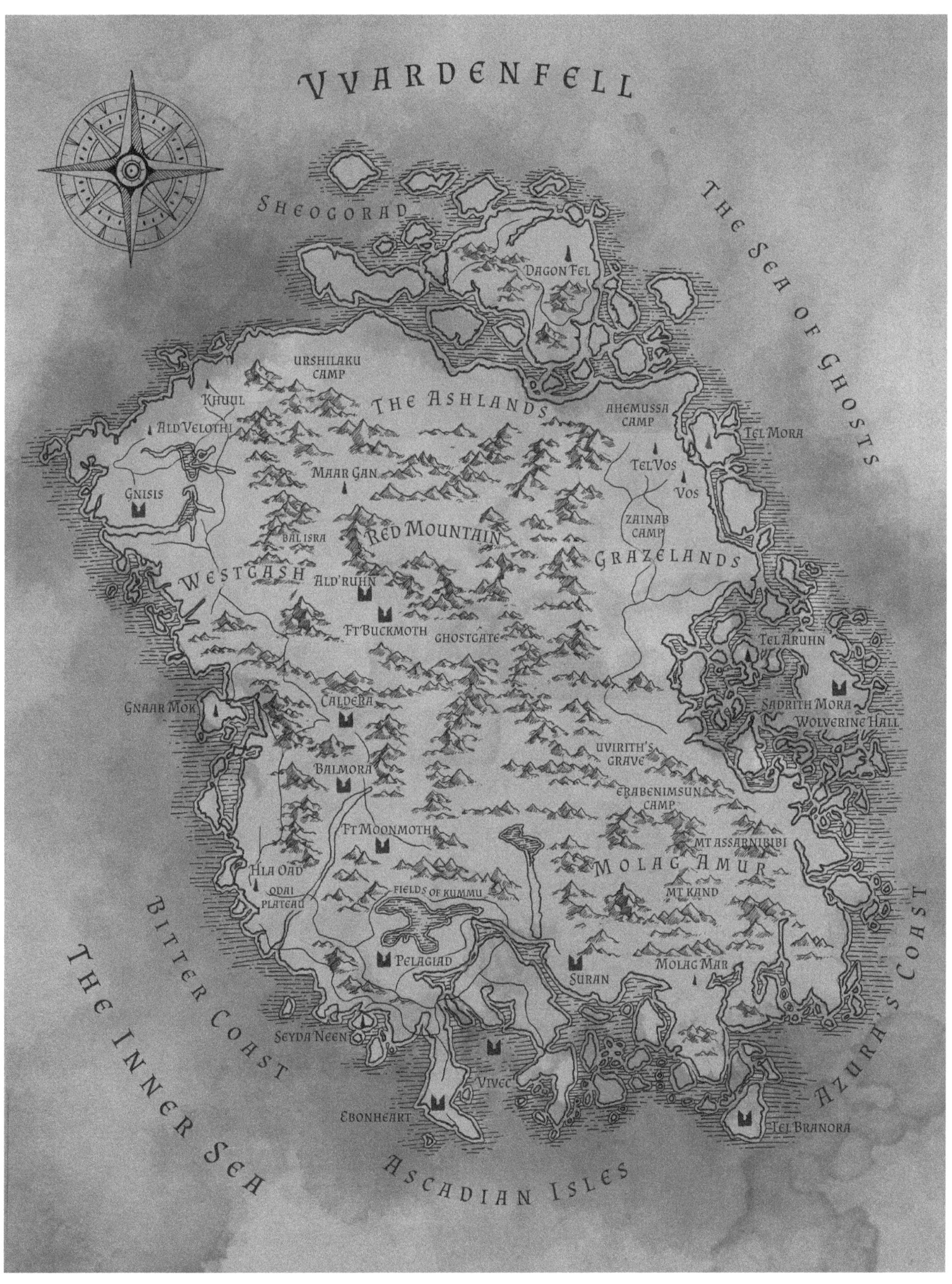
VVARDENFELL
SHEOGORAD
THE SEA OF GHOSTS
DAGON FEL
URSHILAKU CAMP
KHUUL
THE ASHLANDS
AHEMUSSA CAMP
ALD VELOTHI
TEL MORA
GNISIS
MAAR GAN
TEL VOS
VOS
ZAINAB CAMP
BAL ISRA
RED MOUNTAIN
GRAZELANDS
WESTGASH
ALD'RUHN
FT BUCKMOTH
GHOSTGATE
TEL ARUHN
SADRITH MORA
GNAAR MOK
CALDERA
WOLVERINE HALL
UVIRITH'S GRAVE
BALMORA
ERABENIMSUN CAMP
MT ASSARNIBIBI
FT MOONMOTH
MOLAG AMUR
HLA OAD
ODAI PLATEAU
FIELDS OF KUMMU
MT KAND
PELAGIAD
SURAN
MOLAG MAR
BITTER COAST
SEYDA NEEN
AZURA'S COAST
THE INNER SEA
VIVEC
EBONHEART
TEL BRANORA
ASCADIAN ISLES

Chapter One

In late spring of the year 427, in the Third Era, Žaneta Dreyga was working in her forge, hammering the steel as it glowed from the fire's heat. She dunked it in the bucket of water at her side and began sharpening the blade on a grinding wheel. Her brilliant eyes shone in the firelight, as sparks flew where the wheel met metal, before she slid the blade back into the hot coals. She went to two large tubs of water, one on each end of a large carry rod, then, as she placed the rod over her head and onto her shoulders, she lifted the tubs with her extremely powerful legs. Returning to the forge with them, she carefully lowered one side then the other. Continuing her work, hammering and filing, she wiped her brow.

Scale back to the streets and buildings of Balmora, and the location is set. Although she worked in the city as a smith, her homestead lay to the south. At her home, her family was a few miles from town, going about their own days. Her spouse, Sandrew, was chopping wood, while the children sat on the porch and watched their father as the two of them talked and smiled.

Across the vastly different lands of Vvardenfell, unique races carried out their daily traditions and tasks, just as they would any other day. Off the coast, to the west of Balmora, an Argonian—an intelligent race of human-like reptiles—threw his fishing net in a large cast over the water while his young son watched. Happy to have him nearby looking on and proud he showed interest, he placed his hand on the boy's left cheek, giving him a warm smile. Spanning over the center of the island, far over the mountains by the eastern shores, a Dunmer sorcerer was beginning an incantation over the surface of a table to introduce his daughter to the arts. The Dunmer, or Dark Elves, share nearly the same characteristics as humans, only differing in their skin tone—a dark gray ash color—the taller points on the tips of their ears, and their red eyes. Just as he built the energy and signaled his daughter to attempt to cast her spell, a large, thick plume of smoke exploded from the tower window, the sight of which was a common occurrence in the area, where magic was practiced often. The sorcerer stood and waved back and forth, trying to clear the smoke, to find his daughter sitting below the windowsill, coughing and gasping for air as the fog dissipated.

He looked down at her and smiled, extending his hand to help her up as she grabbed for his.

Back in Balmora, hammering the hot blade on her anvil, Žaneta's strong, muscular form was silhouetted against the flames of her forge. Khajiit are magnificent creatures naturally, but even among their race, there are some who possess a beauty that captures the attention of all who meet them—Žaneta was this mold that's spoken of. The human-sized creatures share more in common with cats than they do people. But they, like humans, learn to adapt to their environments, speak different languages, and practice different trades… all while having claws, better hearing, and exceptional sight in the dark.

But her day of work was at an end, and she prepared to head home. She placed another finished blade into the sword rack, removed her apron, and gathered her things for the short journey.

At their cottage, Sandrew had gathered wood for dinner and to warm their home during the cool night to come. Volunteering the children for help, he yelled to them, "Tai! Mazira!"

After a few moments, their youngest, Mazira, poked her head around the edge of the house. "Yes, Daddy?" Her innocence was as captured in the sweet treble of her voice as it was in her appearance.

"Would you and your brother like to help me bring in firewood?" he asked.

But before she could turn around to fetch him, Tai bounded around the side of the house, stepping off the deck behind his sister. "Sure thing, Dad." He swaggered forward, always acting confident and capable of any chore.

These children were quite striking themselves, and Sandrew, a Redguard, was a large, muscular man who stood taller than most people on the island. Redguards (or Yokudan) are dark-skinned humans who hail from the mainland, in the far western province of Hammerfell—an arid country that has a variety of climates, ranging from enormous deserts to beautiful grasslands and mountain ranges. Nearly all Redguards share characteristics common among the race, characteristics that make life in the desert sun and arid region more suitable. His skin tone was dark brown, along with his eyes. His hair was short, thick, and black in color, and he had a thin, dark mustache accenting his upper lip. Despite his large size, he spoke with a commanding calmness, a calmness that masked his unnerving history where, decades ago, he had left Hammerfell in search of a life that showed more promise, away from the fighting and dangers that seemed to be prevalent there, only to trade them for others after finding his way into Elsweyr as a young man. But he'd considered himself blessed above all else. It was those choices that put him in union with Žaneta.

Tai bolstered all the traditional Khajiit traits. He was ashen gray with patterns of black scattered over his body, and he shared his mother's eyes—a mesmerizing, soft gold with a green hue around the center and edges in the right, and a sapphire blue left, both a backdrop to their elliptical pupils.

He was nearly ten years old. Mazira resembled a light-skinned Redguard, but with long, dark hair like her mother's. Side by side, no one would guess Žaneta was her mother if it weren't for those eyes. The five-year-old had the bewitching gaze of both her mom and brother.

Together, the children carried the firewood in, with Sandrew giving the two of them only minor loads, just to give them the chance to be involved. As evening crept closer, the fire popped under the pot of stew that Sandrew was preparing, while he diced up a few remaining carrots. Another fire was going near the living area, where the kids sat on the rug and played—Tai, with his little toy knight, and Mazira, with a doll dressed in the garb of royalty—when suddenly, and expectedly, noise from one particular board on the deck creaked, as it always did when anyone stepped on it.

The family didn't even avoid it anymore as they climbed the step. It was sort of like a knock on the door, announcing that one of the family had returned home. When they heard it, Tai and Mazira gave each other excited glances before turning toward the door, waiting for their mother to come inside.

Žaneta entered, removed her brown, hooded cloak, and hung it on a hook behind the door. Her remaining garb was a green, knee-high, denim fabric that was open on both sides of her legs. It was sewn at the waist up with a tan hide and fabric combination, supported by straps over the shoulders. The satchel she normally wore laid against the rear of her right hip with its thick leather straps resting on her left shoulder. Her ancestry was an obvious influence on her height. Her digitigrade legs were one of the physical features all too common among Khajiit, along with her lower shins and ankles being wrapped in leather bindings with an open toe, providing relief for her paw-like feet.

Žaneta herself was covered in dark brown and tan fur. Starting from her upper chest, though, she was mostly a dark tan with beautiful, white markings on her neck and face. They traced around her eyes and down to the corners of her mouth, with spotted areas on her cheeks and forehead, and one thin, white line that came down the center of her brow to the bridge of her nose.

Though her appearance was elegant, the people of Balmora knew her from the way she towered over anyone she met. Her stature was immense, and most men she passed, no matter the race, had to look up to have a conversation with her. She stood several inches taller than Sandrew, while most Khajiit are usually shorter than humans, depending on the breed. Žaneta's father was a Pahmar-raht, a very powerful breed of Khajiit that are smart and look to be about the same size as a Sabre Cat on two legs. Her mother was a Cathay-raht, also a larger breed, who are often referred to as "jaguar men" and are known for their extremely capable agility.

"Dras'kay," greeted Sandrew, as the children said, "Dras'kay, fado," saying hello to their mother in Ta'agra, her native language. Mazira and Tai ran up to Žaneta and hugged onto her leg and waist. She returned their love then walked to the flowing water trough sink they'd made, which let the water source come through their kitchen from the outside stream.

She washed her hands and dried them with a towel hanging by the oven. Walking by Sandrew, who was stirring dinner, she softly brushed his cheek with her hand then sat at the table. The kids joined her at their places. As it grew dark outside, it was time to eat and then make ready for bed. Tomorrow they could share the day together; Sandrew wouldn't be at his sawmill that day, as the mill needed a new saw blade that Žaneta would forge when she returned to work the day after.

The morning came, noted by songbirds from the nearby creek. Sandrew was already fishing while the others slept in. He was having a moment to himself where his thoughts took him to over ten years ago, back when he and Žaneta were leaving the mainland due to war and the strange events that made rivalries flare, which later became known specifically as "The Warp in the West." The chaos had driven Žaneta's mother and father to insist the two of them try for a life where war was not at their doorstep.

Sandrew was snapped back to consciousness by Tai's, "Good morning, Dad."

Thoughtfully, he replied, "Good morning, son." In the distance, Žaneta and Mazira were standing on the house deck talking, and Sandrew smiled, pleased with what his life had become.

The afternoon came. They packed a picnic, and the whole family sat on a blanket in a field a short way from home, eating bread and salted meat. Mazira and Tai had gotten up and were playing in close proximity to their parents then began giving chase. Taunting his sister, he'd bob and weave whenever she thought she'd make contact with him. Then Tai gave in and let her tag him. The two laughed tirelessly then plopped back down on the blanket and talked back and forth, while Žaneta and Sandrew chuckled and watched. Then the two's conversation went a bit sour, as siblings sometimes do.

"I'll always be faster than you!" Tai smirked.

"Because you're like Mom!" snapped Mazira.

Then Žaneta broke into the conversation. "Don't hold your own attributes over someone else's."

"I have your eyes!" replied Mazira.

"You have your *grandmother's* eyes," Sandrew cut in.

Žaneta nodded. "It's true. We each have our own unique, inherent parts. Vanesci—your grandmother—was a master healer, and that's where you'll excel, Mazira. You, too, Tai… if it doesn't bore you," she finished, as Tai's attention had already been stolen by a distant vvardvark—a small, two-legged animal with tiny front arms, a long tail, and a narrow snout—near the tree line, instead of his mom's words. But he did hear his name and responded, obviously artificially, with, "Sure, Mom!" Žaneta and Sandrew looked at each other in disbelief and smiled.

"Will you teach me?" Mazira asked.

"When you're young is the best time. Your character hasn't been affected by meanness or anger yet," Žaneta replied.

Mazira tilted her head to the side. "What's a 'carrot-ter?'"

Žaneta laughed softly, smiling at her and Tai. "It's how you behave or think through situations. When you're young, your love makes healing magic come easier." She opened her hand, revealing an amber-colored energy coursing from it to form a sphere of healing magic, resembling a small sun suspended above her palm. Both children looked on with excitement, as did Sandrew, who always had a deep appreciation of the art.

"There are many words you will practice, and with mastery and focus, eventually you will need only think them to channel your effort," said Žaneta, closing her hand.

Tai looked between his parents, his face still showing real enthusiasm. "Will you teach me swordplay when we get home?" They both nodded happily.

"Can we race there, Mom?" Tai pressed.

Mazira began to pout. "No fair! I can't keep up with you!"

"I'll carry you, Mazira," Žaneta soothed. "And your brother can carry our things from lunch." She smiled, looking down at Tai.

He just dropped his shoulders and frowned, muttering, "Fine."

Sandrew nodded and said, "I'll see you at home, then."

This wasn't the first time Žaneta had run with the kids in tow, but it was the first time she raced one while carrying the other. They all reached the cobblestone road, and Tai slung the bag over his back with the strap across his chest.

"Hold onto me like that!" Žaneta said to Mazira, looking at Tai. "One arm over my shoulder, the other underneath, and grab your hands so I don't choke."

Mazira hopped onto her mother's back, wrapped her legs around her waist, then positioned herself to get somewhat comfortable, and Tai took off. Žaneta shook her head, smiling, then looked back at Sandrew and gave a wave with her right hand, while supporting Mazira with her left. With that, she started off into a smooth pace, slowly ramping up to catch the little boy ahead.

Tai was in a flat-out sprint, giving it everything he had, which was enough to outrun a grown man, but not enough for his Khajiit mother. Žaneta had already reached his side, but she pretended to fade back a bit, trying to encourage him and make the race a fun confidence builder. She and Mazira both started to giggle loudly, while Tai fought to remain serious.

On the road, there were low, overhanging branches from the trees, which always made the trip home more enchanting from any direction. They also made training this young boy thoroughly exciting.

Žaneta jumped and reached out with her right hand, grabbing onto a branch with the razor-sharp claws she usually kept retracted away. Influenced by this, Tai decided to venture into the trees as well. Žaneta's effort to make it fun had caught on. She swung and released, still holding onto Mazira, and landed into a comfortable running pace, but not fast enough to leave her son behind. He strode from branch to branch then dropped gracefully to the ground before leaping again toward the trees. But with his next jump, he stopped short, landing on his chest on top of the target tree limb. Žaneta had vaulted up to him and pulled his tail, causing his abrupt stop, then crouched next to him on the branch. After ruffling his hair and giving him a wink, she swung down to the ground again—they were home.

Žaneta lowered Mazira to the ground. Tai, still lying chest-down on the branch with his feet dangling in the same position his mother had left him, sulked with his chin resting in one hand.

"Come on down and grab your trainer!" Žaneta called. In a flash, Tai was off like a bolt again, scurrying into the house to grab his wooden sword. "… and mine!" she hollered after him.

Mazira was a bit scruffy from tearing down the path so fast; Žaneta swept back and straightened her daughter's hair and asked, "How was that?"

Mazira giggled. "Amazing! But I think I need a saddle!"

Žaneta, taken by surprise at the response, grinned and laughed a little. "Dear gods."

Tai came blasting out of the house with the two wooden swords. Žaneta and Mazira had walked to some tree trunk seats Sandrew had made for sitting around their fire pit. Mazira, sitting down, said, "I'll just watch… Those sticks hurt!"

Tai handed one of the practice swords to Žaneta. She turned to the small girl, who was eyeing the swords warily. "We'll just be going easy, Mazira—the goal is to not get hit," Žaneta said.

"No way!" Tai challenged. "I'm going to take you down!"

Žaneta gave him a sly grin. "Okay, that sounds nice," she replied sweetly, taking her stance.

They squared off, with Tai holding his sword like a bat and Žaneta relaxed and waiting. He lunged, swinging as if he were chopping down a tree. She sidestepped, redirecting all his energy in the direction of his swing. Then, with a quick swipe, she smacked his butt with the broad side of her wooden sword. His pride was almost as sore as his rear, but they'd always played, and, even then, he couldn't touch her— except now he was trying. He just wanted one tag. He turned around and found his mom smiling. Then, he reset before attacking again, this time slicing across his body toward her. Žaneta leaned to her right, dodging the stroke, as Tai followed through with another tree-chopping swing—this one aimed at her ankle. Žaneta swept her leg up, letting the sword fly underneath it, while she maintained disciplined footing. Missing, Tai spun around and fell to the ground. Žaneta was as balanced as the blades she made in her forge—both were the result of a life of meticulous practice.

Tai grew frustrated, more tired from his overpowered swings than from the run home. "Slow down when you're learning, Tai… You have to learn the moves to a dance before you can perform it," Žaneta encouraged.

As they continued, Sandrew rounded the bend on the path home. He took a seat next to Mazira. "How long have they been at it?" he asked quietly, leaning over to her.

"They just started… but Tai already looks tired!" replied Mazira. Sandrew grinned and nodded.

"Hey Dad, come help me get Mom!" Tai called.

"No thank you, son—she'd put me on my head!" Sandrew laughed.

Tai smirked. "Oh, are you afraid of her?" he teased, daring Sandrew.

"Anyone who knows her like I do, son, definitely is."

With that statement, Tai dropped his arms to his side. Standing there relaxed, he looked at his mom and asked, "How are you so good?"

Žaneta walked over and sat down by Sandrew, wiping her brow. "Your grandpa, Tun'Tarro, was part of the honor guard in Torval; he was also a smith. Traditionally, Khajiit learn everything they can from their parents in Elsweyr."

"That's why you're such a good healer, too!" Mazira proclaimed.

Žaneta smiled at her. "That's right! From my mother. But don't worry, you two… everything we know, we'll teach you in time."

Time moved on, and the afternoon passed. The family was getting ready to prepare dinner and turn in for the evening. Žaneta and the kids sat on the sofa together while Sandrew returned a few items from the picnic to their places. The kids were back to playing with their toys, while Žaneta's thoughts drifted, considering the next day. "Tomorrow I will be finished with the mill saw; we'll just need the cart to take it there," she mentioned, running her fingers through Mazira's hair.

"Outstanding. These last few days with work on hold weren't good for income… even though the family time was nice." Sighed Sandrew. "And you, my children, only have one more day—then it's back to your lessons in town." Both kids grumbled.

"Mom… is it okay if you bring home some of that sweet bread Tofiri makes at the bakery?" asked Mazira.

"I will when I'm done with work, yes," she replied.

Mazira grinned. "Why is she so small? I mean, she's half your size!"

Žaneta raised an eyebrow and joked, "Maybe she doesn't eat her dinner?"

Mazira ignored her and pressed on. "No, really! All the other Khajiit are different from you." The conversation had gained Tai's attention, too.

"Well, my mother was a Cathay-raht, which are naturally larger. My father was a Pahmar-raht, who are—" Žaneta began, right before Sandrew interrupted.

"As big as damn walking Sabre Cats!"

The kids' eyes lit up. "We've only seen sketches of Sabre Cats in class!" Tai blurted, sitting up straighter.

"That's more than some. They like to sneak up on you, but there are none on this island," Sandrew continued.

"Have you ever seen a Sabre Cat, Dad?" Mazira asked.

"Yes… and I love her very much!" Sandrew chuckled, grinning at Žaneta.

Mazira sat motionless with her mouth open, confused by his comment, and Tai wrinkled his nose. "Ah, come on, Dad!" The whole time, Žaneta giggled at their facial expressions.

"All right, now off to bed!" Sandrew said, clapping his hands to speed them along.

Night fell on the woodlands, and the only light in the area glowed from the family's fireplace and table lantern.

***

The next morning came quickly. Žaneta had left for work some time ago, while her family stayed home for the day. But there were no birds singing; it was simply silent, which Sandrew found a bit odd. Tai practiced his fishing a little way from the house, while Mazira sat on the riverbank, just watching.

Sandrew was in the house boiling water to brew a drink as he watched Tai and Mazira from the kitchen windows. Making a cup for himself, he took a sip as he observed Tai's cast, when suddenly, his concentration was interrupted by the creak of that board on the deck. Sandrew turned to look out the window, and what he saw made his heart catch in his chest. On the other side of the glass stood a masked man, suited in leather padded armor, staring back at him.

Time seemed to all but stop.

Shaking off his shock, Sandrew snapped back around to see two men, dressed similarly, creeping up behind the kids. They loosed bolas onto Tai's legs and torso, causing him to fall off the bank into the water. But before the first bolas was thrown, Sandrew had dropped his cup, turned, and was charging to the front door. He reached above the doorframe to unsheathe the sword they kept there then flew outside, only to be greeted by the man standing on the deck.

The marauder stared up at Sandrew and had obviously been expecting the farmer type; facing this burly man, he stepped back a bit. Sandrew had already begun his charge, with the marauder backstepping again, then again, uncertain of how to defend. Before the stranger could even raise his sword, Sandrew had already run him through and was on his way to the children. These people hadn't come to visit with good intentions—that much was apparent. And with the kids in immediate danger… he was in a blind rage.

He rounded the side of the house and saw a horse-drawn prisoner's cage stopped alongside the road, with the men already throwing Tai inside. Another man had scooped up Mazira close to the stream and was making his way to the transport. Sandrew sprinted right by his wood chopping block, where his axe was stuck fast. Placing his sword in his left hand, he tore the axe free and threw it into the back of the man carrying Mazira. They went down, and Sandrew was on them in seconds.

Mazira's feet were bound by the same type of bolas that had been thrown at Tai. Sandrew knelt and quickly started cutting it loose. "Run to town… Get to your mom!" he gasped urgently, helping her to her feet and pushing her in the direction of town. Suddenly, his whole back and right side seared with pain, and he fell to his hands and knees.

He had been hit in his lower right back by an arrow.

Mazira, just feet in front of him, turned to stare at him in disbelief, paralyzed. With his eyes full of tears, he lifted his head, caught her gaze, and screamed, "RUN!" Mazira teared up and choked a little with fear but stumbled her way toward Balmora.

The archer watched the girl head off and, believing Sandrew was down, immediately started in pursuit. Sandrew saw the man come from the tree line to his right onto the path, chasing after Mazira. He mustered his strength, and, pulling the axe out of the back of his first target, he readied it over his head with both hands and threw it into the side of the archer's head and neck, who fell into a lifeless heap by the road.

Sandrew reached down, picked up his sword from the grass, and prepared himself for the two men who had just finished loading Tai.

At this point, outpost guards had been scattered thin from the coastal woods, west of Balmora and to its south, by these marauders, who were seemingly out to kidnap individuals—with children being easy prey. At the same time Sandrew had started fighting against the intruders, a scout had come from the woodland path, yelling as he sprinted up the street into town. He reached two uniformed guards just down from Žaneta's forge, where the commotion had interrupted her work. The scout, out of breath from the run, gasped, "Marauders on the coast and to the south… they're attacking settlements! Patrols are already fighting, but we need help!"

Žaneta's blacksmithing hammer fell to the ground with a loud *clang*, but she was already in full stride before it touched the cobblestone.

Sandrew was engaged in battle with the two men. The pair were obviously clumsy thugs he could've taken without too much effort, but the arrow he'd been hit by had handicapped his movement. One of their group was sprinting with a girl hoisted over his shoulder toward the horse-drawn cage—Mazira. But Sandrew could only focus on the men in front of him.

Back on the path, Žaneta ran, pushing herself with every ounce of strength she had. Her sight was blurry from tears, and her breathing came in sharp gasps from her breakneck pace and the pure terror pulsing through her chest. She approached a scene where three marauders were fighting two guards, one of which lay dead. The other was on his knee with an arrow in his belly, holding himself up with his spear.

The thugs weren't watching for her, and before the archer could call out or do anything to alert them, she tore past the knelt guard, grabbing his spear and lobbing it through the archer in the tree. The two marauders, surprised by her attack, were too slow to react. As the first man reached to unsheathe his sword, Žaneta grabbed his wrist and put her left foot into the bend of his elbow, then out came the razors on her feet. Simply stomping her foot down to the ground, she removed his arm and pulled his sword from its sheath.

She swung the sword into the remaining man's incoming attack. He held a shield and had only one hand on his blade. For this instance, she went against her lessons with Tai, swinging fiercely with both hands; she knew she needed to bat away his attack. When their blades collided, his was knocked from his hand, and her next swing sliced right across his throat, cutting through a yellow fabric sash he wore around his collar.

Žaneta turned to look at the one-armed man, who was on his knees, then came around slicing up… removing his head. The man whose throat had been slashed pressed against the gash with his right hand, trying to stem the blood flow. Not sparing another thought for the two men, she dropped the sword to grab her attacker's shield with both hands, tearing it from his limp body, and was off in a full sprint again, with that whole confrontation costing her only seconds. She was as good with a shield as any blade. In fact, she favored the shield over the terrible iron sword she'd just used.

Sandrew was struggling. The arrow had done its work. Both men rushed him, and in their inexperience, one found the point of Sandrew's blade. The other, though, managed to slip his sword through Sandrew's defenses and stab him in his upper abdomen, just below the ribs. Sandrew collapsed to his knees. The marauder, leaving the blade where it was, made off to catch up with the already leaving prisoner cart.

Žaneta closed in on their home. With only the shield in hand, she approached two more marauders on the path. She jumped and, with the shield in her left hand, spun counterclockwise, bringing it down onto the first one's leg with all she had. His leg was destroyed with a *crack*, still housed by his pant leg but broken into a gruesome shape, twisting awkwardly to the left. Spinning clockwise, she threw the shield at the remaining marauder—who was readying an arrow—like a discus. The shield smashed into him, staggering him, but she'd already taken off toward him as soon as she'd hurled the shield in his direction. She cut his bowstring with her thumbnail, and as he snatched for the blade on his belt, she grabbed his wrist with her right hand, releasing her claws at the same time. With them all embedded in his arm, he screamed. But ignoring his pleas, she sunk her claws into his throat with her free hand, causing him to drop the ruined bow and fumble for his neck, then she reached over his head, pulled a few arrows from his quiver, and ran them up into his ribs.

This fight was over, and never had she thought she'd be fighting so viciously against people—without knowing why. She feared the worst with all that she'd encountered on the road thus far, and the horrifying possibilities waiting gnawed at her. But her family was near, and she knew, within a few moments, she'd be home.

Sandrew was sitting back on his feet, his hands lying still on his legs as he stared at the ground, struggling to breathe. Žaneta, eyes full of tears, fell to her knees beside him. She reached up with her right hand, brushed his cheek, and said, "Ahziss ari," or "My love" in Ta'agra, slipping into her native language. He raised his head and smiled at her as best he could.

"How can you smile?" Žaneta whimpered.

"Because… I was the luckiest man in Tamriel," he whispered. This made Žaneta wince and cry even more. His face swam and blurred before her eyes as the tears came faster; she tried to fight them back. She inhaled a deep breath and started to focus her healing magic, failing the first time due to her raging emotions. She regathered her efforts and began to make a glorious orb. Sandrew reached and gently gripped her right wrist, and the energy dispersed ineffectively but caused a shockwave several yards around them that livened up plant life and flowers in its wake. "It won't work… not with this in me," he said. "And if you pull it out… I'll die quickly."

Žaneta lowered her head in defeat and placed her hand in his. "The children… they left here by carriage. Those men said, 'Get these ones to the B-Briar,'" Sandrew stuttered, then he squeezed her hand and started speaking in her native tongue. "Tell them I love them… I will be waiting for you."

Žaneta laid her head on Sandrew's shoulder and slowly cradled his head against hers. She knew he was dying but refused to let him slip away. Leaning back, she could see the distant stare he wore, only confirming the end was near. Causing him pain—in an effort to save him—she broke the broadhead off the arrow, leaned forward, and pulled it from his back in one abrupt motion. The blood was almost black, and she knew it had hit his liver. With no time to spare, she briefly stood and steadied herself as she held onto the sword's handle. With a quick tear, the sword was out, and she was horrified as she fell back to her knees. Blood spilled from the wounds—the blade had kept him from bleeding out as quickly, she desperately summoned her magic once again.

Straining, she built up the strongest healing fire she could muster—only to find it was too late. A brief moment passed, and as his muscles relaxed, she could see the life leave his body. She stared down right in front of him—not looking at his face—as she continued casting her magic, refusing to stop, knowing he was already gone. With her teeth clenched and tears pouring down her face, she released the breath she'd been holding and let out an agonized cry. Her hands and clothes were drenched in blood, and her soul felt hopelessly lost.

A moment passed. With Sandrew dead, Žaneta stood and looked over at the dead marauder lying on the ground just feet from where she'd sat. He wore the same leather armor as all the others but had the family's sword stuck fast in his chest, driven through him by Sandrew. Her hands started to shake as she looked down at the other sword in her hands, the one that had killed Sandrew. She threw it as hard as she could and screamed, overwhelmed by grief. Then she picked up her husband and carried him into the house, placing him on their bed. She straightened him out, laying him in a peaceful position, and stared down at him. Her face was expressionless… disconnected.

She walked to the kitchen sink and ran water over her hands and forearms to remove the layers of drying blood before returning to their bedroom and heading straight for a trunk they kept in the corner. Removing a few linens and grabbing the gold that was their savings, she reached for the heavy sack at the bottom. It contained her plated forearm bracers, lower leg plates, and a sword her father had made—a beautiful scimitar with a knife stowed in its handle. These items hadn't been touched for the better part of ten years. The armor was hers from long ago—the finest set she'd ever made for herself—while the sword was a gift from her father, made to honor Sandrew and his daughter's courtship. It was inscribed with "Jazrab di Remorgo," or "Edge of Oblivion" in her tongue, a warrior's understanding between Tun'Tarro and Sandrew—*If you take her from me with ill intent, no place is safe.*

Her palms were cold and clammy as she recalled those moments from her youth. Snapping out of it, she stared down at the items on the floor and the clothes she was wearing. She needed something that wasn't marked by the nightmare she was living. She changed into a good clean set of clothes, donned her things, and set about the house looking for anything she might want or need.

In the living room on the sofa, she saw the children's toys—Tai's knight and Mazira's doll. With her grief fading in the face of fury, she grabbed them and shoved them into her satchel then walked back to the bedroom. She sat on the side of the bed and leaned down to kiss Sandrew on his forehead, heartbroken she couldn't even give him a proper burial. They'd crossed Tamriel together, and for them to be torn apart like this made her blood boil. Now, with her children gone, her heart had been stolen—and it was being taken farther and farther away. Knowing he gave his life trying to prevent this, she couldn't linger any longer—

she had to set out after them.

The tears she cried had formed salty trails that had dried on the fine fur of her cheeks. She looked down at Sandrew and brushed his cheek one last time with the back of her hand then stood and walked to the kitchen, picked up the lantern from the table, lit it, and smashed it on the floor. Her intent was to leave the home in ash, as she knew she could never return here after all that had happened and so necromancers wouldn't disturb Sandrew.

If she could find them, the children would never feel safe here again. They would always be reminded of his death here—their home was forever gone from this place. She grabbed her cloak and left the house, slamming the door behind her. She ached for Sandrew, and fear was creeping in, trying to paralyze her. But nothing else mattered—she had to find her children, the only pieces still left of her heart, if it was the last thing she did.

Her house ablaze at her back, she knew, not having passed any horse carriages en route to her home, the group must have headed toward the bitter coast or to the south. With this in mind, she set off. It was late in the afternoon, and she was losing light. Khajiit naturally have great ability to see in little to no light with their unique eyes—this would prove invaluable.

Tracks made off the side of the road by her home gave her a lead to follow—it was all she had to go on.

Chapter Two

*T*he horse-drawn prison cart rumbled along the road, moving quickly in the evening light. At some point, the marauders covered it with a linen tarp to keep its contents from drawing attention. Two of the men rode in the back, tasked with keeping their valuables quiet. Several children taken that day stayed huddled together opposite the marauders in the cage. Tai and Mazira sat next to each other, and Mazira, crying for comfort, pressed closely against him. At that moment, they were all each other had.

Tai listened closely as the wagon slowed; he heard men talking, then the wagon picked up its pace again. He could barely understand anything they said, but the parts he could make out seemed to be some sort of negotiation. After a short distance, he heard waves rolling in, but he still didn't know where they were. The wagon came to a stop, and the two marauders riding with the children stood—one began putting burlap bags on the kids' heads. Tai, being a brave young Khajiit, tried to claw the man approaching with the bag meant for him. But knowing escape wasn't possible with Mazira, he quickly calmed himself when the other marauder raised his fist at him. The bags went on and, one by one, the children were lowered down, hands tied, and led onto a path of wooden planks, like a deck or a dock. Tai could still hear the water, but the sound was much more subtle. However, he knew exactly what was happening when he was led up the slight ramp with notable wooden slats going across it—they were being put on a boat.

***

Žaneta had been running for miles, paying close attention for any breaks in the road. When she left home, she'd noticed wheel tracks from a heavy cart circling around in the dirt from the cobblestone path. The wheels hadn't left a trace on the stone, so she needed to see if there were markings that showed a change in direction, had the cart made contact with dirt in its haste.

Following along the river before reaching the bridge that crossed it to the west, the path diverged and she found her first sign of hope. The path to the right, leading west to the Odai Plateau, showed nothing, but grooves could be seen carved into the outer turn of the road to the left going east, pointing toward more civilization. Žaneta ran and ran, heartbroken from the day's loss, but she never lost sight of the road. Coming across no more clues in the dirt, she kept on her trek. That is, until she came upon a fork in the wide cobblestone street with two choices. Her heart sank. The stone path had turned toward the south, and she stood at a break in the road with a decision to make. Further to the south would take her to Ebonheart, and directly to her left was the city of Vivec.

Already at its doorstep, she decided to enter Vivec. The hour was very late, and she was exhausted. There wasn't a gatehouse to the city, but rather roving guards. She began asking all she came across about any recent carriages or children.

***

Back on board the ship, some of the crew began removing the bags from the children's heads. Handing out bread and cheese, one man—a Dunmer in ragged clothes—hollered, "Eat!" Another passed around a jug of water for the children to share. Slowly, some of the kids rearranged themselves with their friends and siblings. The marauders allowed this. They didn't want to deal with any whining they didn't have to, and the voyage would still take quite some time.

Mazira and Tai found each other and sat down. "What's going on?" Mazira whimpered.

Tai squeezed her hand. "I don't know, but I heard waves, what sounded like the coast, and now we're on this boat. Mom and Dad will come for us," he said.

"Dad got hurt!" cried Mazira, tears running down her cheeks as she leaned into him.

"It's okay, sis… We'll be okay. They'll find us," Tai tried to reassure her, but he couldn't stop the tears from coming either, struggling to believe his own words.

It was early in the morning, still not yet sunrise, but the ship was far from land, and though the children were scared, many began to fall asleep. Tai and Mazira drifted off as well, holding onto each other.

***

The sun rose on Vivec, as the changing of the guard took place. Žaneta had spoken to all she'd seen so far, before the new ones would replace them, and yet… nothing. Not a single guard had seen anything, or some were being paid to stay quiet—she hadn't decided which. But if she was going to make progress, she needed to turn over rocks in the right places.

The new guards were even less helpful than the night guards. Most were tightlipped and near mindless, offering no cares. Finally, one showed a bit of compassion when Žaneta, her eyes wild with desperation, asked, "I'm looking for my children. They were taken yesterday by horse and carriage. I *know* they came at least this far! Who would be helpful that I might speak with?"

After a moment, the guard replied stiffly, "Foreign Quarter—northern-most canton. You're wasting your time here otherwise." Exhausted and growing more and more tired, she headed to the northern part of Vivec.

The cantons that made up the great city were each an enormous floating community—a multi-leveled building over the water, all of which were connected by bridges to make one giant, oddly-arranged collection of homes, merchants, bars, and guilds. The town was highlighted by a unique floating rock—the Ministry of Truth—that hung over the city like the moons over the planet. It was the size of one of the cantons themselves but hovered above them, offering an ominous reminder to the people below. It was once a moonlet that threatened destruction of the city but had been stopped before impact by Vivec himself. Its current use was unknown to her, but she could see scaffolds along one side and a man walking along them. *How did he get up there?* she wondered.

All Žaneta knew about the Ministry of Truth was that it had been stopped by Vivec long ago, when he saved the city that bore his name—the first time she'd seen it had been with Sandrew years ago, when they had arrived on the island. But they didn't worship the Tribunal; they only respected the magic required to hold the rock in limbo.

Once she reached the Foreign Quarter Canton, one of the several buildings built over the water, she started at the Lower Waistworks and began questioning everyone she passed on her way to the Plaza, on the top floor. Her desperate introduction made her come off as awkward at first. "Have you seen any children here recently?" or "My home was attacked, and I'm searching for my kids!" But, "No, sorry!" was becoming all she heard. She tried to walk confidently but felt hopeless. Exhausted and hungry, she ignored her body's pleas and continued her line of questioning to every person she met—spending hours searching for information but learning nothing.

As midday neared, Žaneta stopped at a cantina—the Black Shalk Cornerclub—to get food and talk with the patrons. It was an establishment known to frequent thieves and swindlers… which should prove to be good for gathering information. As soon as she entered, nearly all eyes were on her; her stare flicked to the faces of several individuals as she walked to the bar and sat on a stool, her right foot propped on the ground.

A Dunmer bartender approached her. "What do you want?" he asked rudely, leaning on the counter.

"What do you have to eat?"

"No, I mean… what are *you* doing here, *cat*?" he pressed, raking his eyes over Žaneta's fur-covered hands resting on his bar. Žaneta pulled a few gold coins from her bag, and clinking them together in her hand, she started, "My children were stolen, and my husband murdered… the tracks I could follow came at least this far. Someone who is kidnapping children has help, and I'm not going to stop looking." She leaned closer to him, glaring. "Now… what do you have to eat?"

More interested in her coin than hassling her any further, he said, "I can make you a plate of meats and cheese—we haven't much else. Most come for the drink." He stepped toward the kitchen. A few moments later, he returned with the food, set it down in front of her, and leaned in to whisper, "Ask for Gentleman Stacey in the Plaza."

Žaneta dropped the coins in his hand but knew she was still being watched by the others. She took this break to eat her food and drink some water the bartender had left for her. Turns out, he was more helpful than he was willing to make known around his patrons. Before she stood to leave though, another Dunmer man approached her to talk. "Hello. Excuse me—my name is Graydin, and I heard about your misfortune… I think several did." He looked around the bar. "My niece, Calette, was taken nearly a week ago from Vos. I've found nothing, and I'm afraid if you don't have leads or the skills to learn what's needed, then the trail will go cold, as it has for me," he said.

"I'm sorry—I know what you're feeling. As you've heard, I've just lost mine. How can I help you?" Žaneta replied, calmly turning her attention to him. This entire experience had been like a nightmare she was desperate to wake up from, and she was horrified there were others going through the same thing— most likely, these children had been taken by the same people.

"Just keep watch for her. She's a young Dunmer girl, around eleven years old. Her father, Aryon, asked me to help look for her while he consulted others to seek her out," Graydin explained.

Žaneta nodded. "Calette, was it? I hope this list doesn't keep growing… Please excuse me—I have someone I must speak with." She stood to leave the cantina and walked to the door, passing other patrons with their drinks as they stared at her on the way out.

Usually, the criminals in the cantina were more likely to press newcomers on their business and take their coin. But Žaneta was the largest Khajiit most of them had ever seen, and this left the crowd more inclined to hear what she had to say. With the way talk spread amongst shady individuals, it wouldn't be long before her presence would become known to many in the area.

It was late afternoon as Žaneta entered the large doors leading into the Plaza. Inside, she looked at the tall vaulted ceilings and around at some of the guilds and businesses. She went to an Ordinator—a guard—

and asked, "Where can I find Gentleman Stacey?" He stared up at her through his blank-faced mask and turned toward one of the buildings, nodding his head in its direction.

A couple of fairly well-dressed individuals outside the building were talking when they noticed Žaneta approaching. One left the wall he was leaning against and intercepted her. The Dunmer, about a foot shorter than her, immediately started asking her business.

"Are you Gentleman Stacey?" she asked.

The Dunmer smirked. "New around here… as if you yourself didn't give that away." He gestured up and down, his eyes roving over her appearance. "Name's Crazy-Legs. And you are…?"

"Žaneta," she replied curtly, striding past him toward the building's door. Žaneta entered, followed by Crazy-Legs, who had left his companion behind. "Tell me your business, and I'll pass it on to the Gentleman!" he urged, motioning with his hands for her to stop while he backed up, obviously not wanting to make a scene in the Plaza.

"No. I don't have time for middlemen." She noted the direction of the room he was impeding her progress to and again moved past him. But the room she entered was empty. She spun and looked at Crazy-Legs. "Where is he?"

"What's your business with him?" Crazy-Legs asked stubbornly.

 "South of Balmora—at our home—my children were stolen, my husband murdered… and now I'm here, looking for anyone who may know who's involved," she explained quickly.

Crazy-Legs listened to her plea, knowing she could tear him apart, but she hadn't hurt anyone in the city, as far as he knew. "Look, come to Simine's bookshop downstairs in the Canalworks. Give me a couple of hours, and I'll meet you there," he said.

"Let's go now! Why wait?" Žaneta pressed.

"We can't leave here and go straight there. There is evil that would take advantage of us exposing ourselves. And the next time you go barging into buildings… know where you're going. This is the Mage's Guild, and the guard I saw you talking to was motioning to me… not the building," he said, chuckling a little. Crazy-Legs left the guild ahead of her, and Žaneta stepped out of the building, closing the door behind her. Shaking her head, she thought, *I'm getting sloppy and careless. I need to get some rest.* She was grateful the guild was empty for her intrusion; it saved her the embarrassment.

She stepped outside the Plaza, noting it was getting late, as evening was coming. She took a deep breath and said a short prayer to her Lady Mara, who she had followed since her mother had led her down the path when she was little. As the Goddess of Love, Mara was the foundation of a good heart. Vanesci—Žaneta's mother—shared Mara's words with her as if they were nightly bedtime stories. How her warmth and love is eternal, that none will be forsaken who seek her company. As she walked, one command came to mind: "Preserve the peace and security of home and family." Žaneta knew that everyone leaves this world and to not blame the evil deeds of people on a lack of intervention from the Divines, that trials would always test one's faith; however, her desire to share love—for whomever she found responsible for the tragedies she'd endured—was fading from her list of possibilities.

Leaning on the rail overlooking the land to the north, she stared off into the wilderness, watching as a small herd of Bull Netch glided slowly over the terrain. The large animals looked like something from the sea—with tentacle appendages dangling from their vapor-filled bodies. They were a common sight and were used by the locals for their meat and hide. While she observed them peacefully floating along, she was drifting to sleep just standing there. Knowing this, Žaneta started making her way to the Canalworks.

After briefly searching for this bookstore, she came across a sign that read "Simine Fralinie: Bookseller" and entered. As she walked into the store, she saw the clerk talking to another individual with their back to her. This person, a Dunmer woman—judging by the sound of her voice—wore a hooded cloak and was asking about a specific book called *Progress of Truth*. The clerk shook his head and said, "No, try Jobasha's… I don't have a copy of it." The hooded individual thanked the clerk and turned to the door, revealing very little of herself to Žaneta. As she approached the counter, the clerk raised his head and looked at her, giving her a small smile. He was a short Breton man with brown hair who seemed to be quite at home around his books and the comfort of his shop.

"Hello, I'm Simine. How can I help you?" he asked.

"A Dunmer named Crazy-Legs told me to meet him here. Have you seen him?" Žaneta glanced around at all the shelves then back to him.

"No. But I don't close for a few more hours. You're welcome to wait if you'd like, and please… feel free to read something. And if you like it, please buy it. You can have a seat at the corner table," he said, smiling.

Žaneta cringed at the notion of sitting and waiting, but when she thought about taking a short nap, she reconsidered and took a seat. Seconds after she'd settled, she was out.

***

Hours later, she awoke to the sound of the door being locked. Simine had closed shop for the night with her inside. Still a little groggy, she slowly lifted her head and, staring at him, put her hand on the grip of her sword, uncertain of his intentions. "There, now we can talk. You looked tired, so I let you rest," he said.

Žaneta slowly relaxed. "So… what's next?"

"Would you please follow me?" He kindly gestured toward the back of the store and led the way. In what appeared to be a storage and supply room, there were shelves upon shelves of books and rolled parchment and a locked cabinet in the corner. When he first unlocked it, it looked like a perfectly normal cabinet, complete with stocked shelves. Then he slid the shelves to one side, exposing a hidden doorway.

In the hidden room to the rear waited two people. One was Crazy-Legs, sitting next to a small, well-dressed Redguard man she hadn't met before.

"Good evening. I'm Gentleman Jim Stacey… and you must be Žaneta." Standing up for a proper introduction, he extended his hand to welcome her.

"Yes. Žaneta Dreyga," she replied, taking his hand.

"It's a pleasure, my lady. My associate said he had the honor of meeting you upstairs and told me about your dilemma. You are a rare sight… I'd heard of a great Khajiit smith near Balmora, but rumors come and go around here. I should've paid more attention," Stacey said. Crazy-Legs got up and moved his chair in, then stood next to Stacey for the conversation.

Žaneta gave them a small nod. "Thank you, but I'm after my children and their father's killers," she said, the impatience seeping through her tone.

"Absolutely. You came across some of the men then, correct?" Stacey asked.

"Oh, yes! A few."

"Did they take your belongings, any valuables, or livestock from your home?" he pressed.

"No, nothing like that… just my children. Before my husband died, he told me they said something about taking them to the Briar… does that mean anything to you?" she asked, hoping for just a shred of good news.

"No. Doesn't sound familiar… Crazy?" He looked at Crazy-Legs, who shook his head no. "I'm sorry, that could be anything. A place… a person… a business… but nothing I know of. But, these intruders, did any of them have any markings or similar clothing amongst them?"

"Their leather armor was fairly common. But they all had yellowish tan collars, or sashes, on," she explained.

Stacey and Crazy-Legs exchanged looks, and Žaneta immediately realized they knew something. Her eyes narrowed, and she leaned toward them. "Who are they?" she hissed.

Stacey didn't respond for a moment; eventually, he sighed and met her eyes. "They're the Camonna Tong," he said slowly. "They hate people on the island who aren't Dunmer. Often, their calling card is to remove or enslave all who are of a different lineage."

Žaneta clinched her teeth so hard her jaw ached. She'd heard of disgusting people like this before but had thankfully never encountered them—until now. "Where do I find them?" she asked calmly, composing herself.

"Oh, they're everywhere. They usually only don the yellow sash when they're operating. But most who know about the Camonna Tong know who calls the shots—Orvas Dren."

"Then where do I find Orvas?"

Stacey thought for a moment. "He'd either be with his brother—Duke Vedam Dren of Ebonheart—or on his plantation, north of here. Unless he decides to hold up somewhere; if that's the case, he has several fortifications to lock himself in." Stacey stopped for a moment and met Žaneta's stare. "It's mere chance that you stopped in Vivec to ask around before going to Ebonheart. It may well have been the end of the road for you there."

"Well, I'm sure everyone knows I'm looking now and that the trail leads to Orvas. Thank you for the direction. I'll need to get some things when the stores open in the morning before I leave, but for now, I need to find a place to sleep," Žaneta said.

"It's getting late now. You're welcome to use the bedroll in the corner. I'm sorry—I know it's not much."

"It's perfect," Žaneta replied, giving him an appreciative nod.

Crazy-Legs stepped through the entryway with Stacey behind him, but before they left, Gentleman Stacey turned back and said, "We've been freeing slaves for some time now and have always managed to get by with the small number of people we have. The Camonna Tong don't have rules, Žaneta, and they have resources we can't begin to compete with; their organization is massive." Stacey paused, waiting for her response.

"Well, I *will* get my children back. So what are you telling me?" Her expression turned curious.

"Just that some of the people we have are embedded throughout the slave trade on the island, but it's so bad here at times that it's tough to know if we're making a difference. Please watch for slave drivers who don't wear yellow… they will be the ones *not* coming after you. But you've got quite a road ahead of you, especially if you're after Orvas. If you need anything, just come back here. If we're gone, check for Crazy in the Plaza."

Žaneta nodded and thanked him as they left, just as Simine came around from the front of the store with some water and cheese and placed it on the table.

"Is there anything you'd like?" he asked.

"You all have been more helpful than I could have wished for. Do you have any blank books I can use as a journal? I have a lot of details I need to keep track of."

Simine went back to the front and returned with a blank, brown, leather-bound journal and a small bottle of ink. "No charge. Quills are in the cup on the shelf," he said with a warm smile, pushing the items into her hands.

Žaneta's eyes grew wide. "Nonsense. Either you take the money now, or I'll leave it on the table when I go," she insisted, her hand out, full of more than enough money to pay for the items. Simine hesitated then gave her a polite bow and accepted the payment.

"I'm going to close you in for the night. The bathroom's through there." He motioned to a door in the corner. "I'll give the pantry a knock in the morning when you're okay to exit. If you hear talking… please wait," he instructed.

"I understand," she replied.

With that, he softly slid the shelf closed then shut the cabinet doors on the other side. Žaneta set her things down, sat and ate the cheese before drinking the water, then turned in. She lay there with the lamp still burning, her thoughts spinning out of control. The kids… Sandrew… killing those marauders… the tasks ahead… Calette… and how many others had been taken? She rolled to her side and positioned her arm under her head. Thinking of Sandrew, Tai, and Mazira, tears ran over the bridge of her nose and down her cheek as she remained motionless, staring into the flame of the lamp. She thought about her parents, too, and how much she missed them.

As a child, she'd trained every day in healing magic with her mother. Then there was swordplay, archery, and smithing with her father—expertise she was about to unleash on the Ascadian Isles and wherever else her path led. She thought hard on some of the words her mother had taught her. Some she'd never really used. With all these scattered thoughts, she couldn't stop herself from drifting off to sleep.

Morning came, and with no lit candles or windows in the room, it was pitch black. Once again, Žaneta's natural night vision made this irrelevant; she could see everything. She gathered her things, not knowing what time it was, and lit the oil lamp on the table—after feeding a bit more wick through it to burn—with a spark from the flint next to it. She looked around the room and, on a shelf, found a small bottle of ink with several quills in a jar beside it. So, she sat at the table and wrote down all the events that had happened up to this point, while awaiting her exit knock.

Žaneta wrote for what felt like over an hour. She had written down most of what she'd gone through over the last couple of days—places, people, and her experiences. Anything that could prove useful, should she forget. Reading her own words began to infuriate her. The drive she'd always lived by to love and respect those in her life—people who had never earned any of it—was dwindling, and she began to just want these *faceless* people dead. Then, there was the knock.

Žaneta walked to the false cabinet and leaned close to it, listening for any sounds of people, then after extinguishing the lamp and packing her things, she slid the shelves over to exit. She made her way to the front, waved at Simine, and said, "Farewell," before striding out into the sunshine.

Figuring the best place to outfit for the coming endeavors was upstairs, she headed for the Plaza again, this time to visit the smith there. She approached one of the businesses and met a Redguard sweeping his floor—a man with messy, short, wiry hair—and interrupted his work. "Hello, do you have any looking glasses, and maybe grappling hooks with some rope?"

The smith turned to her and nodded. "Yes. Supplies for your ship?" he asked.

"Not quite, but I am going fishing," Žaneta replied.

"Name's Alusaron. I'll grab some of the things you're after. Have a look around." Walking around to more stock in the back, he came out with a good-sized crate and set it down at her feet. It didn't take her but a glance to see the spyglass she wanted. Small enough to fit in her satchel, it was made of brass and trimmed in brown leather. She opened it to check its clarity then closed it, satisfied. Some of the grappling hooks were nothing special, but there was one set that caught her interest; they folded flat—ideal for her to travel with. After selecting what she liked, she paid and was heading toward the north Plaza doors when she heard a familiar voice call her name.

"Žaneta!" She turned her head to see Crazy-Legs walking toward her. "Would you come with me? I want to show you something I think will help."

Saying nothing, she nodded and followed. He led her inside the building she'd intruded on the day before, but he had an arrangement with the proprietors, so took advantage of the quiet space to talk. They both sat down at a table, and he pulled out a few different locks from a sack he was carrying, placing them in front of her. He started by asking, "Can you pick these?"

She stared at them then up at him, raising her brow and pursing her lips. "No."

"Then let me give you a quick lesson. You can't go making all that noise swinging hammers at locks and doors, now can you?" he said with a smile.

"Okay. What do I do?" she asked, surrendering to her ignorance and paying close attention. She dedicated a good hour to the practice before finally standing.

"Thank you—I think I have the basics," she said.

"Here, take these." Crazy-Legs slid a tension wrench and a handful of lockpicks to her. "You're going to need help, Žaneta. I'll spread word through the right channels to share news of what you're doing," he assured her, giving her a brief smile but with a questioning eyebrow. "And… what *are* you doing, again? You have a plan, right?"

"I've told you—I'm going to find my children… maybe tear down their clubhouse while I'm at it. Why haven't you and your friends gone after these people?"

"Well, I'm not a fighter. Some in our ranks have had some experience with combat, but even they're not warriors. I'm just good at getting in and out of places. Now that you've come into the picture… things are looking up. We haven't been able to fight the Camonna Tong, but you're as intimidating as you are beautiful, and I don't think they know what they've got coming," he said. She fidgeted a little and glanced down at her feet. "Are you okay?" he asked, looking concerned.

"Yes… it's nothing." She fumbled with the picks he'd given her, placing them in her satchel. It was the same old comment she'd always gotten—people were captivated by her, but also afraid. She couldn't help but feel self-conscious every time she heard it. Her natural drive to show compassion, that her mother had always taught her, had always conflicted with her appearance.

Žaneta opened the door, acknowledging Crazy-Legs as he stared up at her from his seat, knowing that he meant well by the comment; yet, she gave him a serious nod to imply farewell. Focusing on the threats to come, she closed the door behind her.

Walking through the atrium of the Plaza to the northern doors, she stopped at a merchant's table to buy food before moving on.

Little did she know, two men, a Dunmer and a large Nord, stood in the shadows, watching her pass. The Dunmer, named Toryn, whispered to his partner, "That's the one!"

The Nord squinted at her then looked back at Toryn. "She looks like a handful."

Toryn scoffed. "I don't care, Sjoring. I'll think of something." They continued to watch her progress as she left the city behind.

Chapter Three

Zaneta set out to the north. Gentleman Stacey had told her the plantation was east of Pelagiad, a city to the northwest, between Vivec and Balmora. She'd have passed the turnoff to it on the night she ran to Vivec, but still, it was not her destination. The plantation had the river on its eastern bank, so she decided to cut over and follow the river north until she found it. After a short time searching, she came to the edge of a tree line to the sight of high walls. There were some individuals in light armor walking the perimeter and casually talking, while she stayed listening, unnoticed.

Žaneta needed to see what was inside, and lucky for her, several of the trees were much higher than the walls. To her left, however, a guard tower sat on the inside of the southwestern wall, making her choice—of moving around to the other side of the compound—an easy one. She started climbing up one of the trees on the north side, and once she was pleased with the viewpoint, she found a good place to perch. Sitting on a branch, she pulled out her new spyglass and started surveying the plantation. What she saw filled her with disgust. She had heard of servants being sold for work as maids or housekeepers, but this was forced hard labor. There were enslaved Khajiits, Argonians, Bretons… the list went on. Several different races, except for Dunmer, were being lashed to work harder. Even while working, they were hindered by the fetters they were forced to wear. She knew this had to be the place, but there were no kids, at least not in sight. She decided she would start in after nightfall.

So, she waited in her tree. As midday approached, she decided to eat some of the things she'd bought from the vendors back in Vivec and pulled a sweetbread muffin from her satchel. It wasn't nearly as good as one of Tofiri's that Mazira had asked for, but it would stop her hunger pains. *And it's much better than tree bark*, she thought.

With the reminder of the request of Tofiri's sweet bread, her mind flooded with thoughts of Tai and Mazira, and she couldn't hold back the tears that began to burn her eyes. Her vision was skewed, which made her more upset. Suddenly, she was immediately focused again as riders appeared on the horizon to the west, moving fast toward the plantation. Angrily wiping her eyes, she looked through the spyglass and noted two men—an Orc and a Dunmer. They were both wearing expensive, heavy armor and tan-yellow neck cloths, but the Orc looked to be more hired muscle than anything else, while the Dunmer appeared callous, with his nose up. She took in what details she could of the pair and watched as they rode into the plantation, as far as the walls and other buildings would let her see. She slapped the spyglass closed and sighed.

Leaning back against the tree, she finished her snack. The breeze was nice, and she decided to just sit and observe the compound… waiting for night to come. The afternoon rolled on, and, far to the east, she could see Silt Striders carrying fares to their destinations. The three-story-tall creatures glided across the land on their six legs, having been used for transport here for longer than she knew. One was headed north, while the other went south. She'd much rather ride those than run all over Vvardenfell. Nevertheless, she looked to the west, inviting the sun on her face, and closed her eyes.

With night coming, the air was cool; a light mist blanketed over the land. Workers lay in their assigned huts, most asleep, but some were still awake from aches due to work and hunger. Many were slowly starving because of the meager rations they received. They couldn't fill up on just hope, even though they had more of that than anything else.

The gates were locked, and all but a few watchmen had already headed to bed some time ago. Žaneta wrapped a cloth around one of the folding grappling hooks and readied it in the spot she'd chosen. Over it went, making a dull thump against the wall on the other side; the cloth wrapped around it aided in preventing most of the bangs and scrapes as she lowered it. Once she felt it go slack, she began dragging it back up—a practice used to hook onto objects below.

She pulled slowly enough to keep the noise down and waited for a snare. Eventually, the rope tightened, and she knew she had hooked onto something solid; she quickly started up the wall. Once to the top, she looked around, but all was quiet. She released tension on the rope to allow the hook to swing loose from whatever she'd snared then pulled it up.

Scanning the compound from her vantage point, she saw the shacks on the plantation were just crudely assembled with planks of wood—poor was an insufficient description. She had no way of knowing who lived in any of them—she assumed slaves but wasn't certain—so she'd have to check each one. Directly down to her right was the large gate the riders had passed through earlier, leading straight up the path between the two rows of shacks that gave way to larger, nicer buildings on the eastern side of the plantation, which boasted importance—there were three. The back of the one closest to her lay just past a row of shacks on the right. Past it was a larger building, a mansion—as far as she could tell—and just to the left of that was another big building, just not as well-lit or ornate. She knew she'd definitely be checking those; if her children were here, they'd be there.

Along the inside of the northern wall was another row of shacks, and to the south—arranged for efficiency—was a garden. Most likely a significant food source for the people here. Just beyond that lay the guard tower she had seen from the south earlier. She could see the plantation in its entirety. She wrapped the hook around one of the corner pillars' top posts and ran the rope over it to secure it before climbing down. When she was a safe distance from the ground, she vaulted off the wall—to clear the object beneath her—and landed quite softly for a Khajiit of her size.

With her feet on the ground, she left the rope flat against the corner of the wall and the slack in a small pile, leaving herself a way out. She could see the object she'd snared. It was a hot box: a metal enclosure used to put people in—as a form of punishment—when they acted out. *Torture* was more like it. In the midday sun, they could reach temperatures that weren't survivable, especially if a person was left for too long. Žaneta's brow lowered in anger, and she couldn't help but notice the chill running down her spine, along with the unfamiliar urge to enforce retribution on these people. Before, she'd felt a tiny bit of guilt for what she was about to do… but she didn't care anymore. Žaneta didn't want the slaves to have to run from anyone that night. So, she was going to shut this place down. First, she would inspect the slave shacks after she tended to the guards.

She could see the two in the tower to her south—an Orc, who looked like he was sleeping, and another Dunmer, who seemed to be reading something. The mist was good, with cloud cover blocking out the starlight, so she hardly needed to make an effort to sneak. Standing at the base of the tower, Žaneta was happy to see the support beams of it were made of wood—something else to quietly climb.

Žaneta was just near the top, right behind the post the Dunmer was leaning against. She moved slowly, looking at the Orc, who was still asleep on his stool across from her. In a flash, she reached from behind the Dunmer and tore out his throat, jumping down in a straight stride toward the Orc, who groggily looked up to see the disturbance. As he raised his head, Žaneta's clawed foot collided with his throat. He smacked against the wall behind him then slid down off his seat to the floor…dead before he touched it.

The tower was quiet. But to maintain the appearance of a guard on watch, she put the Dunmer on a stool and faced him so he was looking out into the wilderness, with his shoulder leaning against the post to prop him up. The Orc had been on a stool but had slouched off and lay drenched in his own blood on the floor, she didn't care to spend the time getting him situated. At first glance, it might've looked like someone was still on guard.

"On to the next ones," she whispered, checking the pouches of her kills for keys—but there was nothing.

Down on the ground again, she decided to be systematic and started by checking the southern row of shacks. Any slaves she found…she would return for. Any slavers she found…she intended to leave there forever. Except for Orvas… they were going to have a little talk.

Žaneta made her way to the southwestern shack and tried the door—no lock.

What luck! she thought. A pleasant start to sneaking into buildings. It was pitch-black inside, but not for her, and this was no slave quarters. Toward the back, through an open door of the bedroom, she saw the foot of a bed and someone under a blanket. She entered the room quietly and spied a sleeping Dunmer woman. Glancing around the room, she noticed a leather cuirass on a chair with one of the sashes draped over the back of it. Žaneta looked back at the Dunmer, her expression cold, drew her sword, and dropped it like a guillotine across the woman's neck. She then wiped her blade on the bed's blanket and began checking the room. On a dresser, she opened a small box with a set of keys inside. *Progress*, she thought triumphantly, stowing them in her satchel.

Žaneta looked out the windows and listened. Nothing. Everyone was still unaware of her presence. She slipped out and moved east to the next living quarters—again, there was no lock. She shook her head. *Apparently, I overestimated them.*

She opened the door, and this time, there was a Dunmer man asleep in his chair with a book on his chest. A lamp on the table put out light but was flickering in its effort to stay lit. He hadn't turned in for the night and instead had fallen asleep in his clothes. And there was that sash—still being worn. It was baffling to her; evil deeds are often committed at random and its victims cry for justice, but here sat evil— literally wearing a yellow flag as his testament to his atrocities—and no one was doing anything. Just like the last, Žaneta's blade found its mark. She blew out the lamp and stepped to the door, creeping it open to look outside before proceeding. Her expression showed nothing except extreme concentration as she focused on the tasks at hand.

She moved toward the *classy* end of the compound, toward those big buildings. Žaneta could see an archer on the northeastern building's flat rooftop but didn't know if he was alone, only noting he held a long bow and slowly paced back and forth in his padded armor and helmet, which came down over the back of his neck. He wasn't watching inside the compound. And why would he? He was supposed to keep people out… like the first two. To the north of that building was another gated entrance and a couple of horse stalls. She hadn't thought it all the way through beforehand, but in that moment, she knew she'd have to kill every slave-driver she could; otherwise, there'd be no way of getting through those gates with the slaves she'd seen—and over the wall would be out of the question.

The next house to the east—somewhat larger than the rest—was directly in view of the building beyond it with the archer on top. She thought she'd start with the building south of the next house instead, as it was poorly lit outside, making it easier to gain entry. From the wall, she'd been able to see the back of the building, but from the front, this one was different… more warehouse than anything.

Inside, a very familiar aroma filled her nose, smelling like rich buttercream icing and honey. Sack upon sack of moon sugar lay piled on top of each other, probably tons of it. By itself, it's perfectly legal. In fact, using it as a cooking ingredient was very common; however, in high amounts—especially this quantity—it can be refined into the drug she'd also seen plenty of. Bottles of Skooma—it looked like they'd been making it here for some time. It would put you into a euphoric state with just a tiny amount on your skin. But used in a large amount, on the skin and inhaled, it could render a person unconscious, or lethargic and delusional for days. Along with that, she found racks of weapons, small chests—containing gems—and shelves loaded with food, jewelry, and clothing. Obviously, this building was full of valuables that were the lifeblood of the business, but she wasn't there for trinkets.

Outside of the surplus building, Žaneta stayed near the southern wall, moving around the back of— what looked to be—the main plantation house, probably where she'd find Orvas. But first, she needed to take care of the lookout and check the interior of the building he stood on.

She could see the target building. But from the angle where she stood, she couldn't see the archer on top of it. Instead of making all that noise climbing a building, she decided to simply go in the front door. But before she did, she looked back at the surplus building with an idea. A few moments passed while she went back to get a couple of bottles from the warehouse. Once she retrieved what she was looking for, she went to enter the building, but it was locked.

You've got to be kidding me! She set the bottles down and stood at the entryway—in the light from its hanging lantern—but didn't fret. She took a knee and pulled out a few of Crazy's lockpicks and the tension wrench then started at it. Softly applying torque on the wrench with the tip of her left index finger while holding the picks—like she would to write with a quill—she tapped and slid them along the tops of the pins inside the lock. Then *snap*, the pick broke off. Immediately concerned, she gasped, but was relieved to see its edge protruding from the keyhole. She backed out the tension wrench—dislodging the piece of broken lockpick—and started over. Taking extra care to feel the sensations of the tiny parts moving under her fingertips while trying not to overpower the delicate tools, the pressure finally released and the cam began turning. It was amazing, the thrill she got from the tiny, yet extremely significant task. Successful, she scooped up the bottles and entered.

There were lamps on in the entryway that Žaneta softly extinguished. She quietly continued down the hallway, and what she found made her excited but nervous—a room full of guards, sound asleep in their bunks. She couldn't believe her luck. She wasn't scared of the men— she just knew she would need to be extremely quiet in order to avoid waking any of them as she picked them off. And she still had rooms to search.

Opening one of the bottles of Skooma—being careful not to get any on herself or breathe it in too much—she began pouring a small amount on the pillow of each guard. *I'll just give that a few minutes*, she thought, as she leaned against a wall, placing the cork back in the bottle.

Well, their time was up. The drug should have set in, and they'd be harder to stir than a pub-crawler. Eight more lay dead in their beds, and she hadn't broken a sweat yet. So, on she went to the other side of the guardhouse, this time to a room with five in it, but six beds. She knew where the sixth was… on the roof, keeping an eye out. She repeated the process again then snuck upstairs; everything was going perfectly.

The next level seemed laid out more for upper management, with much better lighting and a more *costly* appearance, along with only two inhabitants. Two Dunmer men shared a room, but like everyone else, they were asleep. Žaneta scanned the upstairs and found them in a large room asleep on her left, but against the wall straight across from her, she saw a cage with a young girl trapped inside. The sight made her heart pound at first, but it wasn't Mazira; it was a small Dunmer girl wearing a tan fabric shirt and pants, with black shoulder-length hair—cut short on the left side of her head and swept over to the right. She had to think this through. Back in the hallway, she passed a ladder that led up to a ceiling panel, which had to be the roof access for the guard. Good—she knew where he'd be coming from.

She decided to finish off the rest of the Skooma on the two men here, so she emptied what she had left and slowly went over to the young girl. She was sitting upright with her head resting on her arms and knees, when Žaneta lightly tapped on the bars as she knelt in front of her. The girl raised her head, surprised at first, but quiet. "We'll be leaving soon. But could you do me a favor? I need you to cover your eyes… Can you do that?" she whispered. The young girl looked confused then nodded—slowly understanding what was about to happen—before burying her head back into her arms and knees.

Žaneta turned and looked at the two men, lying in beds opposite each other, then positioned herself in between them and readied herself for the first one, just like the others. She took care of the first easily, but the other one sat up in bed, jolted awake by the noise. Žaneta, likewise surprised that he wasn't drugged, spun and came around swinging at his head with her sword. He saw her coming and threw himself back in bed, as her blade sailed right over top of him, into the bed's headboard.

He reached under his pillow to grab his dagger, but Žaneta's blade was already on its way down, pinning him to the bed; as her sword pierced his chest, he let out a strangled scream before falling back on his pillow, dead. The noise was enough to alert the guard on the roof, who sounded an alert with a burst from his bugle. Žaneta tore her sword from the bed and readied herself by the door. Lights began turning on in the buildings she hadn't visited yet, and scurrying steps on the roof told her the guard was on his way down. The ceiling panel flew open in the hallway, and after a couple of seconds, Žaneta heard the sound of boots jumping down and racing toward her. Timing it for when the footsteps reached the doorway, she swung her sword…slicing the guard in half. It wasn't a man—it was a Dunmer woman. But the outcome was the same.

The young Dunmer girl in the cage looked up in terror. She was paralyzed with fear at the sight of what had happened. Žaneta looked at the girl with pity—unable to do anything to console her—and said, "I'll be right back for you!" as she quickly moved up the ladder to get a view from the roof.

Just as she climbed up, she heard the sound of something hitting the plantation gate to the north. She turned and saw the same Orc from that afternoon slamming a warhammer into the gate, busting it open, with the Dunmer riding through as the Orc climbed back onto his horse and followed. It had to have been Orvas Dren, but she could do nothing to catch them. Then, activity caught her eye near the shacks she'd visited earlier. She saw four Dunmer sprinting around with lamps—three women and a man. But only one had on a yellow sash: the female Dunmer that left the house directly west from her.

Not hiding anymore, Žaneta jumped down into the light of the buildings' lanterns to confront her, but as she approached, allowing her a chance to look upon her death, a sword tore through the woman's back and out her chest. The Dunmer man removed it, and as she fell to the ground, he raised his hands, shouting, "Friendly!"

The other two women came sprinting into view and looked on in shock at the dead Dunmer woman then up to Žaneta and the man. "Unchain the slaves and grab what you can. We have to leave very soon!" one of them said to her group. "Here!" Žaneta replied, throwing her the set of keys she'd claimed earlier. The woman caught them, stared at them for a moment with wide eyes, then nodded to Žaneta. She and the other woman raced to the slaves' quarters and got to work.

The Dunmer man slowly walked toward Žaneta. He'd already sheathed his sword and continued to show his hands. "My name's Suvryn. Me and the others have been here a while, but what are you doing here? Who else is with you?" he asked. Her gift of the plantation's keys seemed to have reassured him, but he still narrowed his eyes with suspicion as he searched her face.

"It's just me." Žaneta sheathed her sword. Daylight was starting to peep over the horizon.

"We've got to get you out of here… Guards had to have heard the warning!" he urged.

"Not yet! I've got to get the girl!" she called over her shoulder, already hurrying back toward the barracks.

"Hold on! That's the guardhouse," Suvryn said, lowering his voice.

"They're all dead," she replied calmly, as she walked in the front door with Suvryn on her heels.

"What? By the nine…" he muttered, lighting the halls to see where he was going. "Who in Oblivion are you?" He could only stare at her in disbelief as they climbed the stairs to the room at the far end.

She turned to look at him. "My name is Žaneta. Now, let's get this girl out of the cell!"

They reached the second floor, and she started patting the bodies of the two Dunmer for a key. But instead, she looked up and found it sitting on the desk—in plain sight—for all to see. She opened the girl's cage and looked back at Suvryn, who was going through a footlocker full of gold and jewels that belonged to the recently deceased.

"What are you doing?" she hissed, as he poured all he could into a couple of pillowcases.

"Funding the fight!" he replied.

Žaneta refocused on the girl. "Hello… are you okay? I'm sorry this happened to you, but I'm here to take you home. My name's Žaneta," she said softly with tears in her eyes, reaching out a hand. "We have to go."

The girl looked up at her and slowly offered her hand. Žaneta gently helped her out and picked her up, making her way to the exit. She and the girl, followed by Suvryn, left the guardhouse. At the same time, the two Dunmer women were leaving the surplus house with the freed slaves and all the valuables they could manage carrying after arming themselves with swords and food. They all gathered in the open area between the guardhouse, the warehouse, and Dren's house.

Žaneta looked at Suvryn and said, "Burn these down," motioning toward the buildings around them. "But leave that one… I need to look inside," she added, staring at Dren's place. Without batting an eye, he set his loot bags down and ran into the buildings—each time using one of the several oil lamps that were lighting the area.

The women approached Žaneta and looked at the girl but said nothing to either of them. They just whispered to each other, obviously wondering what they were going to do next. One of them wore an extravagant blue shirt with tan trim and an expensive pair of shoes. The other—a younger woman—was wearing a chitin cuirass with Netch leather greaves, gloves, and boots.

"Excuse me, will you stay with her? I need to check something," Žaneta said to the women. She set the girl down and drew her sword, walking into Dren's house.

Inside, she called out, "Tai! Mazira!" then waited and listened in the eerie silence. Nothing. She stomped through the home, quickly looking through every room she came across. Then she found a door that was locked on the lower floor. *No time for lockpicking!* Žaneta kicked it in, but it was empty. She slowly began to realize the horrible truth—they weren't here. She was back to square one. Since the group outside was waiting, she decided not to waste anymore time. On her way out, she smashed all the lanterns and set fire to every tapestry she passed then stepped out to join the others. For the moment, she tried not to think of Tai and Mazira, where they could be… She had to focus. A few moments later, Suvryn rejoined the group, and Žaneta called out, "Are we ready?" They looked around at each other and nodded, then all set off across the river and south to Vivec.

Dren's plantation was visible for miles as it glowed in the distance behind them. It gave off a trail of smoke that would draw attention the next morning from farther than the fire alone was capable of reaching. The group looked back occasionally, relieved to see an end to that place.

Žaneta and the others continued through the hills to Vivec as they dried off after crossing the river, with Žaneta giving the young Dunmer girl a ride on her back. She opened conversation with her, worried about the child and what she'd gone through.

"I'm sorry for all of that back there… I tried everything I could to make it as quick as possible, as well as quiet. I even drugged them."

"The Ienith brothers? Those two used drugs a lot; I watched them," she trembled out, her eyes wide.

"Probably why it didn't work on them," Žaneta said thoughtfully.

"Yeah, they'd mess with Skooma then say how much they were going to get from my ransom, while throwing food at me in that cage," she proclaimed, slowly opening up.

Žaneta paused for a moment, unsure of what to say. "How long had you been there?" she asked.

"I dunno. Several days, maybe a week or two?"

"What's your name?"

"Calette," she replied.

Žaneta stopped. She lowered the girl to the ground slowly then crouched down in front of her. "Are you from Vos?" she asked.

"Yes, but—" Calette started, but Žaneta interrupted her.

"Your uncle is in Vivec. He said you went missing about a week ago," she shared, smiling.

"Uncle Graydin?" the girl asked excitedly. "I knew my family was close—I could just feel it! But I was… they hadn't come for me." Calette looked down, trying to hold back tears.

Suvryn suddenly approached, interrupting their conversation. "What's the word?"

Žaneta looked up at him then back at Calette. "I met this one's uncle in Vivec when I was searching for my family."

The two Dunmer women walked up, still followed by the newly-freed slaves. One of the ladies asked, "Who are you looking for?"

"My children, taken nearly three days ago."

The women glanced at each other, and the one in the blue shirt replied, gesturing to Calette, "I'm sorry, the only child brought to the plantation was her!" Žaneta avoided their eyes. What they said only confirmed what she already knew, but that didn't make hearing it any easier. Looking around at the thin, wan faces of the slaves, she tried to convince herself this journey hadn't been a waste of time. She done a great thing by freeing these poor people… but her heart felt shattered and exhausted. She just wanted to find her children. The woman spoke again, breaking into her thoughts.

"I'm Guldrise, and this is Ivrosa. You've already met Suvryn. We've cared for the slaves while under the guise of slave drivers, but we couldn't reveal ourselves. Now being the only ones left alive from the plantation, accompanied by Dren's prior property, we'll all be marked. We have to leave Vvardenfell… Dren's informants are everywhere."

Žaneta nodded. "Where would Orvas have gone?"

"Well, we don't even know what direction he left in!" Ivrosa said.

Žaneta lifted her head. "North. I saw him."

"Then after he left, he probably went east, to Suran. It's a friendly place to those in the slave trade, especially if you have coin," Suvryn pointed out.

Žaneta looked between the three of them, becoming serious. "Who are you? Why work against him?"

"We're with the Thieves Guild. Several people have been looking for family members for years. They'd pay whatever they could to get any details that may help find their loved ones. So, Jim Stacey started to organize an effort. There are several of us scattered all over, spying on the slave trade operation from within," Guldrise said.

"Well, I'm glad I didn't kill you. Anyone wearing that yellow sash around their neck lost their head," Žaneta said grimly.

"When a fight breaks out, we've been informed to 'forget them!'" Ivrosa said, smiling mischievously.

"I'm sure! I met your man Stacey back in the city… He's who put me onto Orvas."

Žaneta felt a tug on her fingers. "Hey, Žaneta." She looked down at Calette's small face. "Can we eat something?" The girl had a hand on her stomach, stopping the conversation.

The freed slaves had already begun going through their loot bags and eating some of the food, once the others had stopped to talk. One slave, an Argonian, came up with some rolls from his bag and gave them to Calette.

"Here you go! My name's Neet," he said with a small smile.

The other slaves slowly approached as well. Two Khajiit women stood behind Ivrosa, staring up at Žaneta. One tentatively spoke up. "Madam Ivrosa, what are we going to do now?"

"We need to get as far away from here as we can, 'til no one is asking about our ties to this place," replied Ivrosa, patting her on the shoulder. "Do you have a plan?" Ivrosa asked Žaneta.

"I didn't plan on leading slaves to freedom. I just want to find my children and kill those responsible. No one else need ever go through this," Žaneta admitted. "But with the gold we just took, you said you should leave Vvardenfell… so let's get you to the mainland…"

"I lost my son. I don't know if he's in Vvardenfell, or…" the Argonian man cut in, his face falling. "They put me to work, too, and none of us could escape!" He motioned to the other slaves.

"Your boy? How long ago was this?" Žaneta asked with concern, narrowing her gaze.

"A year? I don't know exactly…"

"What's his name?" she asked kindly.

"Xuzu," he replied, his eyes welling with tears, looking for a sign of hope from hers. But she didn't know how to reply, except only to offer her efforts in her search.

"I will keep watch for him. I won't let this happen to another child. I'll find Orvas, but first I'm going to take this girl back to her family. Let's keep moving—none of you are safe on the island," said Žaneta.

Chapter Four

The group had traveled a good distance, and, for the slaves, the cool morning air on their first day as free individuals—who also had money to start anew—felt invigorating. Dawn was coming. With the light unveiling the land, they could see the city of Vivec a short distance away, with the Inner Sea at its back and the—unmistakable—Ministry of Truth above it.

"I'll take you straight to the docks and see to it that we find you a ride to the mainland. Unless any of you need to stay in Vivec?" Žaneta asked, looking around. No one spoke up, so she turned to Calette and said, "You and I are going to find your uncle." She looked down at the little girl warmly, who was still stuffing rolls in her mouth bits at a time. "And we'll get you something more to eat while we're at it." Žaneta grinned at her.

The sun was up as the group walked through the city to the docks. As they neared, the sound of ship bells grew louder. "Maybe I should negotiate passage," Guldrise said to Žaneta before they reached the ships. "If these fishermen and sailors are asked about passage to the mainland by me, while being followed by slaves, there's nothing out of the ordinary."

Žaneta shook her hand. "Then I suppose this is where we part, but I'll stay around to make sure you get on."

"No need," Suvryn cut in. "With the coin we have, we're all about to be the richest unfortunates to walk off a plantation." He gave her a big smile. "It's been an honor meeting you, Žaneta. If helping slaves and fighting the Camonna Tong are in your interest, the 'Twin Lamps' have been at it for some time—it's the little name we've given the effort. Oh, and here…" He handed Žaneta two small bags—about the size of her fist—filled with gold and jewels. "Give one to Stacey… the other is for your journey." He smiled, placing his right hand on her shoulder, then turned and walked down the ramp to the docks. Ivrosa nodded thankfully and followed Suvryn, with some of the slaves behind her.

Guldrise stayed standing with her while the others left. "If you're going after Orvas, you'll need to get to him, and him alone. His supply of paid men will never run out. His brother, the duke, is likely not involved with Orvas's abductions; he can't risk being seen with his hand in the pot. So that's why Orvas gets a free pass on many things. He keeps a ledger on him to know what's going on and where… He must sleep with the damn thing. Find that, and I'm sure it'll help you find your kids. Tell Jim I said, 'Hello and goodbye.'" With one last grateful smile, she continued down the ramp to join the others.

Žaneta looked down at Calette. "Let's go see Graydin. I know he'll be excited, to say the least." She gave the group a parting look before turning and heading to the Foreign Quarter.

Walking to the canton, some of the wrong eyes were already watching them. Žaneta knew of the risks, but sneaking around wasn't her intention. Instead, she preferred her presence be known, since she didn't exactly blend in anyway. Once at the Foreign Quarter, they went by the cantina, but Graydin wasn't there. "We'll have to check again in a little while. Let's go see some friends of mine, and we'll come back," Žaneta said, turning with Calette to leave.

They worked their way up to the Plaza, and as expected, there was Crazy-Legs. "Hello, Crazy, I've got some news," Žaneta started, surprising him, "I need to meet with Stacey, but first… I've got to take this little one to her uncle."

He gaped at her with a grin, shaking his head. "You really are something. I'll fetch the Gentleman and be at the usual. I'd say stay safe, but maybe I should pray for the other people," he said, causing her to chuckle softly.

"I'll see you in a couple hours." Žaneta and Calette chose to depart through another exit instead of leaving with Crazy-Legs, but they walked in plain view of Toryn.

They left the Plaza, and Toryn stormed into the Fighter's Guild to find Sjoring. "This has to end… now!" Toryn growled, as he slammed his hand on the table where Sjoring sat.

Sjoring looked up at Toryn, waiting for him to explain. "That Khajiit just walked through the Plaza with the Telvanni girl Orvas had. Scouts said they've seen smoke coming from his plantation, and we haven't heard from him here. His brother is going to have us all on the headsman's block if we do nothing!" he yelled.

Sjoring shushed him, "Quiet down… and tell me what you want to do."

"We need to kill her! Or was I not making that obvious enough?" Toryn snapped.

"I meant how do you plan on doing that?" Sjoring asked calmly, ignoring his tone.

"She's been asking around about her children, most likely taken by one of Dren's recent raiding parties, but I don't know where they are. However, I'll approach her with the hope of information. Somewhere public, and when you're ready, you hold onto her, and I'll do the rest." Toryn pulled out his dagger for Sjoring to see.

"Did I ever tell you my mountain lion story?" Sjoring asked.

Toryn sighed, trying not to roll his eyes. "You've told everyone that story. Shot it with your bow, then you had to fight it off before it finally died," he finished sarcastically.

"That's right. I stuck a hundred-and-sixty-pound cat with an arrow then had to fight it off with my sword before it—finally—died. And now you want me to grab this cat from hell—I can only assume, if she burned down Dren's place—and hold onto her? She looked like she was at least four hundred pounds, and probably a hell of a lot smarter than that damn mountain lion!" Sjoring replied, shaking his head and exhaling a long sigh.

"Look, we own you… just as they own me. I'll see to it you're paid well enough from this that you can retire. We both may, when it's all said and done!" Toryn said.

"If either of us live!" Sjoring snarled. He knew the Camonna Tong would kill him for not cooperating—they'd controlled the Fighter's Guild there by keeping him, the guild's leader, under their thumb. "Just say when and where so we can be done already," he complied, grimacing as though he'd just been punched in the stomach.

"I knew you'd see it my way. Follow me… I just saw them head outside, and my people have told me the girl has family loitering around the cantina downstairs. That has to be who they're meeting," Toryn said in a hurry, slapping his dagger back into its sheath as he spun around to the door.

"Well, may the gods help us then if we're going to rush into this," Sjoring muttered, looking dumbfounded. They left the guild and started downstairs.

Ahead of them, Žaneta and Calette were already entering the Black Shalk Cornerclub. "Uncle Graydin!" Calette exclaimed loudly, surprising everyone in the place, including her uncle, who was looking over notes at a table. He jumped and spun around, wide-eyed.

"Calette!" he shouted joyfully. "Thank the gods!" He picked her up and kissed her on both cheeks, hugging her tight.

He caught sight of Žaneta closing the cantina door behind her as she looked on. "I can't tell you how indebted we are to you," he said.

Žaneta shook her head. "I was after mine and found yours—you owe me nothing," she replied simply.

"All the more reason you deserve our help."

"I just need to find my children. So, the only thing I'm after is Orvas Dren. I think he may be near Suran, but I'm not sure," she told him.

Graydin thought about it for a second. "My grandmother and family may be able to help, but we'll need to get you to Tel Mora."

"Who's your grandmother?"

"Dratha Telvanni. Not only did you return her great-granddaughter, but you're also a woman. She's, umm… made it a point to share her distrust of men. Aside from me, because I'm her own, she has only women working in Tel Mora. But she may be able to shine some light on where to look for Orvas, and maybe—hopefully—your children," Graydin explained. "Please, have a seat. At least let me buy you lunch."

"That would be very much appreciated. From here… I wasn't sure where to look next, except for Suran. Having some kind of known direction would be better than wandering around." She nodded gratefully then looked at Calette. "But for lunch, yes. Calette deserves more than I, but we're both hungry," she replied.

"After we eat, I'll take care of the tab, then we'll be on our way," he said, gesturing to the table he'd just stood up from.

Lunch came and went, and they talked a little during the meal. But being tirelessly pressed for time, Žaneta asked, "Can we get going soon?"

Graydin, forgetful in his own happiness with Calette's return, realized she must be in dire stress, needing to get on with her search again. "Forgive me. I'm going to go to the bathroom, then we can leave. Calette, do you need to go before we head out?" He turned to the girl.

"No, I'll sit with Žaneta," she replied.

Graydin excused himself and went around the far corner of the bar, where the bathrooms were. Several customers had come and gone during lunch, and some had been there drinking most of the morning. But no sooner had Graydin gotten around the corner, a Dunmer man approached their table. He wore a dark blue shirt with a leather belt around his midsection, and a dagger hung just on his left. His long, dark hair was swept back, and his red eyes had a look of prejudice about them. "May I sit?" he asked.

Žaneta looked up at him warily. "We are about to leave," she said, turning her attention to him. The man leaned closer, looking around cautiously before inching nearer to whisper, "I have information about your kids, but I'd like to keep from announcing it if possible. May I please sit?" he insisted.

Žaneta's eyes narrowed, and she glanced around the tavern. "Please do," she replied, as he pulled up a chair to join them. "What do you know?" Žaneta asked, concern lining her face.

The Dunmer leaned in and said, "I know they were taken for the slave market, but there's something I wasn't quite expecting." Žaneta was hanging on to every word. "I didn't expect for a parent to be so successful in gumming up the works!" His hand flashed to his dagger under the table just as Žaneta was grabbed from behind by a second attacker. As his arms wrapped around her, Sjoring pushed his weight against her, trying to keep her in her seat. Calette let out a scream, frozen where she sat just to the left of

Žaneta. Toryn, directly across from her, drew his dagger.

Sjoring had been correct in his apprehensions. Žaneta pressed up and back, unintentionally turning the table over in the moment and causing Calette to fall backward, remaining uninjured. She reared up for a kick then slammed both feet into Toryn's chest, sending him flying back and smashing into the bar behind him. The whole cantina was watching, and Graydin had come rushing back after hearing the outburst.

Žaneta reached up and into the forearms of her attacker, all claws in both arms, prying his hold loose. Sjoring let out an agonized plea and released her. "Yield! I yield!"

Freed from his grasp, she picked up the dagger Toryn had dropped and drove it through Sjoring's leg. "Don't run off," she hissed.

Sjoring let out another yelp and fell to his rear, whimpering, as Žaneta walked over to Toryn who, upon inspection, appeared to be choking on blood he was coughing up. She had broken so many ribs on his left side that several must've punctured his lung. Every breath he took suffocated him more and more—Žaneta knew he was dead.

She then turned around to Sjoring and knelt in front of him. "Why'd you do this? Who sent you?" she breathed, strangely calm and deadly serious in the face of the attack.

Sjoring, sweating profusely from the pain, looked up at her as he winced. "That man on the floor behind you offered m-more than I could turn down," he gasped.

Žaneta tilted her head to look at him and asked, "Did he pay you?"

Sjoring shook his head. "No. Not yet."

"Seems like most people who obligate others without a deposit often never expect to have to pay their debts," she said, giving him a hard stare.

"My leg's done in, and I can't feel my hands… I don't think I'll be able to pay for much of anything from here on." He began to shiver.

"My husband was murdered, and my children were stolen. I will find them and leave your employer just like your friend over there. But… I'm not going to kill you," Žaneta finished coldly, tearing the blade from his leg and stabbing it into the floor beside her.

The bar was quiet, aside from the bellows of pain coming from Sjoring. Žaneta concentrated hard and brought her hands close together. Drawing energy, she channeled her healing light and watched as it started closing Sjoring's wounds. But she stopped just short of the injuries healing completely, leaving scars on his arms and leg. The cantina was completely silent. Every person who had watched her lay waste to the two men saw the magnificence she was also capable of.

Žaneta looked at him like a disappointed parent does a misbehaving child, then finished with, "Do better." She stood and looked down at him while he stared at his arms in disbelief.

Graydin and Calette gawked at the scene with wide eyes then met Žaneta's stare. "Let's go," she said. Calette opened the door with Žaneta behind her, as Graydin quickly dropped money on the bar counter.

Walking to the outer doors of the Waistworks, Graydin was full of questions. "That… that… I've never seen anything like that! That Nord I've seen around and thought he looked to be a tough one, but…" he stuttered.

Žaneta abruptly stopped in the hallway and looked to her side, with her hand raised—signaling him to be quiet. "Please stop. I didn't enjoy any of that. I embarrassed him and healed him. Hopefully, he'll choose other avenues for income from now on," she replied as she continued walking.

Graydin scoffed. "I doubt it. Hired muscle doesn't know how to do regular work. But I'm sure he, and all the others, are going to be spreading the word about you."

"Great," she said sarcastically. "Notoriety just brings challengers."

They stopped on the balcony to look at the land, deciding on the fastest route. "Let's take a Strider! They don't go all the way to Vos or Tel Mora, but one should be able to get us close to the Grazelands," Graydin suggested.

"Please! Oh, I'd love to ride back home on one!" Calette said happily.

"Would a boat be faster?" Žaneta asked.

"Yes, by a little, and the boat would take us straight to Vos. But on a Silt, we'll go right by Suran, maybe get you a good view, if that's where you'll be headed. Problem is the boat doesn't leave except for mornings, noon, and evenings. We'd have to wait. Silts go when they're paid," Graydin replied.

She weighed both options and wasn't interested in loitering around the city waiting for a boat. "All right, where's the nearest Strider then?"

"Just up ahead. They're how I came into town." He motioned in that direction.

Žaneta nodded. "I'll meet you there then."

"Wait, where are you going?" he asked, surprised.

"I've got to meet someone first, then I'll join you. Don't worry—I'll be fast."

Graydin nodded, and Calette stared at her, slightly worried. The uncle and niece took each other's hand and proceeded to the Silt Strider, with Calette looking back over her shoulder.

Žaneta headed down to Simine's bookstore. When she got there, Simine was reading at the counter and didn't even look up from his book. "Good day, my lady," he said, gesturing to the back with his thumb. Žaneta walked to the cabinet, which was already unlocked, and proceeded through the hidden door. Gentleman Stacey was sitting at the table and smiled when she entered. "I'll be damned. I've heard and seen what you've done. That damn plantation is still smoking!" he said, laughing a little.

"There were friends of yours there, but don't worry, they survived. But Orvas got away. Suvryn and the others thought he may be headed to Suran," Žaneta replied.

"Well, I'm glad you're okay. Where are the others?" he pressed, concerned.

"They're on a ship to the mainland. Guldrise asked me to tell you, 'Hello and goodbye.' She, Ivrosa, and Suvryn, along with a handful of slaves we freed, left to avoid being targeted. Apparently, Orvas's thugs already got wind of something because I was just attacked at the Black Shalk. The girl I brought back was pretty valuable to them, I guess," she explained.

"Crazy said you had a girl with you. What's her name?"

"Calette Telvanni."

Stacey almost choked, staring at her in shock. "Oh gods, Žaneta! They're a powerful family—be careful," he said.

Žaneta furrowed her brow and waved her hand. "Of course. But I need to be on my way. I'm going with them to Vos or Tel Mora to her great-grandmother's, where, hopefully, I can find out where I need to go next."

Pausing, Žaneta remembered what she'd accomplished so far was because of Stacey, and she slowed herself to properly offer appreciation. "I wanted to thank you for your help thus far. No one offered anything, except for you and your friends. Please… keep me in the know if you hear of a gray Khajiit boy or young Redguard girl, with eyes like mine. Tai and Mazira are their names," she said, setting one of the bags of gold and jewels on the table before walking to the door. "That's from Suvryn."

Stacey looked at it but didn't touch it, only keeping his focus on her. "If I learn anything, I'll make sure you hear about it," he replied, nodding. He waved farewell, and she headed back outside to the Strider.

Graydin and Calette were standing at the corner of the boarding station, looking over some snacks they'd bought from vendors. Graydin saw Žaneta approaching and asked, "All set?"

She gave Calette a half smile and nodded to Graydin. With that, they all went up the stairs and climbed aboard their chariot to the northeast.

***

The ride was a long one, but much, much shorter than it would have been on foot. About a half hour into the trip, Calette was questioning Žaneta about her magic. "That was great back there! I've seen healers, but they usually take hours, or even days—you had him mended in seconds! My dad teaches me how to use fire, but I haven't gotten the hang of it yet," Calette spouted out, probably still hyper from the snacks.

"Your dad? Why are we going to her great-grandmother?" Žaneta asked, looking at Graydin.

"She'll be under the watch of the area's senior—in this case, Dratha—while she undergoes her formal sorceress training. But we will be stopping in Tel Vos to see her dad, Aryon. He'll be overjoyed to see your return." He smiled down at Calette.

"What was pressing enough to keep him from coming after her himself?" Žaneta probed.

"The Houses are in turmoil. Aryon is high in the council for Telvanni. If anything happened to him, or if he left in the midst of all the unrest, then it might have meant fighting between the Houses and families," Graydin explained.

"So, he asked you to come in his stead? I give you merits. Nothing could hold me back from my family," Žaneta replied.

"So we've seen!" Graydin grinned.

Žaneta gave him a small smile. "What other families make up these Houses?"

"Well, you already know Telvanni. Then there are Dres, Hlaalu, Indoril, and Redoran. Only Redoran, Hlaalu, and my family have any real vested interests in Vvardenfell. You've been here a while—surely you've heard the names before?" Graydin asked, sort of surprised.

"They're familiar. The Hlaalu had a good presence in Balmora where I worked, and I've seen some of the Telvanni towers—how they're grown instead of built. But my family has always made a real effort to not be involved in things. The island had only been open to outsiders for a few years when my husband and I moved here. Some of the natives weren't as… *hospitable* as others." She grimaced. "Still, we ignored the bias. Seems though, now, it's been forced on us by the Camonna Tong." She sat back to stretch her legs as she leaned against her side of the Silt's hollowed-out shell with Calette.

Directly across from them, Graydin got a little more comfortable as well and responded, "My brother and I have broken away from our family's ways a little. Most in House Telvanni have dedicated years to the art of magic. Hate is an understatement for outsiders, and many in my family believe that power gives them right…so much so that they'd sell out their own," he explained.

"Maybe a break from all that made this a welcomed endeavor then!" She raised an eyebrow.

"To some degree, but as I said, the Houses aren't always a pleasant gathering in general, and isolation doesn't make a person good at conversation. As far as the other families, House Redoran is an honorable group of warfighters. Their values and traditions leave them… unwilling to change. To me, it looks like they're going to be left behind in way of progress." He shook his head. "And that's where House Hlaalu comes in." He bristled in disapproval, bringing his eyes back up to hers. "They are, by all appearances, directly in line with Imperial influence. They've welcomed the Empire's policies and money into every aspect they control, saying they're about 'peace and equal value for all races.' But they lie! The Hlaalu have been known to provide the Camonna Tong with the ability to operate all over the island, because their crimes are often dismissed as coincidence or hearsay. Most of us think they're just one in the same but can't prove a direct connection. This makes them very dangerous." He finished.

Žaneta, with her mouth slightly pursed, listened in silence. These were people she'd been around for years, unaware of what they'd been the cause of. *They can't all be this terrible!* she thought. As Graydin had said, he and his brother had left their family's ways, in some regard. *But how can I tell the difference between the Camonna Tong and a good member of the Hlaalu—if one exists?* She didn't think she could.

"Although I've no love for the Empire, they should know they have an enemy beside them, poised to slit their throat. You should know that Orvas Dren and his brother, Duke Vedam, both belong to House Hlaalu; however, Orvas doesn't hold any official place with them. His brother is more in line with Imperial practices, and Orvas hates him for it… but that's no secret," Graydin explained.

Žaneta's eyes narrowed as she sucked in a sharp breath. "Then all this makes sense, Graydin! If Calette was taken in a hard time between the Houses, and I found her at Dren's plantation… by getting her father to come after her or, at the very least, keeping him busy looking for her, Orvas could have murdered him or caused problems for his own brother in Ebonheart!" Žaneta leaned forward on her knees.

"Then… you think this was a failed attempt to start a war between the Houses?" he asked slowly, his eyes growing wide.

"Yes. But not thinking about Orvas's intentions, I'd consider finding out who was around when she was taken. It would seem that with all the Houses not getting along, you've got people with close ties who could be doing bad things while no one's paying attention." Žaneta glanced at Calette, and Graydin considered his niece, agreeing she had to have been a victim of this sick political power game. But he became distracted by the landscape; he looked to the southeast, over her shoulder, and said, "There… that's Suran."

Žaneta turned and looked at the good-sized city, observing the buildings and their layout. "If he's there, you'll have a mess of guards and a labyrinth of halls to get through to find him. But let's find out if he's in the city first," Graydin suggested.

Žaneta stared at the buildings and market areas, making plans in her head for if she were to try to enter. But, listening to Graydin, she knew not to get her mind too set on planning a visit. Yet, her desire to have a destination frustrated her. She just had to calm down and have patience. She turned back around and let out a sigh. If he was in there, she knew she'd have to observe the area for some time before proceeding. *Focus on the task at hand*, she thought, knowing she needed to return Calette to her father, hopefully getting help with Dren's location in the process.

"Do you want to see my fire spells?" Calette asked, anxiously waiting for a yes. "Nothing dangerous, just some visual art that helps me practice," she elaborated quickly.

Žaneta welcomed the distraction and nodded with a smile. "Molag alda'hirad!" Calette said firmly, with her hand held in a specific position. With all fingers separated and pointing toward her Uncle Graydin, she spun her wrist, bringing her fingers and thumb together pointing up. A small double helix left her fingertips, glowing reddish-orange, then smouldered and went out when it was about a foot from her hand.

"Good job!" Žaneta said happily, clapping.

"It's okay… Dad was teaching me to hold my hand differently. He says, 'The words are part of it; the rest is in the presentation,' whatever that means!" Calette sighed, shrugging.

"You'll get it. I think I was still very small when my mother started with me. She strove to teach me the magic arts soon after I started talking," Žaneta said, letting out a quiet yawn, which made Calette follow suit.

"You two must be tired, I'm sure. Why don't you rest? I'll wake you if there's anything important," Graydin assured them. Calette and Žaneta didn't disagree. Leaning back, the two of them got comfortable and fell asleep fairly easily under the shade from the awning, even with the afternoon sun over top of them.

***

A couple of hours passed, and the Strider was gliding smoothly over the mountainous terrain of ash and volcanic vents. They were in the uplands, moving toward Azura's Coast, where further east, the territory was claimed by House Telvanni. A number of small islands and coastal towns marked the area, including Tel Mora, Tel Aruhn, Sadrith Mora, Tel Fyr, and Tel Branora—all home to the magically-grown Telvanni Towers. However, these places were farther east than they'd be traveling.

Žaneta stirred and squinted at her surroundings, shielding her eyes from the midafternoon sun. "Where are we?"

"At the southern edge of the Grazelands. Ahead, we'll disembark on some of the rocky outcrops before we reach the lowlands… I made arrangements with the driver to take us this far. From there, we'll head straight north on foot, and we should reach Tel Vos this evening," Graydin told her, reaching over to give Calette a gentle pat. "Calette… time to get up. We're about to get off. Come on," he said, shaking her softly.

The Silt Strider was steered next to the best location available for them to disembark; once they arrived, they all stepped down onto the rocks of the canyon and thanked the driver. Žaneta looked south at the Ashlands and turned to the north, viewing the completely different Grazelands, which were much more inviting with their lush green fields. They started down the rocks and began their way north. Only a few minutes into the walk, however, all of them were thinking about eating. "Do you want me to hunt for something, or do we still have things in the bag?" Žaneta asked.

Graydin reached in, remembering there were several oat wafers he had rolled in paper. "Here we are! We can keep moving until dinner in Tel Vos." They each took a share, and, satisfied, continued on their way.

After about an hour on the trail, Calette broke the silence with, "I wish we had horses—we'd be there already!"

"Getting there faster would be nice… but we'll have to make the most of it." Graydin grunted as they topped a hill. "We saved a good day's travel just being on the Silt. On foot, we wouldn't even be to Suran yet."

Žaneta smiled at both of them encouragingly. "We'll all get there together—no worries."

"STOP!" Graydin suddenly whispered loudly.

An Ogrim had come down out of the mountains to the food-rich Grazelands, which happened more often than not due to the lower populations of people in the area. The group knelt close to the edge of the path where the grass was taller, making for better cover.

"He's eating Hackle-lo plants. They love the stuff. But set it on fire, and they'll nearly kill themselves trying to put it out!" Calette whispered nervously.

"Well, it's right in our way, and if it sees us, I'm sure we'd look way more appetizing than those leaves," Graydin breathed.

Žaneta watched cautiously; she'd seen one before, near old ruins years ago, but changing directions then was an option—one they didn't have anymore. "Fire, you say? Can you be ready to run? If I get close and set one of these on fire, I can lure it away," she said.

Graydin nodded slowly. "That should work, but where there's one here, there may be many more on the road up ahead."

"Then go slowly and wait for me to return. Or should I just kill it?"

"No, don't kill it. A dead Ogrim would draw out Clannfear and Daedroth for days to eat off of. Better lead it away and not spoil the road for other travelers, or yourself coming back, if this be the way," Graydin instructed.

"I'll be right back then," she said in a relaxed voice, as the others looked on anxiously. Žaneta knew there was no chance the Ogrim would catch her. She was just going to keep it close enough, with the "flaming carrot" dangling in front of it to keep its interest. Žaneta pulled off a large piece of a Hackle-lo plant and crouched down in the tall grass. Moving closer and closer, she crept around the creature to avoid the breeze giving her away. She wanted to be just the right distance before she stood up and set her shrub on fire, while also being careful not to start a blaze in the whole field. With the piece of bush in her left hand, she stood and whispered, "Maliat Molag," igniting it with her right. It was a small fire spell that literally meant "Soft Fire" in Dunmer—one she'd used to keep her fires going at the forge.

The Ogrim, who was tearing out Hackle-lo plants and devouring them, was oblivious to her, but its head snapped in her direction at the odor and sight of the burning plant. Its eyes dilated, and it belched out a roar, immediately starting in pursuit of her. Although this house-sized creature was a frightening sight, as it clumsily rushed after her, it was as if a toddler were chasing a grown adult—the monster had nothing compared to her agility. Ogrim look like they are part horned gorilla and part troll, walking upright on legs shorter than their arms. Regardless, she led her chaser away, causing dull tremors in the ground with its immense weight as it followed.

Žaneta led the Ogrim nearly half a mile, looking back constantly to see the distance Graydin and Calette had made, before tossing her plant into a growth of other shrubs. She ran to the side, and just as she was foretold the beast would do, it lumbered over to the smoking pile and stepped all over it, pulling some of the plants out and eating them in the process.

Žaneta took off in a full sprint back to the other two. Once she reached them, they continued at a pace more suitable after Žaneta picked up Calette and stayed at a jog next to Graydin.

Chapter Five

Hundreds of miles away, a ship full of frightened children was moving up the River Thirr. Wildlife could be heard on the banks, and the waters were calm. But the sun was sinking low in the sky, and the men on deck had cooked fish and prepared baskets of fruit to be taken below.

A Dunmer man opened the floor panel, letting light into the cargo hold. All the children in view looked up. One little boy scrambled forth, trying to climb up in desperation, but was stopped and pushed back by the foot of the man. The Dunmer continued down the stairs with a basket of fruit, followed by a Breton with a basket of fish, while a third followed behind them. This last man was an Imperial; he had stubble on his face, dark hair, and dark eyes, and was dressed in a tunic overlaid by a muscle cuirass, with a fancy-looking sagum resting on his shoulders. He stood at the staircase entrance, while the two other men handed out food. He waited for his eyes to adjust to the darkness, scanning far to the back of the hold—as best he could—to ensure he had the attention of all his captives. "Your home is gone. I will take care of you until I find you your next one. For now, eat and rest. Hard times lie ahead!" the man proclaimed. With his message hanging in the air, he turned and went back up the stairs.

A Nord man with a beard came down with a pitcher of water and a ladle to give drinks. As hungry as all the children were, none offered rebuttal—all they could do was sit and eat.

All were scared, though, wondering where they were… where they were going. Most of them huddled in small groups for comfort. Dust would drift down from between the cracks of the deck boards as the crew above walked around. These cracks were also the cargo hold's only source of light when the panel was shut.

As nightfall approached, the men returned to the stairs with their empty baskets and pitchers, handing them up to someone above deck, who in return handed them blankets to be shared amongst the children. The men then went above deck, watched the whole time by a boy at the stern of the ship with his sister, who could both see easily in the low light. Tai peered angrily at the exit, but the two of them sat quietly and ate their food as the panel closed.

***

Back in Vvardenfell, Žaneta, Calette, and Graydin had reached Tel Vos. Žaneta placed Calette down, and she quickly scampered in the direction of her father's tower, yelling, "Follow me… this way!" Graydin followed close behind, while Žaneta, who walked with them, looked around at the structures and buildings. They shared many characteristics of traditional Telvanni and, oddly, Imperial-style castles and buildings. She'd never been around this mixed architecture before and found it intriguing. They all reached the door to the tower, and Graydin pulled out his key, unlocking it, and they entered.

"Dad!" Calette shouted, entering the empty entryway to the main room. They heard a chair scrape across the floor of the next room—Aryon was at the table having dinner and stood, shoving his chair behind him. He rounded the corner in a panic, but relief flooded his face when he saw Calette. "Julikal!" he cried, which meant "daughter" in the Dunmer language.

Aryon and Calette met in the middle of the room and held each other tightly. "Hello, Aryon," said Graydin, striding forward.

"Welcome back, brother." Aryon grasped his hand. The Dunmer sorcerer stood tall. He wore a brown long-sleeve shirt with the cuffs rolled up. His pants—tucked into his brown leather boots—matched the color of his top, and he had a red cloth shoulder cowl draped over his chest. His black and gray hair was cut short on the sides of his head, with medium length hair on top that was naturally swept up. He had a distinguished look about him with his sharp beard and mustache. "And who do I owe the pleasure of meeting?" he asked Graydin, looking over his shoulder at Žaneta, who stood by the entryway.

"This is who we have to thank for everything. She's seen us through to safety at least three times in the last two days," Graydin said, as she approached.

Aryon hugged Calette close to his side and looked at Žaneta as she stared down at them. "I'm grateful beyond measure for your help. I will compensate you with all that I can."

"Thank you, but I don't want money," Žaneta replied, tilting her head in greeting.

Slightly confused by this, Aryon gestured to the dining room. "Please, let's all eat, if you'd like. Then we can discuss how I may be of help."

"That sounds great—we're hungry!" Graydin declared.

The group found themselves empty seats as Aryon went to the kitchen and prepared some more things for his guests. He told his houseman, "Put one of our Nix-Hounds in the oven. Calette has returned home, and we should celebrate! Oh… and some wine, please."

He grabbed a basket of bread and returned to the table. "I've got a meal cooking, but try these to hold you over," Aryon offered, as his houseman came from the kitchen with a tray of cups and a jug of table wine. He set the table then went back to the kitchen for a pitcher of water. Aryon poured Žaneta and Graydin a cup, asking her, "So, tell me what happened… and what you need." He smiled as he filled his own cup then sat and listened.

Žaneta explained the last few days in detail. How, in searching for her family, she'd come across Calette but lost Dren. Time was of the utmost importance—where were her children? Or at least, where was Orvas?

Dinner came out of the kitchen steaming, causing a break in the conversation with its welcomed aroma. "Okay. I understand everything thus far, and I myself have been lost… up until you brought Calette through that door. I have to object with your plan on seeing our grandmother though!" Aryon stated, checking for Graydin's response, but he just waited for his explanation along with the other two. "She has been increasingly lost in her ways. And though she's a master in the Telvanni House council, her hostility toward outsiders, and even family who think differently, is getting worse. I worry you'd run around aimlessly, and for too long, if you went to her. You explained, in some detail, how you're working against time, so I will call for a meeting in the morning with some of the council. Tai and Mazira, was it?" Aryon clarified, looking up at Žaneta. "We will cast for clairvoyance to get answers. But for tonight… let's eat and rest."

Žaneta nodded, feeling as though he understood her stress. She stared down at the food in front of her but was lost in deep thought. Eating was something Žaneta had increasing difficulty with; her stomach turned with guilt as she wondered what her children were eating, while she had a feast in front of her. She sat a moment and stared at it. Aryon reached and put a hand on the table in her direction. "I know," he said softly, acknowledging that he understood the look she wore and how lost she was—he'd gone through it himself. Her eyes had misted up. She broke out of her trance then began eating at a faster-than-normal pace to mask her emotions until she could get ahold of them.

Once they'd all finished dinner, Calette was very tired, yawning in her chair. "We've got a big day ahead of us, so let's turn in. I'll carry this one upstairs…" Aryon said, picking up his daughter, "and I'll show you to a room." He smiled at Žaneta. "Graydin, you're more than welcome to stay here if you'd like. Unless you miss your own bed."

"I think I will walk home; it's the same distance as me walking to a room here," Graydin joked. "I'll talk with you tomorrow. Good night.”

Žaneta stood, told Graydin good night, and followed Aryon to the strange platform at the rear of the main room. She glanced around, and seeing no stairs, she looked at Aryon curiously.

“You've never used one of these before?” She shook her head no, and he continued, “I'll take us up.” Holding Calette with one arm, he used his other hand to generate a blue energy that made an odd aura flow from it; this began lifting the three of them up a shaft to his study room floor. The platform contained the energy; he just knew the magic to turn it on and off. In the study, books and charts filled the room. He led her through it to a hall with a couple of doors on each side and into one of the bedrooms that sat prepared for guests. “Here you are. This is usually for family or other House members. There's a wash basin and towel in the corner, with gowns in the armoire. I'll see you in the morning. Good night!”

“Thank you! Good night,” Žaneta replied. She set her things down and sat in a chair by a small table with an oil lamp on it, already lit. Across from her was the armoire, so she decided to investigate. As she was told, there hung night gowns and bath robes. She pulled out the largest one available for her height—a dark gray bath robe—and changed out of her clothes, folded and placed them on the chair she'd been sitting in, turned the lamp down, and got into bed. She prayed to Mara, asking for guidance and protection over Tai and Mazira. After lying there for only a few minutes more, she finally passed out.

***

The sun was rising, and its light woke Žaneta. She sat up and stretched her arms then glanced at the chair—her clothes were gone. Her blade stayed leaning against the wall to her side, where she'd left it. Tossing the blanket off of her legs to one side, she stood up and decided to go in search of her things.

Stepping out into the hall, she met a cleaning lady carrying a basket full of linens out of the room adjacent to hers. “Hello,” Žaneta said, gaining her attention, “do you know where I may find my clothes?”

The Dunmer woman smiled and said, “Yes, my lady. I took them down to be washed earlier. I will return with them shortly.”

Žaneta nodded and proceeded down the hall to the study room she'd passed through last night. She looked over several volumes of history books, notes on incantations, and spell tomes. As she opened one of the books, a dull blue light emanating from the shaft caught her attention. Using the levitation magic she'd seen last night, Aryon came down from the next floor and found her looking over his collection. “Does anything interest you?” he asked casually.

“I don't know what I don't know. There's so much here—I'd have to read for a week before I had questions to ask,” she murmured, running her hands over one of the books.

"I'm a master in the art of Destruction; however, I don't like the term, since I'm not out to destroy. But that is what fire has a tendency to do," he said.

"I only dabble in flame, but I'm extremely versed in healing." She looked up from the reading material to Aryon.

"Yes. Calette told me of your ability. I haven't seen anything like what she described ever achieved by our healers," he admitted, "but if you'd like, I could share some powerful manipulations of fire with you. I only offer because you're so capable of healing magic. Fire and healing would complement each other quite well," he said with an excited gleam in his eye. "Of course, after your things have been returned to you." He gestured to the robe she was wearing.

Žaneta looked down at her garb then back up to him. "Yes, that would be best," she replied, chuckling at the idea of her *magical* bath robe. It just went below her knees, but at least it covered her.

"I'll go down and get them. In the meantime, look over this book…" he said, scanning the shelf for what he wanted. "Here, this one. *Piercing Fire*. I'll go over the words and presentation when I return." He placed the old tome in front of her on the desk and left her to look it over.

She sat at the table and read. Some of the text relayed a sort of poetry of hand motion and thought—how thinking of something counterintuitive to fire, to destruction, could dampen any efforts of a successful cast. She read the words in Dunmer, in which she was not fluent, but didn't say them out loud. *Tralsid Molag*, she thought. The tips of her fingers and thumb glowed, as the corner of the book, where they touched, ignited in a flash. She popped up quickly and patted out the fire with her other hand. Her right one, dwindling out, hurt like she'd put it in hot coals. "Ouch!" she gasped, shaking it.

At that moment, Aryon returned with her things. "Sorry, they were a bit damp, so we had them warming by the boiler to…" He stopped midsentence at the sight he'd walked into. "Made some progress, I see!" He raised his eyebrows.

"I'm sorry about this!" she replied, gesturing to the burned book.

"No, that's incredible! Students usually take days, or weeks, to produce something, and yet you nearly started a fire in my office in twenty minutes! Some just aren't to the point in their reserve where they can create a powerful cast." He walked around the desk. "There's more to you than you're aware, my lady!" he finished with a serious expression. Žaneta bowed her head in appreciation as he handed her things to her.

After a few minutes of being in her room to change, she returned to the study, where Aryon had set up a steel shield on a wooden support in front of a large open window. "Good, now that you're here… we'll get started. I'm going to refine, with you, the text you were reading earlier and teach you one other spell. But I called for the council to meet today at noon—so we'll have to keep the lesson short. I want to get there early to get a feel for my reception," he said.

"Then let's get started!" Žaneta replied eagerly.

He agreed, while gesturing with his hand where to stand. "Let's."

Žaneta stood nearly thirty feet from the shield. "Okay. Now position yourself as if you were going to throw a punch. This is where hand presentation is everything," he said, showing his hand to Žaneta.

"When you're saying the words, or concentrating and thinking them, while bringing your hand back with your pinky and ring fingers together, you then throw that hand forward. Right as you finish the word, 'Molag,' only your index and middle fingers should be touching as they point to your target," he explained, demonstrating the motion.

She nodded, concentrating hard. "All right. Let me give this a try." She readied her stance, pulled her hand back as instructed, and started saying, "Tralsid…" She could see the glow in her peripheral vision and feel searing heat collect in her fingertips. "Molag!" she bolstered, with her hand pointing at the shield in the correct position. A flash lit their faces as a bolt of fire shot at the shield's upper half, bouncing up and smacking the ceiling then extinguishing itself as the shield fell to the floor.

"Outstanding… though incomplete, outstanding!" He stared at her, amazed. "I've been trying to teach one of my pupils that for weeks. The only thing you did incorrectly was you bent your middle finger on delivery. But the bolt will go through the shield if you're pointing straight to the target," he explained, still in awe.

"This next one is far easier than the last. It is meant to envelop an area, so it's not precise at all. Please, come to the window." He moved the fallen shield and the frame he'd hung it on to the side. "Now, focusing your effort out the window, draw your hand back in the same motion, pinky and ring finger together, but throw forward with all fingers apart. The words to this one are *Finred Molag*, which means 'spread fire.'"

Standing at the window, Žaneta reached back as told and, this time, tried thinking the words instead of saying them. Throwing her hand forward, she released a steady inferno that could've started the very tower they stood in on fire. She looked at Aryon, maintaining her aim out the window, and smirked, then closed her hand to stop the flames.

"Now you're just showing off!" Aryon chuckled, smiling as he stood at her side.

Happy with herself, she lowered her still outstretched arm. "You just said the words needed to teach me… Why didn't you explode or something?" she asked jokingly.

"With my years of practice, I've learned to focus on control as much as casting itself. Knowing all the words that I do by heart, I spend more time trying not to incinerate everything around me than I do trying to cast anything," he replied.

"I understand. I am this way with healing. Destruction… Restoration… we are a paradox," she said respectfully.

"Come with me downstairs; we'll get you something to eat. Calette is already down there! Then I'll need to prepare for the meeting," he said.

The two of them stood at the shaft opening, while the energy could be seen fluctuating within it. They both stepped in, and Aryon lowered them to the first floor, where they joined Calette in the dining room. There was a good breakfast spread out to choose from. Eggs, bread, jams, meats… all being enjoyed by a couple members of the house staff and Calette.

"I've already eaten, but please… help yourself to whatever you'd like. I'll return in a few hours—hopefully with some answers," Aryon said, kissing Calette on her cheek and stepping out.

Žaneta put some food on her plate and sat next to Calette. "Where is this council meeting?" she asked the girl.

"In Tel Mora, at my great-grandmother's tower. I heard 'the bell' ring—was that you upstairs?" Calette asked, grinning.

Žaneta gave her a puzzled look.

"When you hit the shield, it makes a loud clang—we call it 'the bell,'" she explained.

"Oh, yes…" She paused to swallow her breakfast. "That was me. Your dad helped me with spells that should prove pretty useful."

"I told him you were amazing. A lot of fun to watch!" Calette said.

Members of the house staff finished eating and went to the kitchen with their dishes—leaving Žaneta and Calette to themselves. Žaneta finished eating and put her fork down. "Well, we've got some time. Is there anything you'd like to do while we wait?"

"Nah! Just sit with me. I never really get visitors who spend a lot of time here, and I like having you around," Calette told her.

Žaneta gave her a thankful smile. "That's a great compliment, Calette. Thank you."

Calette, glancing at her, offered a sincere smile in return.

"You know, I could share a couple of healing words with you. If you're going to be practicing with fire, a little healing could help with those lessons. Would you like to learn a bit of my art?"

Calette stared at her with big eyes and a cheek full of eggs as she nodded her head.

Žaneta couldn't help but grin at her and the sweet response. She turned her chair to face Calette. "Okay, give me your hands," she said, offering hers. Calette, swallowing her bite of eggs, spun in her seat and placed her hands in Žaneta's. "Now… think of something you love!" She gave her a moment to consider.

"Sweets!" Calette said joyfully.

Žaneta laughed, then took in a deep breath and started over. "All right… that was my fault. I'll try again," she responded, thinking for a second then smiling. "Close your eyes. Now think of something that you *truly* love… your dad, perhaps! What makes you the happiest?" Calmly watching Calette's face, she could tell she was thinking hard. "Have you got it?" she asked. Calette nodded her head, concentrating.

"Now, say the words, 'Zalith ako.'"

"Zalith ako!" Calette grinned and opened her eyes to see a glowing mist flowing from between their hands. She burst into laughter and became so overwhelmed by the sight that her eyes welled with tears. Concerned, Žaneta stopped and squeezed her hands.

"What's wrong, Calette? What's the matter?"

"Nothing… It's great. I can never make my spells work right… and that was just so easy!" the girl said, with happy tears trickling down her face as she wiped her nose.

"That's because you're not heartless, Calette. Hold on to that joy you found!" she encouraged. "You did well. Remember those words—they mean 'healing fire,' and they'll only grow stronger." Smiling, Žaneta ruffled her hair, bringing her back to a lighter mood, then turned to take a drink from her cup.

Calette looked down, and then up to Žaneta. "You said you have a daughter?" she asked. "How old is she?"

Žaneta tilted her head and said, "She's going to be six soon." She bit her lip and tried to look calm, to hide the terrible grief she felt at the thought of Mazira, but she could feel her eyes misting up.

Calette noticed, too. "I'm sorry… I know you'll find her. You have a son, too, right?"

Relaxing, Žaneta took a deep breath in through her nose. "Yes—Tai. He'll be ten soon. Both of them have birthdays coming up," she replied, leaning her elbows on the table and turning toward Calette.

"That's close to my age! I'd like to meet them… What do they look like?"

"Well, Tai is a young Khajiit boy. He has gray coloring, is getting taller every day, and he's got my eyes."

"I've never seen any Khajiit like you… I'm sure he's different, too, like his mom." Calette smiled. "Does your little girl look like you at all? I remember, at dinner last night, you said she looked like her dad… a Redguard?"

"Yes, she has her father's appearance but shares some of my traits. She has my hair, not my fur," Žaneta said, "and my eyes. But what about you, Calette? All I think about are my kids, and when I leave here… that won't change. So, what do you do here? Any games?"

"Nah, I read a lot. Dad really believes I'm going to be the greatest sorceress of my time, so we practice pronunciations and mindset… kind of boring. But I thought a lot about it in that cage, and I'm just happy to be home."

Žaneta smiled. "You've got time to decide what you'll do, but practice things while you're young so when you're older, they're easy," she advised. "How about a little swordplay? I do it with Tai—I bet you'd like it. Let's go find some sticks outside to practice with." Žaneta stood and pushed her chair to the table.

Calette jumped up and moved her chair in, too, then followed Žaneta outside. Searching for a couple of good, straight sticks to practice with, Žaneta looked around at the trees and noticed how curvy they were. "This may be harder than I thought!" she said.

"We've got some cut firewood in the back that might work!" Calette piped up. So they walked to the rear of the building to look at their options. Finding some fairly straight pieces, Žaneta placed Calette in a starting stance and slowly began going over positions—blocking, moving, and maintaining good footing, above all.

Time went by quickly, and the pair had so much fun. But before they knew it, it was midafternoon, and Žaneta grew anxious. Halting the practice, she asked, "Would you like to go and get a snack or drink? Your dad should be back soon."

Calette, still swinging the stick back and forth, replied, "Okay. I'd like a drink, and my arms hurt from all this sword stuff."

Žaneta laughed. "Then let's take a break."

"You could heal my sore arms!" Calette said with a grin.

"Healing is for sickness and injury—not exercise," Žaneta replied, raising an eyebrow as they both chuckled.

Once inside, both had cups of water. Calette was actually very thirsty and drank most of hers. Žaneta, having sipped some, drew her finger around the top of the cup as she began thinking about her children and Sandrew again.

"May I see your sword?" Calette asked politely. Žaneta broke her stare from the cup and met her gaze. She stood and pulled the blade from its frog. With both hands, she laid it on the table in front of them. Calette, very interested, touched the handle and put her other hand under the blade. She lifted it a little. "That's big…" Calette noticed the lower part of the handle had a seam that moved ever so slightly. "Did I do something?" she asked, setting it down.

"No," Žaneta reassured her with a casual smile. "Watch." She pressed the lock-back lever that held the lower handle secure until it clicked then pulled it, exposing the knife hidden within.

"Oh!" Calette gasped. "What does that mean?" She pointed to the words engraved along the back edge near the ricasso.

"It means 'Edge of Oblivion,' but it's pronounced 'Jazrab di Remorgo' in my native tongue," Žaneta told her.

"Did you put that on there?" Calette asked.

"No. My father made this sword and placed the words while the blade was still hot."

"It's gorgeous… It suits you!" Calette said happily.

The main entrance door opened abruptly, and in came Aryon, looking rushed. He closed the door and walked straight to Žaneta. "We need to talk, in private. But Calette… you come with us… I'm not leaving you alone again. I'll take us to the study—please, follow me to the lift!" he urged. The three of them stepped onto the pad together, and Aryon took them up to the next floor.

As they all stood in the study, Aryon said, "Hold on." He went to each room in the hallway to see if they were empty before returning—the whole time being watched by Žaneta and Calette with narrowed eyes, both eager for an explanation as to why he appeared so upset.

"Okay. After completing the clairvoyance ritual, I was struck by a few visions I wanted to share. First, I saw several instances of secret meetings near here in a building I'm familiar with, but only silhouettes— no faces. I heard voices… but they were distorted, leading me to believe they were using a spell or an enchanted item to mask their meeting. One of them did say they needed to return to Tel Vos before their absence was noticed. The rest of the conversation talked of planning and turmoil between the Houses. Graydin told me there may be spies about, but this only confirms it. Also, the reason this is so strange is that I didn't delve into pursuing the safety of my House; I started by searching for Orvas Dren, and all of this rolled out.

"I believe I saw the initial meeting before Calette was taken. But there's more. After that vision, cold came over me… I didn't know who to trust, or if there was someone in our council circle planning against us, but I concentrated. I searched for a path that would lead me to Tai and Mazira, but Žaneta… I saw nothing. Instead, it felt like the ground quaked, as if the buildings would break apart from the shaking. In the vision, I ran outside, and the mountain was on fire… ash blocked out the sun, then I was pulled back into the ritual chamber, as if time had reversed. All was calm, like it is now, and I had one final vision. It was of cliffs and a stronghold, far to the west… but it was unfamiliar to me. With the ocean at its back and no trees seen, that puts it north of Gnaar Mok; I believe it holds significant importance in your quest," he said, collapsing into a chair and rubbing his face.

Žaneta thought about every place she'd ever heard of on the western coast. She stared off, thinking and considering everything else he'd relayed, then looked down to the frightened face of Calette and back to Aryon, trying to make sense of it.

"Žaneta, I want to thank you again. Your coming here saved both of our lives." He placed a hand on Calette's arm. "But we must leave. What I saw… none are safe here, and Calette doesn't need to bear witness to it," he said.

"Where will you go?" Žaneta asked.

"Away from Vvardenfell. But Žaneta, I don't know when these events will happen! There's no calendar in these visions. But they're never of what "may" happen—only of what has or will. Start your search of the western coast. Time seemed to be pressing in these visions, which has never happened before," he explained, concern written all over his face.

"What's the fastest way to the other coast from here?" Žaneta was determined to begin her search at once.

"With the mountains in the way and probable bounties on you from Orvas… ship. There's a boat that leaves port every afternoon from Vos. You have some time to make it—" He was suddenly interrupted by an outburst from Calette.

"No!" she cried. "Don't leave us!" She ran and hugged Žaneta's leg.

Žaneta found herself tearing up. "Oh, sweet girl, I've loved meeting you. But, somewhere, my children also feel as you do." She knelt and hugged her. She leaned back and held Calette's arms. "I will find and see you again. Here—here's something to remember me by." Žaneta reached around her neck to unclasp an amulet of Mara. "Maybe with something of mine, you and your father will be able to see me… and find me," she said, placing the amulet in Calette's hands and closing them around it.

Calette reached out to Žaneta, hugging her neck as she cried on her shoulder. While they shared the moment, Aryon lowered himself to the ground floor and stepped into the kitchen to gather a small bag of food and a water bladder to go with it. In his absence, Žaneta and Calette spoke. "Practice the words I taught you, Calette."

Calette was distraught; her lips quivered as tears poured down her cheeks. "But I'm not strong!" she whimpered.

"Your strength is your love… just think of who and what you love!" Žaneta took her hands and looked in her eyes. "Try it."

Calette sniffed and wiped her eyes with her sleeve. "Zalith ako." She giggled as the fiery, soothing mist returned. She cried even more, overjoyed by her success but lost with Žaneta leaving.

Žaneta could see Aryon approaching slowly in her periphery. He looked on in astonishment at the magic his daughter had created and treaded lightly to not disrupt it as Žaneta closed her hands around Calette's, ending the cast. Sad yet enthused, the girl happily hugged Žaneta again. Aryon walked to his daughter and placed a comforting hand on her shoulder, encouraging her to let go. Žaneta stood and Aryon handed the bag to her. "Something for your journey," he said. She took the bag and slung it onto her shoulder while she wiped her eyes, and they walked to the shaft. He lowered them down to the first floor, where she grabbed her sword from the table. Looking at Calette then back to Aryon, she sheathed it and walked to the front door—once again wearing her stoic mask to hide her emotions. She didn't turn around again, knowing it would make the goodbye unbearable. Taking a deep breath, she left the tower and headed for the Vos dock.

***

On the other side of Vvardenfell was the stronghold. Its gates were shut, lookout towers were manned, and patrols made their rounds wearing their yellow sashes. A large Orc climbed up the steps to a corner tower and entered, passing right by the two guards. He was clad in heavy armor from head to toe, with only his lower face visible from under his half helmet. He closed the door behind him and went up a winding staircase, then approached a Dunmer man standing behind a desk, who was looking over maps and documents.

The Dunmer's face was clean-shaven, his black, medium-length hair had been carefully styled into wild spikes. His high cheekbones and gaunt cheeks gave him a sinister look, which was fitting—he was a sinister man. Wearing Orcish armor, greaves, and boots and a black tucked-in shirt with the sleeves rolled up, he simply stood there and didn't acknowledge his visitor.

"Orvas… all profits on the plantation have been destroyed or are missing. None of our people have reported anyone trying to move the drugs, so they believe they were torched," he said.

"If you're coming in here, you better have something better to report than, 'Your shit was burned!'" growled Orvas, sneering at the Orc.

"Our sources in Vivec said a large Khajiit was with the girl, then was last seen leaving on a Silt Strider—" he started.

"And none of our people tried to stop them?!" Orvas shouted, pounding his hand on the desk. Orvas thought for a second and remembered what one of his men had told him. "I received a report from one of my raiders on the road, about three or four days ago. He said all of the others were killed; he crawled into the woods after having his leg shattered by a big Khajiit with a shield. Now you tell me there's this one seen in Vivec. Who is he?" Orvas pressed.

"It's a woman. She was asking around about her recently missing kids. But when seen entering with the girl, Toryn tried to kill her with some hired muscle."

Orvas waited impatiently, tapping his fingers on the desk. "AND?"

"She killed Toryn and tore up the other guy… but that's not the best part." The Orc smirked. "She healed him… in seconds."

Orvas stood there grinding his teeth, forcing himself to think of a plan and failing. All the efforts he'd made to bring a fight to the Empire and reclaim power were falling apart. He calmed himself and exhaled slowly through his flared nostrils, staring back at the Orc.

"Mash, I want you to listen. Send a runner with a message. Tell our agents they'll get their weight in gold if they bring me her head! Gather supplies and tell everyone who to watch for," he ordered.

Mash stood there listening, afraid of nothing. But Orvas was his bread and bottle, and he respected the fact that he was boss. So, he left the room with his orders and went downstairs, out the same door he'd entered through.

Orvas turned and looked out his tower window, leaning on the sill with both hands. "A damn cat." He breathed.

Chapter Six

It was evening on the mainland of Morrowind, marking the fifth day since the children were taken. Nothing changed in the routines of the crew. Bring water and food—that's it. There were a couple of toilet seats near the stern that let out straight into the water, but they left no room for modesty, and they were too small of openings to consider an escape through. The events of the children's time on the boat was quickly fading from their minds, though, because they could feel the ship slowing down. Waves from the shore rocked the boat, and voices could be heard from the side of the ship.

They were docking.

The floor panel opened, and the man wearing the muscle cuirass and sagum came down the steps. "We'll all be leaving the ship and getting on carriages. Stay quiet and together, and do what you're told," he ordered. He turned and climbed the stairs just as two of his men took his place, rounding up the kids and dividing them into groups.

"Hold close to me," Tai whispered, and Mazira grasped her brother's arm. When one of the men reached the group of children, they all were ushered forcibly to the steps. Since they didn't want to draw any attention to the docks late at night, the crew didn't bother pulling children apart from each other.

With four other children, Tai and Mazira approached the carriage, which would soon carry them deeper into the mainland. It had no windows, just high panel boards with a roof and a wooden door on the back; they looked like cargo boxes, not transports. To one side stood the man in the Imperial-looking garb.

"Tobias, this is the last of them," one of the crewmen informed him.

"Then let's load up and get on the road," Tobias replied, watching the rest be shoved into the carriages before the doors were closed and latched. The horses were wound up and ready to work, tugging at their yokes in an effort to start pulling. Horses near the town stables could be heard whinnying at the commotion, and Tobias didn't like the noise it was causing. He climbed up and sat next to the driver of the first horse carriage, motioning for him to proceed. Four carriages in total began their trip from Narsis to the west, through the Valus Mountains.

***

Hundreds of miles to the north, Žaneta had passed through the Sea of Ghosts along the northern shores of Vvardenfell and changed boats for passage to Khuul, where she would begin searching. It was early in the morning when she made port, and the sun had yet to show any sign of itself.

Khuul was a small fishing community, not her target, and the hour of the day would work in Žaneta's favor—she wouldn't be seen coming into port nor heading along the coastline southwest under the cover of darkness. She started in hard, running at a good pace until she reached the next coastal site, Ald Velothi. Her ability to see at night revealed nothing but disappointment here; this was a public pier and harbor, not fortified by any means, so she carried on.

Stopping to take a drink of her water, she also ate a quick snack before she continued. The sun was creeping up, and the light made things more visible at greater distances. Knowing she'd been running for hours, she started becoming more and more beside herself—she'd come across *nothing* yet.

In the distance, she could see Gnisis as she looked through her spyglass, which offered nothing to support the vision Aryon had described. It was an actual town, not a stronghold. So that meant the River Samsi was to her south, something she was aware of from maps but never had reason to visit or cross. From what she could remember, the West Gash lay beyond its rocky ravines and scattered Daedric ruins, with mountain ranges on its eastern and southern borders. Then past those, to the south, was Balmora. She had nearly come full circle, and though she had slept a short period on the boat rides, she was tired from the pace she'd maintained since leaving Khuul.

Regardless, she pressed on, passing caves and irrelevant landmarks until late morning, when she came across an unkempt Dunmer stronghold. There were no signs of activity outside, no recent tracks around the perimeter, and no cliffs or high rock formations like Aryon had described. *Another bust*, Žaneta concluded. But still, she couldn't rule it out without seeing for herself. She inched closer to the large structure, and after approaching carefully, she began to feel vibrations in the ground and heard a humming that became more pronounced when she got within a hundred feet of it.

She entered, and never before had she seen anything like what was constructed inside. Two towering structures emanated light and were the source of the energy felt outside. Otherwise, the chamber was empty, but these resonating things had a purpose; they were magical, without a doubt. They held two identical platforms, both with a large steeped pillar in the middle, and were encircled by four crescent-shaped pillars that leaned toward the center. A bright red energy was sent off in rolling waves from the devices; yet offered no injury. It was just a big show of light, and aside from being fascinating beyond anything she'd encountered on the island before, she had no idea what they could be for. She stared at them and observed the strange markings on the center pillar, each of which had a small hole next to it—*a keyhole, perhaps?* she wondered. But they were all the same shape and size. She wasn't sure what the markings meant, just that they gave her more questions than answers. But she had no sorcerer to confide in, so she left how she entered.

Just in front of her was a smaller building with one entrance. She moved nearer while listening closely, but the area was silent—not a threatening silence, but rather like this place had been forgotten about. Žaneta opened the door, and her senses were immediately assaulted with a pungent, foul odor. The air was stuffy, and an aroma of vermin and the waste they had left behind filled the hall. But there was no real death to speak of, so she advanced a bit farther to see its contents.

As she moved quietly down a descending corridor, she began hearing a voice on the air. She couldn't find a source; it almost seemed like the voice was in her head. It grew louder, more unnatural, and its beaconing message was insistent, spiking her curiosity. She peered back and forth, squinting and listening as her ears turned different directions, trying to home in on the sound. The hall was pitch black, although she could see a few Skeevers up ahead. But every instinct she had told her this place was evil, luring its visitors into its dark depths.

As much as she felt inclined to find out what was in these tunnels, her focus was dead on, and her target was Orvas, not whatever was down these passageways. Having not come close enough to the large rat-like Skeevers to get their attention, she returned to the surface and back outside to the courtyard.

Shaking off the chills from that place, Žaneta looked around for a good vantage point, and the structure that housed the two magical devices was the tallest thing in sight. She was able to scale it with a few jumps using its outcropped edges and angled walls. Žaneta, standing on top of the building, removed her spyglass from her satchel and observed everything around her. To the north, she could see the highest rocks beyond Gnisis and the tops of some of its structures, but the town sat too low to see.

To the east lay the rocky projections that were the start of the Red Mountain. She could see the tops of crumbling buildings that were part of Daedric ruins at the base of the first line of mountains in that direction. *Too far from the coast and too many Daedra for Orvas to have chosen there!* she thought, so she continued panning. To the south, the cliffs fell into the ocean, and beyond them were more mountains.

Žaneta knew something was about to work out, and those mountains in the south were probably her mark, because beyond them lay the Bitter Coast and Gnaar Mok—where Aryon had told her was too far south from what he'd seen. It was midday, and clouds had rolled in from the sea. Not wanting to lose visibility because of the weather, she climbed down from the building, grabbed some food to eat from the bag, and started following the path south along the coast.

Staying off the main roads, Žaneta chose to keep close to the shoreline. She had to cross ocean inlets in a couple of places before she could reach the high rock formations that spanned the southern coast, forming the ridge of mountains that went east toward Red Mountain. Climbing the northwestern edge of that range took nearly two hours. She finally reached an area of rocks that were more leveled off than the jagged cliffs she'd been scaling, a fitting place to catch her breath. Once she was near the top, she noticed there were no more steep points in the terrain. But moving farther over the ridgeline, she could see they formed an enormous horseshoe that must've gone on for miles. Then, there at the base, nestled in the bowl of rocks, rested a large stronghold.

Žaneta moved down the inner face of the rocks, looking for a good place to observe from, but stayed high atop the mountainous spine until almost directly north of the stronghold. She came across an old bedroll and lantern next to a crudely arranged stone fire pit. It looked to be a scout post that hadn't been used for a while… so using it for that purpose seemed only fitting.

She approached an edge that offered all she needed. With her spyglass in hand, she could already tell this place had significant traffic. She counted at least thirty strong, an archer's tower at the main gate, and men on the inside, patrolling or talking with one another.

Then, she saw him—the Orc. He headed up the stairs to a guarded tower and went inside. *That's it… Dren's there!* she thought. She looked for potential entry points as raindrops started to lightly kiss the lens of her spyglass. She noticed large wooden beams that pierced through the walls, probably supporting the high walkways on the adjacent side of the stronghold for archers to get a clear view of all who approached. However, even though she could get inside by using these beams, she needed more—some sort of distraction, or help, once she was inside. There wasn't a way she could fight all those men without the risk of losing Orvas again… but she had an idea.

The rain was starting to come down heavier; she lowered her spyglass and looked down at the lantern to her side then back at the stronghold. Žaneta picked up the empty lantern by its old, frayed cord and worked her way down the northern outer face of the ridge line, heading northeast. It was late afternoon, and she had to go round up some friends before coming back after dark.

From where she stood, she could see the break in the mountains to the east—the canyon entrance to this charming estate and where she'd be coming back through. Žaneta looked over the land. There were small pockets of mines in the area below to the north, but the northeast was undisturbed. After making her descent, she hurried across the road, making sure not to be seen. It was getting dark. Along the way, she passed some plants and dry bark under the few trees nearby and stuffed them into the lantern. She closed it to keep the kindling as dry as possible, hanging it under her cloak.

She ran, as hard and fast as she had the first night her children were taken. Scattered lightning dotted the land, and she could see the Daedric ruins she'd passed before in the distance.

She was hopeful they'd be there—her "friends." As she got closer to the ruins, she could see Clannfear in the clearing before her. Three of them. The rain was coming down hard, and she was drenched. Still in a full sprint, she drew her blade. Clannfear were more ferocious and hungry than they were smart, but they were also fast. So she needed them gone.

The closest lizard simply stood there, oblivious to Žaneta's charge until it was too late. The rain, darkness, and thunder left them all up to slaughter. Žaneta passed the first, lobbing his head clean off, but making more noise than she cared to with the glass and metal lantern—it rattled, giving away her presence. The other two came lunging in toward the noise, and Žaneta went on defense. The Clannfear simply saw food, with no concern for self-injury.

It's now or never! she thought. Switching the sword to her left hand in an icepick grip, she held it by its ricasso and steadied her feet. Reaching back with her right hand, she thought the words, *Tralsid Molag!* as she pointed straight at the closest Clannfear.

What looked like a bolt of red lightning flared in the darkness and sent a spark through the chest of one lizard, killing it instantly.

The other moved right past it and was already in a leap toward Žaneta. Flying in her direction with its enormous, long claws on its hands and feet extended, she had a split second to jump to the left of the creature. Bringing about her sword in a sweep, she thrust off the ground in her attack, dragging the blade across the Clannfear's belly while holding it like a boat oar. But the Clannfear still managed to slash its foot and hand across her left thigh and shoulder. The disemboweled lizard thrashed on the ground behind her, and she came down hard—her wet cloak had gotten snagged on the Clannfear's claws. Žaneta reached up to remove the cloak and the full sensation from her injuries set in as she screamed.

She rolled to the side and tried to stand—but failed. Her left thigh was split wide open, the muscles torn. Žaneta dropped her sword to the ground. Her shoulder was bad, too, but the wound wasn't as deep. She closed her eyes and relaxed her breathing. The pain was fierce, but as she focused her efforts, her magic started to heal her injuries. She concentrated on herself then watched her wounds close as light emanated from them. As she healed, the darkness once again closed about her like a shroud, the glow fading.

Žaneta stood and walked to the Clannfear. It still lay breathing, obviously suffering, so she quickly cut off its head then inspected her things. She sheathed her sword and put her cloak pin back in her satchel, leaving the torn cloak where it lay. The rain was starting to let up, as she walked back to the lantern, which she'd dropped during the fight. It was still intact, but the glass on one side had broken. Despite this, it would serve its purpose.

The ruins lay just in front of her. She looked around the base and up to the peaks of its crumbling structure then scanned the entrance. Before approaching and pushing open the large iron door, she lit the lantern she'd stuffed with that familiar plant—Hackle-lo shrubs—the smoking lamp doubling as a large incense burner. She went inside.

The eerie glow the lantern cast on Žaneta did nothing to light the temple, but she could see their eyes glowing. She let out a challenging battle cry to make her presence fully known before turning to the door and running.

Outside, she let her speed carry her south a short distance before turning to see what she'd lured out, and she was very happy with what she saw. A Daedroth, a couple of Scamps, and four enormous Ogrim. The Daedroth, an enormous and powerful creature, had the head of an alligator, ran on its hind legs, and had arms like a human. Though not as large as an Ogrim, they were faster and armed with more tools they could use to tear something apart. Scamps were little, nasty, and gremlin-like; she'd run into these before, years ago in the woods a little way from her home. They were half the size of a man, had long pointed ears, big eyes, and terribly sharp claws. Although, the blades on the ends of her fingers would probably make them turn and run… if they weren't so brainless.

The Daedroth and Scamps just wanted to chew on her and would never catch her; they'd probably just give up chase. Those Ogrim, however, would follow the Hackle-lo all the way back.

She continued heading south, passing the Clannfear carcasses, and as expected, the Daedroth and Scamps started eating those instead.

The rain had abated to a sprinkling, and Žaneta casually jogged with her Ogrim in tow. She could make out the barrier mountain range just a little way off to the west on her right, and she had come to the road leading through the canyon entrance. Never letting her clumsy guests get more than a hundred yards from her, she recharged the lantern with a little more Hackle-lo she'd gathered in passing and another zap of fire.

***

It was very late at night, if not after midnight. An archer sat in his lookout tower back at the stronghold, still soaked from the sideways blowing rain from earlier… despite its shanty roof. The guard was tired, just wanting to rest. But he still made the effort to peer out from time to time. Then, something caught his attention in the darkness—a dim light, too dim to be a torch or an oil lantern, but it was a light.

Žaneta, approaching the fort at a sprint, came into the light from the moon as it peeked between the thinning clouds and threw her smoking lantern over the gate before running around the outer walls, out of his view.

"Enemy!" he shrieked, ringing the bell to alert the others. Then, he gasped. He could see the enormous silhouettes in the darkness as they trampled closer.

Men in the stronghold streamed into the courtyard, half prepared for an attack, and a few had run out to the overlook walkway, when they all heard the scream from the man in the lookout tower. "RUN!" he shouted, as the gate smashed apart, the tower collapsing under the Ogrim's advance.

Arrows found their marks and did nothing as men were swatted or torn in half. Some ran back into the buildings only to be crushed beneath them as they were leveled by the Ogrim in pursuit. Another Ogrim was just focused on eating the lantern, swallowing it while getting struck by arrows it was unaware of.

On the outer wall, Žaneta had used her remaining grappling hook to latch onto one of the support beams sticking out and started climbing. She jumped to the next beam, then the next, while holding on to the hook and dragging the rope along, keeping steady with the claws on her feet. Standing on the last beam, as close to the tower entrance as she could get, she threw the hook over the top of the wall and was up and over with her sword drawn. An archer was feet from her left side, as he readied a shot at one of the Ogrim below. She ran her sword through him so hard that it pinned him to the post on his other side.

Just behind them, one Dunmer guard was headed straight for her, while another stood back with his bow. Žaneta unlatched the knife from the sword's handle; weaving under and out of the way of the first man's swing, she brought her knife up into his left side. Looking over his shoulder, she could see his partner set to loose an arrow from near the tower entrance. She pulled her Dunmer shield in close as she removed her knife then threw it into the archer's chest. The man stumbled back against the tower and collapsed.

Žaneta released the Dunmer over the edge of the walkway to the ground below and turned to her sword. Putting a foot on the man it was through, she yanked it out then ran up to the archer lying by the door and took back her knife, inserting it into the handle of her sword before going into the tower. Finally, there stood Mash, holding his ridiculously heavy war hammer. Behind him, that bastard Orvas went scurrying up the stairs that hugged the wall of the cylindrical tower.

Žaneta looked Mash over for a chink in his armor, and besides his lower face and jaw, there wasn't one to be seen. He started in on her aggressively, swinging his hammer wide, knocking a sword rack over and smashing a table, as she leapt over him and darted to the other side of the room. He spun and threw his weapon at her, missing her by less than a foot. It smacked one of the stones in the wall, shifting it noticeably to the outside.

He charged her, and she attempted to thrust her sword into his weak point. He laid his head and shoulder down into the attack, and the blade grinded across his armor, causing sparks to fly. He came up with a backhand, and the sword went flying as he grabbed her arms and forced her backward, pinning her to the wall. He tried to headbutt her straight on but failed, only scraping her left cheek when she moved her head.

With her back to the wall and a foot on the belly of his cuirass, she walked up his breastplate and pushed as hard as she could—off he flew, all the way across the room. He lost his helmet when he slammed into the winding staircase and fell forward to his hands and knees. Giving his head a shake to clear it, he staggered as he tried to stand. Žaneta noticed when he grabbed her, and when he put his hand on his head, that the backs of his gauntlets were armored while his palms were covered in leather— probably so he could swing that hammer.

Another weak spot! she thought, as she stared at them, then back at his face. The Orc had returned to his feet; focused, he came rushing in, and she did little to stop him. He put both hands around her neck and slammed her against the wall. "I'm gonna choke the life out of you!" He growled, squeezing tighter. Žaneta looked down at him and forced out the best smile she could. Bringing her hands up, she wedged her fingers just under his hands and let her claws out. He screamed and loosened his grip, allowing her to increase hers.

"Gotcha!" she hissed, putting one foot on his belly again and pushing him away while tearing his hands to shreds.

His eyes were red and furious, but they flashed with hopelessness as he looked down at the bloody remnants at the ends of his arms. He could do nothing with his hands, and they were drenching the floor in scarlet. He screamed in rage and pain just as Žaneta lunged at him. She sank her claws into the sides of his scalp and threw all of her weight into his left knee, bending the armor and shattering the joint.

He fell into a heap, writhing in agony. Groaning with every breath he sucked in, he was done fighting… permanently.

Žaneta picked up her sword, grabbed a shield from one of the racks, and rushed upstairs. Orvas was standing behind a long table on the next floor; she made eye contact with him then scanned the room to take in its arrangement before looking back at him. An oil lamp burned on her end of the table, lighting the room. With the storm passed and the moon revealed, two windows let in dim light. He was leaning forward over some papers and books, one of which was open. Under its binding, he had hidden a dagger coated in a paralytic poison.

Žaneta stood in front of the lamp and stared at him. "What do you want… your kids?" he asked, suspiciously frozen in place. Orvas stayed leaning on the table, fighting the impulse to move from his spot. He wanted her close before springing his poisoned dagger at her, only needing a scratch to be effective.

"With all the children you've taken, how would you know mine?" Žaneta spat.

"Oh, I wouldn't—but they're gone all the same!" he responded happily, giving her a sinister smirk.

Žaneta reached for the lever on the lamp and turned it off. Orvas could see nothing—the low light from the moon wasn't enough to make out anything. In a panic, he pulled the dagger from under the book and backed closer to the wall.

"Turn the light back on, you damn cat! Stay back… I'll cut you!" he said, nervously raising his voice. She was still standing where she had been but knew the dark would force his hand.

His breathing was heavy, and he listened for her to come closer. But he only heard a *click* in the near pitch-black room, then there was a dull thud and pressure in his belly, followed by pain. As Orvas backed against the wall, the immense, dull ache he felt in his abdomen forced him to slide down to the floor after dropping his dagger. He moved his hand to his stomach and felt something that hurt even more when touched.

Žaneta had thrown her knife into his gut. She walked to him and, with the tip of her sword, tossed his dagger out of reach. "Where do you send the children you've taken?" She breathed calmly.

"The mainland." He panted, occasionally holding his breath from the pain.

"For what? Or who?" she pressed, waiting a moment for a reply, but nothing came. "My husband said something about 'the Briar,'" she said, kneeling toward him.

"Not my detail, Khajiit. Others manage… the handling when en route. My ledger on the desk tells me the ships in dock and headcounts, but no names," he winced.

She stood, laid her shield on the table, then walked around his desk and opened the book, skimming the pages for dates. She came across the closest thing to success she could've hoped for—a ship named "Cliff Racer" left port just over six days ago with twenty-four "passengers" from Ebonheart, heading for Narsis.

"How can you read that?" Orvas interrupted, squinting at her. "Oh, right! Your eyes. You freaking cats all see in the dark, don't ya?"

Žaneta walked back to him, reached down, then turned and pulled her knife from him—causing him to let out a yelp—wiped it on his pant leg, and placed it back in her sword as he splinted his belly and leaned over writhing in pain. "You've ruined so many people's lives, and still you sit there bleeding and spitting insults. Don't forget to say hello to your 'guests' downstairs, unless you choose to stay here… in which case, that wound means a slow, painful death." She placed the ledger in her satchel and walked down the stairs.

Mash was unconscious in the room below, either from pain or the loss of blood he was lying in. Maybe he was dead, but at that moment, Žaneta found she didn't care. She opened the door leading outside and left. Looking in the courtyard, there were no sounds made by men—Dunmer or the like—just Ogrim eating the dead.

She climbed over the wall and, using the grappling hook she'd placed earlier, slid down. Not quite morning yet, she ran from the area and headed south to Gnaar Mok to catch a boat.

Chapter Seven

The sun was rising on the small fishing village. The townsfolk had not begun their day yet, except for a couple of fishermen who were throwing their nets into the shallow waters, one a Breton and the other an Argonian. Walking on the beach, Žaneta called out to them, "Hello! Who can I hire for a boat to Vivec?"

The Argonian came up to the edge of the water. "Talk with Valveli, but don't flash your coin around—there's no law about," he warned, holding his net.

"Valveli? Thank you," she said, nodding, then continued down the beach.

Across the water to the southwest, she could see the boat moored to the dock area of Gnaar Mok, which was a poor community built on a small piece of land. It was separated from the shore by only a waist-deep amount of water when the tides were in but was connected by crudely-assembled plank bridges. Žaneta crossed, walked to the dock, then sat on a bench and waited for the ship's owner to arrive.

Some time passed, and the sun had come up when she saw a couple of the townspeople start their daily routines. Then, she caught sight of something interesting. A Dunmer woman walked up to the door of one of the shops on Žaneta's right to unlock it and open for business; she wore a tan-yellow sash around her neck. Žaneta turned her focus to the woman and watched as she was shortly joined by three more people, all wearing the same attire.

This place has a Camonna Tong presence! she thought. None of them had seen her sitting on the dock, and not wasting any time, she drew her sword and casually walked to the store, holding it backward by its ricasso.

When she entered, she saw the woman who'd unlocked the store standing behind the counter. Two of the others were leaning against the side of the counter talking with each other—a Dunmer man and woman—with the last Dunmer man sitting to Žaneta's left at a small table. He'd just sat and begun reading over papers.

"Are any of you Valveli?" Žaneta asked.

Surprised by her presence, the man and woman at the counter spun to look at her. "No," the man replied sharply.

The shop owner leaned over and whispered, "That's her!"

"What gave it away?" the woman replied sarcastically.

Aware as they were, they were not prepared. The man at the counter had a short sword, the woman, a dagger, and the man to her left had nothing—probably the most dangerous one of them all, with no need to carry a weapon. Žaneta swung her sword at the man to her left, striking him on his left collarbone in a downward motion that ended under his right armpit. His head and right arm slid off from his top half, and suddenly, the danger of the situation became very real to the other three.

Never seeing excitement out here in the sticks, the Dunmer man, both stunned and slow to react, hesitated to put his hand on his sword and draw it. Too late—Žaneta swung hers through the top of his right arm, below the shoulder and partway into his chest, as his arm fell to the floor.

The woman to his left stumbled back as the man toppled sideways and slammed into her. Armed only with the dagger she hadn't even thought to unsheathe yet, she, too, was too late. Žaneta pulled her sword from the man, spun around counterclockwise, and sliced across the woman's chest. Turning next to the storeowner, the Khajiit thrust her sword toward the woman's neck, but missed as she fell back in a panic. Žaneta reached down to her side and pulled the dead man's short sword from its sheath, leaned forward, and threw it through the woman's chest, where it lodged itself into the wall she had fallen against. Žaneta knew there was a bounty on her and that Orvas, dead or dying, wouldn't be alive long enough to pay it. Even so, anyone with a yellow sash was a mortal enemy. Žaneta left the store after getting the keys from the clerk, then she closed the door behind her and locked it.

Walking back, she tossed the keys into the shallow waters and rinsed her sword as well, giving it a couple of swishes back and forth, then returned to her seat on the dock and quietly waited. Žaneta appeared unphased by what had just happened. She looked out at the boat as it was gently rocked by the surf. For a moment, she considered that she should pray, having just slaughtered a group who hadn't attacked her yet. But she was reluctant—the danger she was in required swift action on her part. Although she couldn't think of the fear on their faces without shuddering, she accepted the difficult position she was in. She didn't get to wait for them to all come find her—she had to act.

Around thirty minutes passed. The ship's operator walked toward the dock and, seeing Žaneta, said, "I'm sorry, are you waiting for a ride?"

"Are you Valveli?" Žaneta replied, looking up at her.

The short, black-haired Dunmer woman was poorly dressed due to a lack of means, but not self-respect. She'd done enough to make herself presentable with the little she appeared to have.

"Yes, where would you like to go?" she asked.

"Vivec, please."

"Okay. But let's be off before the town takes notice… Some of the other 'service providers' make efforts to hassle me about profits," Valveli said.

Wasting no time, Žaneta stepped onto the boat while Valveli untied it and hopped in. She lowered the single sail and caught a small breeze to take them out. Žaneta said nothing about Valveli's statement about people bothering her—she knew she'd just eased the burden of the town. Pulling a handful of coins from her bag, she leaned forward and handed them to Valveli. "My ferry service doesn't cost this much," she said, staring down at the gold with raised eyebrows.

Žaneta just shrugged and looked back at the land from the water. "Any rumors going around?" she asked, changing the subject.

"Bandits and marauders have been causing trouble all over, missing persons and looting… pretty much instability throughout Vvardenfell. If you're looking for work, the city leaders often have rewards posted," Valveli informed her.

"You don't say?" Žaneta replied, acting falsely surprised. "You don't have any issues with the Camonna Tong?"

Valveli looked at the water and maintained her steering then replied, "I don't know much about them. I've heard they're a bunch of cut-throats. If you're Dunmer and don't interfere with profits, I've heard they usually don't bother you… unless you *are* their profit."

Žaneta looked at Valveli, wondering how she was unaware of their presence in the very village she worked from. "Better not tell anyone I was your fare then… The Camonna Tong and I don't get along. It'd be best if you let me off north of Ebonheart, on the western shore—I'll make my way to Vivec from there."

Valveli avoided her eyes, acting wary of Žaneta after that. However, since she obviously didn't care for the Camonna Tong, she agreed and didn't sway from her route.

A short while later, the boat turned north into the body of water west of the peninsula where Ebonheart was situated. Valveli landed the boat on a beach directly east of a small island. Žaneta stepped out onto the sand, turned, and pushed the bow of the boat back into the water.

"Farewell, Khajiit!" Valveli called.

Žaneta lifted a hand in a gesture of goodbye and ran up the hill to the road leading to Vivec. She knew agents of the Camonna Tong would be looking for her, but using the gondola service of the city, she made her way to the Foreign Quarter without alerting everyone to her presence. She headed straight to Simine's once in the canton for one last visit.

After entering the shop, she looked around for customers, but only Simine was standing there. Leaning on the counter while reading a book, he looked up and saw her enter; she nodded at him and walked to the back without saying a word. The cabinet was unlocked, so she opened it and slid the shelves to the side, entered, and closed it behind her.

Gentleman Stacey was having a conversation with two other people—a well-dressed Dunmer and Imperial. But he fell silent when she came in.

"I'm glad you're here!" she said slowly then turned her gaze to the others present.

"Gentlemen, let me introduce you to Žaneta!" he announced, smiling. "She's made problems for our common enemy… and in short time."

Žaneta nodded at the two men as they acknowledged her by lowering their heads out of courtesy then looked back at him. "Stacey… I wanted to give you this," she said, removing Orvas's ledger from her satchel. "It's all of Dren's business details." She handed him the book.

"Good gods! Where did—how did you…?" he stuttered.

"From Orvas," she replied in short.

"Is he…?"

"Likely… by now."

The two men exchanged shocked looks before turning to stare at her with wide eyes.

"You see!" Stacey declared, looking at the men.

"There's enough there to come down hard on them, and you can put your people in the right places to put an end to it. But I'm off to Morrowind… after my children," she said.

"I'm glad you found where to go. It's been my pleasure meeting you, and I wish you well. Take whatever supplies and food you need before you leave." He gestured to the chest and pantry against the wall.

Žaneta walked over to them and gathered food, placing it in another burlap bag from the shelf. She slid the shelves of the hidden door out of the way then stepped through the cabinet, turning to look at Stacey. He stared at her confidently but seemed a bit sad as well, as he gave her a wave goodbye. Žaneta, straight-faced, had more to be grateful to Stacey for than she could express, so she kept it inside. "Thank you!" she said sincerely, then slid the shelves closed and shut the cabinet. She went back outside and started heading for the shipyards.

Since Jim Stacey had the ledger and she'd gotten what she needed from it, she could leave this place without caring who saw her anymore. The Camonna Tong had a presence in the city, she knew that. But if they challenged her in view of the public, then all that meant to her was their deaths would be public.

She was in tune with the whispers and stares from people on the cantons' balconies outside. It was then she realized what Stacey meant—they're everywhere. But not a soul attacked her; these people must've been the ones looking to make a profit off of information, not true members of the Camonna Tong's ranks. Though not immediately dangerous, it was how their network was so vast; she ignored it.

Once at the docks, she asked various sailors for their destinations and who might be heading to the mainland. Although she was met with several "nos" or "not headed theres," she was told by a dockworker, "Ask Davir. I think he's got a shipment going out… down on the end there."

Žaneta walked to the last tie off on the pier and found a man fastening some supplies together—a Nord with short, blond hair, a beard, and wearing dark pants tucked into his tall boots, with a white button-up shirt. "Are you the captain?" she asked.

"Aye, name's Davir. What can I do for you?"

"I need passage to the mainland," she said.

"I've got a shipment going there this afternoon, but I don't take passengers."

Žaneta tossed a dinner-roll-sized bag of gold at the man's chest, which he caught and opened. He looked in the bag and up at her. "Climb on board, and we'll be off after I get the rest of my shipment," he said, grinning.

A couple of the crew members helped the dockworkers finish loading the order then pulled the boarding plank onto the ship. One untied the tie off and threw the line to the crew.

With one sail up, the ship pulled out of the harbor and slowly made its way into open waters. "Ya know… now's a good time to be leavin' Vvardenfell. There are a lot of strange rumors, and noises, coming from Red Mountain," Davir mentioned, standing at the helm, with Žaneta sitting a little in front of him against the portside.

She looked at Red Mountain in the distance. "My family's not here… so neither is my home," she replied, stoically glancing back at him.

"Fair enough," he said and let it drop.

The large mainsail opened up, with all three sails working to carry the vessel. Suddenly, with Vivec a short distance behind them, there was a muffled *boom*—as if underground—from the direction of Red Mountain. Trees could be seen shaking, and everything on the water swayed as a shockwave swept through the city and into the sea.

Davir twisted around and looked over his right shoulder in confusion but kept his left hand on the wheel.

Žaneta, frozen, could hear the distant screams from the city. Fear ran through her mind, not for herself, but for what she'd been told… concern for the people, families, Calette and Aryon—she knew he'd been right. Red Mountain hadn't erupted, but this was the start of something horrible, and she knew it meant death. She turned her stare back to the deck in front of her. With her head down, her eyes welled up with tears, and she closed them.

END

Žaneta's Chronicles

Part Two: Edge of Oblivion

MORROWIND
BLACK MARSH
SKYRIM
LAKE CANULIS
THE VALUS MOUNTAINS
THE NIBENAY BASIN
PANTHER RIVER
SILVERFISH RIVER
COUNTY CHEYDINHAL
CHEYDINHAL
THE REED RIVER
LAKE POPPAD
THE NIBENAY VALLEY
COUNTY LEYAWIIN
BLACKWOOD
THE COLOVIAN HIGHLANDS
THE JERALL MOUNTAINS
LAKE ARRIUS
COUNTY BRUMA
THE BLUE ROAD
THE YELLOW ROAD
NIBEN BAY
THE LOWER NIBEN
LEYAWIIN
TOPAL BAY
BRUMA
THE SILVER ROAD
COUNTY CHORROL
THE REALTH
THE UPPER NIBEN
BRAVIL
COUNTY BRAVIL
IMPERIAL CITY
LAKE RUMARE
THE NIBENAY VALLEY
SIBILUS RIVER
THE ORANGE ROAD
CHORROL
THE GREAT FOREST
THE GREEN ROAD
THE WEST WEALD
ELSWEYR
THE BLACK ROAD
THE IMPERIAL RESERVE
COUNTY SKINGRAD
SKINGRAD
KVATCH
THE GOLD ROAD
COUNTY KVATCH
THE STRID RIVER
VALENWOOD
HAMMERFELL
THE GOLD COAST
COUNTY ANVIL
ANVIL
BRENA RIVER
ABECEAN SEA
PROVINCE OF CYRODIIL

Chapter One

Ripples on the ocean's surface shimmered in the midday sunlight. Marveling at the vastness of the mainland, Žaneta gazed across the landscape at the beautiful hills and a line of mountains to the southwest that bordered the land on the right, farther than she could see. The river ahead snaked through the center of Morrowind, the first region across the sea from Vvardenfell, which was marked with several scattered waterfront cities. Turning to look up, she watched the ship's sails stretch taut in the wind, with Davir's flag flying proudly. As the ship sailed up and over the rough sea, the waves lapped at the bow as it pushed through the water.

The land's abundant growth of trees and rich vegetation boasted of a prosperous life for the people who lived there. Žaneta stared at the rich, green terrain, knowing its bounties could feed generations to come. But, as history and her own situation had shown her, there are always those who find ways to bring suffering wherever they go.

Far across the land, a group of wagons were en route through Cyrodiil, west of the Valus Mountains. The four carriages split paths, two to the west and two to the north, around the Imperial City. The horses pulled their carriages along the road quickly, kicking up dust and dirt while they continued to keep up their strained tempo, like machines.

But back over the mountains behind them, over the wilderness of Morrowind, Davir's ship came busting through the waves of the Inner Sea, pushing toward its destination. Captain Davir held steady to his course, and the crew worked their stations in the planned orchestration that came with life on the ship. Every member of the crew knew their place, and working in unison, they cut through the tides.

Žaneta stood on the portside, comfortably holding on to one of the ship's shroud ropes with her eyes closed, letting the breeze move through her hair as she took in a breath. She opened her eyes and set her gaze on the sight of the mainland. Over a decade had passed since she'd been there, and the visit, though unplanned, would likely be very unpleasant for whoever she caught up to. The ship rode through rough waters at the mouth of the River Thirr, but after hours of travel, the sea had calmed. It was midafternoon, and it would take days to reach Narsis at the southern edge of Lake Hlaalu.

Advancing down the river, it had, in fact, taken them nearly four more days before the ship made port at daybreak after sailing through Lake Hlaalu the night prior. Thirteen days had passed since she'd last seen the children, and since the Great Houses here largely operated under Imperial law, slavery was part of regular business—but not the theft and sale of children. With Žaneta's main concern being that time was not on her side, she was eager to get started. The ship bells ringing across the harbor were a pleasant testament to landfall, and Davir's ship would be the first to bring news of the recent events involving Vvardenfell.

Davir had his crew begin offloading their shipment to the dockworkers and took a moment to speak with Žaneta in private. She was gathering a few of her things and standing to sheathe her sword as he approached. "Things are about to heat up around here, what with the earthquake, or whatever we were witness to when we left Vivec. Žaneta… I know you're after your kids, and if they came here by the boat you mentioned, find it. Or talk with the dockmaster. This place is a political beehive, and it would be best to find what you need then be ready to move on. You don't want to linger here longer than you have to." He knew her full story from the trip in and was also aware of the inherent danger of the Great Houses.

Žaneta simply gave him a kind smile and reached out her hand to shake his. "Farewell!" she replied, then she stepped down the boat ramp onto the docks. Looking around, she noticed the city was bigger than she remembered, but it had been some time since she'd last seen it.

Narsis was a place where several roads intersected on their way to the surrounding cities. Hundreds of years ago, it was known for the Llodos Plague, which ravaged the countryside and its settlements. Sadly, the plague was a staple in the history of Narsis, and some thought the sickness might still linger in certain depths of places less ventured. Nevertheless, it was still bustling with travelers and traders.

Knowing no one, Žaneta decided it best to follow Davir's advice and speak to the dockmaster. She walked east along the pier toward the only small building near the docks with a sign out front that read, "East Empire Trading—Office." When she entered, a small bell rang to alert the staff. There was one man inside, a Dunmer who looked as though dealing with the public wasn't his strong point. He had mutton chops and a small bun on the rear of his otherwise balding head. "What ya need?" he asked, brushing his hand across his shirt as if getting rid of crumbs.

"A ship made a delivery here roughly a week ago. Twenty-four passengers arrived. I know you've got a lot of business coming through here, but they would've stood out because of their age… any idea where they went or who they were with?" Žaneta asked. Her face was stony as she analyzed the man's reaction.

"I don't know what you're talkin' about… Go ahead and shove off!" he grunted.

Žaneta was through with games. Being shut up on the ship for days as she traveled here only made her feel even more behind; she didn't need some slob getting in her way. "Where's your record book?" she pressed.

He sidestepped in an effort to go around her toward the door, but she blocked his path. He looked up at her again, knowing he couldn't challenge her. "Look… I don't need any trouble here. I don't know 'bout no kids, so don't try anything foolish. Now let me pass!" he sneered, waiting for her to move.

She didn't. Instead, she slammed a punch into his stomach, causing him to double over. She placed her foot on his shoulder, pushed him down, then stood on his chest lightly enough to still let him breathe as she stared down at him. "I never said the word 'kids!'" she hissed through her teeth.

He'd messed up, let fear cause his tongue to slip. He knew he couldn't get out of it. Either the big cat lady was going to kill him, or the Drens would. But Orvas wasn't the one standing on his chest at the moment, so he chose to live another day. "Look in the bottom right drawer of the desk. The book details shipments going in and out… Please get off me!" He struggled, rolling to his side when she lifted her leg.

She walked around the desk and pulled out the book, flipping a few pages back in the ledger. "There's no record of twenty-four people being brought through here! So, what am I looking for?" she said impatiently, staring down at him with narrowed eyes.

He sat up and leaned against the wall, rubbing his chest. "Barrels. We don't keep headcounts here. My job that evening was to have four horse-drawn transports of the 'discreet' nature ready for the shipment coming. So, look for the date with barrels of brandy and the carriages," he explained as he stood up.

Žaneta scanned back down the list and saw his entry. "That was eight days ago, and you signed for a man named… Tobias!" she growled, slamming the book shut. "Where'd they go?"

The shipping clerk backed up. "West, or-or southwest—I don't know for sure!" he squeaked, wide-eyed and panicked.

"You smuggle kids through here! I should throw your head into the bay!" she snapped, gripping her sword handle.

"Please… I didn't know they were kids! Slaves are traded through here, but that night, Tobias knocked on the office door to let me know he'd arrived to load onto the carriages. But he told me to stay in the office… so I did. I couldn't help myself, though—I had to see what was so secret. I saw kids in bindings get loaded up, and off they went!" he said in a rush. Žaneta, unconvinced, kept her hand resting on the hilt of her sword. Nervously shaking, he pressed back against the wall with his hands up. "Who could I tell? I've had a bit of a drug problem, and House Hlaalu keeps me taken care of. But if I told the guards, or anyone else, they'd have killed me."

Žaneta took her hand off her blade and replied, "Two of them are mine."

The Dunmer swallowed hard. "Please don't! Gods, I'm sorry!" He could barely meet her stare as he shook his head back and forth, staring down at the floor with tears welling in his eyes.

She could see the guilt weighing down the man's shoulders and knew he'd made many mistakes he wasn't proud of. Against her better judgment, a degree of sympathy was all that kept him alive. But in the moment, his guilt wasn't enough for her—she needed answers. "I'm after my kids. I suggest you quit this job and go do something useful. They snuck them by you this time, and you obviously live in a corrupt city… Great!" she scoffed, smirking coldly. "Whatever you do, you better not deal in children again and let me find out about it. Good day."

Slamming the office door behind her, Žaneta ran up the stairs and toward the main streets of the city. Infuriated from the conversation, she had to bite her tongue to keep from crying out, trying to keep it together since she was in public. Momentarily lost in thought, she gathered herself and started thinking of a plan. *West or southwest… I need to get supplies and transportation.* Staring up and down the street, she wandered through the city's market and stopped to ask about horses. She passed vendor after vendor, glancing over the items for sale, then approached the stables at the edge of town.

An Imperial woman was shoeing a horse as Žaneta approached. Wearing green pants and a black denim blouse, she obviously wasn't afraid to get dirty as she held the hind leg of the horse between her knees and filed its hoof.

"I'm looking to buy a good horse. What have you got for sale?" Žaneta asked, briefly interrupting the woman from her work.

"The four in the stalls, plus this one. Let me know if there's one that interests you, and I'll give you a price," the woman replied, sweeping her dark hair out of her eyes. The horse she was working on was a bay, as were two of the others. The last two were heavy horses—one a Shire, and the other a large black draft, standing at least eighteen hands tall.

"How much for that boy on the end?" Žaneta asked, half smiling.

"Twenty thousand," the woman answered without missing a beat.

"That's a bit much, but he is beautiful." Žaneta walked up and rubbed his mane.

"He's the best I've got! I'll even throw in the saddle and bags if you take him," the woman said with a smile. "They won't fit the other horses, except for maybe my Shire, but he's a loaf." She retrieved a halter to bring him out. "My name's Claire," she said, opening the gate. She walked him in a circle then stopped with him at her side. "What do you think?"

"How old is he?" With an eyebrow raised, Žaneta's interest was obvious.

"He's going on seven… will be this summer." Claire looked up at him proudly.

She made up her mind before Claire even finished her sentence. "I'll take him. Does he have a name?" Žaneta couldn't stop staring at how strong he appeared as she placed her hand on his cheek.

"Gus—he was my father's."

Žaneta stared at Claire and didn't hesitate too long, not wanting the girl to change her mind—she was unsure if it was an emotional sale. She reached into her bag for payment. "Do you have a place to count this?"

"Follow me!" Putting Gus back in his stall, Claire led Žaneta inside, where she counted the gold out on a small table. Žaneta watched with a grateful smile as Claire picked up the saddlebags and carried them over to her.

"I'll put an extra couple of diamonds in there if you'll put new shoes on him. I need to grab some things from the market, then I'll be ready to go," Žaneta said, grabbing the saddlebags and placing them on her left shoulder.

"Done!" Claire's smile grew wider.

Žaneta walked back to the market vendors and bought maps, food, a quiver with twenty steel broadhead arrows, thin cord, and a short recurve bow. Walking around the displays, she noticed some clothing and travel cloaks. She purchased a new one, since the Clannfear had ruined her last one back in Vvardenfell.

After Gus and all of her supplies, more than a third of her money was gone, but she was ready to head out. While loading her food into the saddlebags, she noticed one vendor had a basket of apples next to some other fruits. *Gus needs a treat, too!* she thought, smiling. She purchased a bag, putting all but one, which she kept out for herself, into the saddlebags. Biting into the apple, she caught sight of a twisted tower in the middle of town that almost looked like a root, similar to the ones she'd seen of the Telvannis' back on the island. She turned to the vendor and pointed at it. "What's the tower in town there?" she asked, chewing on her bite of apple.

"That's the Hlaalu Kinhouse. Largely, the city's body of government," the vendor replied.

Žaneta swallowed hard and clenched her jaw. She was angered by the fact that Orvas Dren had ties to House Hlaalu but wasn't sure of their involvement. *Fight the enemies you can see, Žaneta,* she thought to herself. It was just before noon and time to leave. But where to next?

 Back at the stables, Claire had fastened the saddle to Gus. His hooves were trimmed and fitted with shoes, and he was brushed and shining. "All set!" Claire said.

"Almost," Žaneta replied as she adjusted the stirrups to their lowest setting to allow for her height.

"Oh yes, sorry." Claire smiled.

Žaneta placed the saddlebags on Gus then reached in her satchel and felt Tai and Mazira's toys. She pulled them out gently and stared down fixedly at the worn dress on Mazira's doll. She couldn't speak for a moment and felt frozen—she wanted more than anything for it all to be over, to hold them close. She was growing weary, but also angry—and it drove her. She looked at her brave boy's toy knight and prayed he was with Mazira, that they were giving each other some form of comfort. She looked up and saw Claire watching her with a concerned expression. She quickly placed the toys in the saddlebag and snapped out of her thoughts. "Do you have another horse blanket I can buy?" Žaneta asked.

Claire nodded and went inside, returning with one under her arm. "No charge," she said, handing it to her.

"Thank you." Žaneta unsheathed her sword, rolled it in the blanket, and tied it behind her saddle with the rest of her things. "I don't want to poke him in the side," she explained, pulling an apple out of the saddlebag to feed him, along with the core from hers. Žaneta stepped in the stirrup and threw her leg over his back. She looked back at Claire and asked, "What are the nearest places to the southwest and west from here?"

Claire reached down to pick up a piece of apple for Gus that he'd dropped. "Far to the southwest, the road will take you into Stormhold—in Black Marsh. The western road out of town ends up heading southwest when you get close to Malak's Maw, through the Valus Mountains into Cyrodiil." She furrowed her brow. "Why? Where are you headed?"

Žaneta adjusted herself in the saddle and stared down at the saddle horn thoughtfully. "I'm trying to decide. Around a week ago, several carriages left from here after dark; I'm going after them."

Claire's eyes lit up. "Four of them. There were four white horse-drawn carts. I was awake and watched them leave." Smiling, she explained, "When my horses start to whinny… I checked to see why. Those carts all went west."

Žaneta closed her eyes and let out a relieved sigh. She thanked her Lady Mara and grinned, relieved she'd found the information she needed—and all by chance. "I can't thank you enough! Farewell." She flicked the reins and gave Gus a nudge with the stirrups, putting Narsis behind them in an instant. Žaneta kept him at a gallop—the road would be long, but she had planned for it.

***

Days prior, when the carriages had taken separate paths, two of them had traveled the Red Ring Road to the Gold Road, west through Skingrad on their way to Kvatch. The other two, led by Tobias, had headed north, pushing for the Jerall Mountains.

The horses pulled their cargo up the switchbacks leading into Kvatch. Night had fallen, and a deal had been struck in the city. The man on the lead carriage, wearing common clothes, was nothing fancy to speak of, but sat high on his coach seat when he and the other carriage stopped to meet his contact: a dark-haired woman who wore a full-length, dark-red robe and waited on the steps of the Great Chapel of Akatosh. The carriage driver climbed down from his seat and was approached by the person in robes, who handed him a thick leather bag the size of a small pumpkin, full of precious stones. After inspection, he walked to the back of both carriages and unlocked them.

Another individual wearing the same dark-red attire came from the building across the street from the chapel and joined his colleague. Together, the two of them lowered the children down, who, looking around scared and exhausted, were led back into the building the second man had come from. They then returned to the second carriage and repeated the process, with the man in the red robe telling the carriage driver, "For Lord Dagon!"

Not knowing what he'd done, the driver climbed atop his carriage with their payment and left the city in the night. Normally, nothing goes unseen by the guardsmen, but for the right price… anything can go unnoticed.

***

It was nightfall on the Valus Mountains. The temperature had dropped with the elevation, and it was cold enough to see their breath, but Žaneta and Gus were fine. Her cloak provided an extra layer to shield her from the windchill, and she, along with the equipment, helped shield Gus. Žaneta could see everything while guiding Gus through the mountains, so they rode all night, with the sun breaking over the hills behind them as they neared the Nibenay Basin. From the descent out of the mountains, the landscape was beautiful.

The mountains gradually turned into rolling hills that held no shortage of trees and green grass and the Imperial City's White Gold Tower in view to the west, built on an isle above the water surrounding it.

Žaneta saw a body of water to the southwest and, looking at her map, knew it must be Lake Canulus. It seemed an obvious choice for a place to rest and drink, so she and Gus trotted through the countryside toward it, where she could finally make camp and get herself and Gus something to eat while she got her bearings.

On the northeastern bank of the lake, she dismounted and tied one leash of the reins to a branch then laid the other over Gus's neck, allowing him to eat all the abundant grass he could while she looked around. Across the lake, on the southern shore, were old fort ruins; observing them through her spyglass, she saw they seemed to be abandoned. The banks all around the lake were quiet, a perfect place to let Gus get a drink and make a small fire to cook on.

Žaneta took off her cloak and stuffed it in the saddlebag; it was too warm here to need it. Then she untied Gus and led him to the water before unpacking some food from one of the saddlebags and set it on the rocks by the water's edge. Gus plunged into the lake, dropped his head, and gulped down the cool water. Žaneta chuckled and began to gather some dead sticks and branches for a fire. When she returned, Gus had come out of the water, and she took the saddlebags, saddle, and blanket off of him, laying it all on the rocks. He rolled in the grass, sat up, and started eating again. She watched for a while in amusement then started to work with the materials she'd bought. Removing an arrow from the quiver, she began carving a groove around the shaft just above the fletches with one of her nails. She then knotted the cord around it. Unwinding about thirty feet of it, similar to fishing line, she tied the other end under the bow's grip.

Some time passed, and Žaneta sat quietly on a boulder overlooking the water. Her bow and arrow at the ready, she'd just scattered more breadcrumbs on the water when her meal presented itself. She let fly an arrow that broadsided a large trout then pulled it in slowly. She took it back to her things, where she'd made a small stone fire pit, and arranged the sticks and kindling. Holding the fish with one hand, she reached out with the other and cast a fire spell onto the pit. Žaneta then filleted the fish before cooking it over the fire.

She enjoyed the catch, but her thoughts kept drifting back to Narsis. She'd seen no yellow sashes on anyone, and though she'd left the area in a hurry, it was well-known Cyrodiil had always been under Imperial rule, having little to no influence from the Dunmeri Houses. The more she thought about it, the more she was aware she need only follow the carts; any Camonna Tong would just be an added bonus and, at that point, were a distraction from reaching her children. *But,* she thought, *they'd started all of this*—she wouldn't forget that.

After she'd eaten, she stood and loosely tied Gus to a tree branch with his bridle then arranged her things to continue her search. She doused the fire and threw dirt on it, but she soon realized the smoke had caught someone's attention; on the northwestern bank of the lake, a couple hundred yards away, she saw three people staring at her.

Once aware she'd seen them, they all began walking toward her. Žaneta could tell they were probably just bandits by the way they were equipped, looking for an easy mark. They all wore light armor of various types. Their boots were of one variety, their cuirasses another, like they'd stolen and pieced together their things from their previous victims. She unrolled her sword and sheathed it in its frog as she walked closer.

The three individuals, two Imperials and a Breton, and Žaneta stopped about fifteen feet from each other. One of the men spoke first. "Good morning, my lady! We noticed you were enjoying our lake and wanted to say hello."

"Your lake?" replied Žaneta, callously raising a brow.

The men were silent for a moment. The one who had greeted her just smiled and said, "That's a beautiful horse. What did you pay for him?"

Žaneta glanced at Gus then back to the man. "A lot. Where do you boys live? If this is your lake and you all came down here together, do you belong to an orphanage nearby?" she said sarcastically, looking them up and down.

All three of them scowled. "Leave your horse and things—they're ours now!" the man sneered as an archer stepped from the tree line. Žaneta saw the archer in her peripheral vision but stayed focused on the three men in front of her. They were all armed with maces except for the one talking, who carried a sword. She smirked—a mace was the worst weapon they could have chosen to use against her. She lunged toward the man with the sword and kneed him in the groin, drawing her blade at the same time. In a single motion, she pulled him up in front of her and swept the head off of the man to her left.

The bandits were so surprised, they barely even had time to move. In their experience, people usually just negotiated or cowered. The archer loosed his arrow and hit his own man, who was being held in front of Žaneta. The last man standing had already taken off running down the lake's shore back in the direction they'd come.

Žaneta, still holding her human shield, turned to face the archer, who was nervously trying to nock another arrow onto his bowstring. She dragged the man with her and put her sword in her left hand, drew back her right hand, then pointed toward the archer. The spark she cast tore through his head and sent him tumbling back into the bushes.

Žaneta turned the man she held to look at him. "You all just want to hurt people… but you're no good at it." Disgusted, she sheathed her sword and let the man fall backward, dying from the arrow's injury.

Tired of wasting time, she left the men where they lay, readied Gus, and left the area, heading west on higher ground. She came to the Silverfish River, which was one of three large rivers spreading over miles that came off the Niben Bay farther into Cyrodiil and provided the Nibenay Basin and Valley with water. She then continued following its southern bank to the west until she cut across the Nibenay Valley onto the Yellow Road before stopping to look at her maps again.

To the south was Leyawiin, a southern coastal city that guarded the waters of the Topal Bay. Straight across from her, over the Niben Bay, was Bravil, a poor, rundown waterfront hovel of a city that was home to very unfortunate individuals—the castle offered the only glimpse of beauty within the city walls. Just beyond it, miles to the west and south, was Elsweyr. It was strange to think she was so close to her birthplace and yet was too pressed with current matters to return. But home was calling, and her memories of her mother—when they'd go walking near the coast—rushed over her, distracting her for a moment.

She recalled meeting Sandrew for the first time in the market, how she always caught him staring at her on the days she was with her father when he smithed. She noticed how interested he was in her father's blades, but after a while, she realized how often his gaze flicked to her—it took less time for her parents to notice.

For a moment, she almost found herself smiling. Then she snapped to and looked back down at her map. To the northwest was the Imperial City. The last time she was there, she and Sandrew were passing through in search of a new home, which eventually led them to Vvardenfell.

While deciding on a route to take, she suddenly had the feeling she was being watched. Something was convincing her to head north, and though hard to understand, it felt… right. She decided to trust the feeling; so, the Imperial City it was. She turned right on the Yellow Road and headed north.

The path through the valley was beautiful, and several hours into the ride, Žaneta was daydreaming about when she and Sandrew had stood on the bridge northeast of Fort Alessia almost eleven years ago, the very bridge she was about to cross. Approaching it on her left, she felt her eyes brim with tears as she turned toward it. Continuing across it at a steady gallop, she remembered her and Sandrew's conversation.

***

"I don't know where to go from here." Sandrew gazed over Lake Rumare then turned to meet her eyes as they both leaned against the barrier rail before staring back out over the water. His arms were crossed, and she was resting back on her hands.

"We'll find our way… We've got each other. So who cares if we're lost!" She reassured, giving him an earnest smile, and Sandrew placed a hand in hers. "I love you, Žaneta…"

***

The view of the Imperial City from over the water was mesmerizing and recalling that brief moment in the past with Sandrew was agony. She refocused and picked up the pace, swallowing back her emotions before they got the best of her. She was sinking back into the terrible despair she'd felt when she'd lost him. But knowing it would do her no good to dwell on it, she wiped her eyes and kept riding, putting it away for the moment.

It wasn't until late afternoon, when reaching Pell's Gate, that she stopped to give Gus a break and a couple of apples from her bag. She looked at the village and noticed an inn's sign that read, "The Sleeping Mare." She figured she'd get herself and Gus some rest here, instead of the countryside-ambush option. Žaneta took Gus to the stables and went to pay the boy who was tending stalls to board her horse.

The young Imperial boy was caught off guard by her initially. Startled, he jumped and looked up from his work. "Good gosh… You're, umm… That sure is a pretty pony!"

She gave him a kind smile, ignoring his stammered greeting. She was used to getting shocked looks wherever she went; not many people had ever seen a Khajiit who shared her features, much less her size. "Hello, may I keep my horse here overnight?"

The boy stopped what he was doing and walked up to take the reins. "Yes, I'll take care of him."

She took her sword from the horse blanket, sheathed it, then walked into The Sleeping Mare, the whole time being eyeballed off and on by the stable boy.

Žaneta closed the door behind her and was immediately greeted by the barkeep. "Good evening! Welcome to The Sleeping Mare. How may I help you?" the woman asked. She was a Breton who seemed like an honest, hard-working individual.

"I'd like a room for the night."

"Absolutely. Would you care for some dinner? I've got stew cooking in the kitchen." She smiled politely.

"That would be great!" Žaneta replied in mild relief, half smiling. She walked to the small dining area to sit at one of the several vacant tables.

The woman came back with a glass of water, spoon, and napkin, then returned to the kitchen to retrieve Žaneta's meal. She placed a bowl of steaming beef stew on the table in front of her. "There ya are… enjoy. Just let me know if there's anything else you'd like!" she said, walking toward the stairs.

"Actually!" Žaneta started, gaining her attention, "have there been any horse carriages through here in the last week or so… several at once?" She tried to seem only mildly interested.

"Imperial carts come through here often. But not many stop since it's so close to their forts, where they can stay and eat for nothing," she said.

Žaneta's stare drifted down. She prayed she wouldn't have to start searching for clues all over again. Then, the woman continued, "But ask Antonius—he's usually outside during the day. Maybe he could tell ya."

Žaneta smiled and nodded at her then took a bite of the stew and realized how hungry she was. She stuffed in another bite before replying, "Who is Antonius?"

The barkeep stood there, happy to see her food being enjoyed. "He's the farm boy in town, and he also works the stables. My name's Candice. I'll leave ya be while you eat and go get your room ready." Turning, she headed upstairs.

Žaneta quickly finished eating and downed the glass of water just as Candice returned and said, "Room's all set up! Would you like me to wake you in the morning?"

"Yes, dawn if possible, or whenever Antonius is up and at it." Žaneta stood up. "I didn't even ask… how much for the room and dinner?"

Candice gathered the bowl and cup from her table and set them on the counter. "The room's ten Septims, and the dinner wasn't a bother," she said.

Žaneta reached into her bag, felt around the bottom—past the gold coins to some of the loose gems— and pulled out a small emerald, placing it on the counter.

"Oh, ma'am… that's too much!" Candice murmured with a grateful look.

"Thank you for dinner." Žaneta smiled and walked up the stairs to her room.

"First one on the right!" Candice called.

Žaneta entered and set down her things. The lantern and a small candle were the only sources of light. The bedroll had been laid out, and there was a wash bowl and towel on a small table. Žaneta washed her face and cleaned up. She took her brush from her satchel and ran it through her hair, removing some of the debris it had collected, then lay on the bedroll.

Clearing her mind as she leaned her head back, she closed her eyes and soon had that same feeling of being watched come over her again. Without warning, a vision snapped into her subconscious. An image of a city that had been destroyed flashed through her mind—structures were toppled, and many still burned. It was dark and raining, and silhouettes could only partially be made out. A cold came over her, and she sat up. *What was that?* she thought, lowering her head onto her knees. The vision had stopped as fast as it had started, and she was wide awake.

It seemed someone was trying to tell her something, but it was like a dream… or a warning. *Maybe the stew is messing with me!* she thought. She lay back down and remained motionless, trying to rest.

***

Morning came, and there was a knock on her door. "Good morning, ma'am! I'll have breakfast downstairs when you're ready!" Candice said through the door.

Žaneta had been up for some time, sitting at the table and thinking on what the dream could mean, where to go, and who to talk with. She knew people in the Imperial City from the last time she'd been there; hopefully, they were still there and could offer some help.

After breakfast, she thanked Candice then stepped outside to the stables. Antonius was raking hay into a pile by his wheelbarrow as she approached him. "Antonius?"

He looked up from his work and grinned.

"Good morning! How's Gus?" she asked politely.

"Brushed and pampered, my lady," he replied.

She walked to Gus's stall and held his chin, rubbing his forehead. "Antonius, over a week ago… did you happen to see multiple carriages pass by at any time?"

He stopped working and leaned on his rake. The gesture made her suddenly notice he must be only a little older than Tai. "Often, ma'am—we'll probably see some today. Soldiers are by here all the time."

"These wouldn't have been soldiers—more like prisoner carts or containers, traveling together and moving fast," she elaborated.

He tilted his head. "I remember, last Middas, two carts moved through in a hurry. I couldn't see their contents, though… maybe they were transports due to the door on the back. I don't know—first time I'd seen 'em."

"Just two… which way did they head?" Žaneta asked casually.

"West, but you'll have to ask in Fort Virtue. If the carts didn't check in there, they'd have gone west before the fort on the Gold Road, toward Skingrad." His eyes lit up at her grateful nod, and he puffed out his chest with pride.

"You're certain?" asked Žaneta.

"Yup. All carriages, carts, and transports require inspection before being allowed into the Imperial City area. There's a fort on every road leading into it."

"You're a wonderful young man! Thank you." She grinned, threw Gus's horse blanket on his back, and saddled up the rest of her things.

Just around an hour after sunrise, she headed west to Fort Virtue, thinking along the way about how Antonius had said he'd only seen two carts. If these were indeed the transports she was after, where had the other two gone? Hopefully, she was still on their trail. She couldn't let herself think otherwise much less dwell on the two missing carts. Out of options, her choice was clear, and she needed to press on, urge Gus to gallop faster. She'd been fortunate enough to come into contact with those who had information she needed, and that gave her hope—it was all she had right now.

Chapter Two

It was later in the morning when Žaneta arrived at Fort Virtue. The guard she approached saw her but stayed silent, waiting for her to speak. "I'm looking for two carriages that may have come through here last Middas. Who keeps track of the traffic here?" she asked.

"You'll need to talk to Captain Evans about it—she'll be just inside," he answered.

Žaneta hopped off Gus, tied him to a hitch post, and entered the fort. Two more guards stood right inside the entrance. "Captain Evans?" she asked.

One Imperial looked her up and down, concerned at first, then said, "Straight down the hall to the right, then through the doors. Her desk will be straight ahead from there." Žaneta proceeded, and the two soldiers looked at each other in surprise—Žaneta wasn't the *usual* passerby.

As directed, she followed the hall around through the doors and found an Imperial woman in plate armor sitting at a desk and writing in a ledger. "Captain Evans?"

The woman looked up. "Yes, citizen?" Her eyes grew wide as she took in Žaneta.

"I'm looking to see if two white carriages came through here last Middas. They would've been large enough for prisoner transports, but they weren't cages. They came from the east."

The captain flipped back several pages in the ledger in front of her and scanned down the list with her finger. After a minute, she replied, "Nothing like that. On Middas last week, only garrison troops came through here."

"What about the days following?" Žaneta pressed.

Captain Evans sighed irritably. "Look… I don't even have to tell you what I have! What's this regarding anyway?"

"My children may have been on them!" Žaneta growled, fixing her with a penetrating stare.

Evans's expression softened, and she began to scan down the pages a little more thoroughly. Žaneta struggled to stay still and calm, fighting her fear and impatience as the captain flipped through the pages. Finally, Captain Evans stopped, her eyes narrowing. "On Fredas last week, carriages that match your description came through and went north. Their contents were empty. My men reported them arriving from the Gold Road."

Žaneta's mind began to race, picturing the map presently lying in her satchel. She realized if they came through empty on Fredas from the Gold Road, then they'd have come from the west after dropping off their cargo somewhere. The turnoff toward Skingrad, which she'd passed on her way here, would've allowed them to travel without checking in at Fort Virtue, just as Antonius had said. That meant, she was fixated on a new target—Skingrad. The Imperial City had been moved further down on her list.

"It would seem you have your heading, ma'am. Times are hard right now—several factions are at odds with new ones popping up all the time. Even bandits have been increasing their activity. I can't offer any guards to help you… but mention my name, and it should afford you cooperation from our soldiers where you ask. Good luck," Captain Evans said, lowering her head to return to her work.

Žaneta marched outside, climbed onto Gus, then rode west to Skingrad, the next city along the Gold Road.

***

Not far from there, in Kvatch, the children were in a room together, sitting on bedrolls and eating food they'd recently been given. The man from before entered, followed by the woman wearing those dark-red robes. He stood by the door as she approached and spoke softly to each child, smiling at them. "Who'd like to meet my Lord?" she asked, looking back and forth at the children. None said a word as the starving children shifted and shivered on their ragged bedrolls. Every few seconds, tiny whimpers rang out from a couple of the kids huddled together as they shrank away from the woman.

None volunteered. The woman turned to look at her colleague. "Bring me a boy and a girl," she said as she left the room. Her pleasant demeanor and smile only made the children more uncomfortable. With that, all the children began whimpering and huddling tightly together. When the man grabbed the wrists of the two he'd chosen, they began to scream and cry loud enough that an old woman on the street outside was alarmed by the noise.

The old woman walked to the city gates, looking back over her shoulder at the house, to tell the first guard she found. But inside the home, in the basement, the two kids were led to the woman in red. She stood in the empty room with only a lantern for light and something in her left hand, but she kept her fist closed around it with a small gold chain dangling out.

The woman motioned to her side and said, "Paradise awaits!" A portal opened, filling the room with an ominous purple light, causing the once quiet room to abruptly erupt into chaos when both kids started screaming again. They both fought back against the man but were unable to avoid being slid forward. The man ushered them closer by force and pushed them in. As fast as the portal had appeared, it vanished.

The house was quiet, then the man and woman returned to the main floor. Just then, there was a knock on the front door. The woman set the lantern on the table and opened the door casually to a city guard standing in front of her, his eyes narrowed as he attempted to look past her into the house. "Yes, sir, how may I help you?" she asked with a small smile.

"Noise complaint. There was a report of children screaming," the guard said, monitoring the woman's reaction.

There wasn't one—she just raised an eyebrow and replied, "I don't have any children. Must've come from somewhere else, but I didn't hear anything!" The guard slowly relaxed as he analyzed the woman's expression. She was confused by his question, and the look in her eyes seemed genuine. Satisfied, he nodded. "Okay, sorry to bother you." With that, he walked to the next building.

The woman closed the door then latched it and let out a sigh, knowing how close that had been. But she knew anything was worth her cause—even the risk of being caught.

***

Back on the Gold Road, Žaneta had come over a large hillside then down through an equally large ravine which lay under a huge arched support bridge. The bridge led to the solitary Castle Skingrad, across from the city itself. Directly ahead of her was the city entrance. She approached the posted guards and greeted them as she dismounted. "Last week, around Middas or Turdas, two carriages came this direction carrying people, maybe through town. I spoke with Captain Evans—have you seen anything?"

"No, ma'am. I've been posted here for three years. But you may need to speak with Sergeant Faven; he usually works the night-guard post here," one of the soldiers replied.

It was already late afternoon, and Žaneta stood in the shadow from the high eastern walls of the city as they blocked out the sun. "Who's captain of the guard here?" she asked.

"That would be Captain Dion. When he's not in his office, he's at the Great Chapel of Julianos, inside to the left," he said, opening the large city door.

Žaneta walked Gus to the stable behind her, unrolled her sword and sheathed it, then handed the reins and payment to the man tending to the horses before heading inside. She stood before the huge walls continuing on her left and right, which appeared to part the city into two halves, each of which was connected by low arched footbridges. The low point, where she was, looked like a cobblestone riverbed that wound between the walls.

She ran under the arched walkway above her then up and left to the Great Chapel courtyard. Žaneta walked toward the building, admiring the beautiful architecture a moment before going in. But on the steps of the chapel stood a soldier with no helmet and unique markings on his armor, talking to another individual.

She walked straight toward him with purpose. "Excuse the interruption… Are you Captain Dion?"

The man turned to Žaneta. "Yes. State your business."

She looked down at the captain even though he was a couple of steps up toward the chapel. "I need to speak to your guard, Faven. After talking with Captain Evans, two carriages may have come through the city last week carrying stolen children. The day guard said he saw nothing," she explained.

Captain Dion, suddenly attentive to her complaint, became heavily concerned, his expression darkening. "Captain Evans sent you? I'll send for our man. Come with me to my office," he replied, before yelling to a nearby guard to have Faven report to him. Žaneta followed Captain Dion and told him some of the details about what she'd gone through to get here. She also convinced him to be so kind as to allow her to question Faven should he start to stumble in his recollection.

After they waited about twenty minutes or so, a guard knocked on the office door then opened it. "Sir, Sergeant Faven is here."

Captain Dion nodded to the guard. "Send him in."

Faven entered and stood at attention in front of Dion's desk. Žaneta was sitting in a corner chair behind him out of view, waiting to hear his statement. "We've had reports of two carriages coming through the city last week. Its contents we can discuss later, but it happened on your watch. What would you like to tell me?" asked Captain Dion sternly.

"What? Nothing, sir. I've seen nothing!" Faven replied.

"So, Captain Evans is lying… Why would she do that?" Dion pressed.

"No… I mean, I don't know…" stammered Faven, both confused and nervous. "Carts came through, but that was on Fredas!"

Captain Dion rose from his seat and leaned on his desk. "You just told me you saw nothing!" he spat.

Žaneta stood from her chair and approached Faven, who turned and was caught completely off guard by the large Khajiit. "Who the hell is this?" he spluttered, breathing more heavily.

"This is Žaneta. She wants to know why you let two loads of children through my city, as do I!" Dion shouted, smacking his desk.

Suddenly, Faven reached across his left hip for his sword. But Žaneta grasped his wrist with her claws; it was becoming a common practice for her. He let out a loud yell as he stumbled backward, bracing himself on Dion's desk to keep from falling back. With her teeth bared, she slammed her right hand down onto his left, pinning it to the desk with her claws.

The guard outside came rushing in with his sword drawn. "Give us a minute!" Dion commanded the guard, who backstepped from the confusing scene and slowly retreated while pulling the door closed. Faven, out of breath from screaming, was sobbing. "Please… continue," Dion ordered.

Žaneta released her grip and took Faven's sword, tossing it away from him. She grabbed the chair she'd been sitting in and forcibly slid it to Faven, motioning for him to sit. "Start talking!" she barked. His hand and wrist were bleeding profusely, so Žaneta, not wanting him to pass out or make more of a mess in Dion's office, reached out and began healing his wounds. With his arms still covered in drying blood, he looked up at her in amazement. Dion couldn't take his eyes off Žaneta either.

"I can put the holes back, if you'd like! Who are you working with?" she breathed calmly.

"I don't know her name," he muttered, lowering his head. "I was at my post a couple of weeks ago when, late one night, she approached us. She made an offer in gemstones… a bag the size of my fist, and said, 'In a week, carriages will be coming through with precious cargo. Let them pass.' Said they'd give the phrase, 'Paradise awaits.' I thought it was nonsense and easy money…"

"Then what about your watch partner that night? Davies? He was reported missing the next day. You said during questioning you both ended your shift together and went to your quarters. But he didn't show up the next night with you!" Dion leaned toward him, his face growing redder as his hands shook.

"Now, I'd swear my life on it, I did nothing to him! I don't know where he is. We disagreed about the payment but said we'd talk about it, then he never showed up. The two carts came through the city, but I've not seen him since the woman gave me the gemstones."

"Where's the bag of gems?" grumbled Dion.

Faven let out a shaky sigh. "Under the frame of my bunk."

"Would you stay with him?" Dion asked Žaneta, and she nodded. "I'll return in a minute." He left the office.

"Who are you in all this?" asked Faven, still looking down.

"My children were taken, and I've been after them since," she replied, still pinning him with her stoic gaze.

"What you did… I've never seen anything like it. I mean, I've seen healers work, but nothing—nothing like what you just did." He stared at his wrist and hand, layered in dried blood that he rubbed and picked off in patches.

Žaneta changed the subject back to what was most important. "Describe the woman. What was she wearing, what did she look like?"

"Looked like any other Imperial woman. But she had brown hair, brown eyes, and was dressed in a red robe… dark red. And she was weird. Just calm and out of place," he said.

Žaneta couldn't believe what she was hearing—could no one be trusted, especially the ones charged to protect the helpless? "Sounds like 'out-of-place' wasn't alarming enough for you. You just took her money, despite what it was paying for!"

Captain Dion entered the room, walked around his desk, and tossed the bag of gems on it. "You weren't kidding, Faven—there's enough there to do nearly anything with. But the woman who paid you made a mistake! This bag is made of fabric from Kvatch. They're about to have their celebration for the Second Planting in a couple of days, and they sell these patterns of gray and black every year to honor the city colors. She'd have been smarter to tear off a piece of her own clothes than use this." He smirked.

"Kvatch?" Žaneta asked shortly.

"Yes. It's a short ride from here to the southwest, then up onto a plateau. I'll have some guards accompany you—men I trust. And you'll have full cooperation from the guard there. This just became an Imperial matter as well!" Dion scowled at Faven then picked up the bag of gemstones. "Guard!" he hollered. "Bring a prisoner cart around for Mr. Faven; we'll be going to the Imperial City directly. Also, tell two guards to get horses ready. They'll be accompanying this woman to Kvatch."

Žaneta waited there with Dion and Faven until the guard returned, saying, "All is ready, captain!" They all walked down together. Žaneta exited through the east gate, wrapped her sword, and mounted Gus. She rode back into Skingrad between its double walls, where she waited for the assigned guards to meet up with her.

After a moment, the two guards joined her on horseback with Captain Dion on his own. "I'm going to deliver Faven to the Imperial City. If you find this woman, we would like her alive for questioning, but that is up to your discretion, as I know you have more to lose than any of us. May the gods be with you on this." He paused and addressed his men, "Do as she asks! She's working under my authority." Then he rode back toward the east gate.

The hour was getting late, but the two guards accompanying her normally worked the night posts in the city, so they were fresh. The three of them headed west out of Skingrad along the road toward Kvatch.

Riding all night, they'd not be there until the early hours of the morning. But there was enough light from the moons and stars to not be completely in the dark, which gave the guards riding with her a bit of relief.

Along the path to the east, Captain Dion rode on the prisoner cart with one of his guards. They stopped in Fort Virtue for the night; Captain Dion wanted to tell Captain Evans the details of what had happened while affording the prisoner a place to stay under proper lock and key. The fort was mostly locking down for the night with torches burning and a handful of soldiers posted outside. Just as always, the primary purpose was to keep watch for travelers at the checkpoint.

***

It was a couple of hours after midnight, and near the Gold Coast, Žaneta approached the gates of Kvatch with the guards from Skingrad riding on either side of her. Two city soldiers stood on watch at the entrance, and one of the riders with her spoke up. "We're here on business for Captain Dion. We'll need quarters for the night and to speak with Captain Matius in the morning." Žaneta looked at him and smiled, grateful the two of them had accompanied her. She was sure their presence would make this part of her journey much easier. Everyone was always asking so many questions, which slowed her down. It was nice to have some support.

"Open up!" the gate guard called as he pounded on the door a couple of times with his fist. The sound of a crossbeam being moved was heard, and the door opened. As the three riders proceeded inside, the large door was shut behind them.

As they dismounted, Žaneta retrieved her sword off Gus before the three of them handed their reins to two guards who were ready to stable their horses for them. A Kvatch guard approached them with a lantern and said, "You need quarters? Follow me." He led them to the guardhouse, which was filled with bunks for all the soldiers who weren't on watch or who were traveling between sites.

Once inside, he showed them the bunks arranged in two different rooms divided by a hallway. "Ladies on the left… Men on the right," he said, gesturing to each of them. "In the morning, we'll take you to the captain—just let one of us know."

Žaneta and the two guards separated, and after picking a cot and leaning her sword against the wall, she got ready for bed and prayed.

The vast distance she'd covered that day wasn't nearly as tiring as the thoughts whirling through her mind. She grimaced, her eyes closed. *You've done everything right!* she thought.

Shifting back and forth on the narrow bed, she was restless. The thought of her children being here, or somewhere nearby, fueled her adrenaline, and she was desperate to check every place in the city. *Find the woman, find your answers!* She reminded herself to keep focused and stay on track. In the morning, she was certain their captain would be of more assistance. But all this thinking—and worry—was exhausting. Overwhelmed with stress, her concern pressed against her chest like a weight—a weight she was tired of carrying. Slowly, her eyes began to drift closed, and she was finally able to rest.

A.L. Zuniga

Morning came, and Žaneta was finishing getting ready as she sheathed her sword and walked to the men's side of the guardhouse. One of the guards that had accompanied her was putting on his boots, and the other looked like he had just woken up. "I'll be outside looking for Captain Matius," Žaneta told them.

She left the guardhouse and had a strangely familiar feeling about the city. But she ignored it for the moment and looked for the captain.

Two Kvatch guards were nearing her when she stopped them and asked, "Captain Matius?"

One of them offered direction, "Go left after these houses, past the chapel, then straight ahead, and you'll find him at the castle gatehouse."

Žaneta nodded her thanks and proceeded to the end of the street. As she went left around the houses, there stood the Chapel of Akatosh. Suddenly, it hit her—the same feeling from when she was in Pell's Gate. This was the city in her vision that was laid to ruins—it all flashed in front of her again. Fire and shadowy figures had been scattered all about, but the city she presently stood in was undisturbed. Pushing away the ominous dream, she felt compelled to go into the chapel.

Žaneta walked straight across the street, up the steps, and inside. Beautiful stone architecture, just like the Chapel of Julianos, was decorated with amazing stained-glass windows and was nearly empty. She quickly found an altar and knelt to pray. She only took a moment, asking for clarity on the vision and guidance to find her children, when a priest laid a hand on her shoulder. "Sometimes prayers are more effective when we do them with others. Can I help you with something, sister?"

Žaneta looked at him, her eyes frantic with worry. "This place was overrun… destroyed. And it felt real in my dream, so I came to pray," she said quietly.

"What's your name?" He gave her a kind smile.

"Žaneta."

"Pleased to meet you. I'm Brother Martin." He reached for her hand with a welcoming handshake and helped her up. "Would you like to talk about what you've seen? Where are you from?" he asked, his eyes widening as she stood.

"I'm sorry, I have to go, but thank you. Just pray for me and my children… and your city," she replied quickly. She turned and walked to the chapel doors then headed to find the captain.

When she arrived, Captain Matius was leaving the castle gatehouse. A seasoned Imperial soldier with short, dark hair and a black headband, he was clean-shaven and seemed to have a no-nonsense attitude from what she observed in his appearance.

"Captain Matius?" she inquired.

"Yes, I'm Savlian Matius. Who are you?"

She didn't hesitate to explain every detail. "My name's Žaneta. After talking with Captain Dion, we discovered two carriages of stolen children were likely brought into your city last week on Middas or Turdas. Captain Evans reported two empty carriages passed through Fort Virtue last Fredas, going north, but my children may have been amongst the ones brought here. Now, I'm looking for the woman who paid off a guard in Skingrad to get the children into your city. She's a brunette Imperial who was seen wearing a dark-red robe. What guards were posted those nights?"

Captain Matius looked a little shocked. His eyes flicked up and down the street, and he seemed flustered as he considered what to do next. The city was bustling with the festival Captain Dion had mentioned, and Žaneta could tell Matius was a busy man. Thinking quickly, the captain gave her a determined look and said, "All right. Let's go wake them up!"

Žaneta followed him as they walked to the front gate. The two Skingrad guards were standing in front of the guardhouse, and they joined Žaneta and the cap`tain as they passed. "Wait here a moment," Matius ordered as he entered the office at the base of one of the front gate towers.

Inside, three men were working. "Lieutenant!" Matius shouted at one, who jumped. "Middas and Turdas of last week… bring all the men who were on night watch those days and have them waiting out in front of the barracks. I'll be there shortly," he commanded, stepping back outside. He walked up to Žaneta and asked, "What were the details from when the carriages passed through Skingrad?"

Žaneta thought a moment. "It was late at night. The guard on duty, Faven, accepted payment in the form of gemstones from a woman in a red robe, an Imperial with dark hair and eyes. The bag she gave him was said to have come from here by Captain Dion's observation," she said.

"Hmm, that's thin info to go on, but still concerning with the potential that I may have a corrupt guard… or guards," he said.

As they continued to discuss the situation, they were interrupted by the lieutenant. "Sir, all the men requested are present and accounted for."

Together, the group proceeded to the barracks where, in front of the building, twelve men stood at attention. Captain Matius stopped in front of them.

"Last week, carriages with stolen children were either brought into my city by guards who allowed it or paid for and snuck in by a woman from the area. Now, I will find out who it was, and if you come forward, I promise only you will be tried… but if you make me wait for long and draw this out into more than it needs to be, I will make sure your whole family is exiled from these lands while you hang."

The men were trained to stand at attention in uniformity, and it was probably the hardest time they'd ever had following this order. The tension was thick amongst them, and they all strained to keep from glancing at each other. But as they subtly shifted, their eyes flicking back and forth, Žaneta was certain the message had gotten through.

"In the meantime, I want to know who this woman is." He paused, looking back and forth between the men. "Not everyone at once!" he sneered sarcastically. "A dark-haired Imperial woman, our sources say, was last seen in a dark-red robe—anyone?"

"Uhh… sir?" a Kvatch guard on duty spoke up from the left side of the detail. "The woman you described… I saw her recently."

Captain Matius narrowed his eyes and approached the guard, as did Žaneta and the others. "Where?" he growled.

"Across from the chapel. A townswoman made a complaint, said she thought she'd heard screams. But when I questioned the houses in the area, there were no noises, and that woman was the only one who said she didn't have kids. You mentioned the dark-red robe… that's what made me remember her," the guard replied, standing straight.

"Lieutenant!" Matius bellowed, still staring at the soldier.

"Yes, sir?" The lieutenant stepped forward.

"These night watchmen are not to leave the city until I've talked with all of them—is that understood?"

"Yes, sir!"

"Dismissed," Captain Matius said. He turned back to the guard. "Show us this house."

The guard took them by the chapel and along the street of houses directly next to the house where the woman had answered the door, cautiously keeping their distance so as to stay out of the woman's sight. "This next one's it," the guard whispered.

Žaneta looked down the street to the right, toward the chapel she'd visited that morning. *I walked past this place twice this morning*, she thought, shaking her head. "With your blessing, captain, I'd like to say hello," Žaneta muttered. She stomped up to the door and knocked.

She waited a few moments then knocked again. A man wearing the same dark-red robe that had been described answered the door. "Yes?" he asked warily.

Žaneta was the only one in sight, as the others stood to the side of the doorway. "Is your wife home?" she asked with a smile.

"I'm not married," he replied slowly.

"Well, does your girlfriend know you're wearing her clothes, then? Or do all of you wear the same outfit with whatever it is you're doing?" she asked, her smile fading.

His face paled, and Žaneta saw his eyes flash with panic as he suddenly began to slam the door with trembling hands. But Žaneta stomped down in front of it, keeping it ajar. "Get out of the way!" she snarled, pushing him back. She was followed quickly by Captain Matius and the three guards. She grabbed the man's collar and held him against the wall. "Where are they?"

The man simply stared at her and pointed to his right, up the stairs.

She let him loose and pushed him to the Skingrad guards, one of whom put him in shackles and took him outside. Žaneta proceeded up the stairs, while Matius and the other two guards stayed at the entry. She opened the door to one empty room then moved to the next. She could hear shuffling from the room and glimpsed the shadow of someone scurrying around by the light seeping out from under the door.

Žaneta opened it and saw six children, scared and dirty with gaunt faces. Distracted by them, Žaneta didn't notice the woman in the red robe lunge at her with a dagger in an attempt to plant it in Žaneta's neck. But in her haste, she gave herself away and only managed to cut across Žaneta's right shoulder as she dove out of the way. Žaneta reached toward the woman's incoming attempt at a second stab and grabbed the dagger's blade, which plunged straight through her left hand. Žaneta didn't scream, but she clenched her teeth as her eyes filled with tears. She made a fist around the quillon then grabbed the woman's throat and forced her down to her knees, not letting her claws all the way out—even though she badly wanted to. "Where are my children?" she asked through her teeth.

Matius and the guards, hearing the noise, barged into the room. He immediately ran to the children. "Help me! Let's get them outside," he commanded the guards, shaken by the sight of them.

The woman still hadn't answered and was smiling up at Žaneta as a light stream of blood trickled from her neck where Žaneta held her.

"Are you good?" Captain Matius asked as he passed with some of the kids.

"Right behind you," Žaneta replied. She released the woman's throat then dragged her out by her hair down the stairs.

By that time, a small crowd had gathered due to all the excitement. The man in the robe sat on the sidewalk with his hands shackled behind his back. The Skingrad and Kvatch guards came out with a couple of children each, followed by Matius. "Go get some food and water… and a healer!" he ordered.

"No… just the food and water. I'll do the rest!" Zaneta interrupted before the guard left. She pulled the woman out of the house and shoved her down into the street.

Žaneta pulled the dagger from her hand and gave it to Matius then slowly walked to the children. She took a knee and spoke to them gently. "My name's Žaneta. I'm looking for my children. Their names are—"

She stopped short as one little girl interrupted her. "Tai and M-M… Mazi?" the little girl whimpered, looking at her.

Tears filled Žaneta's eyes. "That's right! Tai and Mazira. Where are they?"

"They didn't come here with us! There were others, but… it's just us now," another boy replied sadly.

"I saw their eyes—they're just like yours," said the little girl.

Žaneta's tears spilled over as her mouth quivered, and she exhaled sharply. Giving herself a brief moment to recover, she tried to swallow back her grief. She stared up at the sky and blinked away the emotion—as best she could—before focusing on the children.

"Come close, don't be afraid." Žaneta beckoned to all of them. She was down on both knees. She relaxed with all the children by her side and cupped her hands together in front of her chest.

Her magic started to form in her hands. Light glowed from the wound in her palm as it and the cut on her shoulder started to close. The appearance of dehydration, cuts, and bruises faded away from the children as they stood next to her. The city street was in awe. The crowd had become substantial, and no one said a word. Žaneta separated her hands, and the energy stopped. Kneeling there with dried blood on her hand and shoulder, but nothing else to prove there were ever any injuries.

The kids were fine but hungry. Two guards came with food and a pitcher of water, staring around at everyone. They approached the children and handed out all they had. One quietly asked the captain as he stood nearby, "Sir, what's going on?"

Matius turned to the guard but could only shake his head, speechless.

The woman in the robe, still sitting in the street, glared up at Žaneta. "Who are you?" She'd barely moved after watching what had happened.

Žaneta's smile and tears turned into a distant stare as she stood and turned to face the woman. "You came here with more children—six more! Where are they?" she demanded, striding toward her.

The woman stared down at the ground and laughed under her breath. Žaneta knew she was sinister from the vile chuckle and was tired of playing with her. She drew her sword and abruptly jerked her to her feet. "Where. Are. They?" she hissed fiercely.

The woman looked up at Žaneta with wild eyes and smiled. "Oblivion!"

At the woman's crazed smirk, Žaneta lost control. Without thinking, she drove her sword into the woman's abdomen and out her back as hard as she could, lifting her off the ground. The woman let out an agonized gasp and tried to grasp the sword, her hands clutching at it.

Then Žaneta saw it—an amulet in the woman's left hand, clanking against the blade.

With her dying breath, the woman choked out, "Paradise awaits!"

In the middle of that street in Kvatch, a dark portal flashed open, enveloping Žaneta and the woman as it disappeared—with both of them inside.

Chapter Three

The world felt like it had been flipped upside down. Žaneta and the woman seemed as though they were surrounded by a bubble of fire, then *pop!* She stood on a circular stone pad surrounded by hillsides of beautiful green grass and flowers as the woman turned to ash and dust that dropped to the ground. There was no wind… Instead, a suspicious feeling nagged at Žaneta—there was something off about the place. Though she could see it teemed with life, the serenity and perfection seemed false. There was a tinge of death that lay just under the surface, almost as if the entire landscape was artificial, made to seem enchanting.

Žaneta sheathed her sword and looked around, when a male's voice suddenly broke out in her head. But it was loud, as if it were ringing from the sky. "I've seen you, cat! You've been disrupting my efforts, and I am not… amused," the voice boomed.

Žaneta stared down at the ash of the woman and saw the amulet she'd held. "Who are you, and what is this place?" Her eyes narrowed; she decided to be cautious of anything said in this land of lies. She knelt down, examining the amulet, and began to pick it up.

She noticed a symbol etched in the gold that looked like a pointed horseshoe with a dot in the center, a symbol she'd never seen before. The voice replied, "You know nothing of the coming fire! Tamriel will be reborn, and Lord Dagon will reclaim his kingdom!"

Žaneta stood up, continuing to look at the amulet. "Sounds like you have it all worked out. Why am I here, and why tell me any of this? I don't care for your demon," she said stoically.

"You're here for the children my servants sent me from that town, and the gates will open, thanks to them. But my paradise is not complete, and you will be here forever to serve my Lord with your suffering. You won't die here—just live out an eternity in anguish," the voice proclaimed.

"So, they *are* here! I'm going to find them… and then you. Hopefully, you don't disappoint." Žaneta smirked, stepping off the pad onto a stone path, with no choice but to follow it. The land was untouched, undeveloped, and the trees and flowers were all perfect. It was all too ideal to be genuine. Then, just ahead, she came upon a Daedroth. It just stood there on the path, waiting in place—definitely unusual. As she got closer, it charged, arms spread with its huge alligator-like mouth open. Žaneta pulled her hand back and shot a blast of fire through its mouth and out the back of its head. It toppled to the ground and slid a couple of feet on its chest before coming to a stop.

But it only laid still a moment.

As she came nearer, meaning to walk around its corpse, the wound on its head started to close, and the beast began to rise. Žaneta drew her sword and braced herself. The Daedroth stood, completely unscathed, and bellowed out a deafening roar, just feet from her. It swiped at her with its enormous arms and claws as she dodged to the side, then again with its other hand, missing her when she rolled under the swing. She came up with her blade, taking the Daedroth's left arm off just below the elbow.

It stepped back and lifted its head, letting out a roar of pain. In that split second, Žaneta jumped up and cut deep across its throat, nearly taking its head off as it fell backward, dead. She looked at the creature, took a breath, and sheathed her sword. But as she did, the Daedroth's right arm began twitching; the neck wound and severed arm slowly started to close and heal.

The voice rang out, "You see! This is where my immortals harden themselves… in unending tribulation."

Žaneta drew her sword and fully removed the Daedroth's head to buy herself more time, then left it and continued along the path. She came to a small stone bridge and noted a cave-like entrance beyond it, with moss hanging over the opening. *If the children encountered the Daedroth, they'd all be dead. But can they die here? Or did they even come this way?* she wondered.

That person, that voice, or whatever it was, was testing her, and she knew it. Žaneta slowly entered through the mossy opening and let her eyes quickly adjust to the dark. The walls were cramped as she navigated into a large cavern. Red, glowing light revealed the contours of the cave, and the smell of burnt flesh was offensive. There was only one path to follow—Žaneta didn't even consider turning back.

Echoing off the walls, distant screams could be heard: men, women, but no children. The narrow walls she had to pass between opened to a rock bridge that joined an adjacent open area to the cave floor where she stood. But below the bridge ran a river of molten lava; it was the source of the red light and the heat, which distorted Žaneta's view of what lay ahead, perched on the bit of rock just over the bridge. But she knew exactly what she saw—there was a large cage containing the six missing children.

Two Dremora stood guarding it, evil demons of Lord Dagon who wore black Daedric armor and swords. It was the first time Žaneta had seen anything like them. Their nightmarish appearance was unnerving, but thankfully, they hadn't seen her yet. She thought the red-eyed demons almost looked like men until she caught sight of their faces. They were knotted with boney lumps that twisted into wicked, jagged shapes, and their eyes burned crimson. They had bald, spiny ridges on their heads and small, wicked horns scattered about their skulls.

They both stood there maliciously looking at the children, when one Dremora stuck a hot metal rod through the bars of the cage toward an exhausted boy's foot. He squealed in pain as he quickly withdrew it.

The next thing the Dremora felt was all of Žaneta's weight coming down on him.

She ran her sword through the back of his neck and out his throat as she crushed his man-sized body. The Dremora crumpled under her, dead before he hit the ground, but she was already tearing her blade from the first and swinging at the next with an upward slash.

Her sword scratched across his chest plate and pushed him back, causing sparks to jump off his armor. She was furious. Hot tears filled her eyes as she bared her teeth, her ears lying flat against her head.

 The Dremora drew his sword and belched out a garbled battle cry, lunging at her in an aggressive attempt to cut through her midsection with a clumsy, broad swing. He overswung so hard that when she backstepped out of his path, she only had to swing swiftly toward the back of his neck to take his head off. He collapsed to the ground, and she rushed toward the children.

The cage had a heavy barred top and a lid that hung over the front of the doors—keeping them from swinging open. No key was needed since the children were too small to move it.

Žaneta started lifting the top of the cage but saw the arms of her first kill slowly move under its chest in an effort to push up off the ground. She let the top of the cage go, rushed to the downed Dremora, and stomped on his head. She sheathed her sword, dragged his body to the trench, then threw it into the lava below. Turning to look at the other, she was thankful his head wasn't growing back.

"You cannot defeat them," the voice rumbled. "Your strength will leave you eventually, and then you'll be mine. I'd say run, but you've nowhere to go."

Žaneta ignored the voice and approached the cell. Several of the children stared off into nowhere, while the others cried when they saw her near the door, fearful of the torment she was there to bring. But she lifted the top and flung the gate open.

She didn't know what to say as she looked at their sallow faces. They appeared starving, shaking, scared, and to put it simply… in hell.

Žaneta fell to her knees in front of them. Despair felt natural here as she teared up and tried to touch one of their faces, but they nervously withdrew. Then she remembered her own children. Their smiles, their lives… Sandrew's. She was heartbroken. She swallowed a sob and buried her face in her hands. Anger and anguish crashed into her as she started to channel her healing magic like she never had before. Her effort made the walls of the cave tremble as she focused the energy between her hands, watching the radiant light grow brighter and brighter.

The Dremora never had reason to fear anything—when they were killed in combat, they would simply continue to come back over and over. But while Žaneta gave her attention to the children, the previously beheaded Dremora was standing fully formed behind her. He looked on as the orb she created with her magic formed a sphere around her and most of the children. Then, when he reached out to touch it, his hand burst into a form eerily similar to a human's before the energy burned the flesh down to the bone. He withdrew it, shrieking in pain.

Žaneta stopped concentrating, hearing his cry, and slammed her hands into the ground, sending out a shockwave like the one from the day Sandrew had died, but much more powerful. The wave of energy struck the Dremora and blew him apart, searing his flesh and scattering his bones along the ground while the armor he'd worn fell into a pile.

"Impossible!" screamed the voice with a tinge of desperation. "What are you?"

Žaneta lifted her head and looked over her shoulder at the remains of the destroyed Dremora then replied, "This is going to be easier than I thought!" She wiped her eyes and stood, helping the children up. They all flocked to her. They finally had a spark in their eyes, and their gaunt faces looked a little fuller—heathier.

"You've accomplished nothing! The Mythic Dawn has been set in motion, and I will bring Oblivion to Tamriel. Be gone!" the voice bellowed.

As suddenly as she had been teleported there initially, so too was she sent back, along with all the children, away from the confines of that hellish place.

Žaneta reappeared exactly where she had left in Kvatch, and the scene was still the same, as if no time had passed. The only difference was the six fresh, young faces she was surrounded by, aside from being very, very dirty. Though shaken, they clung to her.

Captain Matius stumbled toward them in disbelief, his mouth hanging open. He gave orders to the guards, never breaking eye contact with Žaneta. "Bring more food and water!" He thought for a moment. "Hold that! I think this deserves an audience with Count Goldwine. We'll feed them all at the castle… and throw that prisoner in a cell. Nothing to eat or drink, not even a bucket to crap in!" he ordered.

Žaneta knelt and gazed at each of the children, happy but still upset by the ordeal.

"Žaneta… are you okay? What in the world just happened?" the captain asked.

She stayed on one knee, shaking her head silently, unable to tear her eyes from the children.

"Please, follow me," he said gently. She stood, and the children, along with some of the guards, started toward the castle.

Once inside, Matius led them to the castle's guest dining hall and summoned the count's clerk by telling one of the many castle servants. He also asked for fruits, meats, and bread to be brought in. They sat at the large rectangular table, but the children needed some direction. They'd never been in a castle before and were still confused by all that had happened. Žaneta helped them get into their seats one by one as she wondered where home was for them.

Kitchen workers began bringing trays and placing them on the table, along with cups and pitchers of water. The kids were propped up in their chairs as they sat on their feet, leaning toward the trays. For a moment, all was quiet besides the clattering of silverware and the children's giggles as they munched on sweet rolls and fruit. Many gulped down their water without coming up for air.

Žaneta couldn't begin to imagine the horrors they must have experienced… what Tai and Mazira undoubtedly were *still* experiencing. She clenched her fists under the table, and her appetite vanished while more trays were brought out.

Then the count's clerk entered through another doorway and stopped. Looking at the scene of dirty kids, Žaneta, and Captain Matius, he asked, "What is the meaning of this? Who are all these people?"

Captain Matius set down his cup and approached the clerk. "Tell the count we have a critical report to give him. Terrible things have been happening in the city that he will want to know about."

"I asked who these people were!" the clerk blustered.

The captain's eyes narrowed dangerously. "Your job is to discuss matters in the count's stead, not use his command as your own. When the Captain of the Guard tells you to do something—you do it! Now move! Or I'll throw you in a cell!" Matius yelled into the clerk's face, who stumbled back to the doorway and scurried off with the message.

Captain Matius turned back to the table, where his captive audience was frozen, still eating but staring at him. "I apologize," he muttered. "My patience has worn thin." He sat near Žaneta and began talking more with her about what had happened and what she'd seen.

A short time passed, then a man rounded the corner. Dressed in a black and burgundy robe accented by noble features, he spoke to Matius. "Captain… this had better be important. Otherwise, I know you wouldn't have made my dining hall into the school lunchroom!"

The captain stood and replied, "Yes, count. I have been witness to strange events this morning. This woman has pursued stolen children since Vvardenfell and worked with Captains Evans and Dion, exposing not only treasonous actions in Skingrad but potentially here as well. My concern is it's bigger than that, though. The children you see before you are twelve of the twenty-four children, two of which are her own," finished Matius.

Count Goldwine looked past Captain Matius at Žaneta and motioned for her to approach. As she stood from the table, the count's eyes widened at her size and appearance. As she presented herself, he said, "You're not like any Khajiit I've ever seen!"

The captain nodded at her appreciatively and added, "I can vouch for that, sir."

Changing the subject, she got straight to the point. "My name is Žaneta. When I came into the city last night, I was after the woman believed responsible for paying guards to obtain these children. At the house where we found her was an accomplice, the man currently in custody. They both wore red robes, and I've learned they are Dagon worshipers. We found six of the children in the house," she explained.

"Then where were the other six children? I count twelve at the table," asked the count.

"I asked the woman where the other six were, and she said, 'Oblivion!' My heart sank at her confession. I thought she meant she'd killed them, so I ran her through in the street. Her death, and this amulet, took me to another realm." She took the amulet out of her satchel. "A man's voice spoke to me after I arrived there—a cruel voice. Following the path, I fought a Daedroth that I killed two times over, but it wouldn't stay dead. Then I came across the entrance to a cave. When I entered and traveled a short way inside, I found the children in a cage guarded by what looked like two Dremora… from what I've heard of them, anyway. And they, too, simply wouldn't stay dead. It was only after healing the children that I noticed it destroyed the Dremora. I was only trying to bring them comfort, but it burned the demon… like fire does to us. That infuriated the voice, and that's when he sent the children and me back here. But before doing so, he told me the Mythic Dawn has been set in motion and that he means to bring Oblivion here," Žaneta finished.

Captain Matius gawked at her then turned to the count and said, "And by her account, sir, she fought there for hours before returning with the children. But here, to us, she simply disappeared with the woman and reappeared with the children seconds later."

The count stared at the amulet and the markings on it. "You need to take that to the battlemages at the palace and tell them what you've told me. If Dagon worshipers were practicing their filth here, I want it out of my city. So, captain… put your prisoner in a cart and offer this kind lady a ride to the Imperial City, where the right people can make sense of all this," he said, turning his concerned gaze up to Žaneta. "And I'll send two more carriages with you for these children. Emperor Septim will know better than I how to help them from here."

Captain Matius nodded, acknowledging his orders, then turned and began talking with the children about meeting the emperor, making sure all their needs were taken care of before they departed.

Count Goldwine stood for a moment with Žaneta. "Thank you for what you've done for Kvatch. Even still… you've asked for nothing. I know finding your children is what truly motivates you. But if you ever need anything, come back here anytime," he said sincerely.

Žaneta said nothing, but nodded her thanks to the count. With that, she turned to the children, who were still shivering but seemed to be in better spirits. She was determined to see them back to their homes and was ready for the next part of her journey. Somehow, she knew she was getting closer and closer to Tai and Mazira.

Chapter Four

Once outside, Captain Matius ordered for two nice carriages with snacks for the trip to be brought around for the children, as well as the prisoner cart for the man. Captain Matius rode on the prisoner cart with another guard, and they led the caravan. They were followed by the first carriage of children driven by two guards, and in the rear carriage rode the rest, along with one more guard and Žaneta.

"Please attach my horse to the team on this carriage—I'll not be returning with you," she said as one of the guardsmen prepared the horse team. He then went to retrieve Gus.

It was midafternoon as the transports headed out of Kvatch.

***

Entering the Imperial City, Captain Dion made his way to the bastion in the prison district. The prisoner cart stopped in front of the Legion offices, and Dion entered. At the desk sat a man wearing beautiful brushed steel armor with a gold inlay that had been placed with meticulous detail.

Captain Dion closed the office door behind him and approached the desk. "Lex… you look as pretty as ever!" he chuckled.

Captain Lex was all business, good at putting pressure on the people he felt needed it, and his work was his only pastime. His attention to detail came first and foremost, with his armor as polished as his respect for the job. The Imperial man had a reputation for being incorruptible, and his dark-brown hair, marked by streaks of gray, proved he had a lengthy career at it.

"What do you need, Dion?" he asked without looking up from his paperwork.

Dion became serious. "I've brought a gift. One of my guards has committed treason, so he'll be staying with you for a while."

Captain Lex looked up, always appreciating swift justice. "What did he do?"

"In charge of Skingrad's eastern gate eight nights ago, he let two carriages with kidnapped children pass through the city. We believe they headed to Kvatch, so you will likely be getting more guests soon," Dion replied.

"Do you have any proof or just a confession? And who's *we*?" Lex asked, still sitting in his chair.

Captain Dion dropped the sack of gemstones on Lex's desk and said, "The payment my man Faven accepted from the woman we're after. And by we, I refer to Žaneta, the Khajiit woman who had her children taken and who has been pursuing them since Vvardenfell."

Captain Lex looked in the bag. Re-tying the top, he set it down and replied, "A Khajiit woman? And you're working with her? What has she asked for?"

Dion raised a brow. "Nothing. She came in strong, had our boy Faven confessing in minutes, then rode out after we knew where to head next. She's got some healing power I've never seen before… Faven got a little 'over-motivated' during our talk, and she fixed him right up after he tried to draw his sword." Dion smirked slightly.

Lex shook his head, looking down at his desk, and replied, "Great… A magic cat! Did it ever cross your mind that maybe she's after something bigger than gold and gemstones? I mean… she's a Khajiit. So, the prerequisite for being a criminal has already been met!"

Captain Dion's eyes grew wide, and he tilted his head. "Same old Lex… I can't believe you! Her actions thus far have earned more respect than the speculation coming out of your mouth. But you can tell me what you think when you meet her."

Captain Lex stood, full of pride. "So, where is this Žaneta?"

"In Kvatch… probably busting heads." Dion nodded. "I haven't seen such tenacity in anyone I can think of. It's… inspirational. Now, to the matter at hand. Could we get Faven introduced to his new home?" he asked.

"We'll get a cell for him, sure, but violent offenders and acts of treason offer the prisoner a choice—you know this. He can serve his sentence behind bars, if we don't hang him, or he can go to the Arena. If he survives there, he will serve a reduced sentence."

"Yes, yes. I just need my cart back and to return to Skingrad. Now, how about a receipt for the evidence and a form for my report? Then I'll be on my way," Dion said, annoyance seeping into his tone. He shifted impatiently, ready to be out of Lex's office. The man had always been an insufferable know-it-all, constantly regurgitating laws the other officers already knew. Dion could only tolerate him for so long, and he was ready to hit the road.

***

It was late afternoon, and Captain Matius and the other carriages approached the western gate of Skingrad. The sun was shining down on their backs, and Žaneta had leaned back against the top of the carriage to relax while the driver kept them on course. They passed through the gateway into the double-walled street of the city and stopped to water the horses. Žaneta jumped down and checked on the children. The ones in her carriage were all asleep, and she smiled as she peered in.

Captain Matius approached her as he removed his leather gloves. "Now's the chance to eat something and take care of business, if you need to," he said, motioning to the barracks. "Bathrooms are just inside. I'm going to wake the kids and ask if they need to go." Looking in the carriage, he found them all fast asleep.

"I'll help with taking them in," she replied.

The children were startled at first but pleasantly surprised to see the city when they woke up. They climbed down from both carriages and were led into the barracks. The Skingrad guards had come to help tend to the horses, which were led to the east gate where the stables were.

The prisoner stayed in his cart under watch, while the others prepared to return. All the children and guards came back to their transports. Žaneta held two apples—one for Gus and the other for his partner. Captain Matius climbed onto the prisoner cart and looked back to see everyone ready. He flicked the reins, and they started off on the Gold Road, heading east from Skingrad.

Hours into the journey, the sun had begun to set behind them. The light crept through the woods on either side, throwing golden beams whenever a break in the heavy foliage allowed it. Žaneta closed her eyes and started to think a prayer to herself but felt increasingly tired as she concentrated while being rocked by the carriage.

Another set of images flashed before her in a dream-like state. Mountains, an evil chanting echoing over them, words that sounded familiar but none that she'd ever heard. Then, she awoke to another carriage coming toward them on the road. She shook the vision from her head. *What just happened?* She couldn't stop thinking about how the last one had only shown catastrophe, the destruction of a city…

She sat up and focused on the approaching travelers. The cart had lanterns on either side of the two men who rode on the driver's bench. All of the carriages slowed and stopped, as did the oncoming one. It was Captain Dion and one of his guards.

"Good evening! This is a sight worth seeing!" Dion proclaimed as he leaned over to shake hands with Captain Matius from their opposite seats. "I see you've got another prisoner… Any trace of the woman we were looking for?"

"Oh, yeah. But I'll have to stop on my way back through and talk to you about it over drinks—it's going to take a while. For now, I've got to get this one to the prison. We have a lot of questions that need answering. Then there's the matter of all these children!" Matius glanced back at the carriages.

"I'll be damned… You found them!" Dion grinned.

"All twelve… well, six. Žaneta returned with the others," Matias added, nodding seriously to Dion.

"I knew it! Where is she?" Dion said, smiling and standing to see further to the rear. He saw her sitting next to the driver of the last carriage with her legs up on the footboard. "Damn good to see you, lady!" he hollered, raising a hand to say hello. She looked up at him and returned the gesture with a half smile. "Well then, tell me all about it on your way back through Skingrad. Safe travels!" Dion said to Matius as he sat down and motioned for his driver to proceed. He nodded to Žaneta as they passed.

The brief stop was enough to allow Žaneta to wake up more, though it was getting dark and they had no intentions of stopping for the night. Well past midnight, they reached the checkpoint at Fort Virtue and continued north after declaring their contents.

The drivers switched to let the others rest. So, from Fort Virtue, Captain Matius and Žaneta drove their carriages along the Red Ring Road. They could all see the Imperial City to their right, the ships at harbor, the city's tall walls, and the White Gold Tower—a beacon to all travelers from any direction. But it was especially beautiful as the city cast its reflection on the surrounding Lake Rumare.

Continuing along the road, Žaneta tried to recall what she had dreamed earlier. *Was it a dream? Was it another vision of someplace I need to go?* She remembered seeing Kvatch in ruins—had she prevented something terrible by finding these children? So many questions… *and now, this image of the mountains. But the voices… What were they saying?* Žaneta had to shake it from her mind. In the moment, it was more confusing than helpful. All of it was. She thought about how, just over a week ago, her family was happy, together at home. She didn't dwell on it for too long, however. The thought of losing these children to the depths of hell, the insurmountable suffering they'd experienced, and the fear she felt of not knowing where to search for Tai and Mazira were almost unbearable. It was dragging her to a dark place, unfamiliar to her—where failing seemed to have a chance. The whole situation continued to test her confidence, as well as her ability to keep focused on a positive outcome. But in the end, she knew things happen for a reason… even if the effects weren't seen for generations to come.

The light from the two moons broke her train of thought as the carriages trundled down the road. *It'll be my birthday soon*, she thought, noticing the two moons, Masser and Secunda, would be lining up. The occurrence only happened once every so many decades. She was much younger the last time she'd seen it, and before that was when her mother said she was born. Letting her mind wander helped the trip go by quicker. It was early in the morning but still hours before sunrise when they passed through Weye, a small town on the western bank of the lake before the city's main bridge.

They crossed the largest bridge in Cyrodiil that connected the Imperial City to the mainland around it. There were other bridges that connected to the island, but they all paled in comparison.

Captain Matius pulled over to the stables just outside the main gate to the city, and the others followed suit. He jumped down and went into the stable office.

He stood at the counter and knocked before voicing a loud, "Hello!"

The stable's ostler, an Orc, came from the back room, scratching his head. He looked at Matius and tightened his belt around his shirt tunic. "Official business? What have you got?" he asked courteously.

"I have three carriages, five horses total. Would you please put the black draft horse on the last carriage in a stall? The others can be kept corralled together… and yes, it is Imperial business," Matius stated.

"Very good. Sign here. I'll bill his Imperial Majesty," the Orc replied.

"I've got a prisoner in one and will return with that cart after I've dropped him off," Matius explained. The Orc nodded, and Matius stepped outside.

"All right, everyone! We leave the horses here, except for the prisoner cart… I'll take him to the jail," Matius said.

Žaneta and the other guards hopped down from their seats, and she approached Matius. "Where do we stay in the meantime?" She glanced back at the children.

"As soon as we enter the city, we'll be in the Talos District. Straight and on the right, you'll find the Tiber Septim Hotel. Just follow me in, and I'll show you before I head to the jail."

Žaneta returned to her carriage and began waking up the rest of the kids. Some were awake and already asking questions.

"Is this the empire city?"

"Where's the emperor?"

"Can we eat?"

Žaneta smiled and laughed, trying to answer all their questions. "Yes… here somewhere… and I'm sure we'll find something to eat." She slowly helped them down as she looked at the empty snack basket. "For now, let's get down and go inside. We'll get a room until morning."

The Orc came out of the office with a lantern and began taking the first carriage that had brought the children, which the guards had already unloaded. Žaneta saw him and spoke with the children, "Okay, everyone, join the group over there. I'm going to take the horses around, but I'll be right back."

She grabbed the reins of her carriage and began leading it around the side to help the ostler. He was tying the horses from the cart he'd led to a hitching rail. Žaneta followed him and led hers to the one right beside it. He looked up at her as he took the bit from the first horse and removed its yoke. "Thank you!" he said, continuing his work.

Žaneta rubbed along Gus's mane and replied, "This one's mine! I'll come see you soon to pay for his care."

The Orc looked at her suspiciously for a moment then nodded.

Žaneta returned to the group and walked with the children and guards as they followed Captain Matius's cart into the city.

Imperial guards closed the gates behind them as they proceeded to the intersection ahead. Matius stopped his cart, pointed right, and said, "There! That's the Tiber. Tell the clerk we'll need four rooms: three for you and the kids, and I'll share one with my men. It'll be much better than using the city barracks, and I'll pick up the tab when I get back." He nodded, dark circles below his red-rimmed eyes from the long day. Then he turned the horse left, going north toward the jail.

Žaneta and the three guards walked to the Tiber Septim Hotel and entered with all the children; she stood at the entrance holding the door while they all followed inside. At the counter, one of the guards made arrangements with the clerk, received the keys, then came back to the group. Žaneta and the children gazed at the hotel lobby, admiring how nice everything was.

"Beautiful place," Žaneta mentioned, smiling at the guard as he approached.

He handed her a key. "Indeed, nowhere better in the city. I got you a suite that's large enough for you and most of the kids, along with two other rooms for them and us, once the captain returns," he said, pausing briefly and looking at the two keys in his hand. He met her eyes. "I know the captain said to get four rooms. But this was cheaper, and those kids wouldn't sleep by themselves. Hell, most of them don't want to leave your side, my lady!" He grinned. "Second floor… Sleep well."

Žaneta took the key and started for the stairs. "Come on, children. Let's go to the room," she said softly, with all twelve following her. The guards watched and chuckled as Žaneta gave them a teasing glare. Her group walked quietly down the hall, the children staring at the paintings and decor, then they stopped as she stood in front of their door. Opening it, the kids flowed around her into a place fit for royalty. Some of them jumped onto the couch, some onto the beds of adjacent rooms within the suite, while others dug into the fruit and snacks the room was stocked with.

Žaneta entered and closed the door behind her. It was very well lit, and she glanced at the fixtures, noting there wasn't a trace of dust in the place. She examined the small kitchen area in detail, and as she ran her hand along the marble countertop, she noticed a tub sink with a hole in it, a spout, and what looked like two door handles fixed to the counter. She went to pull on one, but it was stuck. She turned it, and water began to flow from the spout. Her eyes widened as she smiled. She turned the other handle and noticed the water changed temperature. With the kids bouncing around the room and her discovery of the amazing water source, they were all entertained.

Before long, the children began yawning, and some were already asleep in whatever places they'd found. Žaneta shut the water off and began tucking them in or positioning them on the couch. But even with three beds and the couch, they seemed cramped. There was a knock at her door as she stood with one of the little girls in her arms. She positioned her on her left side and went to the door to open it.

One of the guards from Kvatch was standing there, smiling. "Could we take any of them from you? We've got plenty of open beds. One of us will stay with them."

Žaneta handed him the one she was holding and replied, "Yes, that would be great. They won't all be comfortable here. How many more can you take?"

"Probably three or four."

"Perfect! Would a couple of you come back for the others? They're falling asleep quickly." She was relieved at his offer. Then her eyes lit up. "Did you know this place has running water?"

The guard grinned and laughed. "Yeah… Wait 'til you try the shower!"

She didn't know what he meant by that, but he was already walking down the hall to the other rooms. She closed the door and looked at a few more children who were hanging off the couch or asleep at the foot of one of the beds.

Two of the guards came back to the room as she was walking to the door with another child. She handed that one over then grabbed two off the overloaded couch, giving them both to the other guard. "Good night." She smiled and slowly closed the door. That left her with three kids in one bed, three more in another, and two on the couch. She hadn't even finished looking at the rooms, so she grabbed a sweet roll from the basket on the table and explored.

She found a pantry with food, a closet with linens, and the only other unclaimed bed in an empty room. She unsheathed her sword and leaned it in a corner, took off her bracers, and removed her leg plates and lower leg wraps, setting them in a pile. Then she sat at the foot of the beautiful bed. Not thinking, she stood and noticed the dirt she'd left on the clean, white blanket. *Yikes… I'm dirty!* she thought as she looked around the room. She opened the armoire to check for a robe or something else to wear, then opened what she thought was a closet door.

It was another room, all tile, with a larger version of the sink she'd seen in the kitchen. Then it clicked—"the shower." Walking up to it, she savored the notion of how nice it was. She turned it on then closed the bathroom door, taking in the steam from that fantastic creation before learning how to get the warmth set just right. The robes and towels were on the wall, and once again, all the robes were too small or short for her height, with too short being the better option. But she made ready for bed afterward and passed out.

***

The next morning, light streamed in through her window, which overlooked the intersection of the street down below. Žaneta slowly woke up to the sound of children laughing. Her eyes still closed, for a split second, she thought she was home with her own children. Her heart pounded as she sat up fast, aching with disappointment when she reaffirmed where she was. She grew tired of being mentally exhausted at the start of each day, but she pressed herself to keep moving forward, trying to avoid being idle. She threw off the blankets and began getting dressed.

The kids were all awake and eating fruit and muffins. She sat with them and grabbed her own apple and salted meat from the baskets. "Good morning!" She smiled, and the kids returned the gesture. Žaneta looked at the children then saw the little Breton girl she had spoken with in Kvatch. "Hey, young lady, remember when you told me you were with Tai and Mazira?" she asked with a calm smile. "All of you were together when you came here, right?"

"Yes, ma'am, we were on a boat together," she replied.

"Where is home for you?" asked Žaneta.

"Gnisis, at my grandpa's," she said, her gaze dropping to the floor.

Žaneta's eyes filled with tears. "I'm sorry, sweetheart… I'm sorry that any of you had to go through this." She looked around at the rest of them.

The kids were chewing slower, and it was quieter at the table. Trying to stay away from sadness, Žaneta changed the subject. "Now I need to find mine. Do any of you know where they were headed? A city, or a direction? Maybe something you may have overheard?" She waited, hopeful for a positive response.

The kids looked back and forth at each other, but none had anything to say.

"Sorry, Zan 'Etta, they kept us closed in the whole time, even where you found us," piped up one of the little boys, an Argonian. "I can't stop feeling scared when it gets dark out…"

"You're safe now," she reassured him. "The people here will help. What's your name?"

"Tibiar, after my dad. I do feel safe with you, but when you did what you did for us in the street… I'm much better now."

Žaneta smiled at the boy, recalling the Argonian she'd met in Vvardenfell—he wasn't Neet's son, Xuzu. But she hadn't forgotten to consider him.

"Yeah, what was that?" asked a Nord girl.

Žaneta looked down at her apple and said, "My healing? I guess it's something I've taken for granted for too long."

"Well, it was great!" The girl smiled. "Like sitting next to a warm fire in winter."

"I'd been coughing and sick since home, even before we were taken, until you did that. Now I feel good!" added another little Imperial boy.

Žaneta smiled but was interrupted by a knock on the door. She opened it to Captain Matius. "Good day, my lady. Did you rest?" he asked.

Žaneta moved to the side and invited him in. "I did… We all did. Any news this morning?"

The captain walked to one of the chairs by the couch and plopped down. "Yes. After I checked the prisoner in at the Legion offices and wrote a report, I was in my room for only a couple of hours before two Imperial battlemages came asking for me. Did anyone knock on your door this morning? I mean, before me?" He looked up at Žaneta.

"No, just you. Kids?" They all shook their heads no.

"Well, for the last four hours, they've been questioning me. It seemed that nothing in my report about the prisoner mattered until the right people read about the portals and the words 'Mythic Dawn.' Now, I know they're very interested in meeting you. Apparently, Žaneta, we've stumbled onto something big here. The White Gold Tower was buzzing with activity, like a beehive that's just been kicked," he said, wide-eyed. "Do you have the amulet you showed the count?"

Žaneta reached into her satchel and pulled it out.

"Good, they'll want to see that piece." He broke his stare from it and turned to the kids. "Children… you'll want to say goodbye to Žaneta before we leave."

"Wait! What about these kids? Their families will be looking for them!" She was surprised—why did she need to leave them so quickly? She'd just torn them from the clutches of hell, and the thought of letting them go made her entire body tense up.

"Žaneta… Vvardenfell's in chaos. Something has happened there. Sickness has spread across the land, and the last report stated 'things' were coming down from Red Mountain. The people still there are fighting, but it's not an option for the children," Matius explained quietly, turning to Žaneta. "I have, however, begun working on finding them temporary homes here in Cyrodiil with families willing to take them in. I told the Legion offices I'll stay and help get something organized. Siblings will stay together until we can return them back to their loved ones, but so much is happening… I'm sorry." He let out a heavy sigh and looked down, shaking his head. His worry and concern were tangible.

Žaneta could only stare off into the distance, lost in thought. She sat in the chair opposite him, and her sight became blurry with tears. Snapping out of it, she quickly popped up from her seat and walked around to the table. "Come give me a hug, kids!" she said, taking a knee. The eight of them almost plowed her over. "What of the other four?" she asked Matius.

"They're down the hall in our other room. I'll return with them and my guards to stay with them here." He stood and excused himself.

"We don't want you to leave!" whimpered one little girl as the others joined in her protest.

"I'm sorry… It breaks my heart, but I have to find the others. Just think—there are ten more of you with my children somewhere. They're lost and scared, just like you were before we found you. Do you understand? I have to go," she said calmly, swallowing past the lump in her throat.

The door slowly opened, and the other four children came in, followed by Matius and the guards. The four ran up and joined in the sendoff. It was a hard goodbye, but she finally stood and walked toward Captain Matius and the guards. Matius opened the door as she turned to the children and said, "After I've found Tai and Mazira, I'll check on each of you again someday."

With that, she turned and left the room without looking back, once again leaving behind people she'd become so close to. But the terrible journey was leading her toward Tai and Mazira, and her heart ached for them, driving her forward.

"Lead the way," Žaneta said to Matius, her brow furrowed. "And I meant what I said back there. After all the work you do is done, I want the kids' names and the locations they're sent to," she demanded seriously.

"Absolutely. That information will be here at the Legion office regardless. I'll make certain it's kept together for you."

Chapter Five

aptain Matius took Žaneta to the center of the city, to the Green Emperor Way District, where before her stood what everyone in the surrounding countryside could see—the White Gold Tower. On constant patrol were guards of the Imperial Watch, whose armor was almost too nice to dirty in battle. He led her up the stairs at the base of the tower and entered. They were immediately met by battlemages—soldiers wearing the same Imperial armor as the others but with a mage's hood to identify their specialty—and directed where to go. Heading to the right through a continuous corridor that crept higher in a steady incline, they went through a series of doors and overlook areas that allowed the ground floor of the center of the tower to be seen up to a certain point, as if the whole building was set up like the layers of a cake.

Eventually, they came to a door on the left and stopped. One battlemage took out a key and unlocked it, saying, "We go no further from here on. Captain, you may wait here or return to your duties, but she goes alone. The priests have questions."

Žaneta gave Matius a reassuring stare and said, "Go see to it that those kids are looked after—that would mean more to me."

Captain Matius nodded with a determined look and turned to the other battlemage, who accompanied him out.

Žaneta looked at the battlemage by the door and asked, "Who am I here to see?"

"They'll come talk with you. Just head to the left and tell the man at the gate your name. He'll direct you from there," he replied.

Žaneta walked in, and the door was shut and locked behind her. Looking to her left and right, she saw two halls that also followed a cylindrical path, just like the exterior of the tower itself. Going to the left placed her in front of the gate the battlemage had mentioned, and behind it sat a man in a gray robe with a long beard and a blindfold over his eyes.

She approached the gate and gripped one of the bars. As she was about to speak, the man said, "Hello, Žaneta… It's good to talk face-to-face."

Žaneta slid her hand from the bar. "What is this place, and why all the secrecy?" she asked suspiciously.

"We've observed your travels since you came into these lands. Every time the woman in the red robe opened portals, we could see those who were drawn to the children. Their loved ones, so far away—except for you! You were always right on our doorstep. More will be explained. Beyond these gates is a collection of books and scrolls, of which we are sworn to protect," he said.

"Wait… if you've seen me, then you know of my children—Tai and Mazira." She became desperate. "Please, tell me where they are! You have to know something."

"Not entirely. Please follow me. We need to delve a bit deeper to bring this mystery to light." He stood and unlocked the gate, leading her around the path to yet another gate, which he opened.

Žaneta stepped through, and the priest locked it behind them. He led her around the hall to the opening of a large room in the center of the circular walls. Shelves encompassed the inner room, filled with rare books and scrolls. A great spiral staircase corkscrewed up through the ceiling above them and into another chamber from the center of the room. The priest started up the stairs, and she followed, still staring about.

"You said 'we'… Who are you? And I'm not trying to be rude, but if you're surrounded by books, why the blindfold?" she asked bluntly.

"I was waiting to see what you'd say about that. We are the Moth Priests. At some point, many of us lose our eyesight due to our studies with the Elder Scrolls. Their properties and knowledge can leave the reader with more clarity and foresight than their natural eyes ever could. However, this is with training, of course. To simply pick up an Elder Scroll and read it without preparation may just leave the individual blinded. The risk is great," he explained as they reached the top of the staircase.

Four people were waiting for her. She recognized three of them based on their attire. One was another Moth Priest. He had no beard but was draped in the gray robe and blindfolded like her companion. The second was a battlemage, with Imperial armor and a mage hood. The third was a ranking officer wearing Imperial palace guard armor, with a thin streak of gray in his brown hair. However, the fourth looked of a different stock. He wore an elegant purple and red robe and a white shoulder accent piece, along with a large red jeweled amulet made of gold. He wore a calm but concerned expression as he approached.

"Žaneta… it is my pleasure to introduce Emperor Uriel Septim the Seventh," announced the Moth Priest, smiling.

Žaneta immediately dropped to a knee and bowed her head in respect while keeping her eyes fixed on the emperor's face. "Forgive me, Your Majesty… I didn't know I'd be with royalty," she said respectfully.

The emperor approached and smiled warmly at her, more with his eyes than his lips. His presence felt more fatherly than she'd envisioned. Before, she'd always assumed he'd be more… pompous.

"Nonsense, young lady. The sight of you is like having art walk the palace halls. But my compliment, unfortunately, is the only positive thing that comes to mind in these troubling times. And melodrama is not usually in my practice." Pausing briefly, he tried to be inviting. "Žaneta, is it?" He reached out a hand, which she took. He raised hers and kissed it, and she stood—his stare followed her as she towered over him. He motioned to a small table with enough chairs for all of them. "Please sit with us… You've become a focus of the priests, so I've been told."

They all moved to the table and sat. The emperor was to Žaneta's left with the battlemage on his other side. The Imperial officer and both Moth Priests completed the circle.

"This meeting is obviously informal, and for good reason. After word of the report from Captain Matius reached our mages, it quickly worked up the chain. Your name was mentioned as well as your description, which rang alarms with the priests," the emperor explained.

"Do you remember your vision of Kvatch, Žaneta… how you saw it laid to waste?" a Moth Priest asked.

"That was your doing?" She squinted at him.

"Yes. Tears in our plane of existence present us with visions of where they occur or, sometimes, what they may bring. Based on our vision, it seemed as though Kvatch would be lost!"

"I saw the vision you shared… What does this have to do with me now?" She glanced at the table then up to his covered eyes.

"We never know when these things will happen, or even if they will. But you've made us consider something else. When we saw you disappear with the Mythic Dawn woman and reappear with the children, the vision of a destroyed city faded. We think you bought us some time," he explained.

"Another man I met in Vvardenfell told me about his visions after I helped reunite him with his daughter, and when I was leaving the island, it felt like it was going to explode. So, these Mythic Dawn people… what do they want? Besides to go to hell on purpose," she muttered, scowling.

"All guesses thus far. Maybe they believe if they feed the demon, then they themselves will not be eaten. People who practice the Daedric arts often gather strength that, in the end, destroys even them. But from all I've ever learned, Dagon, the Daedric Prince of Destruction, is not known to take on lasting partners," the emperor elaborated.

"Yes, Your Majesty. But is their plan to just continue stealing children, and if so, where are mine?" Žaneta asked, keeping her calm exterior firmly intact as her mind whirled. She suddenly felt her claws digging into her thighs, so she relaxed her grip. She hadn't realized how tense she was.

"This is when the priests said everything was altered," he replied, looking around at them.

"Žaneta, something bounced around with time, and we don't know what to make of it yet. After you returned with those kids and the city seemed saved, we began seeing visions of an empty throne, and they've become increasingly clearer since. We couldn't see you and have no certainty about the other children. If they were used by the Mythic Dawn, we would've seen them if another portal had opened," one priest said.

Žaneta looked down and simply felt lost. The battlemage leaned in to join the conversation. "Žaneta, this morning we dispatched couriers to Chorrol, Bravil, Leyawiin, Cheydinhal, and Bruma, as well as the forts in between, under order from the emperor for any noted sightings of transports that look like these to be reported to the Imperial Legion office at once," he said, sliding her a copy of the leaflet. It had an image of two wooden transports with no windows and a door on the back.

"Who saw these carts?" she asked, perking up as she scanned it.

"These, we believe, were the transports from Kvatch. We spoke with Fort Virtue and saw they were logged in as passing through empty. Then we found them abandoned near the lake, just south of Fort Empire."

Žaneta sat back in her chair, noting how poor the carts looked—a box unsuitable for animals. Her emotions began to boil, and she could feel her jaw tightening.

"So, Žaneta, the word is out. If anyone has seen anything, we'll hear of it! Stay in the Imperial City, if you can. The Legion office will be the first place notified of any news," the battlemage said, trying to lift Žaneta's spirits.

The officer, who had so far sat listening quietly, broke his silence. "Žaneta, I'm Captain Lex. I spoke with Captains Dion and Matius prior to your arrival. I must admit, I had my suspicions of what this was all about, but I won't stand for these crimes. I'll be sure to let my men know of your work here, and as he said, we'll keep you up-to-date on any details we learn!"

She understood it had become a waiting game. She met the emperor's eyes. "How many children do you have, Your Majesty?"

"I have three sons. Even though they're grown men, the influence of recent events has led me to send more protection to them, and even I myself will be moving under more guard until we can sort this out," he answered, concern lacing his tone.

"Have you any idea where to find more of these Mythic Dawn?" Žaneta asked.

"Not yet, but we've got the one from Kvatch under interrogation as we speak. Fingers crossed, he'll give us something," replied the battlemage.

"Žaneta… I know some of what you saw after you went through the portal." Žaneta met the emperor's gaze—from the look in his eyes, she felt that he somehow knew exactly what she was going through. "I was betrayed by one of my own nearly forty years ago and imprisoned on a plane in Oblivion, in which I lost all sense of time."

Žaneta looked at him, speechless for a moment. "How did you escape?"

"After being there almost ten years, in Tamriel time, the one I gave the title 'Eternal Champion' to found a way to come in after me and slayed my captor. I guess what we probably both already know is… I don't want any more of that place here in ours," Emperor Septim concluded.

She nodded her head in agreement then looked at the others, her eyes resting on the blind priests. "Here, this amulet is all that was left from the woman. Maybe you have a use for it." She laid it on the table. One handed it to the other after feeling its details, puzzled. The second priest then slid it back onto the table.

The battlemage slowly picked it up and inspected it. "Strange… I'll have to show it to the others."

Žaneta nodded again then looked back to the priests. "I'm sorry, but this has been bothering me since I met you." She said to them. They both became unsettled at her comment and turned toward her, waiting for her to continue. "May I return your sight?" she asked. Both looked surprised and leaned closer to the table.

"Do you think you could? Other healers have not been able, but that goes without saying," one replied, gesturing to the blindfold.

Žaneta didn't even let him finish his sentence—she began charging an orb in her right hand. She leaned in on her elbow, bringing the orb to the center of the table, and said, "Lean in and remove the blindfolds. Tell me when you begin to see us."

The priests did as they were instructed, and she held strong—it proved different from any injury or disease she'd ever healed. She began to focus, and the table started to vibrate, while the attempt made her hand numb. Her arm and head began to ache. She saw strange images of an unknown text in her own vision, when one priest spoke up, quickly followed by the other.

"I see!"

"I can see you!"

Žaneta closed her hand, and a soft, warm pulse sent all the men's hair and hoods back, as if moved by a breeze. Color returned to the Moth Priests' eyes as they both stood and looked around, laughing. Žaneta watched them with a grin of her own as the emperor simply looked on in amazement.

"As fierce as you appear, it amazes me to see the joy you get from healing what all others could not. We should be bowing to you as royalty, my dear," he said with a genuine nod.

Žaneta slowly stopped smiling. "Thank you, but… I only wanted a simple life for my family. I never wanted this. This recognition and praise—it's kind. But all I want is my family back," she said sadly.

He reached out and gently took her hand in his own. "It would seem the Divines have called on you for more, Žaneta."

***

Back at the prison in the Legion office stood a large man by the name of Owyn. He was a giant Redguard who stood even taller than Sandrew had—close to six-foot-six—and wore his heavily-muscled physique with an obvious confidence in his stance. He oversaw fighters in the city arena and had recently received a prisoner wishing to become a combatant.

"Hello, good sir," he greeted the guard at the desk, who was working on the record books and not paying him any attention.

Owyn tapped on the desk. "I got a prisoner yesterday wanting to fight his way from life in prison, and I told him, 'Or lose it in my Arena!' But he didn't laugh. So, I got him sized up for his gear, and then he started talking about the woman who landed him in shackles. Funny thing is, he only ranted for about ten seconds before I knew who he was talking about. Her name's Žaneta—have you seen her around here?" He paused, waiting for a response.

The guard finally looked up at him, nodding. "I've been told her name a couple of times today, but I have yet to meet her. I can tell her you're looking for her if I do, Mr.…?" The office door opened and closed as another person entered behind Owyn, who stayed focused on his conversation.

"Owyn… just Owyn. I'm Battle Master at the Arena. If you see her, ask her to come see me. She's got two different colored eyes and stands about this tall…" he said, motioning just a little over his own height with his hand.

"You must've grown… or I shrank!" Žaneta replied from behind him, smiling. "How are you, Owyn?"

"Žaneta!" he exclaimed, spinning around. He walked up and bear-hugged her. "I heard you were in town and have gone full circle looking for you. What the hell brings you to the Imperial City? Where's Sandrew?" he asked, grinning.

Žaneta felt like she'd been punched in the gut. The strain from the journey so far had worked as a distraction against thoughts of Sandrew, of burning his body, their home… She let out a heavy sigh and worked to keep the tremor out of her voice. "He's dead." With effort, she was able to keep her emotions at bay.

"Žana… I'm so sorry," he replied, his smile fading.

"It's okay, Owyn. How would you've known?" She dropped her eyes to the ground then looked back up at him. "'Žana!' No one ever called me that except for my mom and you guys," she said with a half smile.

His grin returned at the memory, then he gave her a confused look. "Then what's going on… Why are you here?"

Žaneta was vaguely aware the guard at the desk had stopped writing and gone very still, listening intently. "Excuse me a minute," Žaneta said, turning to the guard. "Hello, I'm Žaneta. The emperor has dispatched posters with an order for information to be reported."

"Yes, ma'am, about sightings of the prisoner transport carts," he replied.

"Yes, I wanted to introduce myself. I'll be by often to check on progress." She turned back to Owyn and motioned to the door. "Let's go for a walk."

Walking across the connection bridge from the Legion offices and prison, then back into the Market District of the city, she explained what had happened over the last couple of weeks and how she was in limbo until she knew her next move.

"Žaneta, my heart bleeds for you and Sandrew, but I know you'll find your kids. You two were just kids yourselves when we met here over a decade ago. Do you remember my boy? He was about thirteen the last time you were here," Owyn said.

"Vaguely. How is he?" she asked.

"Great… and terrible." He sighed, and she narrowed her eyes, confused. "He always wanted to fight in the Arena, and we trained constantly. He's gotten good, honestly. But Žana… he's extremely arrogant. He just ranked up to a gladiator, and my concern is he's going to get himself killed. I mean, most fighters come to the Arena for a chance at some coin or to prove something. But I've watched some of the up-and-coming challengers, and I'd prefer he get some training before meeting them on the sand."

"And you want me to do it, I assume?" she said teasingly, already knowing the answer. She'd known Owyn for a very long time, and she could tell from the gleam in his eyes that he had a plan brewing.

"Would you? Every trainer I've put him against, he's cleaned house with. I wish he would've just joined the Legion some days… But he hates being told what to do—he needs to be shown! And he won't listen to his dad," he explained, crossing his arms and scowling.

"That's a shame. You were a great champion in the Arena," she replied, sitting on a stone bench along the street.

"I couldn't beat you!" he bounced back.

"I didn't fight in the Arena! Tell your son he's got a trainer, but once I've received word from the Legion about my children, the lessons are over."

"Thank you. Can I buy you lunch?" He smiled.

"Yes, that's where I was headed next." She strolled along the street by his side, happy to catch up with an old friend.

Evening came, and Owyn showed Žaneta around the Arena. First, he took her to the coliseum's spectator seats, then through the announcer's podium, and ended with the fighter's staging area—the Bloodworks. As she walked with Owyn, the other fighters looked on curiously, and some nervously. She observed several individuals wrapping their wounds from previous fights, some of which didn't look good. Žaneta broke from Owyn's lead and approached them all one by one, leaving not one unhealed. The last woman, an Imperial whose leg she'd repaired, looked to have taken an arrow. After she was done, she stood and turned to Owyn, who'd followed and watched.

"Looks like more than your son needs help in the Arena," she said.

"You are one of a kind, Žana. Everyone, listen up! This is Žaneta. She will be training Cyrus while she's here. I'd suggest making sure you're topside to watch during those lessons if you care to improve your game!" he shouted, turning to the surrounding fighters then back to Žaneta.

"Let's get your things picked out. Cyrus won't be here until morning," he said, leading her to the armory, where swords of different types were available, as well as axes, war hammers, bows, maces, shields, and armor. "If you were a combatant, you'd have to choose from the armor we have. It represents team colors and uniformity. If you remember?" Owyn started.

"That would be a deal breaker. I'm not wearing one of those miniskirts for anything!" she replied, smirking. "I saw there was a forge near the market and a couple of weapons dealers—I think I'll make myself something there and call it good."

"I'm sorry, but you have to choose from these weapons—nothing special, except for enchantments."

"I wouldn't use another sword besides my own, but for this, I'll just take a stick. What I want from the forge is to make a shield that doesn't have to be stuck on my arm," she explained.

"No sharp edges or spikes? The last person who had an edge on their shield got the whole team disqualified," he teased.

"Good gods, Owyn, I'm not trying to kill your son!" She smirked.

Owyn raised an eyebrow. "Everyone else does."

Žaneta continued looking at the shields available and found an old Blades shield she thought would be perfect. *Why's this here?* she thought. She knew the Blades were highly regarded among the Legion's ranks—the elite. To come across great craftsmanship here was good fortune. She looked at Owyn, and he shrugged. "Be my guest." She took it from the rack and jogged to the market. With the sun setting, she knew some places would be closing up.

Passing through the Market District, she stopped at the first arms dealer she found. On the left was a shop called "A Fighting Chance." The business appeared to be more of a "sales only" establishment, but she questioned the proprietor, "Hello, do you know where I can find a smithing table and anvil I can use? Or maybe a forge?"

The woman looked up at Žaneta and said, "You can use mine downstairs for a fee. Do you need supplies, or did you just want to straighten and fix some things?"

Žaneta was relieved as she sat the shield on the counter between her and the woman. "Seven feet of thick, one-inch-wide leather strap, a D-ring with a shield mount, and leather clasps to fasten it," she replied, her experience around a forge showing itself.

"All right, I've got all those things. How would you like to pay? It'll be fifty Septims for the supplies and another fifty for the equipment use."

Žaneta pulled out a small ruby and placed it in the woman's hand, its value worth far more than her price. The woman's eyes widened, and she turned to lead Žaneta downstairs. "Okay then, follow me."

The basement was dark until the woman lit the lanterns on the walls, taking one down and placing it on the worktable. "The name's Rohssan. If you need anything that's not here, let me know. Buckles, clasps, and rivets are in the drawers on the table. Here's the leather strap you wanted." She turned toward rolls of cord and leather straps of various sizes. "Seven feet of one-inch?" she confirmed with Žaneta, who nodded. Rohssan then turned to the forge and opened the flute to allow the heat to escape.

The coals in it weren't hot, but they weren't out. She pumped the bellows to bring them back to life and added some more from a bucket next to her. "I'll be upstairs. I don't close for about another hour and a half," she said. Žaneta got straight to work, and the woman left her to it.

She cut the forearm strap from her shield, leaving the D-rings that had mounted it in place, then set it on the table. Grabbing the handle and resting her elbow on the shield to lay the strap across her arm, making note of the placement, she installed another D-ring—after heating it in the forge and using a little Soft Fire from her hand—to the side of the top one. Letting it cool, she ran opposite ends of the leather strap through each of those rings then folded them over, pinned them, and placed clasps before binding them with heavy stitches. Before long, she was finished.

All she had done was taken the taut forearm strap and replaced it with a longer one, which allowed her different options for combat. She tried it out. Holding the handle, she pulled the leather strap over her arm and through the lower D-ring, then around the handle and into her grip. It made it act like a regular shield, but if she let go of the strap, the shield would fall loose, letting her use the strap to swing it like a meteor hammer. A leash for her shield—very simple.

She slung it over her head, under her left arm, then to her back. Satisfied, she went upstairs, told Rohssan good evening, and returned to the Arena.

Žaneta entered the Bloodworks and found Owyn as he was finishing up with details from the day and waiting for her to return. "I finished at the smith. I wanted to talk about your son—what do you think he would benefit from the most?"

"Just kick his ass. Then he'll listen to whatever you have to say," he replied seriously. "Žaneta, I'm telling you… he's really hurt some of his trainers in the past, but he's reckless and thinks I'm just getting long in the tooth. If he's knocked off his pedestal, he'll start paying attention."

She considered his words. "All right, I'll head to a hotel and be here in the morning. What's close? I saw something in the market."

"Probably the Merchant's Inn—good rooms and food. It's also the closest. Although, you could always take a cot here!" he joked.

Žaneta grinned and raised her eyebrows. "Ah, why didn't I think of that? I'm sure the Arena's cots will offer more comfort than all the city's inns combined!" They both chuckled, and Žaneta gave him a wave. "Well, I'll be at the Merchant's Inn… See you tomorrow."

They parted ways, and she went to the Market District. After checking into the hotel, she had a quick meal then told the owner she'd like to be woken at dawn before retreating to her room.

This place had a shower and running water, too, just like the Tiber, but not nearly as nice. She liked that about the Imperial City but didn't favor constantly pampering herself—it wouldn't last once she was back on the road. But after a brief workout with what was available in the room—the end of the bed for lifts, a chair for dips, and the floor for push-ups and sit-ups—she enjoyed the shower and was off to bed.

***

Morning came with a knock on her door. Žaneta's eyes crept open, and she slowly sat up into a stretch. "Hello… This is your wake-up!" the barkeep called.

Žaneta proceeded to get ready. She fastened her leg plates to her shins, thinking about all she'd had to deal with lately. Her children were missing, and her entire life seemed so chaotic. But she tried to clear her mind and finish preparing for the day. She brushed her hair again and left it swept over her shoulder to one side, sheathed her sword in its frog, picked up her shield, then left, ready to start the day.

Walking slowly down the street toward her first day of teaching, she breathed in the cool air, appreciating the stillness of the resting city. She arrived at the Arena, where Owyn was waiting out front.

"Good morning, Owyn. Where's your man?" She smiled.

"Good morning. I'm waiting for him… He should be around soon. How'd you sleep?" he asked politely.

Žaneta noticed his bloodshot eyes—it seemed that he himself hadn't rested well. She shrugged and gave a so-so expression. "Now I'm going to go in and pick an item to beat your kid with!" she said, and Owyn burst into laughter. Then he refocused and thought on what details might help her. "He favors two Imperial short swords."

"Good, tell him to use what he's comfortable with." She paused, giving him a brief doubletake. "Sounds like he's all offense. I'll be on the sand waiting."

Žaneta entered the Bloodworks and browsed over some of the wooden maces. *Too clumsy*, she thought. The practice swords were simply too thin to work against a real blade. Then she saw thick wooden rods—about four feet long—in a bucket. She asked one of the fighters passing by, "What are these for?"

The Nord man stopped and quickly answered, "They hang event ribbons on those when we have a ranking match."

Perfect, Žaneta thought. She pulled one out, got a feel for it, and took it to the arena floor.

Once on the sand, she unsheathed her sword and set it to the side against the wall below the announcer's podium. She walked out closer to the center and looked around, wondering what the place would look like full of spectators. She knew, before long, it would be—then she'd see for herself.

Little did she know, word of Cyrus getting a new trainer had drawn interest among the fighters. She sat down, placed the rod on the ground and the shield on her lap, then closed her eyes and cleared her mind. Minutes went by, until, one by one, people began to enter the stadium seating. The clamors and rattles from the audience did little to distract her from concentrating, despite the noise growing with the size of the crowd—the fighters of the Arena had come to watch, and the place began to pulse with anticipation.

Owyn stepped up onto the announcer's podium and leaned on the rail, which offered a center view of the arena below. Then, up from the Bloodworks walked Cyrus. He wore a heavy raiment, leather boots, and gloves, with an Imperial short sword on each hip. He had fairly short hair and a clean-shaven face, stood a little over six feet tall, and was in good shape for Arena life—essentially a poster boy for the business.

Listening to his footsteps as he approached in the sand, Žaneta opened her eyes and watched him as he swaggered nearer.

"Žaneta? My dad said you were here to give me a lesson," he called arrogantly.

Žaneta said nothing, not taking her eyes off him. Then she stood, revealing her imposing size. She grabbed the handle of her shield and wrapped the strap around her forearm to secure it, then reached down and picked up the rod.

"A stick!" Cyrus smirked.

"Your father wanted me to train you, not kill you," she answered stoically, loosening up and squaring off.

He drew both of his swords and stood at the ready. "Funny… I didn't get that message."

They stared at each other briefly with the Arena watching and waiting, anxious for the fight to begin. Cyrus struck first, starting with an aggressive barrage of attacks. He didn't like leaving any opportunities for an attacker to make a move; however, Žaneta blocked every attack, letting him burn himself out. He swung his right sword high and into her block, then low again into her shield. He swung with his left as she met it with the rod, too thick to cut through, then followed around with another swing from his right into her shield.

She knocked it back hard, spinning away from him. Seeing his left sword coming toward her in a thrust, she deflected it inward, redirecting the blow.

Not wanting to give her his back, he quickly spun to bring his right sword around. In an instant, she dropped the rod and released the leather strap on her shield, allowing it to fall free. She intercepted his right hand, grasping underneath the sword's cross guard over his hand, and as he came up with his left sword over his right shoulder to jab back at her, she ducked to the side. It missed its mark, almost grazing her head.

She grabbed under the cross guard and brought it over the top of both their heads then stepped her foot into the middle of his back. He tried to pull her over top of him by crouching forward, but it wasn't enough. Žaneta pressed out and sent him flying, sliding in the sand, while she held both of his swords.

The small crowd was in an uproar around them, and Žaneta could tell Cyrus's hurt pride was pushing him toward anger.

Žaneta turned and threw one of the swords hard across the sands behind her then tossed the other in front of Cyrus, who had rolled over and sat up. He grabbed the sword quickly and got to a knee, thinking she was about to charge him.

"Slow down!" she hollered, picking up her shield strap but leaving the shield on the ground. It would double as a flail.

He took off toward her, and up came the shield, hitting him in his right side before he was close enough to strike with his sword. He stumbled to his left, well past her. She spun the shield with her right hand and released it into his chest as he turned to face her, knocking him to the ground again.

The onlookers cried out, some clanging their weapons and shields together or banging the ends of their spears on the floor.

Žaneta stood up, unarmed, and waited for him to charge with his sword and pride. She was unafraid. Combat came as naturally as walking to her, and she had her arm and leg plates—more than enough to get her through.

He lunged in and swung low at her left leg, but she lifted it out of the way. Swinging more fiercely, he sliced toward her right leg. She stepped into his move with the leg plate on her shin, stopping the attack hard, so he spun around, swinging toward her upper half.

Žaneta raised her armguard into the attack and reached beneath his underarm, pulling him around then pushing him away. At the same time, she jerked the sword out of his grip by its cross guard.

He went stumbling forward but stayed on his feet. Then he turned and looked at his father. "She's got the strength of a man but the legs of a horse!" he yelled to Owyn.

"Then stop trying to overpower them, son—stay out of their way!" He chuckled.

Cyrus looked back at Žaneta warily. "Easier said than done," he muttered to himself.

She threw the sword, just as she had done with the first. He looked to some of the fighters in the crowd and yelled, "Spear!" One was thrown down to him, and though it was against common practice, Žaneta didn't care—she simply stood there, waiting.

Cyrus got within range and swung the blade edge of the spear around in an attempt to cut across her chest, but she weaved under it. He followed through by grabbing the middle of the shaft with his left hand and brought it in a downward slice that she sidestepped, leaning back to her right. Cyrus pulled back and tried to thrust forward with a piercing blow, and yet, coming forward from her last dodge, she spun right around the spear and grabbed the wood just below the blade.

Grasping it tightly while he tried to pull, she threw it over her head as hard as she could while he maintained his grip. Like a tetherball on a pole, he spun around with the spear while she closed the gap. Grabbing the shaft as she gave a short jump, she
she slammed her left knee into the middle of the weapon, breaking it in half.

Leaving Žaneta with the sharp edge and him with the shattered stick, his confidence sank, and fear started to set in. He tried not to let his guard down, but he was growing exhausted. He panted hard, and his face was covered with sand and sweat.

Žaneta threw her piece of the spear then stared at him, again waiting for his attacks, which were becoming more and more tired with every swing.

Armed with only the stick—like the one he'd mocked her for using; she smirked at that fact—he began swinging at her desperately. He slashed toward her belly, missing. Then her face—another miss. He swung at her foot next, and she lifted it. Then her upper body, and she met the blow with her armguard. He was exhausted, so she left a tempting target out for him to strike. Exposing her right leg as she stepped forward, the poor boy spun around and smacked her thigh with a solid *thwap!* Žaneta didn't react to the pain. Instead, she used his attack to her advantage, quickly grabbing the end of the stick. She brought her leg up to step on the center of it, which jerked him forward. Grabbing his shoulder, she brought her end of the stick up hard into the center of his face.

Cyrus blacked out and stayed standing a moment before finally falling backward, flat on his back.

Žaneta tossed away the stick as the Arena fell silent. She walked to Cyrus's side and waited for him to wake up. Slowly, he began to groan and reached for his head. Sitting up, he put his hands over his nose and face; blood was streaming from his nose, which she'd obviously shattered.

She knelt beside him and pulled his right hand down slowly to inspect his injury. Then, lifting an open hand with her palm facing him, she focused and began healing. Drowsy and startled at first, thinking she was about to cast something dreadful on him, he scurried back on his rear with his hands and feet. But she was already done and standing up, offering a hand to help him off the ground. His pain was gone, and he didn't feel as worn-out as he had a few seconds before. He looked up and grabbed her hand, and as he stood, he touched his nose—besides bits of dried blood, he was fine.

"What the hell!" he gasped in disbelief. "That was… great! You kicked my ass, and I feel great! I don't understand… how did you—what?" he spluttered.

Žaneta patted his right shoulder before turning to pick up her shield, half smiling. "I needed to know how you fought. Now… we can fix some things."

Owyn, beyond impressed with her display of sportsmanship, stood and clapped and was soon joined by all the fighters and onlookers.

Žaneta walked to the announcer's podium to retrieve her sword and sheathed it. Owyn leaned over the rail and looked down at her. "Well done!" he shouted.

Cyrus jogged across the Arena to pick up his swords then ran back to Žaneta and his father. "Where did you find her, Dad? And why haven't I been training with her before now?" he asked, smiling slightly.

"She's an old friend. She won't be here long, son, so take in all she can teach."

Žaneta bowed her head in appreciation to Owyn and looked at Cyrus.

"I'd be an idiot if I slacked on whatever she has to offer!" Cyrus grinned. She turned and gave him an appreciative smile.

Owyn smirked, giving Žaneta a thankful nod.

The crowd had dispersed, and Žaneta motioned to Cyrus to lead the way out of the Arena with an open hand. "After you." She turned and looked up at Owyn. "I'll be back. I'm going to the Legion office to check on any news."

"Thank you for the help, Žana," he replied.

"My pleasure, Owyn."

With that, she turned and proceeded to the Bloodworks with Cyrus.

Chapter Six

Even though the Arena had an open roof, the air when Žaneta stepped outside was substantially better. It was the early part of a beautiful day as she walked through the market, purchasing some dried meat and a piece of fruit for breakfast on her way to the offices. By that time, the streets had come to life while the city's residents began their days.

She entered the Prison District and went into the Legion office, then asked the guard on duty if there had been any sightings reported of the carts. He shook his head no, but when she started to give her name, he stopped her and said, "I've been told of you, Žaneta."

Thankful that word was getting around the Legion, she looked down with a sigh of relief. "I'll be staying at the Merchant's Inn and training at the Arena. Please, if you hear anything, come find me." She turned and left the office, and when she walked outside, she took a moment to lean against the wall. She sucked in a deep breath and exhaled slowly.

She hadn't fully expected a result yet, but she was steadily feeling trapped in this vast world, with no idea where her children were. She was scrambling to find anything, any idea of where they could be. She felt like her mind and body were being pulled apart. Trying not to give in to the sinking feeling overwhelming her, she distracted herself. *Gus, I'll go check on Gus.*

She started heading toward the Talos District and the main entrance to the city. As she passed by people on the way to the stables, she wondered how they could enjoy living here. Or perhaps it was all they knew. On occasion, she found a pleasant "hello" returned to her, but most of the time, it seemed to require too much effort for many of the residents as they hurried by. *Was courtesy sacrificed due to the bustling crowds constantly flooding the streets? It's so crowded! Like Torval*, she thought. She remembered the tranquility of being able to hear herself think after leaving her hometown.

She'd only been in the city for two days and could already tell her coin wouldn't last if she lived here. But since she still had plenty, she'd stick with the plan—training Cyrus while waiting for news.

Once at the stables, she found the Orc taking buckets of grain to the horses as they chewed on hay. Gus was in a large corral with a couple of other horses so he could move freely outside the confinement of the stable.

Žaneta approached the Orc. "Good morning," she said, getting his attention. "I see the captain's horses are still here! Has he been by?"

The Orc hung the buckets on fence pegs so the horses could eat from them. "Yes, ma'am, he was here yesterday evening," he replied.

"I'm not sure when I'll be leaving. So, I can pay daily or simply when I leave if that's okay. What's your preference?" she inquired politely.

"Your bill was paid by Captain Matius for 'services rendered.' I'm also to tell you to give your receipts to the guard captain in the Legion offices to cover your expenses. Sounds important, ma'am… Not every day that we get people through here who are getting their bills paid by the Legion." He leaned against the fence post as he stared at her.

Žaneta scowled at that, surprised. "I didn't ask for that… I pay my own way."

The Orc nodded his head in understanding. "I get it, but I guess they figured they owed you. I don't think they're 'giving' you anything." He nodded respectfully.

"What's your name?" she asked.

"Turk… Turk gra-Bura. My sister and I own the stables, but she's not a big fan of the business, so it's mostly just me."

"Well, thank you for working with the horses. Gus likes apples if you have them," she said.

Turk chuckled. "Yes, ma'am… They all do!"

They both smiled, and Žaneta nodded before heading back toward the Arena. On her way there, she went by way of the temple to take in the sights and use the moment to pray at the Temple of the One, the god Akatosh. Its large domed roof and white stone were unique in design, and it was visited heavily by the many who attended the Blessing on Sundas.

The arboretum in the next district, though, she found very beautiful. As she walked the grounds, looking upon the flowers and trees the gardeners had so meticulously cared for, she appreciated the placement of the statues of the Nine Divines, which were positioned around a statue of Tiber Septim at the center of the garden.

Although she'd never recognized Tiber as one of the Divines, she did acknowledge the facts of his conquests and achievements. But it was the Nords who called him Talos, or Ysmir, "Dragon of the North," and continued serving him as a god. Despite her beliefs, she honored him as the warrior he was.

After making her way around the circular path, the Lady Mara statue stood to her right. She stopped, pulled a coin from her bag, and placed it in the statue's basin. All donations were collected by the groundskeepers—hopefully, for the maintenance of the garden. She asked for a blessing, again giving a short prayer, then stepped back from the statue and continued to the Arena in the next district.

The city was laid out in a circular fashion with the White Gold Tower at its center. If Žaneta kept walking, she'd eventually end up right where she started. Only the prison and the Arcane University were separated from the main city by connecting walkways northeast and southeast from the outer walls, respectively.

When she neared the Arena, cheers of excitement could be heard ringing from the coliseum. At the main gate, men were selling tickets, but the Bloodworks' access for combatants was open to her. However, Žaneta wanted to watch the match, so she purchased a ticket and climbed to the seating area. From the stairwell, the view was so good that she didn't need to find a seat. She looked down at the tired fighters below, who had little to offer in way of skill. The match didn't look like it would last much longer.

The woman she'd healed just last night was hard at work against a fighter from another team, an Argonian woman who had all but won this match. The Imperial woman was trying to stay on her feet after having sustained some nasty injuries. The Argonian darted in and ran her through. Then she pulled out her sword and raised her arms in victory. The crowd shared a mixed roar of boos and cheers, as with every match, but Žaneta just stood there with her arms crossed. *What a waste*, she thought.

She knew the place made an income for many, but death for entertainment was not on her list of things to do by choice. Which reminded her—*where was Cyrus?* She thought she'd better get started on his training before he stepped into a careless match.

After the Arena workers cleaned up the last fight, two new fighters prepared for their battle. The match was between two individuals whose names she'd never heard before—an Orc and a Bosmer from what she gathered by listening to the people talking. She waited to see for herself, and sure enough, out came an Orc in a heavy raiment followed by a small Bosmer in light armor. The Orc looked traditional—with an axe and shield fit for a battlefield against many. The Bosmer, however, was quick on his feet and was armed with a dagger and a light shield.

The announcer gave their introductions, and the fight commenced—it was hardly interesting at first, though. The Orc looked to put up a tremendous fight as he charged, swinging his weapon fiercely, while the Bosmer simply played a game of keep-away. Carrying light weapons, he was able to stay close enough to attack, but bobbed in and out to keep from getting clobbered. His long dagger was his only weapon and was apparently poisoned or enchanted with something—people in the crowd had been yelling, "Give him the strike!" and "Stun him!" The Bosmer was able to drag his dagger along the outside of the Orc's right wrist, and almost instantly, Žaneta noticed the Orc appeared burdened and tired. He was slowed by the scratch, just enough that the Bosmer was able to plunge his dagger into the Orc's neck twice. He fell over dead as the crowd cheered.

Žaneta shook her head in disgust. "How cheap!" she muttered, turning to leave the Arena. She went down to the Bloodworks, thinking, *Maybe I'd better buy potions or something to defend myself against shady fights like that in my travels.* She saw Owyn, which interrupted her train of thought, and walked to him. As she drew closer, she noticed he was laughing and having a conversation with Cyrus.

Žaneta watched as Cyrus talked and talked, waving his arms and laughing. She was so happy to see the two of them getting along. "What are you two talking about?" She smiled as he approached.

"You!" Owyn grinned. "How you did this, how you did that!"

Žaneta looked at Cyrus. "And?" she asked, raising an eyebrow.

"And I'm ready to stop matches in the Arena while I'm taking lessons from you. Then we'll see! And I'm sorry," he replied, stifling a chuckle.

She tilted her head and squinted. "For what?"

"For saying you have the legs of a horse," Cyrus replied, holding back an embarrassed laugh and attempting to look solemn. Owyn bent over with his hands on his knees, roaring with laughter, which made Cyrus cackle as well.

Žaneta smirked at the pair of them. "You idiots."

"He meant as *strong* as a horse…" Owyn said, covering for his son.

Žaneta just shrugged and smiled then looked at Cyrus. "When do you want to train?"

Cyrus was still wiping tears from his eyes. "Will this evening work? After the matches are over? The Arena will be all cleared out by then."

"Sounds good. How about we get lunch somewhere? I haven't had much to eat," she said casually.

"I'm buyin'!" Owyn piped up. "The King and Queen Tavern has a great lunch—let's head there."

They all nodded at each other. Owyn led the group toward the Elven Gardens District while he, Cyrus, and Žaneta talked along the way. The trio gathered a lot of attention in the city, not only because of Cyrus's up-and-coming status as an Arena fighter, but also Owyn's history as well as his size. The father and son were intimidating figures. Walking through the Imperial City with a beautiful Khajiit, who was imposing on her own, there were onlookers wherever they went.

They entered the tavern and sat down in the dining area. An Imperial man came to their table with his hands resting together over his abdomen, holding menus, and said with a smile, "Welcome to the King and Queen. What would you like to drink?" He placed a menu down in front of each of them.

"Beer, please," Owyn answered.

"The same," Cyrus replied.

Žaneta cut in, "He and I will have water."

"Ah… you're no fun!" Cyrus joked. But he politely smiled and nodded in agreement with a resigned sigh.

"Sorry. But let's keep a clear head while I'm here training with you," she said.

"No… I get it. Didn't mean to get too leisurely. I'll stay on my toes," said Cyrus. He gave her a respectful nod.

"I had something I was going to ask you two!" she said, changing the tone of the conversation. "I watched a Bosmer fight today, and he killed his opponent with a dagger. Spectators kept yelling, 'Strike!' or 'Give him the strike!' What was that?"

"Shimmer Strike," Owyn grumbled. "Some of the fighters, though skilled, are lacking in certain areas. They rely on enchanted items to see them through."

"I'm familiar with enchantments. But I was surprised to see them allowed on weapons in an Arena battle. Shields I can understand… Has this always been the case?" Žaneta asked.

"As long as I've fought," Cyrus chimed in. "Some thought this may keep real-world possibilities in a fight between unequal opponents."

Žaneta nodded. "Then that's what I need to make sure I'm ready for when I get back to searching for my children. Where's a good place I can get a few potions… maybe enchantments, something to guard against things like that?"

"I don't think I made contact with you once during our match, besides the stick to your leg—but you gave me that one! However, if you're after those things, I'd cut out the middleman and go to the Arcane University," Cyrus advised.

Žaneta looked between him and Owyn.

"Don't ask me! I haven't kept up with trends lately so far as who has the ins," Owyn said, raising his hands.

As they talked, they glanced over their menus and took very little time to find what they wanted. Owyn and Cyrus went there often, and for Žaneta, hunger was the best spice. The man returned with their drinks and took their food orders. She could smell the aromas coming from the kitchen, only making her stomach rumble even more. Owyn and Cyrus both heard it, and they all laughed. As they continued chuckling, they were approached by a Breton woman who had a calm stare set on Žaneta.

Owyn's eyes lit up with recognition. "Hello, Trelina, how are you?" he said, smiling. "I believe you know my son, Cyrus. And this is an old friend, Žaneta." He gestured to her. "Would you like to join us?"

The woman's brown braided ponytail rested over her right shoulder. With common features and simple clothing, she wasn't a person who stood out. When Owyn spoke to her, her blank expression suddenly shifted into a courteous smile, and she turned toward him. "Oh, no! Thank you. I just saw you all sitting here and wanted to say hi. I need to be getting back to work." She grinned.

Everything appeared friendly as the four politely smiled, but as Trelina passed her, Žaneta noticed her make an abrupt motion toward the dagger on her left hip. Žaneta bounced up quickly, shifting the table, and reached for the woman's forearm as she came around with the dagger.

Stopping the swing, Žaneta jabbed with a left cross and rattled the woman's head, knocking her out cold. Žaneta lowered the woman slowly and took the blade from her. Owyn and Cyrus, staring in shock, were speechless.

"Go get a guard, Cyrus!" Žaneta muttered, rolling the woman onto her back. She turned to Owyn. "Who is she?"

"She's a gardener at the arboretum. I've known her for years in passing… but I guess I didn't really know her at all," Owyn replied quietly.

Cyrus came back with two Imperial guards in tow and pointed to Trelina. One began placing her in shackles while the other asked them questions. Owyn repeated what he'd told Žaneta as well as how the ordeal had transpired. "Have you ever seen her before?" the guard asked Žaneta.

She shook her head. "No… I only saw her going for her dagger as she left our table."

The woman began to stir and was lifted to her feet by the guards.

"That's better… What was the purpose of this?" one demanded as her eyes fluttered open, her head lolling down over her chest. She looked up at him as both guards each held an arm, then spit on him. Drowsy, she grinned and said, "Dawn is breaking."

Žaneta wanted to tear her head off after hearing that. Her vision burned red as she clenched her teeth and balled her shaking hands into tight fists, her claws piercing her palms. She knew Trelina must have ties to the Mythic Dawn. She got right down in her face. "Get her to the prison and alert one of the battlemages that they've got another member of the Mythic Dawn to come see!" she hissed, disgusted.

The guards hauled Trelina out of there as she continued cackling with laughter. Owyn and Cyrus looked on, as did the other people in the restaurant, but Žaneta couldn't take her eyes off her. She scowled as they dragged her away.

"What the hell… the Mythic who?" Cyrus asked.

Žaneta sat and invited them to rejoin her at the table. She began to explain all that had happened to her and who the Mythic Dawn were. As she spoke, with Owyn and Cyrus listening intently as they leaned over the table, their food came out—a welcomed interruption in the tense conversation.

Cyrus stared at her with understanding. "Žaneta, from the one day I've known you, you're busier than anyone I've ever met. Thanks for taking the time to work with me, but maybe teaching me should be set aside," he said slowly, his voice full of concern.

Žaneta stopped cutting into her steak and looked up at him. "It's fine. I'll get the details I need from the Legion when not working with you. Besides, it keeps me busy while I'm waiting to hear back from them. Let's eat!" She was drained from all this talk of the Mythic Dawn, especially since the situation had become even more serious… and confusing. She wasn't sure how this Trelina woman had found her. *On the bright side, I haven't seen one yellow-sash-wearing bastard yet!* she gratefully considered, continuing to cut into her food. Then again, maybe the Camonna Tong would be better to deal with than these lunatics. She'd take an army of thugs any day in favor of the hell these people loved so much. There was one thing that gave her hope—the priests hadn't had a vision involving her children and a portal. At least, not yet. She clung to that hope… She was certain it wasn't too late. There was still time.

They all stopped talking and ate in silence. After they were done, Owyn paid the bill then headed back to the Arena with Cyrus after Žaneta told them she was going to the palace to talk with the battlemages.

Heading straight to the White Gold Tower, she entered then continued up the ramp until she came to the guard at the door.

"I need to speak to a battlemage," she said politely.

"You're Ž… Ža…?" the guard stuttered, struggling to recall her name.

"Žaneta," she clarified.

"My apologies. Please follow me." Slightly embarrassed, he led her through the same tower hall she'd previously taken when she met the Moth Priest. But this time, she was taken to the priests' and battlemages' quarters. The guard left her with a female battlemage, who reluctantly pulled her attention away from her paperwork. "Hello, Žaneta. How can I help you?"

"A woman attacked me about an hour ago at the King and Queen Tavern. Her name is Trelina. A friend I was with identified her… said she was a gardener at the arboretum. But the reason I'm here is because of what she said—'Dawn is breaking.'" Žaneta watched the battlemage carefully, monitoring her expression to see if she was familiar with the phrase. The battlemage didn't disappoint—she sat up straighter, her eyes narrowing. "I know she's part of the Mythic Dawn; there's no other explanation for her to randomly attack me. I told the guards who hauled her off to inform the battlemages, but I wanted to relay it as well," Žaneta explained.

"Good. What do you say we go get some details out of her?" the mage replied, standing quickly.

Žaneta agreed, and they started walking out of the quarters. Just as they left, they were stopped by the priests she'd met yesterday. "Žaneta… we need to talk!" one said urgently.

"We've been bombarded with visions, which happens often. But with these, we just saw you. You were at a distance from someone who was *very* focused on you," the other priest said. "I saw a brief image of your likeness near a woman being led by guards, then the vision slammed shut like a door in my face!" he said, his voice rising. "Does this make any sense to you?"

Žaneta exchanged glances with the battlemage. "We have to go… now!" Žaneta urged, her eyes flashing. Heading to the door, she turned and looked at the priests. "Tell more mages to meet us at the prison. Let them know what you told us and that we are headed there!" she stressed, gesturing to the battlemage next to her.

They hurried down the tower then rushed to the Elven Gardens District, where she'd had lunch. From there, the two of them worked toward the prison. The pair looked up and down the streets for any signs of a disturbance, but the crowds were going about their business as usual. After they passed through the Market District and reached the bridgeway to the prison, they stood facing an enemy who was covered in dark armor and wearing a red hood, leaving only a steel mask exposed.

Staring at the figure blocking the center of the connection bridge between the city and the prison, Žaneta looked at the guards, she'd met in the tavern, lying at the woman's feet, dead. She knew the enemy had to be Trelina. *But where did the armor come from?* she thought wildly, without taking her eyes off her. The enemy was also armed with a strange sword that gave off a blue glow.

"That's a summoned blade! Let me take lead!" the battlemage insisted. She stepped in front of Žaneta and began rushing toward the enemy.

As she strode closer, the masked individual began to form energy in her left hand. The battlemage made a motion with her hands and brought up a strange translucent barrier that Žaneta had never seen before.

A blast of bright lightning shot from the stranger's hand and snaked toward them, crashing into the mage's barrier, which not only stopped it, but seemed to absorb it. The mage took off running toward her, with Žaneta right behind. Bolts of lightning hit, one after the other, and the mage began slowing and let out a gasping cry as they started overpowering her. Žaneta heard the panic from the battlemage, who had all but stopped as she struggled to maintain the barrier. Žaneta braced against her shoulder, beginning to heal her. They continued to inch closer to their attacker.

Žaneta pulled her blade and looked for the best weakness to exploit. But there was only one method of attack on the narrow walkway—straight forward. Over Trelina's shoulder, Žaneta could see a few guards sprinting toward them from the prison—maybe this would be the distraction they needed.

Both groups rushed at their target, with the guards closing in faster. But one screamed at Trelina to stop, which only alerted her of their approach. She turned her focus on them, thrusting her left hand at the first guard. Lightning coursed all over him then jumped to the next guard, shocking them both to death. They collapsed in a heap on the bridge, leaving one to continue the charge.

Žaneta, still bracing the mage, grabbed her sword like an ice pick and pulled her right hand back to cast the fire bolt Aryon had taught her. She sent the flame right through Trelina's left shoulder, sending her spinning to the ground. But she wasn't down for more than a couple of seconds before she rolled to her feet and cut through the last guard to reach her.

Trelina turned to the mage and Žaneta, preparing to attack, but the mage reached her first. Žaneta gave her room to work; yet, even one-handed, Trelina slashed just above the mage's left hip, which was unprotected by armor, causing her to collapse.

Trelina brought her sword up to finish her off, but Žaneta lunged forward, blocking the blow with her blade.

Then, slamming the blades close to Trelina's body to prevent her from swinging, Žaneta grabbed her right wrist, holding her arm up—nearly lifting her off the ground—as she slammed her knee into Trelina's chest plate. Even with the armor, she went flying backward a good twenty feet, as her bound sword evaporated from existence. Žaneta's knee ached from the strike, but she healed it quickly then did the same for the mage before refocusing on Trelina.

The woman picked herself up and ripped off her faceplate, panting. Her eyes gleamed as she laughed mirthlessly. "You idiot—we are immortal!" she shrieked, bracing herself on her knees with a defiant sneer.

At her words, Žaneta scowled and took a split second to remember something her mother had shared with her. Magic words from the past... old magic. It had been so long since she'd used the phrase that it took a moment to recall any of it. Žaneta took in a deep breath and roared one of the magic words at her. *"Joor!"*

The word sent a shockwave toward the prison and rode the air like an explosion, passing through Trelina. She dropped to her hands and knees, crying and shaking, her eyes widening. She clutched at her chest in panic and stared up at Žaneta. "Wha—what is this?" she sobbed.

Žaneta just stood beside her with misty eyes and readied her sword. "Self-awareness," she replied. With a heave of her blade, she swept Trelina's head off her body.

A long moment followed, and Žaneta felt paralyzed as she stared down at Trelina and the slain guards with a weighted conscience. *What could I have done differently?* she thought. She finally sheathed her weapon and checked on the three guards; however, it only confirmed what she already knew—they were all dead.

The battlemage approached her with a baffled look while she was checking the last guard's pulse.

Žaneta stood and turned to face her. "Do you feel okay?" she asked, still somewhat distraught.

"I feel fine. But what did you just do? I heard you start to say something, but then I was deafened by thunder... My ears are ringing!" the mage replied in amazement.

Žaneta looked at Trelina's corpse. The armor seemed to be disintegrating from her body. "Old words I learned from my mother. In my language, it translates to 'Var,' or as you would say, 'Living' or 'Mortal.' It seemed fitting... when she said she was immortal," Žaneta explained. Žaneta could tell the battlemage was trying to hide her confusion about what she'd just witnessed. The way she was looking at Žaneta, she wondered if the mage had ever seen anything like it before. She was in shock herself about what had happened. "My name's Ashlyn." She extended a hand to Žaneta, but they were distracted by the sound of her friends approaching.

Three Imperial battlemages came sprinting from the Market District gate of the city and ran up to the two of them. "What happened?" panted one of the mages.

"She was part of the Mythic Dawn," Ashlyn replied.

"And she killed five guards?" another asked in surprise.

"Nearly six, if not for her," she answered, gesturing to Žaneta. "Did you hear it?"

The three mages looked at each other, then one asked, "Did we hear what?"

"The thunder!"

"That was you?" one said, his brow furrowed.

"It was her," Ashlyn replied, smiling at Žaneta.

"You're full of surprises…" one muttered. They all agreed but appeared perplexed.

Žaneta changed the subject. "Let's get these men picked up. They don't deserve to lie on the ground." She bent down to lift one. The others did the same and led the way to the Legion offices, carrying those they could manage.

In front of the office, they set the men down carefully and respectfully with help from others who'd come from the bastion. Žaneta took a knee and prayed, thanking them for their sacrifice, then started crying.

Ashlyn placed a hand on her shoulder. "There's nothing more you could've done."

Žaneta wiped her eyes. "I know… But they're dead, not us." She stood and turned to face Ashlyn. "The more I kill of their little gang, the more they'll be looking for me."

"I think you can manage against them!"

"It's not me I worry about… It's everyone close to me that makes me concerned."

"Then that's going to be a problem. A soldier could only hope to fight next to people who think like that. Thank you for helping me on the bridge." Ashlyn gave her a small smile.

Žaneta nodded and changed the topic from the murdered men, trying not to focus on their loss. "You'd better tell the guards to check on the other Mythic Dawn prisoner from Kvatch."

"You're right—I'll be right back." Ashlyn made her way to her colleagues, and Žaneta watched the brief discussion as two of the battlemages nodded to Ashlyn and marched inside. Ashlyn rejoined Žaneta and stood in silence, watching as the guards covered their dead with wool blankets. One of the battlemages came out of the bastion and gave Ashlyn a thumbs up, then the two of them turned and left the prison.

"What was that shield magic you used there, the one that stopped her attack?" Žaneta asked as they walked back to the bridge together.

"Oh… the ward? Greater Ward, to be exact. It's a magical barrier that's saved me plenty, but it doesn't stop objects like arrows or anything… only other magic."

"Would you teach me how to use it? If you hadn't been there, crossing the bridge would've proved… interesting. Or suicidal, rather!" Žaneta laughed darkly.

"Of course! With your hand, or hands, out in the direction you desire to block, think the words, 'Arc'gah adurid.' This means, 'Power break.' Then, all that's needed is for the user to gain experience in Restoration." The pair smiled at each other.

"Well, that's a relief to hear," Žaneta said, pulling her journal from her satchel to write it down. "Would you please spell it here for me?" she asked, handing her the journal. She wrote down the spell and handed it back to Žaneta. "I made an agreement with a friend at the Arena, and I should try to honor it. I'll be there if you need me, but I need to stop by the Arcane University first."

"The Arcane University? Why do you need to go there?"

"I'd like to get my shield enchanted," she explained.

Ashlyn raised an eyebrow. "With what, exactly?"

"Protection from whatever I can. Fire, lightning… I haven't run into it yet, but ice. Pretty much whatever can be done to it would be helpful."

Ashlyn stood with her arms crossed and extended a hand. "Give it to me," she said with a kind smile. Žaneta pulled the strap over her head and handed it to her. "I'll make sure you're taken care of. I'll return it to you when it's done."

"Thank you," Žaneta replied. With that, they shook hands and went their separate ways.

Chapter Seven

Back at the Arena, the fights were still raging. The cheers could be heard from all around the surrounding area, and it was getting late in the afternoon.

Žaneta entered the Bloodworks and looked around. The day's battles had left several fighters injured, and she postponed her search for Cyrus for the moment to help them. Open wounds, punctures, blunt traumas, and other injuries gained all of her attention, until there were none left—a blessing they need not become accustomed to with her temporary stay.

When she was done, she saw Owyn talking to another combatant, so she sat and waited for him to finish. Once he saw her, he excused himself after his talk and approached her. "May I have a seat?" He pointed to the bench next to her. She moved over and made a spot for him.

"How'd it go?" he asked casually, smiling.

"It was… surprising. Trelina's dead. She killed five guards, though." She pursed her lips and dropped her gaze to the floor.

He gawked at her in confusion. "What are you talking about? Are you serious? We watched her leave in shackles!"

"Somehow, she freed herself and attacked us when we found her. She'd manifested a sword and armor from nothing, but it ended in her death all the same." She paused and sighed, not sure what else to say. "Phew! Strange day."

"Wow, a damn gardener. Can't trust anyone." He shook his head.

Žaneta suddenly looked around. "Where's Cyrus?"

"He went to my house to grab some things of his. Said you'd appreciate them, but he should be back soon."

Žaneta stood up slowly with a soft smile and said, "Okay. I'm going to go wait outside. It's too nice to be stuffed down here." Walking out, she turned and looked at Owyn. "Let me know if anyone else needs healing—I'll be close."

After leaving the Bloodworks, she sat down cross-legged on one of the stone walls that surrounded the coliseum and laid her sword across her lap. She pulled out her maps, finding the one for Cyrodiil. Skimming over it, she looked where she'd already been and began wondering where the other carts might have gone. *Only two passed through Pell's Gate… Did the other two even come into Cyrodiil after leaving Narsis? Did they go south or stop at a place along the way?* she thought, her head spinning.

Her mind raced with the possibilities. The potential for corrupt guards being paid off was likely, and Žaneta only became more frustrated as she searched the map. She didn't even know what direction to take. Upset, she stuffed it back in her bag.

"Žaneta!" She turned to see Cyrus jogging toward her. "Hey, are you okay?"

"I'm all right. What's all that?" she asked, nodding at the bag he was carrying.

He sat on the wall next to her and placed the bag on his lap. "These are little bottles of what you asked about earlier!" he replied, his grin growing. "Small enough that you can carry many, but potent enough to see you through a fight. Here, this one's resistance to fire." He removed a small bottle with a flame drawn on its label. "… and this one is resistance against frost." He showed her a bottle with a drawing of a snowflake on it. "All of them are protection potions, except for these two. These will allow you to stay underwater for over five minutes!" he said happily, handing the bag to her.

"A gift?" She slowly looked at him, her eyes full of thanks.

He just shrugged and smiled.

She looked into the bag at the variously colored and shaped bottles, knowing they'd all probably come in handy. "Thank you." She nodded seriously. "How much longer until the Arena closes?"

"Not for about another three or four hours."

"Well, how about we train outside the city? No crowds?" she proposed.

"Sure, where'd you have in mind?"

"I saw a large open area past the town after the bridge to the city. Let's go there. Just tell Owyn and grab some things you think you'll want," she replied.

"I'd like to check on my horse anyways, then maybe we could ride there from the stables. You could probably use my dad's horse," he offered.

"Sounds like a plan. But there's no need to borrow his—mine's there, too!"

"Great!" Cyrus hopped down to the sidewalk and went inside the Bloodworks. He grabbed a couple of iron shields and two of the wooden rods he'd underestimated before then jogged back to Žaneta.

She analyzed his selections as he approached her, and they made her smile. "I like your choices!"

They started off to the stables, leaving them with a few hours of daylight as they cut through the Green Emperor Way in the middle of the city. Shortly after, they arrived at the Chestnut Handy Stables. Cyrus and Žaneta both greeted Turk and retrieved their saddle blankets and saddles, while Turk put in their horses' bits. Žaneta went to her saddlebags with the bag of potions she'd just gotten from Cyrus and placed the majority of them inside. She kept out a resistance to fire, frost, and lightning potion for her satchel, as well as the water breathing ones.

After saddling up, wrapping her sword to tie it down, and climbing onto Gus, they headed to the corral gate as Turk opened it. "He's a damn big boy!" Cyrus shouted, admiring Gus. He was riding on a strong— but smaller—bay.

Žaneta grinned. "Thank you… Magnificent, isn't he?"

The two of them started across the city's large bridge and then through the little town of Weye. As the road forked in front of them, they continued straight into the open field beyond it. Scattered trees offered a place to dismount and tie off the horses. The sun was well over an hour from setting, so there was plenty of time before it got completely dark.

As they started training, Žaneta began by praising Cyrus on his ability to use either hand in a sword fight. Many fighters didn't have that skill, and Žaneta was impressed. After boosting his confidence, Žaneta was down to business—they started with practicing his shield work. However, balance was her main focus with him. They went over body positioning, how to use his weight, and how to use others' imbalance against them. She showed him how to, even with a regular shield, release the handle and grab it by the strap before it fell off his arm. This allowed close to an extra two feet of reach that he could swing at someone. "When they step here, swing there!" she grunted. These were all techniques her father had taught her, and she relaxed into the comfortable, familiar positions. This practice went on for a solid two hours, and Cyrus absorbed it like a sponge. Before long, night fell around them.

Žaneta could see, but Cyrus was left with the dwindling light of dusk. "What do ya say we head back?" he asked. She agreed, and they walked to the horses, untying them from the tree limbs they'd used, and began riding to the stables. It was a good start to their first true lesson—thankfully, it didn't involve destroying each other. At the stables, they unsaddled the horses and put them back in the corral. Turk must've been inside, so they put their things back in the tack room before heading into the city, only after Žaneta remembered to grab a small piece of cord and her drinking bladder from the saddlebag.

When they reached the Arena District, they entered the Bloodworks to return the equipment and see who was there. Only a couple of fighters were present, but Owyn wasn't around.

"Dad probably went for food… or to bed. I'm gonna do the same. Can we do this again tomorrow?" he asked with anticipation.

"Yes. Let's get a morning start and go to the same place. I'm going to grab dinner and enjoy this city's running water," she replied with a smile.

They both went their separate ways, Cyrus to his father's, and Žaneta to the Merchant's Inn. Once in the hotel, she went to the reception counter and talked to the owner.

"Good evening, I stayed here last night and would like to continue renting a room until I'm finished with my business in the city. Also, the Legion may need to reach me, so would you let me know if I get any messages? My name's Žaneta."

He looked under the counter and reached down to grab an envelope. "I knew the name sounded familiar—here you are. Would you like me to show you to your room?" he asked, handing her the letter.

She inspected it and noted the Imperial wax seal on the back. "No, thank you. I'd like to get something to eat, though! May I sit at the table?"

He gestured to it with an open hand. "Of course. I'll be right with you to take your order. Just let me see who's in the kitchen while I get you a drink. What would you like?"

"Water's fine," she replied. She sat down and opened the letter—it was from Ashlyn. It read,

> *Žaneta,*
> *Per our discussion, your shield has been prepared. I also had the armorer work on its finish.*
> *Come see me where we met yesterday, or I'll revisit here tomorrow evening.*
> *Best regards,*
> *Ashlyn*

Žaneta appreciated the shield had been completed so quickly, and yet, she felt a little disappointed. For a brief moment, she'd thought it had finally been information about her children. She lightly set the letter down and leaned back in her chair, letting out a sigh. She wouldn't lose hope—she'd keep checking with the Legion every day. But she knew that with each passing moment, the children were getting farther and farther away from her. She placed the letter in her satchel and looked to the innkeeper, who was walking toward her with a glass of water.

He placed it on the table in front of her. "What would you like to eat?"

"Do you have baked chicken? Maybe some rice and vegetables—?" Suddenly, she caught sight of her glass of water. "Wait… there's ice in my cup!" She examined it closely then gave him a questioning smirk.

"Yes, but only carrots and broccoli… We've had a busy day. And we've started doing that to some of the drinks—it's very popular!" he replied.

She took a drink. "That's good!" She lowered the cup, pleasantly surprised.

He smiled and nodded, walking back toward the kitchen. "Give me a little bit, and I'll bring out your food."

While waiting, she pulled out her journal and looked over her entries. It was the weekend, Loredas, so she brought it up to date with her recent endeavors. Her writing just poured onto the pages; some part of her hoped the food would take longer so she could finish her thoughts, but no such luck. Her dinner came out, and she paused for a moment to say thank you. Quickly summing up her entry, she focused on the food.

After she finished eating, she retired to her room. She prepared for the next day, washing her clothes and taking advantage of that wonderful shower. Before too long, the exhaustion from the day claimed her, and she fell asleep.

Instantly, it began—the dream. It came crashing in like she was in another land, on another adventure, and none of it made sense. Žaneta saw a fort, high in the mountains. It was as if she were flying above it. Then she saw a strange green glow begin to radiate from cracks in the walls and the ground itself. In a flash, she found herself standing there. But there was no longer a fort around her—just high winds and ash in all directions, as if she were trapped in the center of a tornado.

The voices returned, too, that evil chanting from before. It seemed to be in her head, but figures began to manifest in the dirt and ash that swirled around her. They held staffs, but the details were impossible to see. Through the darkness grew a light. It became brighter and brighter, an orange-red, as if there were a huge fire on the other side of a wall of smoke.

Then it stood—the silhouette of a jagged, thorny dragon.

Its eyes glowed, as did the heat in its mouth, and it spread its wings, clearing the smoke, ash, and debris.

As quickly as she had fallen asleep, she woke up. Her heart raced as she sat up and looked to the window. Day had come, and it was light outside. She took a deep breath, wrapping her arms around her knees, and sighed as she rested her head on them. "Get moving," she whispered to herself, throwing off the covers. After she finished getting dressed and gearing up, she brushed her hair, folded it into a braid that fell over her left shoulder, and tied it with a piece of cord. She gathered all her things and left the room.

Walking to the Arena, she tried not to give too much thought to what she remembered from the dream. *Could the priests be behind this again?* She'd meet with Cyrus and stop by the palace on their way out of town to pick up her shield and talk with the priests about what they knew.

She stopped and sat down on the wall, the same place she had yesterday, then closed her eyes and tried to clear her mind. She focused on training Cyrus then started a little healing magic for herself. She found it relaxing, but before she knew it, she was glowing. People began to stop and stare. She opened her eyes and brought the effort to an abrupt halt when she realized how powerful she'd let her cast get while concentrating.

Žaneta stood and began to walk toward the Bloodworks, but didn't even make it to the door before Cyrus came out carrying equipment.

"Good morning!" he said with a smile. "You look nice. How'd you sleep?"

Žaneta just smiled and replied, "I'm getting used to not sleeping! You look ready to go."

Cyrus handed her one of the shields and sticks. "Absolutely!" He grinned, and Žaneta could already tell he was motivated to learn more.

With that, they started through the Green Emperor Way again. But along the way, Žaneta paused. "I need to talk to someone at the palace and get my shield. I won't be long. Would you wait for me in the main chamber?"

Cyrus agreed, and they walked up the steps to the large entrance of the tower. When they entered, Cyrus stood across from two guards who were posted by the door. "I'll be right here," he said as she went through the door that led to the mages' and priests' living quarters.

"Nice stick!" chuckled one of the guards to Cyrus. They both scoffed at him. But he just smiled and kept his mouth shut.

When Žaneta reached the guard at the entrance to the upper levels, she told him, "I'm here to see Ashlyn."

He turned to open the door, took her to the locked gate at the library entrance, and left her in the battlemage quarters with Ashlyn and a couple of other battlemages.

"Good morning, Žaneta. You got my letter, I presume?" she asked politely.

"Yes. I just didn't expect it back so soon."

Ashlyn looked at the stick and shield she was holding, even though her scimitar was strapped to her side. "What are those for?"

Žaneta glanced down at them and smirked. "I'm training my friend's son… He shows promise."

Ashlyn raised an inquisitive brow as she tilted her head. "That's good of you. What's his name?"

"Cyrus."

"Not the Arena's Cyrus?" she asked with a wide grin.

"Yes. Why?" Žaneta responded, slightly confused.

"Because that young man hasn't lost a match! How'd you get him to accept training?" Ashlyn asked, crossing her arms.

"I didn't. His dad is an old friend. He found me in the city and told me his boy needed help, that he was going to get himself killed."

"So, what did you do?" she asked.

"I convinced him with one of these sticks and my—"

"Your shield," Ashlyn finished her sentence, nodding. She stood. "Give me a second." She walked to another room then came back carrying the shield. "Here you are!" She handed the polished enchanted shield back to her. "I think you'll be very pleased with what we've done to it!"

Žaneta laid the practice equipment down at her feet then took the handle of her shield and wrapped the leather strap around her arm, holding it securely.

"So *that's* how you wear it! The others and I were wondering," Ashlyn said.

"What were you able to enchant it with?" asked Žaneta, admiring it—it had been restored to its former glory and more.

"All that you asked for. Resistance to fire, ice… and lightning. We even had one of the Master Enchanters bind a ward barrier to it that defends against incoming magic attacks before they reach you, so you don't have to cast a ward while this is up. Now you've got something for physical and magical attacks… the best of both!" She grinned.

"This sounds expensive…" Žaneta looked up at her, concern filling her eyes.

"You have no idea! But it was my pleasure," Ashlyn said with a smile. "Have fun training."

Žaneta took the shield off then picked up the training equipment. "Actually, I wanted to ask—have the priests made mention of any visions? Anything concerning to them?"

"Nothing. Why?"

"I don't know… I had a vivid dream, I guess, more than once. But it seemed real enough." She dropped her eyes then shook her head, dismissing the thoughts.

"What did you see? I'll ask the priests; they're in council with the emperor at the moment."

Žaneta thought for a second. "A mountain fort, green light from underground around it. Dust, ash, and smoke flying around in what seemed like a windstorm, then figures chanting something. Finish it off with fire and a big dragon! Confusing, isn't it? Maybe I ate something that didn't sit well…" She shook her head again. "All I know is that ever since I started after my children, chaos has appeared everywhere. I find it hard to believe no one has had any details to go off of in finding them."

Ashlyn nodded her head in understanding and gave her a sympathetic smile. "The emperor has made it clear to keep a careful ear and eye out for information that will help you. Something will turn up."

Žaneta knew she must be patient and not go mad for lack of direction. She hid her concern well, masking it behind her stoic, calm appearance. But that didn't mean her insides weren't twisted with worry.

"We'll be training outside, in the area past Weye. I'll check back later, and if not, I'll be back at the Merchant's Inn after we're finished," she said, walking to the door. "Would you mind getting the gate? I don't have a key."

Ashlyn followed her and let her out before locking up behind her.

"Thank you for this—I'll take good care of it!" Žaneta said, turning to Ashlyn and gesturing to the shield.

Ashlyn smiled. "You earned it!"

Žaneta returned downstairs to the sight of Cyrus and the guards laughing as they traded stories. He saw her coming around the hall and finished his conversation. "All good?" he asked with a grin.

"Yup." She nodded to the guards then headed to the stables with Cyrus.

"Let's grab a muffin or something to eat before we leave," she suggested as they walked to the Talos Plaza District. "Where should we go?" They stopped next to a dragon statue in the center of the plaza.

"The Flask," Cyrus decided. He led her to the right and up the street, where they came across a business sign that read, "The Foaming Flask." When they entered, there was a mixed crowd of people, some dressed nicely sitting and eating, and some in clothes that obviously hadn't been changed in days.

There were baskets of sweet rolls, blueberry and banana nut muffins, as well as fruit. Žaneta bought two sweet rolls, two apples, and two banana nut muffins. She rolled up the sweet rolls in paper and put them in her satchel for later, then gave Cyrus one of the muffins. When they reached the stables, Turk was mucking stalls. He saw them approaching and waved. "Good morning!"

"Good morning, Turk!" Žaneta replied, smiling. She walked to the corral fence with the apples and held one out for Gus. As she rubbed his head, the other horses trotted closer with interest, but Žaneta only had one more apple. "Here!" She handed it to Cyrus. "You can feed yours. Obviously, we needed to buy a bag!"

Cyrus raised his eyebrows and nodded in agreement. "Wedgie!" he called out. "C'mere, boy!"

Žaneta's face broke into a huge grin. "Wedgie?" she asked, starting to laugh. The horse crowded Cyrus, as did the others, all wanting the apple.

"That's right! He's a pain in the ass at times and just needs straightening out." He snickered.

Žaneta snorted with laughter. "All right… let's get them ready." After about ten minutes, they were saddled, packed, and riding to the training grounds.

It was still morning when they rode into the field and tied off nearly exactly where they had yesterday. This time, they would have a full day to commit to practice. Žaneta took Gus's saddle and blanket off for him to stay cool, laying her wrapped sword near the rest of her things. Cyrus did the same, and the two of them were left with iron shields and two sticks.

Once again, she went over some of the basics she had covered the day prior. They squared off against each other, as if they were about to begin a dance. They walked in a circle counterclockwise, just feet from each other, then engaged.

Time flew by, and Cyrus's efforts started to gain him strikes every once in a while. Instead of constantly being the aggressor, he was learning to counter much more efficiently. Žaneta demonstrated how to battle an unarmed opponent then how to fight against a large beast, where footing and surroundings were everything.

"Watch your enemy's body, ignore their battle cries and facial expressions—they're useless. But after a fight has afforded some exhaustion, look at their eyes. Before I caught you in the face with your own stick, you were blinking hard and your eyes were starting to wander."

At that point, they took a short break. Žaneta grabbed her water and took a good drink, then offered it to him.

"Are you a religious woman, Žaneta?" Cyrus asked after drinking, handing the bladder back to her.

"Yes. Why?"

"Just being that it's Sundas… I didn't think to ask before we came out."

"Although the strength of prayer in numbers is powerful, I can honor my Lady Mara anywhere; I've never needed a building," she said kindly.

"I understand. Shall we?" He tapped his stick against his shield and nodded toward the field.

By the afternoon, there wasn't a cloud in the sky, and it was getting hot. They had been practicing for nearly six hours when Cyrus rested his hands on his knees and said, "I'm famished! Would you like to take a break and get something to eat?"

Žaneta lowered her stick and tilted her head, giving him a judging glare, then walked to her satchel and took out the sweet rolls she'd bought earlier. "Here!" She tossed one to him. "Training isn't all about moves and balance. Let's work on our focus when our bodies are lacking." She stuffed the whole sweet roll into her mouth and raised her stick. After waiting for him to quickly finish his, they began again.

After a couple more hours, Cyrus had regained confidence but was still nowhere near besting her. They were sparring against each other so that, one day, he could implement what they'd gone over when it really mattered. Even with such a short time instructing him, Žaneta could see real potential if he stuck to it.

Suddenly interrupting their lesson, a rider swiftly approached from the Imperial City. Hoofbeats on the road got their attention before they could see the rider; they stopped their practice and looked toward the sound, waiting apprehensively. *Please, gods! Let it be something.* Žaneta trembled with bridled worry.

Was it news? Was it a courier en route to somewhere else? She strained her eyes, her heart pounding in rhythm with the approaching horse's pace. Then she realized…

It was slowing down.

Chapter Eight

A battlemage came to a stop in front of them. "Žaneta, we've received information about the carts. Also, the priests at the palace need to speak with you. We'll see you at the tower," he said in a rush before turning his horse and galloping back to the city.

Žaneta darted straight to Gus, threw on his saddle blanket and saddle, then tied down the rest of her things after she'd slung on her satchel and shield.

Cyrus, still gathering his things, said, "I'll see you back at the city, maybe! Just leave the gear at the stables—I'll take care of it."

Žaneta nodded, spun Gus around, then took off toward the White Gold Tower.

Arriving at the stables, she jumped down and led Gus to Turk. "Turk, would you water him but keep him ready to go? If I'm not back before dark, please go ahead and take everything off of him for the night," she stressed, handing him the reins and sliding her sword from Gus's pack into her frog. She jogged into the city as Turk watched her with a perplexed expression.

When she reached the tower, a handful of battlemages were waiting by the steps. It appeared that something had increased the empire's interest yet again. There were more battlemages in one place here than she'd seen before, only confirming they'd gotten wind of something.

"Good afternoon, ma'am. The others are waiting. Let's get you in!" one said courteously.

They all went up through the same halls and rooms with which she'd become increasingly accustomed, then up the spiral staircase to the table where she'd first sat and spoken with the emperor. There he was again with the same group as before, as well as the small entourage that had accompanied her. The emperor stood and approached, taking both her hands. He gestured for her to join them at the table.

"Hello, my dear. Please have a seat." He smiled.

Žaneta sat and looked at them all, waiting for one of them to say something. But the tension was unbearable. "What's happened?" she eventually asked, anxious.

Captain Lex leaned on the table and met her eyes. "Žaneta… we've got one of the carts. Thankfully, we recovered six more children—but none of them are yours," he finished, his posture stiff.

Žaneta released the breath she'd unintentionally held and fought back her cry of frustration, but she couldn't keep the tears from coming. "Where did you find them?"

Uriel looked at his captain as they exchanged a short glance, and the emperor responded, "Eight days ago, the Bruma City Watch had a problem outside of their city walls on the Silver Road leading into the Jerall Mountains. They reported they saw two white carts coming up the road from the south."

Žaneta looked back and forth between the two of them. "And they couldn't stop both carts? Their horses had to have been faster than the ones hauling carts with children inside!" she hissed through gritted teeth, the wild, raging emotions finally breaking through her composure.

"Žaneta, the guards didn't do anything—they only saw everything unfold from their watchtower," said Captain Lex quickly. "They reported that as they saw the two white carts, a large female Khajiit had come down from the mountains to the east… very quickly. The guards said she couldn't catch the first cart but used a curved blade, like a scimitar, to tear through the back wheel of the last one. The cart turned over near the side of the road, and the Khajiit killed the drivers before busting into the back of it. The guards said they sounded the alarm, but she had already taken off to the north… they assumed in pursuit of the other cart. When the Bruma guards reached the overturned cart, kids had already begun crawling out," he explained. He looked over her shoulder and motioned for someone behind her to approach. "Is this the woman you saw?" Captain Lex asked the man.

The guard stared at Žaneta, and his eyes widened. "Yes, sir!" he replied.

"This is one of the Bruma guards, Žaneta. Now, he says you were in Bruma this last Loredas, but we know you were not in Cyrodiil yet," the captain said.

"What the hell is going on?" Žaneta cried, dropping her head into her hands. The guard was dismissed and left the room with a battlemage.

"Žaneta, none of us understand what's happened, but perhaps you'd be willing to stay with the Moth Priests to learn more. We'd all be relieved to have answers," Uriel said calmly.

Žaneta lifted her head and took in a breath. "Okay."

Uriel smiled and stood. "Thank you," he said as he, his personal battlemage, and Captain Lex left the room.

"Hello, Žaneta… We're sorry for all of this," one of the priests murmured as he adjusted his chair to move closer to the table. "You told Ashlyn of a dream you experienced last night—could you go over it again with us?"

Žaneta, lost with the recent news, stared blankly at the table. *Over a week ago? The carts passed through, and there was no mention of it 'til now?* She tried to rationalize and knew she was just making more questions for herself. She tried to focus and rejoin the conversation.

Resting her elbows on the table with her hands clenched, she recounted the dream. "I was flying, as high as this tower is tall, and I could see mountains below me for some ways. There was a collection of structures beneath me—a city, perhaps—but the focus was on the fort in the mountains. A light… a green light was coming from cracks in the ground and from within the fort itself. Faster than I could have fallen to the ground, I was already standing on it. From there, it looked like I was standing in a tornado. Dirt, ash, smoke… all spun around me," she finished.

"Ashlyn said you heard voices—what did they say?" asked one of the priests, leaning toward her.

"I don't know… I've never heard the language used." Then it hit her. The old magic her mother had shared with her… the word she'd used against Trelina on the bridge. "The word I used yesterday, maybe it… maybe it shares a likeness! The figures I saw were chanting something just before I saw fire and a dragon appear," she recalled.

"What word did you say? Or better yet, who taught it to you? We don't want anything that could be dangerous used in here," the priest said.

"My mother. She was a healer and a devout follower of Lady Mara. I remember going to old ruins by the coast and hearing her share words inscribed there with me. I don't recall who translated them, or if it was her, but I never understood the markings," she explained.

"This fort you saw—did you see the architecture? Was it anything you've seen before?" a priest pressed for details.

"Only that it was Imperial," she replied.

The priests thought on her words then hypothesized with one another. One spoke up, "An Imperial fort, a nearby town, mountains, and this Bruma guard's account of seeing you there days ago. It would seem as though we know which way you need to head. But Žaneta, I don't know of any forts there."

"Cloud Ruler Temple!" exclaimed one of the battlemages from behind them. "The Blades operate from there. Its location is regarded as highly secret, and I would think it best if we didn't have everyone informed of its location. Outside of present company, of course."

Žaneta stood and approached him, determined. "Where is it?" she muttered stoically.

"Northwest of Bruma. The guards posted in the city are tasked with policing the traffic to the mountain path. It's the only thing beyond Bruma's gates in that direction," he said, and she immediately spun around to leave.

"Wait!" he barked. She stopped and turned to him. "The Blades are the good guys, but anyone trying to get in won't… And if they do without an invite, they definitely won't be welcome. I just figured you'd like to make progress," he said with concern.

"I already did… eight days ago, apparently!" she said sarcastically.

"Right, so let's talk with Emperor Septim and get you a pass, a letter with his good graces."

Agreeing with this, she followed him and his colleagues out of the room and up to a part of the tower many had never seen—the emperor's chamber. It was glorious, but she hardly noticed, distracted by the knowledge of her destination. *Bruma, Cloud Ruler Temple, the Blades!* she repeated. She'd been ready to leave for days. Finally, she knew the next place along her journey, and she could barely focus on her surroundings. She waited, drifting in and out of the muffled conversation between the battlemage and Uriel.

After understanding these events were beyond his comprehension, Uriel wrote a letter on a blank piece of parchment, signed it, and sealed it with wax using his Imperial crest stamp. He walked up to Žaneta with sad eyes and didn't meet her stare at first.

"My dear lady, from recent statements about the past, I don't know if I'll see you again in the future! But may the gods guide you and keep you safe." He handed her the folded letter and shook her hand before holding it tightly between both of his. The battlemages all began to leave, and Žaneta followed, looking back at Uriel and sincerely hoping he was wrong about not seeing her again. She nodded to him with one last serious look then proceeded down the stairs.

Chapter Nine

utside of the White Gold Tower, Cyrus was waiting on the steps with Owyn. He'd taken the practice weapons back to the Arena and told his dad of the news. The two of them stood patiently waiting for Žaneta, anxious to learn of what had happened. When she stepped out of the building, it was apparent she was upset. As she walked down to them, she was silent, and no one spoke at first.

"I'm off to Bruma."

Owyn and Cyrus remained speechless. They could tell she wasn't happy with the news. Owyn stood up straighter and reached out a hand to shake hers. "It was good to see you again, Žana." He gave her an encouraging smile.

They shook hands, then Cyrus also reached out his. She took it, and he pulled her into a tight embrace. She suddenly realized the strong impact she'd made on this young man, and his hug was as heartfelt as it was surprising. Žaneta was happy she'd had the opportunity to come into his life and was certain he'd changed her for the better, too. She patted his back as he released her.

"Get out of the Arena, kid. Stop wasting your talent entertaining those who would just as soon cheer your death," she said softly.

"I think I'm going to the Arcane University… be one of these battlemages. They seem to have their shit together." He chuckled.

Žaneta's expression brightened with relief as she gave the young man a small smile, the same feeling she was sure Owyn must have experienced. "Ask for Ashlyn—she already knew your name. I bet she could help you," she replied. She turned toward the stables.

"Oh! I almost forgot… here!" Owyn tossed a small pouch to her.

"What's this?" she asked. She opened it and saw it was filled with gold coins.

"Your winnings from the fight between you and Cyrus! The fighters apparently had a little side bet going. Most of the winners gave it to me to give to you."

She tossed it back to him and said, "I did it as a favor to you. Put him in school—I'm certain he'll make a revered battlemage." She winked at Cyrus. "Farewell." She smiled and waved as she walked away, leaving them behind.

She felt she was always leaving, making friends, and revisiting old ones—all of it was becoming more difficult emotionally than she cared for. But she knew she'd helped while she was there, and the thought of her children drove her forward.

At the stables, she worked with Turk to make sure she had all her things. She grabbed the arrow quiver and bow she'd left in the tack room and unsheathed her sword, rolling it in the spare horse blanket before tying it behind the saddle. Turk handed her the reins as she stepped into the stirrups. Žaneta looked down at him. "Thank you for everything." She gave him a serious nod then took off across the bridge, galloping toward Bruma.

***

It was late afternoon. Žaneta had torn across the Red Ring Road and come up the Silver Road toward Bruma and was looking upon the Imperial City from the Heartlands to the north. She was pushing Gus hard, but too much time had already passed. She slowed him down at times, but never dismounted, never stopped. Her thoughts were everywhere. She couldn't comprehend what she was riding into, but the testimony from the Bruma guard was convincing enough to have them all believe she was involved in the events outside the city. She'd never been north of the Imperial City, not in years past... and definitely not recently. But she recalled the priests mentioning things had changed, that something bounced around with time. Žaneta still only cared about finding Tai and Mazira, and all she knew was this was the way.

They reached the outskirts of Bruma that night, and there along the path, past the turnoff to the city, lay a busted white cart on its side. She approached it slowly on Gus then dismounted. Inspecting it briefly, she looked at the backdoor pieces that had been knocked in. Then she examined the remnants of the back-right wheel, which had blown apart while it was moving, leaving pieces scattered all the way up to where the cart rested.

Žaneta climbed back onto Gus and rushed to Bruma. She approached the gate guarded by two of the city's watch.

"Ma'am, we wondered if you'd ever be back here! Captain Burd has questions!" one guard called.

Žaneta pulled out the letter to the Blades that bared the Imperial crest and showed it to the guard, keeping it sealed. "I just finished speaking with the emperor, and I need to pass through on business. Please tell your captain that if he has questions to contact the Imperial City; Captain Lex can fill him in." She stared at them seriously and placed the letter back in her satchel.

The guards didn't hesitate to open the gate, and one accompanied her through the city to prevent any more hassle.

"Would you show me to an inn? I will head out first thing tomorrow," she asked, her eyes bloodshot.

The guard took her to the Jerall View Inn, and she hopped down and removed the horse blanket with her sword.

"I'll report your passing through tomorrow and refer that the captain speak with Captain Lex. I'll take your horse to the stables, just by the entrance you came in. If you're up early enough, I'll take you through town. My shift ends just after sun-up," he said, holding the reins. He nodded to her then led Gus out of the city.

Žaneta entered the inn, paid for a room, and went straight to bed.

The following morning, she was up before dawn and immediately left the inn, searching for the guard. She left out the east gate and found him standing post right where he'd been the night before. "I'm going to ready my horse, then I'll be good to leave before you're done at your post." Still stoic, she walked to the stables, where she saw shedding brushes hanging on a peg by the stall. She grabbed one and began combing over Gus like she may never see him again. After all, the guard said he saw her… not her on horseback.

A good hour went by, and she saddled Gus, tied down her things, and went inside to pay the ostler before riding back to the guard. Sunrise was coming, and the morning light was radiant as it lit up the landscape. The guard watched her approach and opened the gate to lead her through the city. Bruma had some beautiful buildings—the Great Chapel of Talos being one—and there was a well-built castle along the western edge of the city. But it wasn't a large city, which she liked.

They approached the northwest gate, and the guard hollered to the man posted there, "Open the gate! Official business from the emperor!" The message carried weight with it, allowing her to pass unchecked.

She could have ridden around the town, but had she been seen by the guards, they might have tried to pursue her for questioning, slowing her down. But she also wanted daylight to let her presence be known. She had no intention of sneaking into Imperial forts—yet.

As she rode Gus past the walls of Bruma, it began to lightly snow. The trail ahead of her took a winding path around the outer face of the mountains, but it was the only choice—there were no other paths into the mountains from here. Clouds hung low over them as she and Gus climbed higher. She had ridden him hard from the Imperial City yesterday and decided to climb off and lead him up the rest of the way. Žaneta dismounted, sheathed her sword, took the reins, and started walking.

It was a steady incline up the pass, but she appreciated the hike until the clouds obscured her view. She came around a rocky outcrop and found herself standing before huge doors in the wall of a stronghold. There were no guards posted where she could see them, no burning torches or lanterns. The place looked abandoned. Žaneta pulled the shield from her side and used the edge to knock loudly on the door.

Nothing. Dead quiet.

"Hello!" she yelled. "I'm here with permission from the emperor."

She waited for a response then heard a shuffle from within the fort. "I've got a letter for entry!" she called, waiting briefly.

A metal plate opened down at the level of her knees, and a man responded gruffly, "Slide it through!"

Žaneta did as instructed and only had to stand there a moment before she could hear the gates unlock and begin to open. The doors were huge and heavy, creaking under their own weight as they swung on their hinges. Two men on each side pushed the doors open from the inside, while a fifth stood behind them with Žaneta's letter in hand. She entered with Gus, and the men closed the doors behind her.

The armor they all wore was detailed in the specific accents she was familiar with, and a couple of them even had shields like hers—she knew she had found them. One of the Blades walked to her and said, "Ma'am." He stretched out a hand to take the reins, which she handed to him, and he led Gus away to their horse stalls.

The Imperial holding the letter observed Žaneta. His stern, inquisitive stare was already analyzing her before he started talking. "I'm Captain Steffan. Reading the emperor's letter, it states that, 'Žaneta is to be treated as you would me, and she will explain everything up to this point regarding her situation,'" he finished, raising his steely eyes to hers.

"Would you be so kind as to follow me inside? I'll make us some tea while you catch us up."

He gestured around to the rest of the Blades present.

He returned the letter to her and led her to the great hall at the top of the stairs. He asked a little bit about her history then told her more about the Blades. Žaneta learned they didn't get visitors often and spent their time training daily in one skill or another.

Steffan showed her to the hall. "Please, have a look around. I'll be right back." He excused himself to a door at the east end of the room. As he left, he turned to another Blade. "Baragon!" he said. "Tell everyone to meet here. Whatever this woman has to say, I don't want to have to repeat it to all of you."

Baragon nodded. "Yes, sir!" He quickly stepped outside to round them up.

Steffan left through the east door and was gone for a short time, during which Žaneta admired the decor of the great hall. Arched ceilings were decorated with the swords of the Blades—the Akaviri

Katana—and an enormous fireplace roared from the far side of the room against the northern wall. The room was a testament to their history of war fighting, but it felt underused, like a trophy one locks in a safe or a museum. Nothing was out of place.

Before long, members of the Blades began coming in and sitting. None made a large effort to acknowledge her, but briefly conversed with their comrades before the captain returned with two cups of hot tea. He placed one cup on the table in front of Žaneta then sat with his.

"Everyone, listen up! After Žaneta spoke with the emperor, he sent her here. You will show her the same respect as you would him! Understood?" he commanded. "Now, listen well. She has many important details to discuss, and I don't want to miss a single one."

With that, Žaneta had their attention. She sat in the room for hours going over everything—from Vvardenfell, to making port in Narsis, Skingrad, Kvatch, and all the way up to knocking on their gate.

Her story seemed to sit heavy with each of them, and Žaneta had a creeping feeling they knew something. But it was Jena, one of the Blades listening in, who spoke. "Captain…" she said, and Steffan turned to give her his attention. "The Relic!"

Žaneta's sharp eyes centered on Captain Steffan as he breathed slowly through his nose. "What is she talking about?" she asked. He turned back to Žaneta and considered the best way to share their secret, while she waited for his explanation.

"Days ago, while training in the armory downstairs, a historical item we've held there since before I was a Blade began to… glow. The emperor knows of it and has always ordered it to be kept safe because it couldn't be destroyed—they tried."

"What is it?" Žaneta pressed, leaning forward.

"It's a piece of the Mantella stone fixed to a segment of brass armor plate. We believe it came from the Numidium." His stare bored into her.

She thought for a second, remembering her history lessons. "The Numid… the Brass God! That's why I was seen near Bruma the Loredas before last—you've got a broken time stone in your basement!" She glared at them.

"Perhaps, but it never worked before, not until you showed up in the Imperial City at some point. Then you had these dreams and heard the strange chanting, that you yourself may know without realizing it. I'm thinking this… thing is responding to your presence," he said, his elbows on the table and his chin resting on his fist as he stared back at her.

Žaneta leaned forward on her legs, looking down toward the floor, then met his eyes. "I'm sure you're right." She rose to her feet. "Are you going to show me?"

Captain Steffan stood and nodded to her then turned to the east wing. "Follow me." He started leading Žaneta with the others following. He led them through the dining hall then downstairs. No lanterns were lit, and it would normally have been very dark in the armory and training area without them, but toward the back of the room, sitting on a table by the wall, was the relic… giving off green light. It pulsed like a heartbeat.

The captain reached the bottom of the stairs, gestured to it with an open hand, then looked at her. Žaneta's heart missed a beat as she forced a breath out through her nose. She stepped off the last stair and slowly walked toward it. The other Blades had come down the stairs, with one of them lighting a lantern in the room; none of them said a word. The pulse of the stone seemed to increase with every step she took until she was right in front of it—it glowed solid green.

Žaneta slowly reached out a hand then pulled it back reluctantly—both the relic and she herself felt like they were vibrating. Determined, she touched the stone, and immediately, she and the relic vanished. The Blades stood in shock and looked at one another—not a trace of either Žaneta or the stone remained.

For Žaneta, the situation was immensely different. Her surroundings seemed to peel back as the world changed around her, and in an instant, she was standing within barren mountains that were blanketed in snow. She stood touching the same piece of Mantella stone as a man who had appeared next to her left side. Startled, she drew the knife from her sword handle then swept his feet out from under him, taking him to the ground.

She put the knife to his throat and demanded, "Where am I?"

The older man raised both his hands and calmly replied, "Peace… Peace!"

As Žaneta slowly quit baring her teeth and loosened her grip, he sat up cautiously and rose to his feet. "Who are you?" he asked. As he stood, the Mantella stone fractured and burned out, then the relic vanished again, leaving them there in the cold, blowing snow of a wintery storm. The freezing conditions caused a chill to crawl up her spine, which was only intensified with the disappearance of her only way home.

They watched it happen and looked at each other as they were steadily peppered with snow. The man wore gray robes and leather gloves. His hair and beard were gray and white and in long Nordic braids.

"Žaneta… my name's Žaneta. Where am I?" She squinted into the wind and snow as she placed her knife back into her sword.

"Skyrim, in the mountains east of Bromjunaar," he replied. "My name's Felldir."

END

Žaneta's Chronicles

Part Three: The Lost Mane

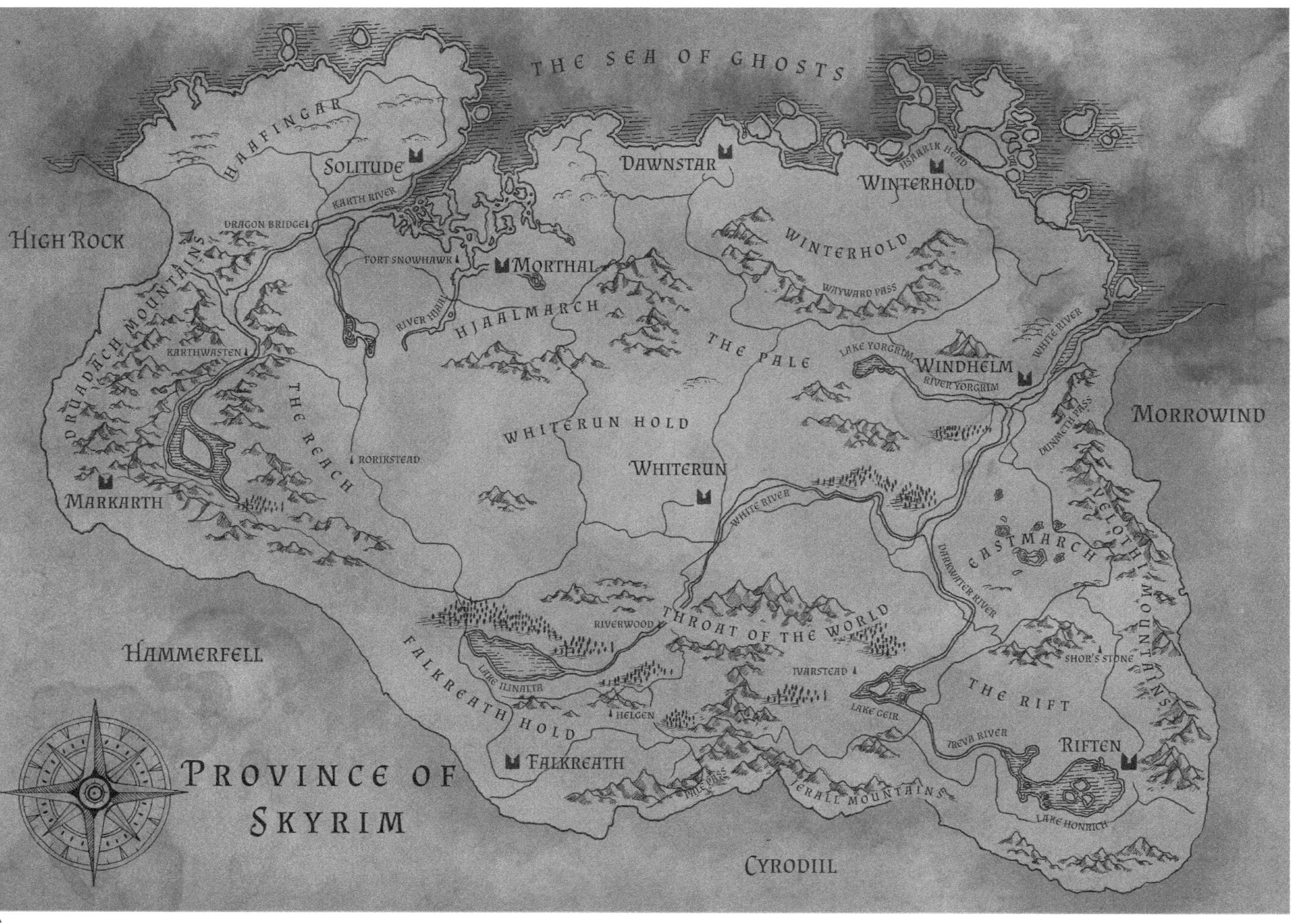
THE SEA OF GHOSTS
HAAFINGAR
SOLITUDE
KARTH RIVER
DRAGON BRIDGE
FORT SNOWHAWK
RIVER HJAAL
HIGH ROCK
DRUADACH MOUNTAINS
KARTHWASTEN
MARKARTH
THE REACH
RORIKSTEAD
MORTHAL
HJAALMARCH
DAWNSTAR
WINTERHOLD
HSARIK HEAD
WINTERHOLD
WAYWARD PASS
THE PALE
LAKE YORGRIM
WINDHELM
RIVER YORGRIM
WHITE RIVER
MORROWIND
WHITERUN HOLD
WHITERUN
WHITE RIVER
DAWNMETH PASS
EASTMARCH
DARKWATER RIVER
VELOTHI MOUNTAINS
SHOR'S STONE
RIVERWOOD
THROAT OF THE WORLD
IVARSTEAD
LAKE GEIR
THE RIFT
HAMMERFELL
FALKREATH HOLD
LAKE ILINALTA
HELGEN
JERALL MOUNTAINS
TREVA RIVER
RIFTEN
FALKREATH
LAKE HONRICH
PROVINCE OF SKYRIM
CYRODIIL

Chapter One

Deep in the mountains of Skyrim, a rickety, horse-drawn carriage flew along the bumpy road alongside one of the land's many lakes. The rocky terrain was blanketed with scattered fir trees, pockets of snow, and the occasional river winding through the countryside. The white transport—driven by Captain Tobias—raced toward its destination, fleeing quickly.

Miles behind him, over row upon row of the jagged points of the Jerrall Mountains, Žaneta came into view as she sprinted along the winding paths. She continued at a blistering speed but had lost sight of the horse cart she'd been chasing for some time.

Sprinting at a pace that would exhaust many, the horse's endurance still outmatched her on foot. Regardless, she pressed on through the Pale Pass. After running for what felt like hours, she finally came to a stop. She caught her breath as her eyes landed on the Throat of the World in the distance, the largest mountain in Skyrim. All the other mountains Žaneta had seen paled in comparison.

Looking ahead, she saw a crossroads. The feeling she hadn't been able to escape crashed over her again—now what? Which way should she go?

Short of breath, her heart was pounding, both from the run and her growing concern. On her map, Falkreath lay to the west. East held many options—including Riften, Windhelm, and all of the eastern provinces—then straight to the north was Helgen. Surveying the land, Žaneta could see that to head west or north, she'd have to go through Helgen. For a horse-drawn carriage, there was no way around it, and the path east was left unchecked to travelers. There were simply too many directions to cover. Tired of guessing, she reached into her satchel and pulled out the letter from the emperor, still bearing his wax seal, which had been broken. Clutching it in hand, she proceeded into Helgen, which flew an Imperial-style banner.

She was going to need help.

***

Backtracking nearly six hours earlier, Žaneta had just returned to the present time—which placed her in the mountains east of Bruma—before she'd begun pursuing the carts full of children. Before that, her story had left off after touching the Mantella stone in Cloud Ruler Temple. Thrown thousands of years into the past, she had sat in a large animal-hide tent as she talked with the stranger she'd met upon arrival, Felldir. The weather outside had grown harsh, and he'd made a small fire to cook on and keep them warm.

"I've never seen anyone like you! From where do you hail?" He lifted a curious brow while he stirred a small pot of stew as it heated over the flames. Snowflakes still peppered both of them but were quickly melting away.

Žaneta sat draped in a fur blanket by the fire with her sword on her lap—her own fur wasn't warm enough for these frigid temperatures. "I was born in Elsweyr… far to the south," she replied, then she paused for a moment. "You said we were in the mountains… east of where?"

"Bromjunaar." He handed her a wooden bowl full of stew.

"I'm not familiar with it. What day is it?" She squinted in question, but he appeared to have no answer for her. "Who's in charge? Is there a king?" she probed. She knew time had been distorted and hoped to find out *when* she was, if not *where*.

"Gunther. He is not king, but still leads many. His bloodline traces back to Ysgramor."

Žaneta listened carefully, trying to fully understand what was happening. "Why are you out here alone?" she asked.

His eyes drifted from hers and stared at the fire. "A friend…" He paused. "We had sought help from others, but were offered none. The Dragon Cult and their deities are tearing Skyrim apart. I've had visions—more frequent of late—that led me here!"

Žaneta thought on this a second. The name Ysgramor was familiar, but she couldn't place it. And she was completely unfamiliar with the Dragon Cult—the name meant nothing to her. But any group labeled as a "cult" made her uneasy. "What did this Ysgramor do to make himself known?" She sipped from her bowl.

"What *didn't* he do?" Felldir bolstered. "He saved many from the civil war in Atmora, bringing them here along with his Companions. The damn Snow Elves gave him hell and killed many of his people. But he and his five hundred fierce warriors took back the land," he explained, eagerly watching her reaction for a spark of recognition. But she didn't know anything about this Ysgramor, and her face said it all. His eyes grew large, and he sat back, looking at her curiously. "He chose where to establish ports, started cities, and taught many to write. His use of runes has helped us document… well… everything!" He stared at her, wide-eyed.

Suddenly, Žaneta remembered something—*the First Man.* History said one man had been credited with the settlement of Skyrim and taught the use of words—in written form—to his people. But that was thousands of years prior to Žaneta's own time. Four thousand years, to be exact, a period in history that was shrouded in mystery. But there wasn't time to share the whole world's future as she knew it with Felldir. She and her children didn't exist yet, but here she was in front of this man who obviously had significant concerns of his own. Something urgent was happening here, and she wanted to know what. Somehow, she had faith it would lead her to her children.

"What exactly did you see in these visions that brought you here?" she asked, taking another sip of the stew.

"A few of us have waged war against the Dragon Cult. Not all dragons are hell-bent on destroying the world or enslaving it. Rather, a number have sided with us; but we have been losing, nonetheless. One of them who is great amongst their ranks has been teaching us their language! Words that have power… but they haven't been enough." He furrowed his brow, growing frustrated, then took a drink from his bowl.

"I'm sorry… dragons?" Žaneta clarified. She stared, transfixed, at Felldir. She was sure she must be missing something. Dragons… It seemed unreal. A cold chill ran down her spine at the thought, the same feeling she'd experienced in her dream. Dragons, fire—her dream was slowly becoming reality.

"Yes. They're not everywhere, then?" he replied, a hint of relief in his voice.

"Uh… no," she said simply. She wanted to keep focused on the matter at hand.

"So, I prayed to the gods," he explained. "Nothing we'd done seemed to gain us any ground. I felt as empty as our attacks on the dragons; they'd simply scatter us and kill any who dared threaten them. But the cult is another story. Our use of the dragon language has given us the ability to kill the bastards! Before, we'd get in some strikes but lost too many in return. That's when the dreams started. I saw the mountains from afar, outside of Jorrvaskr… beyond the plains. I saw a green light in the distance to the northwest. But when I awoke in that very mead hall, I'd venture outside to nothing. Two more times, I had similar visions. I could hear the Dragon Priests spouting their mind-numbing delusions, but the light was growing, and every time, I could feel its pulse calling me. I had to go to it, and even though I couldn't see it out of the dreams… I had a direction!"

Žaneta raised an eyebrow and nodded. "I understand that all too well. It seems as though our meeting wasn't an accident." She finished off the last bit of stew at the bottom of her bowl then set it down. "You said a dragon taught you their language?" she asked, leaning on her crossed legs.

"Yes. He was once a nightmare, having killed many; but this is a war, and perhaps I'd do the same to them if I could. The words used… He calls it their 'Thu'um,' or 'storm voice.'" He stared into his bowl before downing the rest.

Žaneta immediately realized where she fit in here. The word she'd used that exploded across the bridge in the Imperial City… Ashlyn had said it "thundered" out. The term "storm voice" struck her, giving her words a significance she had never before realized. She remembered her mother had stressed their importance to her as a child, as she did with all the magic she taught her. But recalling the wall they were inscribed on, Žaneta did find it strange how, of all the other magic she'd learned, these words had to be studied with help from her mom and one of the shamans.

The words did seem similar to the language Felldir spoke of. She considered the old ruins where her mother had shared those words with her and the one she'd used just days ago… But she'd only said one of the three she remembered. Thinking of the first—*Joor*—jogged her memory, and she suddenly recalled the second: *Zah*. But she was so young, and it was so long ago, she couldn't remember the last—she'd have to come back to it.

"The language he's taught you… you can attack with it?" she asked. She thought back to her fight with Trelina—she'd been able to use *Joor* to debilitate her. But was the language capable of killing?

Felldir smiled. "Oh yes… incredible attacks. You see, for a long time we thought dragons were breathing fire or sending lightning and frost from their mouths—until Paarthurnax landed before a handful of us and shared his wisdom. They were words in their Thu'um, and when pronounced properly, we could use them too."

She narrowed her eyes. "But why the bad blood? What turned some dragons against others in all this?"

"We asked him the same thing. He said that though the dragons are mighty, their practice of giving their words to priests—who'd use them for self-gain—while being worshipped as self-righteous gods destroys their traditions and cheapens dragons to lazy beasts. If the words were going to be shared, then honor had to be at the foundation," he finished with a hint of pride.

"Felldir, was it? I, too, learned some of these words, but from another time and place. I'm sure this has a bearing on why we're here, but what specifically is happening that made you come after the light?" she asked. "For me, it was my children. In their pursuit, I began having visions of the green light, then when I touched the stone, well… You know the rest. Except you touched it and stayed in the same place; I was somewhere far away."

Žaneta knew that whatever happened here, if she stayed the course, she'd be sent back to Cyrodiil and her time. She had been seen a week prior near Bruma—proving she survived this and made it back. But that didn't mean it was going to be easy. She'd heard tales of how the Brass God was used to change things in different places, and—by some accounts—it was seen in different lands at nearly the same time.

Now, she understood how.

"Alduin, the World Eater… he's the strongest and oldest of them, and we can't touch him. Countless have died from his onslaught, and we who would use the Thu'um against him are dwindling in number, as are the dragons who oppose him. I've lost my family, as have others! It has driven many of us to rage and despair. Žaneta… we are dying!" he explained, becoming desperate.

"Who are your allies, the ones who also know this… 'Thu'um'?" she asked.

"Hakon and Gormlaith… and a handful of others. But Hakon has not returned from Bromjunaar. Gormlaith left to seek aid from Gunther and his men, so I set out after Hakon on my own," he said with a hint of urgency.

"So, this Bromjunaar lies to the west? What's the significance? Why would Hakon go there?" She held his gaze.

"It's their capital. Hakon heard rumors of Dragon Priests offering sacrifices to a Blood Dragon. This type of thing is what's been happening all over, but Hakon's village lies to the southwest of Bromjunaar, and it was mostly destroyed when he'd last visited. He said everything was in disarray and the village was empty. Homes had been broken into or ruined entirely… We were at Jorrvaskr several days ago when he learned of what the Dragon Priests were doing in their city, and he left in a blind rage in the middle of the night, convinced his people were there. His actions were suicidal at best. But perhaps dying with them—in an effort to save them—would rest better with his soul than abandonment. But the outcome would be the same.

"Gormlaith was due to return from Windhelm, but I couldn't wait… He's like a brother to me. That's when I came after him and saw it—the light I'd never seen outside of the dreams began to actually appear." He spoke with trepidation as his eyes stared fixedly at the fire, lost in thought.

"Where is Jorrvaskr?" Žaneta asked firmly, bringing him back to the conversation.

"South of here, in the lowlands. About two hours away," he answered.

"Then I'll go to Bromjunaar. You head back to your friends, who, I pray, have brought fighters with them. And Felldir, I can't stress this enough… speed will determine our outcome!" She gave him a serious stare.

"But… Hakon went there alone. We don't know if he's still alive, and it's their damn capital city! We need to wait for more help! What are you going to do?" he said quickly, steadily growing more concerned.

"You were waiting for help—I'm all that came! I'm going to find your man and probably stir up a hornets' nest." Not wasting any time, she pulled out her map of Skyrim. "Here… show me on the map where I'm headed." Moving around the fire, she laid out the map before him.

Felldir glanced over the map and was astonished. "What are these places?! The land looks accurate…

but there are so many cities!"

"I know it's different, but let's just focus on where I need to go. You said we were east of Bromjunaar… Where is it? And where are we?"

He looked it over, unable to read the modern script and ignoring many of the landmarks, then pointed to Labyrinthian. "Here… that's Bromjunaar, and we are right in this area," he said, sliding his finger over to a place called Stonehill Bluff.

"Okay, can you describe Hakon?" Žaneta asked, folding the map and stuffing it back into her satchel.

"He's a strong Nord but blind in his right eye from an injury. Red hair and beard, but that just describes most of my fellow countrymen. I'll hurry to Gormlaith and hopefully find the aid we need there. But from Jorrvaskr—if we're traveling in numbers—it'll be several hours before we reach the city, and we can't just storm up through the canyon. Scouts keep watch on the pass to the north and south, and the mountains on either side make you choose one. What's your plan to get in? You don't exactly blend in with anything here!" he stated, gesturing to all of her.

"I'll have the cover of night, and since you mentioned it… I'm going to need to borrow your blanket," she said, reaching into her satchel for her cloak pin.

Žaneta fastened it in front of her neck and over her shoulders then stooped low toward the entry flap of the tent. Before exiting, she turned to Felldir. "Thank you for the food. I'll try to reach the city this evening and look for the best way in unnoticed. If I can, I won't start anything until you've arrived with the rest of your party. But if I find Hakon and others who need help… I won't wait!" She watched his reaction, making sure he understood. He nodded and narrowed his eyes, his expression growing deadly serious.

"If fighting breaks out, I'll send a bolt of fire into the sky as a signal. And I'll take care of the scouts guarding the southern pass. You and your friends should have a way in," she reassured him. With that, she opened the flap, stepped outside, and was on her way.

Žaneta jumped and scaled the rock wall to the west of the tent then looked back down. She could see the benefits of the location of Felldir's camp; it was hidden from all directions until you were right upon it, and the only way in or out was by way of a narrow pass to the south. But from where she stood, it was also an obvious kill box if they were discovered. Ignoring this thought, she started navigating through the scattered pine trees of the mountain range.

***

Felldir wasn't a young man, but his stamina was conditioned for life here. He ran down the path out of the camp and held a steady pace to the south. The cold air of the snow-covered mountains always reminded him to maintain a certain pace; when breathing began to get painful, he'd slow down and breathe through his nose, occasionally covering it with his hand. But nothing was easy when the elements here became harsh.

Once he descended to the lowlands, the trees doubled in number. Lone travelers usually worried about the wooded paths, which inspired robbers or attackers—an obvious cause for concern. But the coverage in such dire times felt like a blessing. He could stay hidden and avoid running into the wrong people… or worse.

After a couple of hours, he broke through the tree line and could see Jorrvaskr and smoke from the Skyforge just as light was fading from the land. By the time he reached the hall, it was already nightfall; he'd made it without incident. He was beyond thankful, knowing he was the courier of crucial information.

Felldir entered the mead hall to a roaring firepit that was keeping many unfamiliar faces warm. He looked around the room for Gormlaith then made eye contact with her as she approached him from one of the chairs around the fire.

She was a hardy Nord woman with long blonde hair, probably half his age, and dressed from the neck down in heavy plate armor. She had streaks of warpaint down her face and was obviously prepared for a fight. "Felldir… Where have you been? Where's Hakon?" she asked, her eyes searching his face.

"Plans have changed! Who are these people…? Gunther's men?" he asked, staring around at the busy mead hall.

"And then some! Many of the Nords you see here joined Gunther's soldiers in passing, just interested in a good fight." She smiled.

"Gormlaith… things have happened. When I went after Hakon, I started seeing the light again… And this time, I went to it—" he said, but before he could finish his thought, she interrupted him.

"If you left to find Hakon, when did you dream about this crazy green light again?" She raised an eyebrow, trying to keep her chuckle down.

"I didn't dream it, I found it! It came from a piece of green gemstone on a large, curved plate of brass. When I touched it… a large cat-like woman appeared next to me." He paused, almost breathless with excitement. "Gormlaith, we talked… and I believe she was sent to us! She didn't say more than she needed to, just asked me where to go and what to look for, like she was ready to go fight them alone!"

"I like her already!" Gormlaith smirked, a sarcastic gleam in her eye. "A big cat-like woman? You can't be serious!" She stared at his solemn expression then crossed her arms. "You *are* serious!" She straightened up as he nodded. "So… what's the plan?"

"She's headed to Bromjunaar—she may be there already. We need to move. Now!" he stressed.

"Tell the men. We're ready!" she replied with a confident smile.

He nodded then steadied himself, trying to gather his thoughts. He walked to the fire and stood before it. The men and women warriors talked and laughed, celebrating each other's company as they ate. But one by one, all turned their focus to Felldir, who stared at each of them. Eventually, the only noise came from the *pops* and *cracks* of the burning logs on the firepit.

"Warriors! It honors me that you've come. The great war of our time has claimed many, and the dragons, with their priests, mean to continue until we are no more. But we have been sent hope! She came to me today asking for our aid and is moving on Bromjunaar as I speak. She is like nothing I've ever seen… We talked, then she left for the city on her own while I came to gather the strength of our numbers. We've all asked for help before and were sent Paarthurnax, who taught us to use their Thu'um… to start taking the fight to them! Yet *still* we fall!" He stopped for a moment to allow the crowd to quiet their grumbles.

"This woman, Žaneta, is the second sounding of the trumpets. I thought your coming here would only be to save one of our own. But Hakon, and all of us, have been summoned for something greater. So I ask you—did you come here for a fight? Or to get fat and drunk by the fire?! Because I swear to you, these days of fellowship are coming to an end if we do nothing!" he proclaimed.

It was the best speech Felldir could manage, but luckily for him, it was more than enough. They had come ready to die for far less, and as Gunther—a burly Nord with dark, braided hair and a large, wooly beard—stood from his seat, he commanded the respect of his men as he stared at Felldir. The crowd rose alongside him. Many of them began to hammer their tankards on the tables in unison. Gormlaith walked to Felldir and stood at his side as the men and women let out battle cries with each slam of their cups.

Gormlaith drew her sword and raised it up. "Companions… Sigr or fjorlag!" she yelled, which meant, "Victory or death!" in their Nordic language. The hall exploded into a loud battle cry, so loud the call echoed throughout the surrounding hills. Rallied and full of adrenaline, they were on the move, with Felldir in the lead.

***

Late that night, fires burned brightly in the city of Bromjunaar. It was bustling with activity, and many people were already dead and dying from a day full of sacrifice. The cult had bled the innocence from many in the gruesome practice of burning and beheading nonbelievers. Outside, in potential view of their deities, the Dragon Priests had more would-be sacrifices brought to their platform in front of the enormous doors to their underground temple while subservient onlookers watched and relished in the event.

Scouts sat posted on the walls of the canyon entering the city from the south; they numbered six or more on any given night. Under darkness, you could see the canyon floor to the south just enough to tell if something was moving down there, and any approaching group would have the scouts alerting the city. No one ever came up the southern pass—at least, not without being captured or killed.

The north was a frozen set of switchbacks and stone staircases, too narrow for an advancing force to attack all at once. Besides, the mountain range—from east to west—added another day's worth of travel; time Felldir's men didn't have.

The guard positioned nearest to the capital sat high on his perch and casually watched—as he did on most uneventful nights. Light flakes of snow began to fall on his shoulders at first then steadily turned into heavier clumps. He wiped them off as he listened to the distant screams of sacrifices from across the city. Suddenly, he looked up just as Žaneta and the tip of her sword came crashing down on him.

With her capable eyes, she'd been watching and biding her time, waiting for the perfect moment to strike. She pulled her sword from the man she'd just impaled and sheathed it. Then, picking up his bow and quiver, she caught sight of several others as they, too, sat watching the canyon floor, unaware of her attack.

Žaneta shot an arrow into the guard sitting on the adjacent canyon wall across from her then jumped back up and continued moving down the canyon to pick them off one by one. Farther from the city, one after another, they fell victim to Žaneta's arrows.

The hour had to be after midnight. Žaneta had just finished her work in the south pass, and she crossed the canyon and climbed up onto the western ridgeline as she crept back toward the city. The spine of those mountains would put her directly over the door to their temple, but more importantly, she'd be right above the platform where they were slaughtering people.

The air in Bromjunaar was foul with the smell of burnt flesh and putrid blood, and the horrid odors and devastating sight assaulted Žaneta's senses. As the scene came into view, her eyes welled with tears, and rage coursed through her body. For many, she was too late, arriving only in time to bear witness to the muffled cries and pleas from those still awaiting their deaths. Cult Nords brought up three more for sacrifice, all gagged with their hands bound behind their backs. Led out and forced up the stairs to the platform where their dead friends and family had been tied to posts, they were positioned in place after the last victims were removed and tossed onto a huge bonfire behind them. Their captors tied the prisoners' necks around the posts to ensure they stayed upright.

There were two men and a woman, all commoners, but one had a recognizable characteristic—a scar on his right forehead and cheek, leaving the affected eye glazed over, white. Hakon was bound to the center post as one of the two Dragon Priests approached, leering at him. He said nothing. The woman to Hakon's right was sobbing, and the man to his left had already pissed himself out of fear. Hakon simply glared at the priest's blank wooden facemask as the man turned and spoke to one of his cult guards. "Start with her. Let this one hear her sing with the fire beneath her," the priest ordered as he watched Hakon, who hadn't broken eye contact.

At his words, Hakon began to squirm and scream at them, thrashing about on the post. His words, muffled by the gag, could call for no one. But then, something caught his eye near the dark corner beside the temple. Someone—or something—had come down from the sloped roof by one of the decorative pillars, and he saw the creature's eyes reflect the glow from the burning torches.

Žaneta had slowly climbed down and unpinned the fur she'd worn, letting it fall to the ground. In an instant, with all her speed, she leaped toward the platform and swept her sword downward into the priest in front of Hakon, cutting into him diagonally at the collar, almost through to his hip.

In a flash, she jerked her blade out and stabbed through the guard at the priest's side then rushed to Hakon. She slapped her sword flat against his chest, pulled her knife out of the handle, and sliced off his bindings. Thunderstruck, he grabbed for the sword as she gripped the front of his shirt and, with wild eyes, screamed, "Fight!"

Žaneta pulled him back from the post with a quick jerk then tugged him forcefully to the ground, placing both of her feet on his chest as she tumbled backward. Rolling onto her back, she kicked as hard as she could, and he was catapulted up the stairs onto the side of the temple behind her.

The other Dragon Priest near the entrance to the temple watched in shock. In his delayed response, he'd shot a blast of magic from his staff, but it missed and struck the post where Hakon had been tied.

Žaneta rolled backward onto her hands and knees after sending Hakon flying, then leaped toward the woman who was tied up next to him. She cut her bindings then raised her shield as she saw another incoming blast of energy from the priest. Just as Ashlyn had said, the shield projected an absorbing barrier that completely nullified the attack—most likely saving both of their lives. But before Žaneta lowered the shield, a boom sounded, and a wave of force crashed down on the priest. As if an invisible boulder had landed on him, his body was crushed like a crumpled piece of paper.

Amazed by the devastating display, Žaneta looked up and saw Hakon standing over them on the overhang to the temple entrance—he had just used his Thu'um, and what a powerful weapon it was. In awe only briefly, she refocused as more screams rang out, but instead of the potential victims, they came from the onlookers in attendance as they scattered. Guards streamed out of all the buildings nearby as a distant horn sounded, signaling trouble for the two of them. Suddenly, Žaneta remembered to send her own signal and drew back her hand, casting her bolt of fire straight up into the sky.

"Run!" Hakon yelled. He scurried off the arched roof of the building, sliding down the side.

Žaneta cut the last man on the post loose and sprinted to join Hakon. She wrapped the leather strap of her shield around her arm so she could use it properly and ran with him as they moved toward the southern canyon exit. Guard after guard intercepted them, but not one could make them yield. Žaneta stayed close to Hakon, not sure if he had any strength left after being in captivity.

The enemy's numbers were increasing, and as Hakon used his Thu'um while also fighting, Žaneta could tell he was becoming more and more exhausted. She sent out another blast of fire, hoping their allies had gotten the message, then drew her hand back again and cast an inferno around them. The blaze circled her and Hakon, slowing the cult's advance. She stood next to him and concentrated on healing, realizing he'd surely been without food or rest up until his planned death; she needed him fighting at full strength. Her aura glowed brighter than the fire surrounding them, and she could tell Hakon could feel it. He rose to his feet, stumbling a little, and looked south, ready to run. Žaneta stopped healing and quickly reset her attention on more approaching guards, who were sprinting after them through the canyon.

"Get out of here! I'll slow them!" Hakon yelled, raising Žaneta's sword at the ready.

"I'm faster than anything on two legs, and I'm not leaving you!" she snarled. She wasn't about to let him become a martyr.

The cultists in pursuit were oblivious to the fact that no archers were helping from their usual places along the walls, and they were running straight into the advance of a formidable throng of opposition. A roar of retribution could be heard from the south, and it was coming from the Companions, who were in an all-out charge. Gunther and his soldiers were rushing up the canyon unchecked with Gormlaith and Felldir amongst their ranks. The added assistance was a blessed relief to Hakon and Žaneta. She didn't know if the prisoners she'd freed had escaped, but with more men, she hoped to rescue more than only Hakon.

Žaneta turned back up the hill and cast more fire at the incoming attackers. As the group of Companions reached the two of them, her flames had all but died out. Gunther stopped and greeted them as his warriors continued their charge, but he was at a loss for words as he stared up at Žaneta.

She didn't hesitate. "We have no time to waste. They have prisoners inside, but I don't know how many…"

"We'll free whoever we come across. But we're here for blood, and my sword's still dry!" he called, rushing to catch up with the charge.

Žaneta looked at Hakon and motioned for her sword with an outstretched hand. He gave it one last admiring look then handed it to her. She returned the knife to the handle, then waited for him to claim a new weapon from one of the many dead cultists.

The attack had begun. The two Dragon Priests lay dead outside their temple, but the city was vast, and until now, only guards had been streaming out of the doors. What lay on the surface was only the front door to the depths of the city beneath them, and the dangers it housed were numerous—the city had awoken, and more forces began to join the battle.

High-ranking cult Nords began surfacing and joined in the fight, carelessly using their Thu'um against Gunther's men and killing some of their own in the process. There was no honor amongst them, and some fighters used their own Thu'um in retaliation. Arrows were loosed back and forth, and streaks of fire and lightning were cast from all directions as the battle lines began to blur. And they weren't even in the city yet.

Felldir, who was fighting next to Gormlaith, called out to her and pointed over her shoulder. "Hakon lives! Get to them!"

Žaneta worked in close proximity to Hakon, using her shield to protect them both from incoming attacks and magic as his friends fought their way closer to them. They were both refreshed, fighting as if the battle had just started—thanks to her healing. But it still left no room for error.

Žaneta and Hakon started down the stairs of the city entrance just east of the temple. "Follow me! There are more prisoners underground where I was held!" he barked, leading her to the northeast edge of the city. They reached a set of stairs that led underground.

But no guards were on watch at the door; everyone seemed to be engaged in the battle to the south, behind them. Still, the immediate silence as the clashes and clangs of weapons disappeared brought with it an air of ambush. It took a couple of long moments for Žaneta to accept there was no one lingering in the shadows, waiting to lunge out at them.

Felldir and Gormlaith had caught up with them, and both were short of breath. Gormlaith caught sight of Žaneta and initially looked like she'd seen a ghost, but she refocused and asked, "Where… where are you going?"

Hakon stopped and answered, "Below… They've got people below. We're getting them out!"

Žaneta slowly approached the two of them, healing them of their exhaustion, then started down the stairs with Hakon. "Coming?" she asked, glancing back.

She took the lead as they entered a dark, cave-like corridor. They spiraled down the path in a clockwise direction until torchlight could be seen. Ahead of them, through a small opening in the wall, the prisoners were gathered in an adjacent room. They had caught Žaneta's full attention, so the cultist to her right went unnoticed.

Hakon yelled, "Look out!" Pushing her forward, placing himself in the path of the cultist's shout.

It wasn't fire, or any element, just a push of force similar to what Hakon had used on the priest outside, but far less powerful. Yet it was still enough to slam Hakon into the wall and drop him to the floor.

Žaneta had been pushed behind partial cover, and she pulled out her knife as she rounded the corner. The Nord cast up a ward, expecting a magic attack, but through his barrier came her knife, flying into his chest. He looked down in surprise at the handle as his barrier faded and reached up for it with both hands. The Nord looked up just as Žaneta grabbed his throat, and before he could muster up another shout, she squeezed. Blood poured from the man's neck, and as he dropped to the ground, she gripped her knife handle and pulled it out.

Felldir and Gormlaith were helping Hakon sit up as Žaneta approached them. "You took my place… Thank you." She furrowed her brow and nodded earnestly. Kneeling down, she summoned her healing light then placed her hand on his chest, immediately returning his ability to breathe while mending his broken ribs and head injury.

"When we get out of here, I'll fix that eye," she said, giving him a serious nod.

Felldir and Gormlaith each grabbed one of Hakon's hands and pulled him up. Standing, Žaneta turned and looked past the dead Nord to a spiked, steel-rod gate. As they all proceeded toward it, Žaneta and Felldir stepped on pressure plates that made two of the rods drop out of place. Thinking they'd stumbled onto a trap, Felldir quickly stepped off his plate, and one of the rods shot back up, narrowing the opening. Žaneta did the same and watched the last rod to the doorway close.

"It's a pressure plate mechanism, but it takes us standing on it to keep the rods down," Gormlaith said slowly.

"Three plates and four of us… Someone needs to get the prisoners from the next room!" Hakon growled.

"I've got them. Open the gate!" Žaneta affirmed.

With each one of them standing on a plate, the rods dropped, and she hurried through the narrow entryway. Moving through the tight passage leading to the room, she peeked her head around the corner before entering. It was poorly lit, but she could see every prisoner; they all sat on their knees, gagged with their hands tied behind their backs. Some were young, probably in their early teens.

As she stepped into the room, one man stood up from between the others and stumbled toward her. "Thank the gods you've come! We'd given up hope…" he muttered in a panic, but he was quickly silenced by Žaneta's knife against his throat.

"Where are your bindings?" she hissed through her teeth.

"I-I managed… to slip them off," he mumbled quickly.

She could see the handle of a dagger behind his back. His hands and wrists weren't marred from being tied, either. "I'm glad you're all safe," she said as she lowered her knife and put it in her sword.

She placed a hand on the man's shoulder and smiled then slammed her foot down the front of his right leg in a flash, from kneecap to ankle, with her claws. His leg shredded, he toppled over screaming. Forgetting about his dagger, he grabbed his leg.

As he writhed around on the floor, he confirmed what she already knew—he was a wolf in sheep's clothing. "You—you'll never make it out… of here!" he gasped.

Žaneta leaned over him. "You were just thanking the gods that I'd come! But you should've hidden your blade—I can see in the dark," she growled.

His groaning died down to a whimper as he held his leg, then she stomped on his throat.

"Žaneta! Are you okay?" Felldir yelled, hearing the commotion.

"Yes. I'm fine. We'll be right with you!" she replied. She examined the prisoners, ensuring there were no more guards amongst them. One by one, she cut their hands free. "Let's get you all out of here!" she urged as they rose to their feet and removed their gags.

Žaneta finished freeing the last one and left the room—littering it with the twelve cords used to tie the prisoners' wrists—then rushed through the gateway. "That's it!" she announced.

Felldir, Gormlaith, and Hakon stepped off their pressure plates, and the steel spikes snapped shut behind her.

Hakon glanced over the prisoners, getting a headcount. "Okay, folks, there's fighting going on outside. Stay low and keep up with us!" he ordered.

"Perhaps we should try something different…" Žaneta piped up.

The group stopped and looked at her.

"I'm going to heal all of you, and when we get out of here, I want you to stay in a group, but don't bunch up too close to us," she said, gesturing to Hakon and the others. "We need space to swing a weapon. I'll take lead, one of you take the rear, and we'll have one on each side. Let no one through… We're all getting out of here tonight." They agreed, and Žaneta climbed up the stairs and back outside.

The snowfall had increased since they'd gone underground, and the noise from the fighting had faded slightly. Together in the protective formation they'd discussed, they moved through the empty side of the city toward the south pass, hugging close to a building as they rounded a corner.

Based on the structures they passed, Žaneta could tell this place held significant importance to its tenants. Either the Dragon Cult had built a beautiful city or they'd captured it, and it was massive. But the details didn't matter right now—they just needed to escape with as many people as possible. The group had retaken their defensive formation as they reached the stairs that were level with the cult's temple entrance a couple hundred yards to their right.

Bodies were scattered across the city. Žaneta was glad to see three or four times as many cultists lay dead in comparison to Gunther's soldiers and volunteers—the passion for battle was in their souls, but the fight wasn't over yet. Although the soldiers still fought ferociously, more guards began to appear from the temple, rushing toward the battle. Walking behind the guards, two more Dragon Priests strolled casually by, as if they were in no hurry, their gaze focused on the battle at the edge of the city. Their calm demeanor concerned Žaneta, and she had the creeping feeling something terrible was about to happen. But before she could do anything, one of the priests let out a booming shout straight up at the sky. Nothing seemed to come of it… at first.

"Hug the walls… Get to cover!" Žaneta hissed to her group. She motioned to their left—further away from the priests' view. Then, everyone heard it—a thunderous call answered the priests. Žaneta froze and scanned the sky. Then she saw it. Though her heart was racing, her blood ran cold, and she and the entire group stood rooted to the spot. It was their deity… their Blood Dragon. Many of the soldiers threw terrified looks at the skies as the huge beast flew over the canyon walls.

The sight distracted several combatants, costing them their lives as they fought. As the dragon circled back around, men began to scatter. It didn't care who was caught in its inferno as it breathed out a stream of fire right onto the center of the canyon floor. Flying low, it swept underneath huge stone archways in the canyon and landed on all fours before leaping onto the arched entryway to the city. Then it was back in the air with an enormous push of its wings. Screams echoed off the canyon walls, and Žaneta, infuriated to tears and terrified for the men and women lost, clenched her teeth and watched as the dragon flew high to loiter above the fighting. She then turned her attention to the Dragon Priests. *If they love their shouts so much, I'll give them mine!* she seethed. "Stay here!" she growled to the group.

Still relying on the night's darkness for cover, she circled down toward the stairs in front of the temple to get closer then sprinted straight at the priests from behind. As she ran past the remains of the flattened priest from Hakon's work earlier, her prey stood staring at the carnage around the canyon. She'd almost reached them when one turned and saw her coming.

Surprised, he quickly shouted, *"Yol!"* which sent a blast of fire at Žaneta. She slid to a stop and raised her shield; once again, the enchantments on it saved her life as the fire slammed into it and deflected around her. The other priest turned and shouted at the sky again, and she knew what would return.

The fire was intense but brief, and she needed to act fast. The Dragon Priest looked to see the damage he'd inflicted, but all he saw was something spinning through the air toward him. Žaneta had thrown her sword low and hard, and it sliced through both of his shins, cleaving off his legs. He collapsed forward, his blood painting the snowy ground.

As soon as she threw her sword, she didn't wait to see what damage had been done. Instead, she ran as fast as she could toward the men. When the priest landed on his chest, she stepped on the back of his head and leaped forward, twisting her body and slamming her right knee into the remaining Dragon Priest as he started to suck in a breath to attack. When she smashed into his torso, she knocked all the wind and words out of him, throwing him back into the wall where he collapsed.

She picked up her sword and stalked forward, ready to finish off the priest. The powerful priest, who was well-versed in some of the deadliest forms of magic, cowered before Žaneta's searing gaze as she towered over him. Staring down at him, she couldn't help but place all the blame for the innocent lives lost that night on this one man. He lay there struggling to breathe and coughing up blood, which she could see dripping from the mouth hole of his mask. As she moved closer, an ear-splitting roar sounded from overhead again.

"Your time is running out… You're a fool," he muttered, gasping in pain.

Žaneta suddenly let out a laugh of relief. "That's what I forgot!" She smiled and thought back to her childhood. She suddenly recalled the memory tricks her mother had taught her as a young student, lost with time… until now.

When she was young, her mother had taught her magic by using similar-sounding words and phrases. Even for the words of power, she had a saying to remember them by: "You're-a-fool," for the words, *"Joor-Zah-Frul."*

She searched the skies for the dragon as she stabbed the priest in the chest to keep him from interfering. She appeared calm and collected; yet, inside, she battled her rage, focusing the emotion into energy she could use. And she was dead set on her target, her confidence restored.

The dragon flew low around the city then landed on the platform where the sacrifices had taken place. Žaneta was one flight of stairs above where it was poised to attack—but it simply watched her. Then it took in a huge breath and roared, sending out a blast of frost this time and leaving ice in its wake.

With her shield up, she was protected from the deadly ice, but the ground froze beneath her. The pain was excruciating, and she couldn't move her feet from where they were planted. Keeping the shield raised, she suddenly had an idea; dropping her sword, she reached for the bottles in her satchel. Grabbing all she could at once—knowing the dragon wouldn't wait on her—she looked for the Resist Frost potion. Žaneta struggled to remove the cork, eventually biting it and tearing it out. But before she did, help appeared from far off on her right side.

Hakon, Gormlaith, and Felldir had all used their Thu'ums to attack the Blood Dragon. Waves of fire, ice, and pressure slammed against it as well as weaker lightning and fire magic.

"We're just pissing it off!" Gormlaith yelled.

"Spread out and keep at it!" Hakon spat in response.

Žaneta drank her potion and began to heal herself with the time they'd bought her. As she stood, she grabbed her sword, lowered her shield, then looked at the dragon; it faced the three of them and began to inhale. Žaneta took in a small, sharp breath of her own and shouted the only words of power she knew: "*Joor-Zah-Frul!*"

When her words thundered over the dragon, it let out a sharp exhale of pain, as if it had just been stabbed in the belly, then collapsed onto its chest. The great beast couldn't push himself up off the ground, and Žaneta sprinted toward it. She dropped her shield to grasp her sword with both hands and leaped over his neck, slicing at it without effect. Its scales were like trying to cut through stone. Slamming to a stop as she landed, she raised her blade and turned back toward it. The dragon twisted its enormous head to face her just as she ran the point of her sword up into his neck beneath his jaw, which stopped him from voicing his pain. As he collapsed, Žaneta tried to shove the sword in deeper, but as his head hit the stone, she was knocked backward. When he crashed to the ground, the pommel of her sword collided with it, pushing the blade through his skull; his eyes flashed a shade of midnight as they dilated. He lay dead on the platform, which was still drenched in the blood of the innocent from earlier that day. The dragon's blood mingled with theirs, and as Žaneta stared at the broken corpse of the magnificent beast, she almost expected it to begin moving again… but it was dead. The dragon was dead.

Chapter Two

Everything was quiet except for the wind roaring through the canyon. Sunrise wasn't far off, and the light of day slowly unveiled the horrific aftermath of the battle, the lives lost. Despite the carnage, some warriors had survived in the south pass. Gunther and a handful of his men and women lumbered toward the scene. Felldir, Gormlaith, and Hakon had come up the stairs and were standing in astonished silence, while Žaneta was frozen in a state of shock. They'd fought their war against the Dragon Cult but hadn't been able to best a dragon, much less kill one, until this moment.

Felldir looked to his friends and gave them an excited grin. Still in awe, they looked back at the dragon and Žaneta, who was sitting by its side. The three of them approached the corpse.

"Žaneta… are you okay?" Hakon asked, observing Žaneta's distant expression with a look of concern.

She stared at the dragon as it lay there, lifeless on the ground, but her mind was someplace else. The bloody battle had rushed by in a blur. Everything had happened so quickly that prior to her act of fearless courage, she'd simply viewed this beast as another obstacle standing in the way of reaching her children. But as she stared at the dragon's blank eyes, his massive form slumped across the stone, she was suddenly struck by the thought that no one, not even the strongest beast, is invincible. She was reminded that she, too, was mortal. She snapped out of it when she saw Gunther and his group on the stairs leading out of Bromjunaar.

Žaneta stood and turned to Hakon and the others. "Could you help me roll it a little? I need to get my sword." Numb to the feat she'd just accomplished, she had yet to shake off the shock.

The three of them came to her side and began to push. As they did, she sat on the ground, braced both of her feet on the dragon's neck and jaw, and pulled out the sword.

"Let's go—we have people who need attention!" Standing and sheathing her weapon, she looked to Gunther's group and walked to retrieve her shield and the fur blanket she'd left behind earlier.

"I'll go get the others!" Hakon announced, hurrying to the prisoners they'd rescued.

Once the group stood reunited at the south entrance to the city, Žaneta began concentrating her energy as she built up her magic around herself, healing everyone close by. The prisoners and remaining warriors basked in its warmth, as if the sun had just broken from behind the clouds. All their ailments, their injuries… gone. The prisoners had experienced this briefly earlier, but all of them thought her powers were just as remarkable as the slayed dragon lying in the city. After she was finished, the group left the area together.

"Check for survivors!" Gunther commanded his soldiers as they walked through the canyon. But they soon realized they were all that was left. After coming across their fallen comrades, one after another, the mood became increasingly gloomy, and the walk out of the pass was a quiet one out of respect for the dead. There were no dry eyes, and their hearts were full of both sadness and fury. The cost of this battle had sparked a firestorm that was yet to come. As Žaneta walked, she was certain she could never repay what these people had done, what they'd sacrificed. With the dead scattered around her, Žaneta knew she and the others owed them their lives.

"I'm sorry," Žaneta said once they'd reached the greener grass of the lowlands after leaving the canyon.

She looked at Gunther; she didn't know anything about him, but she could tell he cared deeply about his warriors. Like the others, his face was marred with dirt and blood, and his expression was full of grief. He met her stare with tired eyes and replied, "I'm not. Our brothers and sisters suffer no more—they go to Sovngarde. Dying in battle is an honor… but dying in defeat leaves no story to be told. We lost many of our people today, but you saved us from being forgotten… Thank you." He gave her a respectful nod.

Žaneta couldn't keep from tearing up at his praise, but she felt as though she'd done nothing more—and in her opinion, she'd done much less—than the many who'd paid with their lives. Although the walk back to Jorrvaskr was less emboldened than the charge from it hours ago, there was a strong confidence maintained throughout the group of fighters. They'd faced evil on its own ground and had come out victorious.

The day was clear, and the blue sky gave them a warmer passage back to Jorrvaskr. The entire party was hungry and talked of the feast they'd have when they returned. Near late afternoon, they arrived at the mead hall and were met with the chilling memory of the warriors they'd lost. The night before, the hall had teemed with life… voices… friends. But despite their loss, Felldir and the others knew the tides had changed; the dragons no longer held complete sway over them. Now, they could fight back.

Some of Gunther's warriors began rekindling the firepit as Gormlaith looked in the kitchen for food to serve. Felldir approached Gunther, while Hakon started a conversation with Žaneta.

"Thank you… for everything. I was a dead man, as were all these people… everyone!" he said with a courteous nod while she glanced at some of the people who were congregating around the firepit. The two of them were standing by the entryway. "Who are you? Where did you come from, and what were the words you used?" he asked.

Žaneta slowly turned to look at him. "Perhaps we should sit," she muttered with a heavy sigh. He motioned to some empty chairs at the table.

They discussed all of her recent experiences, and she explained just how she, like Felldir, had seen visions of the glowing stone, where she'd learned the words, and that she needed to get back to her time.

"I know there's a way! In my time, people said they saw me in places where I hadn't yet been…" She trailed off, waiting for him to respond.

Hakon looked down at the table and thought for a moment, a perplexed expression taking over his features. "Paarthurnax… he might know. I'll speak with the others; maybe he can help."

Food was brought out, and several people started prepping meals on the fire while others poured wine and mead. With the twelve rescued individuals—some of them family—and the warriors, there were just over thirty present.

They sat and ate as Felldir, Gormlaith, and Hakon talked with Žaneta. The four of them discussed her words of power… knowing their importance if they hoped to defeat the dragons. Gunther joined the group to listen in; he always wanted to learn of any possible advantages when it came to killing the beasts. He never wanted to lose his edge. Then, they went over the details of meeting Paarthurnax. Once their plan was set, they settled in for the evening. After a night of rest, Felldir and the others would set off to meet Paarthurnax, while Gunther and his soldiers would return to Windhelm to amass his army. Seeking refuge, the survivors would accompany them there—Žaneta knew it was the safest choice for them in these uncertain times.

***

As the sun rose again the next morning, everyone began preparing to leave Jorrvaskr. Outfitted with a good coat and better cloth to protect her feet from the bitter cold, Žaneta folded the fur Felldir had loaned her and set it on one of the tables. She helped gather food and supplies, then they started down the hill to the east, taking the path north of the Throat of the World after crossing the White River. The group continued east for hours until the river split to the north and south; they crossed it again to head north toward Windhelm. Far before reaching the city, the four of them parted ways with Gunther after agreeing to regroup in Windhelm in the coming days. Žaneta followed her team across the Darkwater River into

Eastmarch.

While they traveled on foot for over two hours, Paarthurnax had carved his own path through the clouds. Many dragons stayed high in the mountains and only came down to eat, but in recent years, they'd corrupted themselves with self-glorification and gluttony; Paarthurnax's mission was to restore balance. As he rode the winds high over the land, he heard his name—Felldir had shouted for him, which he only did when he was in dire need.

Paarthurnax flew over the Velothi Mountains—which bordered eastern Skyrim—and began descending over the area from which he'd been called. With eyes as sharp as an eagle's, he could see familiar figures on a hillside south of the Dunmeth Pass, so he circled to land. The wind from his wings made the trees shiver, and when he touched down, the ground trembled.

"*Kul Sul,*" he breathed, which meant, "Good day," in the dragons' language. Greeting Felldir, he turned to Žaneta. "Why have you summoned me?" he asked.

Felldir began to speak very respectfully. "Good afternoon, Paarthurnax. Many things have happened, and we've come to you for help. Our last battle involved someone from another time entirely!" he announced, gesturing to Žaneta. "She used words that brought down the Dragon of Bromjunaar. She's shared her ability but now needs to return to her own time."

Paarthurnax stalked toward her, the ground shaking with each step, until he stood right before her. "So, it was you who killed Bokipraan?" he rumbled. "You can't imagine how the *dov*, the dragons, have begun talking."

Žaneta, uncertain of what to say, stared at him for a moment in amazement. His stature made her feel insignificant; she now understood how others, with their probing stares, felt upon seeing her. Talking with a dragon was… surreal. She told him what she knew of her words and where she'd come from. If he was the hope they all saw him to be, then he was the key to moving forward… closer and closer to her children.

"During my childhood, I learned those words that have brought fear amongst you: that nothing is immortal. Death does not concern me… only losing my children to hopelessness and fear. I have to get back to them—I know there must be a way!" she pleaded.

"What is your name?" he asked.

"Žaneta," she said clearly. She was filled with pride at his question, honored that such a magnificent creature would want to know her name.

"Žaneta? Hmm, you're a strange-looking *kaaz*… cat! You've been sent here—as I have, I suspect. Our own interests have placed us before each other, but the Divines are the creators. Though we are important vessels in their plans, what motivates us are our own ideals. We may never live to see the outcomes of our labors, but our deeds now will influence those who will perhaps never know us later. You say you seek your children, whose entire existence has not yet been realized, but here you stand before me. And you don't seem to comprehend that you're shaping the world to come. Which begs the question! What is your year?" His voice was like the deep, rolling thunder of a rainstorm.

Žaneta glanced away then met his eyes. "427… in the Third Era."

"I will remember. If you leave this place, a conversation will be in order. I've taught those with you the strength of our Thu'um, but I haven't the words to return you to your time." Then he elaborated, "However, they may already have the key." He turned his gaze to Felldir and the others.

Žaneta looked around at them as Hakon spluttered, "What—how?!"

Paarthurnax tilted his head and simply considered them, allowing them a chance to think. "The scrolls you were presented. I'm sure they have not been misplaced?"

"No, they are safe. A few have tried deciphering them, but it has proven… difficult, to say the least. How do we use them to aid her?" Felldir raised an eyebrow.

"You do nothing. The one who looks upon it will either gain what they're after or pay for casting their eyes upon the tomes. Take her to the scrolls and find the one sharing a likeness to 'Bok,' or as you'd say, 'A moment in time.' As with all the scrolls, you can control nothing; they use you to whatever end the Divines see fit," he answered.

"Thank you, Paarthurnax. Once again, we are in your debt." Felldir bowed his head.

The dragon spread his wings and, with an enormously powerful leap off the ground, began flapping. The forceful strokes carried him straight up to the sky and into the clouds, leaving them to their journey.

The group looked from the sky to each other as Žaneta stepped closer to the three of them. "Where do we find these scrolls?" she asked without hesitation.

They all looked at each other, and Felldir replied, "Saarthal. The mages have been working on things there, and the scrolls are kept safe with them for now."

Žaneta adjusted her gear, shifting her shield strap off her collar, then stared at him calmly. "So, where is this place?"

"Northwest of Windhelm, over the mountains. But the fastest route would be to travel through the pass north of Lake Yorgrim. Saarthal is northeast from there," he replied.

"Well, what are we waiting for? Let's go!" she urged, looking motivated. Her anticipation rose to the surface as her excitement grew. Not knowing where to go had been her constant nemesis during this journey, but with a clear direction, her drive was hard to contain.

The others agreed, but something was off about their response. It seemed they were holding back information, which piqued Žaneta's curiosity. With the threat of dragons, as well as the other dangers this group had faced so far, Žaneta wondered what could be causing the tension amongst the three of them.

"What aren't you telling me?" she probed, casting her glare back and forth amongst them.

"We won't make it before nightfall. Winter is upon us, and the pass can be treacherous!" Felldir paused, "from the elements as much as anything else!"

"Is there a better way?" she snapped.

He thought for a moment. "Nothing that would get us there quicker." The others looked at him.

"Then why are we standing around?" she asked, giving them a determined nod as she turned north. They knew their destination and were well aware of the dangers between here and there—but it changed nothing.

As they traveled north, they eventually came within sight of Windhelm and the stone bridge that lay before it. But they took the path across the Darkwater River and followed it until they crossed north, over the Yorgrim River. The path curved west and followed near the river and its waterfalls, but as the river grew in width, opening to Lake Yorgrim, the road twisted north through the mountains.

They reached the Wayward Pass at nightfall, just as Felldir had said. From there, temperatures began to drop substantially.

As it grew dark, Hakon asked Žaneta, "You can see at night… yes?"

"I can."

"Good—you'll be our eyes through the pass. If we don't have to use torches or fire, we can get through unnoticed," he said, hinting at the unknown, lurking threats that could be near.

She nodded—by now, she understood nothing was without risk.

Not wanting to gamble with any of their lives, she tread carefully through the mountains, keeping watch on the cliffs and outcrops. They walked up the pass with the cold sinking into their bones, causing the four of them to move slower as the wind picked up. The snow stung Žaneta's eyes as she peered into the dark, but she considered it a blessing. If continuing through the pass was this harsh, being attacked was far less likely. To stay together, the group grabbed the garb of the person in front of them as they pressed forward.

Frostbite and numb hands and feet nearly made them stop, but still, Žaneta pulled them along.

"Keep going!" she hollered through the raging wind. "I'll take care of us when we're through!" And from what she could see, they almost were.

The northern mouth of the pass was just ahead, barely half a mile away. As they broke out of the pass onto the icy, snow-covered lands of the Winterhold region, the wind and snow died down significantly. The passage through the mountains funneled the weather into a violent, narrow bottleneck, but out in the open clearing beyond, you'd never know it. They stood panting in the calm, chill air and dusted the snow from their faces and bodies, shivering.

"Aside from your f-fur, you're the o-only one… w-with any color left in their face, Žaneta!" Hakon chattered from the frigid cold as the light from Žaneta's magic began to glow.

"Ahh… I can feel my hands again." Gormlaith sighed in relief. "I'd take you on every journey… for selfish reasons, of course," she elaborated with a peaceful smile, basking in the healing energy.

Žaneta nodded and closed her hands, and the shroud of darkness returned. After their eyes adjusted to the light, the sight of the night's sky and stars were beautiful to behold. The blanket of white on the ground enhanced their sight, and feeling restored, they started walking, continuing northeast from the pass. Since they could all see the ground in front of them, being led in the dark wasn't as much of a necessity.

"I'll take the lead. We'll want to follow close to the northern face of these mountains for a while. There are uncrossable breaks in the ice over the land up here. We'll have to go around!" Hakon told Žaneta since she was unfamiliar with the area.

She gave him a teasing smile.

"Don't even think about it! Uncrossable breaks, I said." He smirked at her. "I won't be flung through the air anymore… Thank you very much!"

Žaneta shook her head, still smiling. "I didn't say a word."

The two laughed a little, and Gormlaith stared at them. "What are you talking about?"

Hakon chuckled. "I'll tell you another time."

***

Farther to the north, the city of Saarthal was busy with research. The once great capital now lay in ruins after the war between the Snow Elves and humans, but it was teeming with a magical energy the mages had been investigating ever since. Nord soldiers took shifts walking the grounds in pairs, and two more were posted at the main door. The guards stood casually talking with one another as the group of four travelers walked down the wooden plank staircase toward them.

The guards drew their swords, and one hollered, "Who goes there? Show yourselves!"

The group walked into the light of the torches, revealing their—mostly—familiar faces.

"Hakon!" the guard said in surprise, sheathing his sword. The other guard followed suit, putting away his weapon, but they stared at Žaneta.

"It's okay… I'm used to it," she said, giving them a stoic nod.

"Umm… we need to go through, good sirs!" Felldir said, motioning past them.

"Of course, sir." One guard nodded and knocked on the door, shouting, "Bronsen! Open up!"

Žaneta heard the door unlock from the inside, and both guards stepped out of the way as Felldir strode forward and pushed it open. The men never took their eyes off Žaneta as she walked past them, followed by Gormlaith.

"You're embarrassing yourselves!" Gormlaith whispered to the pair, then she closed the door behind her.

Inside, a guard standing by the wall let them pass to the descending stairs and through the cave-like tunnel sloping downward. Carvings on the walls displayed the Nordic architecture and heritage in great detail, and at the bottom of the stairs, the tunnel opened up to a large multileveled room. A huge decorative pillar stood like a totem at the center of the room, and a stone slab ramp corkscrewed along the wall, providing access to the ground floor below with two doors leading to other areas.

Felldir led them down the winding ramp then straight across a wooden plank to a gated door in the uppermost part of the room. The plank creaked under Žaneta's weight, but it was sound and, thankfully, didn't break. Everything seemed to be guarded quite well here, keeping individuals from roaming about freely. Behind the gate stood a young Aldmer in gray mage robes, guarding a passage with the only lever to open it behind him. The light-skinned elf watched them closely as they approached.

"Good morning, Felldir. I see you all made a new… friend," he said, raising an eyebrow as he looked at Žaneta.

"Hello, Iachesis. They have you on gate watch? A young Psijic such as yourself should be practicing the arts, not manning a post!" he replied with a smile.

"The halls beyond me are of great importance, as you are aware. Besides, it affords me plenty of time to go over my studies. Are you expected?" Iachesis inquired, opening the gate without receiving an answer.

"No. But Paarthurnax said we should look over one of the scrolls. Is Brynneth in the study with… it?" Felldir asked.

"Yes. She's been working all night," he replied, watching them with intelligent eyes that followed their progress through the door.

The four of them proceeded through a beautifully intricate set of double doors into a large, empty room that didn't seem to have a purpose. A slope curved up on the right to an entryway through the wall. Beyond it, several lanterns lit a hallway that shared the same carvings and details decorating the main room at the entrance. The hall stood empty, but vibrations could be felt in the floor as they walked through it. At the end of the passage, they turned left and stood in front of another set of double doors.

"Wait 'til you see this!" Gormlaith grinned at Žaneta and motioned for her to enter. Felldir opened the doors, and light surged from the room, emanating from a huge sphere that hovered over a blue concave platform. Both the sphere and platform were covered in strange markings that gave off the same blue light.

As the floating sphere slowly rotated, an Aldmer woman on the other side stood with both hands outstretched, casting some form of magic on it. In fact, she seemed to be drawing energy from it. Her eyes were closed as the group walked around the platform toward her, and as they drew nearer, she spoke. "Not now! Wait for me to finish this!" She strained to concentrate.

A short moment passed, and she completed her practice. The blue, radiant energy left her hands and was absorbed by the sphere, causing the light to die down to a soft glow. The woman turned and removed her hood, revealing somewhat opaque eyes. She wore the same type of robes as Iachesis, but Žaneta could tell she held a substantially higher rank in the Psijic Order. Looking at Žaneta, she squinted somewhat to take in what little details she could see of this stranger before turning her attention to Felldir and the others.

"The Eye has been erupting with mystic properties recently… Have you felt it?" she asked.

Felldir shook his head. "No. Not until just outside." He looked around at the others, who mirrored his interest. "Have you learned anything?"

"Oh, yes! However, it courses with magic that only leaves more questions," she replied, pausing briefly. "You've come for something though, haven't you? I've seen the three of you—a clear image of you all traveling together. But I don't know you," she finished, turning her milky gaze to Žaneta. "In all actuality, you have no aura about you. You don't belong here… do you?" she asked, staring into her eyes.

"No. I don't belong here. I need to get to my time, to my family." She sighed in relief that someone seemed to immediately understand.

"My name's Brynneth. And you are?" she said in a somewhat snobbish manner, but Žaneta could naturally tell this was simply how the woman carried herself. She raised an eyebrow when she spoke, her nose in the air. Her white hair was tucked behind her ears, and her sharp features gave her a somewhat noble appearance.

"Žaneta."

"Well, Žaneta, what have you come here for?"

"We've come here to send me back."

"I think not… Not with this!" Brynneth replied, gesturing to the sphere. "But your expectations may be well-placed. I've spent countless hours researching, and the magic in this place is unlike anywhere else I've experienced. Perhaps I will discover something useful with a little more time."

Felldir looked at Žaneta then back to Brynneth. "We're actually here for the scrolls, Brynneth."

Žaneta watched Brynneth's stare as her gaze drifted away from him, deep in thought. She knew the clouded vision this woman suffered from and the way it came to be—she had seen the same symptoms with the emperor's Moth Priests. She considered her success with restoring the priests' sight and turned toward Brynneth.

"They're on the table behind you. Make sure she knows the risks before using them!" Brynneth said sternly, unconsciously lifting her hand toward her eyes.

Žaneta stepped closer. Brynneth stiffened, and neither said a word. Then Žaneta opened a hand at chest level and started forming the same healing orb of fiery magic she'd used to heal the Moth Priests.

"Hold still," Žaneta said. A moment went by, then she turned to Hakon. "Come closer—I'll return vision to that eye!"

But he didn't move and simply gazed at what she was doing for Brynneth. "I'm okay, Žaneta, thank you!"

Žaneta, though confused by this, was nearly done, and the cloudiness lifted from Brynneth's eyes. "I can see!" she cried, staring around. "Everything's clear!"

Žaneta closed her hand, and Brynneth turned to her, noting her appearance for the first time, and gasped in surprise. Like the others, Žaneta was sure she'd never seen a Khajiit before, and any she may come across in the future would pale in comparison.

"I've had many in our order try to reverse the effects from reading the scrolls, but you did it without any trouble… How? What are you?" she asked.

"I don't know… I just never believed I couldn't," Žaneta replied shortly, shrugging. She considered her abilities were so strong simply because she'd practiced them ever since she was a child; some of her earliest memories were of learning magic. But even she had realized that the more she'd used them of late, the more powerful they'd become. She approached Hakon. "What's wrong?" she asked softly.

He was silent for a moment then took a deep breath. "The day I lost vision in this eye… was the day I lost my son," he explained calmly. "I'll see him again in the next life, but I'll wait for that day."

Žaneta immediately felt her eyes fill with tears. Looking away, she lowered her head, and a couple trickled down the fine fur on the bridge of her nose. His reason resonated deep within her. Feeling empathy for his loss made her think of Tai and Mazira, but she refused to believe their story would have the same ending—no matter what she had to do, they would be returned safely to her. Looking at the sorrow in Hakon's eyes, she respected him even more now that she knew a little of his story. It seemed the group's motivations were one in the same—fighting for family and each other. She wiped her eyes and sniffed, swallowing back her emotions. Nodding at Hakon, she turned to Felldir.

"I'm ready to get back to my family. What do I need to do?"

Felldir and Brynneth walked to the table and opened the decorative gold containers that held the scrolls. They placed the three of them next to each other but kept them closed.

"None of these scrolls have ever 'taken' me anywhere, but after my first attempt with one, my vision was nearly lost. So, I don't know what to expect," Brynneth admitted.

"Let's do what Paarthurnax told us to do—find the scroll marked 'Time.' We just need to find—" Felldir paused, confused. "Brynneth, help me with these. The writing is unfamiliar. What do they say?"

Brynneth scanned along the edge of the scroll. "'*Anar Sil.*' That means 'sunlight,'" Brynneth said, running her finger along the script. She looked at another scroll. "And this one says, '*Akai.*' This is the one I opened—it means 'Dragons.'" She set those two to one side and looked at the third. "This says, '*Tarn*

Lai.' This must be the one… but the word 'Tarn' means 'portal' or 'to go,' and 'Lai' means 'moment.' Since we've ruled out the other two, this must be your option." She picked up the scroll and handed it to Felldir.

"'Moment!' This is the one!" he agreed. He stared down at it as it rested in his hands then walked around the table to Žaneta. "I don't know what will happen, but Paarthurnax said you need to view it. Then we'll see… When you're ready, I'll open it toward you, but remember… reading it can leave you temporarily or permanently blind. However, we've seen you remedy this, so I don't believe it is of any concern." He sighed before taking in his next breath. Growing sad, he stared down and avoided looking into her eyes. "If you do leave from our time, then first I want to thank you!" He reached out a hand to shake hers, holding the scroll under his left arm. "I could not have rallied our people and made it to Hakon without you."

Gormlaith and Hakon approached Felldir's side. "And the dragon would have sealed our fate. Now, I feel like we have a chance against the bastards!" Hakon added.

"Before, we had to fight from a distance and escape to cover—the beasts rarely landed. I agree with Hakon and Felldir; it's been an honor having you with us." Gormlaith half smiled, her way of saying farewell.

Žaneta gazed around at the three of them then nodded—appreciating the sentiment—but feeling as though she was losing time. But she knew it was quite the opposite. She'd helped shape history, or change it, which made her consider, *The gods have a plan I don't understand! But what have my actions affected? Would the future be different without my influence?* She realized she'd not heard of any Khajiit in history linked to this time, place, or circumstances, something she thought crucial to convey. "Don't speak of what I've done here! Your victory need not pertain to me."

Always believing notoriety brought challengers, this situation was no different to Žaneta. If the wrong people ever got wind of a Khajiit's involvement, she might be risking the lives of innocent generations to come from sheer retaliation. Finally, she looked up at them and said, "Open it!"

Apprehensive about its potential power, Felldir slowly raised it in front of her, gripped its rolled edges, and pulled it open. And for them—standing behind it—it was nothing more than Felldir unrolling an ordinary scroll. But for Žaneta, strange markings and words began growing brighter and brighter. She stared at them until it felt like she was looking into the sun, then everything turned white.

Chapter Three

Žaneta stood outside in bright daylight, high atop the rolling foothills at the base of the mountains to her left… in a different time and a very different place. Everywhere she looked, her vision was cloudy and blurred, and none of the others were there with her. She began healing herself by simply closing her eyes. The white became words, fading into markings she could still see, as if they'd been burned into her vision. Slowly, they too began to fade, and while she remained still, concentrating on her efforts, she could hear horses in the distance drawing nearer. Žaneta opened her eyes and could see clearly. Straight ahead of her, miles away, lay the White Gold Tower, and far to the west, she could see the steeple of the Great Chapel of Talos in Bruma.

Then, from the southwest came two horse-drawn carts. Her eyes filled with tears as she released the breath she hadn't realized she'd been holding. Without hesitation, she took off in a sprint.

The carts were moving fast, and the man in Imperial-style armor, Tobias, was relaxing while the driver next to him stayed the course. Žaneta tore down the hill, carrying her sword reversed by its ricasso. She knew how this would end but was still determined to change it.

Tobias saw her coming closer, stirring up dirt and loose rocks a couple hundred yards off to his right, and quickly grabbed the reins from the driver. "Move!" he shouted to the horses, whipping the reins to speed them up.

Žaneta reached flat ground and began turning to the north to intercept them. Her heart ached as she realized how close she was to the children, but she was too far away to reach them or slow them down. Close to sobbing, she screamed, "Tai! Mazira!"

But the horses kept pulling farther away from her—she couldn't catch them.

As she ran up the road, the second cart was coming from behind her just as fast. Moving to the right side of the road, she looked over her left shoulder and gripped her sword with both hands as she jumped and, spinning counterclockwise, slammed the blade down to her left as the cart passed her. Her sword busted through the metal rim around the wagon wheel then into the wooden spokes before it kicked out her blade. She clung to her weapon as she slid on her chest. She eventually rolled to a stop and rose to one knee as she watched the horse carriage.

The back-right wheel began coming apart, and the cart sagged down on its right side as it veered left off the road, tipped over, and landed on its side with a violent crash. The horse on the right was killed from the impact, but on the left, the shaft broke and the heel chain and check line tore loose from the second, allowing it to gallop off, terrified, around the northern part of Bruma.

Žaneta rushed to the overturned cart and stood over the two drivers. As one of the men, a Breton, tried pulling his sword on her while he struggled to stand, she brought her blade down on the both of them. Wasting no further thought on them, she rushed to the rear. She kicked in the wood-paneled door and leaned down to look inside. The precious cargo had been rattled and bruised and were lying on the right side of the cart. But as she brought up her hand and began healing them, they climbed off each other and moved to the back, afraid and unsure of what was happening. After a moment, Žaneta was finished and stood back up.

Reassured the children were all right, she took in a deep breath and let out a sigh. Her heart was pounding as her vision drifted in and out from the tears. *They were right here!* she seethed. But still, she knew her children were alive. She wiped her eyes and sucked down another breath before sprinting toward the Jerall Mountains, in pursuit of the other cart.

***

It was just after midday when the cart pulled into Helgen. The horses grunted and panted as they reached the checkpoint, their first rest since Bruma.

"Captain Tobias," a guard grunted. "Good afternoon, sir!"

Tobias leaned over after handing the reins to the man next to him and asked, "Where's your captain?"

The guard pointed to the tower on his left. "In the office. Shall I get him?"

"No. Tell Captain Rodai there was a Khajiit causing problems to the south. It attacked a carriage on the road outside of Bruma, so I'd pay careful attention and keep watch for any you see up here. Consider it to be *very* hostile—I'd tell your men to kill it! Just report this to your captain," Tobias said. He twisted his expression into one of worry and anxiety, trying to elicit as much concern as possible from the men to spur them to action. He had to get this Khajiit off his tail.

"Yes, sir. Who's he?" the guard asked, gesturing to the man in plain clothes next to Tobias.

"A conscript. My driver. Now mind your post! I'm off to mine in Solitude. Farewell," he said, motioning for his driver to proceed.

The cart left to the north, unchecked due to Tobias's status as an Imperial officer. But since he was the only officer on this trip, it left the other carts—which had been on their way to Kvatch—susceptible to inquiry. Little did he know, all the other carts would soon be recovered.

***

Several hours passed before Žaneta reached the crossroads outside of Helgen. It was far from the freezing temperatures she'd experienced in Winterhold. Taking a moment to shed the layers she wore, she removed the heavy coat and placed it beneath a tree. Summer was upon them, and her regular clothing would more than suffice.

As she approached the city with her letter in hand, she was met by archers and soldiers with spears. "Stay where you are!" one ordered.

"This is odd. Are all travelers met with such a welcome?" she asked blankly as she raised her hands.

"It was reported that a Khajiit attacked a horse carriage on the road, and now you just happen to be here? Mere hours after we were informed? What's in your hand?" the Imperial asked as he slowly approached her, reaching out to take it.

"It's a letter from Emperor Uriel. I spoke with him about certain events that have taken place, and I'm here on his behalf, as well as my children's," she said, slowly meeting his eyes.

The soldier, frozen for a moment by her gaze, read over the letter. His brow steadily furrowed in disbelief before he folded it and handed it back. "Lower your weapons!" he ordered his men. "My lady, I apologize. I'm Captain Rodai. Earlier, one of our Legion Captains, Tobias, told us of a hostile Khajiit along the road south of here before he passed through the city. What is this all about?"

Žaneta lowered her hands and put the letter back in her satchel. "This captain… was he on a cart?"

"Yes. Why?" he asked, his curiosity growing.

Her misty eyes were full of pain as she stared into his. "Then no one saw its contents, or you wouldn't be asking why!"

"No. My men reported it was an enclosed transport!" He raised an eyebrow and looked at his men, who nodded.

Žaneta watched the guards then looked back at him. "I know. I stopped one outside of Bruma and discovered the contents of two more in Kvatch—*eighteen* stolen children thus far, Captain! And Captain Tobias, was it? Just rode through your command with six more. Two of them are mine!" she cried, glaring at them. Before, she'd only known his name was Tobias—she had no idea he was an Imperial officer. Until now.

"Son of a bitch!" Rodai growled, rounding on one of his men. "Spread the word. Send out riders! I want the message to every city and fort. If they see Tobias, arrest him immediately. The bastard said he was going to Solitude… so let's tighten the noose. If he tries to take a crap, I want him doing it on the run!" he seethed.

"Yes, sir!" the soldier barked before running inside to pass the message.

"I need a horse, Captain!" Žaneta said quickly.

"Yes, ma'am!" He snapped to and looked up at one of his men on the gate walkway. "Archer, bring my horse around!"

The man nodded and rushed toward the stables. As he left, Captain Rodai turned to Žaneta. "I'm glad you came in with that letter in your hand instead of your sword. Tobias told my men about you, so we'd kill you for him. We're all in this now—we'll get him! And I'm sorry, I read your name in the letter, but would you do me the honor?" He was trying to sound courteous, but Žaneta could see the terrible news she'd given him was weighing on his conscience. His shoulders slumped, and his brow seemed to be permanently furrowed.

"Žaneta," she replied. Suddenly, two horsemen rode past them swiftly, heading east. She followed them with her eyes.

"They are couriers, Žaneta," Captain Rodai said, following her stare. "The others will leave to the north and west. Nowhere to run!"

"People always have friends, Captain—even the bad ones! I'll feel better when he's been caught. But why not send your men straight to Solitude after him?"

"We need to make sure every fort and city are aware, so he won't be able to lie and cover his tracks, possibly escaping somewhere else. We almost killed you because of his statement, and I don't want it happening again in another city. He said he was going to Solitude, but he probably won't bring the kids with him. Besides, that's probably where you're headed… Am I right?" As he finished speaking, a soldier returned with his horse—a dark brown bay that looked very much like Cyrus's horse, Wedgie.

"Thank you. What's the fastest way to Solitude?" she asked, resetting the stirrups and taking the reins.

"Head north then left when the road splits. Lake Ilinalta will be on your right—just follow the path north around it. Do you have a map?"

"Yes." She stepped into a stirrup and threw her other leg over the horse. She drew her sword to rest it in front of her—at the ready—instead of rolling it up behind her and held it with one hand while she gripped the reins with the other.

"Then you're all set. Just head north after the lake and continue on. You should reach Rorikstead by nightfall." His guilt sat heavy with him, but Žaneta could see the efforts he was making to remedy the situation.

With that, she galloped to the north through Helgen, staring around at the landscape she'd just visited. Even though thousands of years had passed, it looked almost exactly the same. She was dumbfounded at the thought—*a different time!* She would've considered the idea insane if she hadn't just been there and seen it with her own eyes. The landscape did differ slightly with a new air of life about it. Mountain flowers and wildlife were everywhere, but when she'd visited, the cold winter and war offered only emptiness and danger.

***

Far to the northwest, past Lake Ilinalta, Tobias's cart was at the crossroads east of Fort Sungard. "Stop! Give me your hands!" the driver commanded Tai. The young Khajiit boy had made several attempts to free himself and the others from their bindings, and this stop just added to the count. Tai had cut his cords and gag but continued hoping there would be someone around who could help, but whenever the door opened, it was the guards—the children were on their own.

"Give me your hands!" the driver spat. He wrapped the boy's wrists with another cord then extended each finger and cut the tips of his claws off with a knife.

"Where are we?!" Tai hissed, trying to put on his best face and not appear too upset as he stared at Mazira, who looked on helplessly. He was forced not to fight back while Tobias stood next to his sister and the others with his sword drawn. "We're close," the driver said roughly. He re-gagged him and shoved him back into the transport as Tobias forced the rest to climb in and sit. They had all remained terrified throughout the trip, and nothing brought comfort anymore except for the fact that they were still together.

Walking around to the front of the cart, Tobias unlatched the yoke from one of the horses and set it next to the driver's seat where he'd been sitting. Taking the reins of the freed horse, he jumped and threw a leg over its back.

"Get the cart to Riften. I'll return to Solitude. Being required to check in at Helgen slowed us down, but I have to be in the city by morning. They'll need to be fed, but don't stop in Whiterun. See what one of the farmers has for sale along the road, and don't approach the estate until after dark. Now move!" he ordered.

The driver flicked the reins, turning the cart east, while Tobias spun around and set off toward the north.

***

Riding alongside Lake Ilinalta, Žaneta took in the beauty of the mountains towering over it. She knew she was tiring the horse—she'd been riding hard since leaving Helgen. She slowed for a moment then led the horse to water. She dismounted and looked him over. His saddlebags were interesting upon inspection; on the right was a normal flapped bag with gloves and a rope, and on the left was a hard cylinder-shaped container. Letting the horse rest, she opened the container to inspect its contents—it was full of steel broadhead arrows. *Now I just need a bow!* she thought.

Suddenly, she considered how she and Gus were probably somewhere to the south before realizing they hadn't been introduced yet; at this moment, she was still on Davir's ship. This entire situation was so odd.

She stared at the peak of the Throat of the World and the dense cloud cover surrounding it then gathered herself and climbed back on the horse, continuing along the path. Setting a pace that wouldn't exhaust the horse, she rode around the western shore of the lake when, probably a quarter mile ahead of her, she saw another rider galloping quickly. She whipped the reins and leaned forward, tapping her legs against the horse's sides to speed him up. Closing the distance after passing a break in the tree coverage, she could see it appeared to be one of the couriers who had been dispatched earlier. She whistled loudly, gaining the rider's attention. After she caught up, they slowed to a walk beside each other.

"Where have you come from?" Žaneta asked.

"Falkreath. Do you have business?" he answered.

"I was in Helgen with Captain Rodai. You're an acting courier, yes? Your Legion's Captain Tobias is wanted for treason… along with being a piece of shit!" she spat, her lip curling in disgust.

"Yes, ma'am, message received. Where are you headed from here?"

"Rodai told me Rorikstead."

"Okay." He nodded. "About twenty miles ahead of us is a crossroads. You'll go straight through to the north, then it's the first place you'll reach!"

"And where are you headed?" she asked.

"I'll stop at Fort Sungard then head to Markarth—far to the west."

"I'll ride with you 'til the crossroads then," she said, and they spurred their horses into a gallop.

***

Miles away, Tobias had been on the road from Rorikstead for a while after getting food at the Frostfruit Inn. His reward for his payload was sure to be in question—since half of it had been lost. *And why the random ambush near Bruma?* he wondered. *Was it someone looking for the children, after all this time? Or just a thief looking to attack and steal from travelers?* He recalled the Khajiit yelling something but hadn't been able to make it out.

His concern had steadily grown during the ride, and he wasn't able to shake the feeling he was still being followed. All of his trips in the past had been a piece of cake, but this one was proving worrisome. The assault near Bruma was messing with his mind, but he eventually convinced himself it must've been a random attack. He was just being paranoid. He'd eaten and taken his time doing it at the inn, which he hadn't been able to do in weeks, then left the town with enough time to make it to Solitude so he wasn't reprimanded. He needed to be back by first thing in the morning and report in to avoid being over his leave time and declared absent. He traveled light and rode hard, making it to Dragon Bridge by dark.

***

The night was clear, and the sky was dotted with stars. The two moons' outlines, Masser and Secunda, had not even made contact yet when Žaneta finally reached Rorikstead. Before she'd traveled back in time, they had almost been aligned when she was nearing the Imperial City with the children from Kvatch. There were no stables for boarding, just a fenced area with a couple of three-walled shelters in front of the inn, a water trough, and a place to tie off the horse. She dismounted, sheathed her sword, and tied the horse to the hitching rail, looking up at the sky as she patted him.

It's still a couple weeks until my birthday! she thought, staring at the two moons. She'd lost track of the days during her journey, but the lunar alignment confirmed it. And when it did happen, it wouldn't happen again for decades to come, if it did again in her lifetime. Her parents always told her she was special, that the day of her birth was not shared with anyone. And as she grew older, she knew being born on a lunar eclipse meant committing their daughter to a life of servitude to Elsweyr. They wanted her to have a choice. A freedom she was grateful for. She lowered her gaze to the sign on the overhang of the building, which read "Frostfruit Inn." She took the saddle and bags off the horse to set them on the rail, along with the blanket underneath, then walked up the steps and entered. The room held a large, welcoming firepit in its center, chairs and tables against the walls, and the proprietor's counter off to one side.

Being the only tavern for miles in any direction, it was a popular establishment. At the moment, there were only a handful of customers inside having drinks, but it was getting later in the evening, and Žaneta was sure some of them would probably be there 'til early morning. All heads had turned, and the patrons' eyes were fixed on her.

"Dear Talos!" slurred a drunk Nord.

Žaneta, ignoring them, looked at the innkeeper and started toward him. "Welcome to the…" he started, but he was distracted by her unique appearance as well. "I'm sorry, we've had Khajiit through here, but—"

"I know—I'm uncommon," she interrupted softly, placing her hands on the counter. "But I would like something to eat."

Composing himself, he replied, "We've had beef on the smoker all afternoon, and vegetables are in the pot over the fire. A plate's just fifteen Septims."

Žaneta pulled the coins from her bag and laid them on the countertop with an extra five. "And something to drink, please," she added as she settled on a barstool.

The man returned with a plate of food and utensils, brought her a cup of mead, then scooped up the coins. "Do you need a room for the night?" he asked politely.

Žaneta stopped cutting into her meat. "No. But do you have any apples?"

He looked confused about the change of subject for a moment, but nodded and replied, "Aye, I've got apples."

"I'll take a bag, if you'd be so kind—they're for the horse." Taking a bite of her food.

The man smiled. "I see."

Žaneta began stuffing food in her mouth as if short on time, and a few minutes later, the innkeeper came from the basement with a small bag.

"Here you are… There are seven in there," he said, placing the apples on the counter next to her. "That'll be eight for the apples."

Žaneta wiped her mouth and placed ten more coins on the counter. Then she finished her drink and stood to leave. Grabbing the bag of apples, she took a step toward the door then stopped and turned back to the man. "Have you seen any Imperial officers today?"

The innkeeper didn't hesitate. "All the time! We're halfway between everything north and south," he said, clearly oblivious to anything out of the norm.

She'd hoped for a more definitive answer. But knowing the man she was after was established here, it changed nothing. Her destination remained the same.

"Okay, never mind. Good night," she replied, curling her lip.

Once outside, she walked to her horse and fed him apple after apple then stowed the empty burlap sack in the saddlebag. He ate the last one, and she carefully placed the bit back in his mouth and ran her hand across his mane. "You know… I don't even know your name!"

Žaneta walked around to his left side and picked up the saddle blanket from the hitching rail. She was about to throw it on when she heard a distant voice call out in a muffled, unclear growl, "*Kaaadg…!*"

With the high rocks to the west behind her and the inn directly in front of her, she couldn't tell where it came from. She crept around the southern side of the inn to look and listen, but all she could see was the thick tree line on the ridge ahead. To her right were cattle and a small farm, but nothing else.

Turning around, she walked back toward the horse then heard it again—more clearly this time: "*Kaaz!*"

The voice was deep and familiar and was coming from the trees to the east. She turned and started up the hill behind the inn, disappearing into the darkness. The dense fir trees eventually gave way to a rocky clearing; Žaneta could see his eyes before she left the foliage.

"*Kul wah koraav hi…* Good to see you, Žaneta… I knew you'd arrived! I wondered where I'd see you again," he rumbled.

She couldn't believe her eyes. "Paarthurnax! How did you find me?" she asked, shocked.

"When I spoke with you and the others on that day so long ago, you left that moment in time but told me the year from which you came. It has been nearly forty-three hundred years since then, and I see for miles. I've been watching you from the Throat's peak, wondering if it was indeed the *kaaz* I'd met," he answered.

"You stayed here this whole time? Are there others?" Her eyes were wide in question.

"The *dov* have all left… or been killed! After you were gone, Felldir and the others battled for years. It wasn't until they challenged Alduin—and nearly died for it—that they chose to use the scroll you used to banish him to a future time, when, hopefully, we'd be better prepared for him. I've trained others, in secret, to use our Thu'um in preparation for the day he returns… but I continue to wait."

"So, you've gone unnoticed all this time? Who are these 'others?'" she pressed, looking around.

"Over the millennia, they've gone by different names, one secret group or another… But they are all devout in not misusing the power. As for me, I take to the sky at night. I've become accustomed to seeing in the dark, as you do. But I have questions for you as well." He brought his head down closer to her.

Žaneta wasn't sure what she could possibly know that Paarthurnax didn't, but she gave him a respectful nod. "I'd be honored," she replied.

"What have you learned?"

She knit her eyebrows. "I don't understand."

"You traveled on the currents of time, looked upon the Elder Scroll of Time itself, and here you stand with your vision, staring right back at me. You saw the texts, the words—do you remember them?"

She thought for a moment. "I can see them, but I don't know what they mean."

"Perhaps we can determine their meaning together. Start by writing the symbols on the ground in the dirt."

Žaneta picked up a stick and began carving the markings that had been burned into her memory. They spent hours together deciphering their meaning, and Paarthurnax helped put them into a Thu'um she could pronounce. They practiced them over and over in the wilderness. He even taught her other words of power, further developing her arsenal. The power made her feel nearly unstoppable. Like all magic she'd learned, she memorized using simpler phrases, just has her mother had taught her. Yet, it was a difficult art, as all new skills are.

The sound of thunder across the countryside made all creatures in the area suspicious of an approaching storm, but the training continued. At Paarthurnax's request, fire boomed against his armored scales, not injuring him in the slightest. Žaneta couldn't believe she'd made it. A thunderous force pressed against his body, forcing his head to bow while staggering him ever so slightly. Her success lifted her spirits as she spoke the same words Hakon had used against the priest those many years ago. As their training ended, she finished by perfecting her most recently acquired phrase, saving it for last. Before they finished in the wilderness, he appraised her and asked again, sternly this time. "Now… what have you learned? Show me!"

She stood confidently before him and gave her answer.

In an instant, she vanished from his sight, only to reappear next to him with the tip of her sword held to his neck. He slowly turned his gaze to her and met her cunning smile with his own.

Chapter Four

I t was early in the morning on Sundas, and Tobias was on the outskirts of Solitude. No messengers had made it there yet, and he was none the wiser about the information they carried. As far as he knew, all he needed to do was clean up, change clothes, and report to his detail today, like any soldier returning from leave. He'd been away for weeks, and his colleagues were going to have questions about his "time off." He'd lie, and they'd move on, as they always had. Well before dawn, the gates to the city opened as he approached and entered.

***

Like Tobias, Žaneta hadn't slept for some time, and while Tobias was getting ready for work, the sun was rising on her. Leaving Rorikstead on the road north, huge rocks and tall trees lined the path. The rock formations became larger and larger as she descended from the higher elevation to the craggy, rolling landscape surrounded by mountains in the distance.

Ahead lay a small stone bridge that crossed the River Hjaal, and just beyond it were boulders on either side of the road that stood as tall as most houses, with the rocks on the right forming a large hill. The natural rock formations created a narrow pass after the bridge, after which the path followed alongside the river as it flowed north.

This pass was a bottleneck, and she knew it—perfect for anyone laying a trap. She began looking around cautiously but continued riding in a swift gallop. A moment too late, she sensed danger just as she reached the northern half of the bridge. She suddenly heard the *zip* of an arrow. It pierced the horse's right shoulder, startling him. He whinnied in pain, and Žaneta was sent flying out of the saddle. She rolled onto the path, her sword and shield clanging as they crashed against the cobblestone. She jumped to her feet and lunged toward the rocks for cover. Captain Rodai's horse collapsed from the injury and grunted loudly, struggling to breathe.

Žaneta looked left and right, not certain where the arrow had come from—but she knew they'd be working to find a better firing angle. With only her firebolt for a ranged weapon, she knew she'd have to expose herself to lure the archer out. Strapping her shield to her arm, she left her sword sheathed then cast an envelope of fire all over the boulder she stood against. As she turned and sent the blaze in an arch to push back anyone potentially sneaking over or around it, she ran around the left side and raised her shield, scanning the area for her attacker.

She saw two.

With the riverbank behind her, she noticed an archer in the rocks high above the right side of the road, and directly in front of her—about twenty feet away—stood a man with an axe. He was standing with his back to her, watching the path from behind cover. Not wanting to get pinned down again, she drew back her hand, which caused the glow of fire to reveal her position. The archer saw this and quickly loosed an arrow, just as she sent her firebolt and lowered her stance behind her shield. His arrow missed its mark, sticking in the ground behind her, but he was positioned within the rocks. The small space left him unable to move out of the way, and her firebolt burned through him. His lifeless body slumped forward and fell to the ground as Žaneta drew her sword and turned to the other man.

The commotion had gotten his attention, and he started running at her. He swung his axe from over his shoulder, staggering himself in the overpowered attack. Žaneta quickly sidestepped to her left and kicked out her right foot to trip him. He slid in the dirt as he spilled onto his chest, and before he could roll over to get up, he was pinned to the soft soil of the riverbank by her blade. With her sword through his back, she stepped on his shoulder and pulled it out. She rushed back to the bridge to check on the horse. He was lying there suffering, unable to move.

Žaneta pulled out the arrow and placed a hand over the wound to slow the bleeding. She concentrated. There was no noise except for the flow of water as she began healing him. His breathing slowed, and he rolled onto his belly before getting up. She stopped and stepped back, looking at him. He was fine. She smiled and sighed in relief then climbed on his back to continue traveling.

As she picked up the reins, she gave the area a second look. Those men had turned sloppy in a hurry. She wasn't certain if they were here just to rob people or if Tobias had paid them to help slow her down. *Probably just bandits…* she thought. She didn't think there was any way he could know she was on his trail, especially since he'd planned to delay her—or kill her—in Helgen. Then again, she knew where he was, but not who his accomplices were.

Riding north alongside the river, the rocks on both sides of her were remarkably high. *This would be an excellent place for an ambush if archers were along the tops*, she thought, continuing at a gallop.

Noticing the road forked ahead, she stopped to look over her map.

Right led to Morthal—a city located in the dense, cold marshlands of Hjaalmarch, she noted—with Labyrinthian only a short distance to its southeast. *Amazing, I'm so close to that awful place!* she thought.

The road to the right first ran into Fort Snowhawk and continued east—not her path. Left would take her over a bridge to the northwest, across the River Hjaal. After another bridge, eventually she'd head northeast to Solitude. Putting the map away, she tugged the reins to the left and crossed the bridge that led her up the hill on the cobblestone path then to the viewpoint at the top. To her left was the base of the high rocks she had ridden between along the path here. But to the northeast, she could see the coastal city of Solitude in the distance.

It was unmistakable due to the Blue Palace, which sat nestled on the natural rock bridge that connected the adjacent pieces of land and allowed the Karth River's estuary to flow beneath it into the Sea of Ghosts. The palace was inaccessible from the east because of the completely vertical cliffs behind it. She would have to enter from the west.

She'd heard stories about this city, but it was a magnificent sight in person; the books hardly did it justice. Looking toward it, she noticed storm clouds were rolling in from the northwest over the mountains, so she nudged the horse to continue.

A short distance ahead, she approached an ancient-looking bridge that passed over the Karth River. It arched to connect the lands the river divided far below, and the gorge was fed by a waterfall further to the southwest. Six large pillars on both sides created ominous supports for the bridge, but the true marvel was the archway at its center. It held a double-sided dragon skull statue that greeted travelers from both directions.

Žaneta kept the horse at a walk over the bridge then trotted into the small town just beyond it, the name of which—not surprisingly—was Dragon Bridge. It had a tavern and a few homes but was also an outpost for the Legion, based on the Akaviri banners hanging from the building. A post on the corner had a sign pointing north that read, "Solitude," with two others pointing back toward the direction she'd come that read, "Morthal" and "Rorikstead." Her maps were spot on and had been extremely helpful so far. There was no mistaking the huge city, Solitude, to the north.

Pausing briefly, she considered the outpost. She needed to stop here. If Tobias hadn't continued on to Solitude, every outpost needed to be checked, and she didn't exactly know what he looked like. She'd only seen his cart from a distance outside of Bruma, and she'd never glimpsed more than the back of his head. She dismounted from the horse, tied him off, then went inside.

Sitting at a table by the fireplace were three Imperial soldiers. "What can we do for you?" one asked. The other two had stopped talking, and they all gave her their attention.

"Captain Tobias?" she asked, scanning the three men's faces.

"Haven't seen him, but he should be reporting back to the Solitude barracks soon," the guard answered. He paused then looked at the man next to him. "Jerald… isn't he supposed to be back before you go on leave?"

"Aye—I won't be seeing you boys tomorrow!" Jerald replied with a laugh.

The other soldier scowled at him then gave Žaneta a courteous nod. "What's your business with him?"

"He's wanted for kidnapping… and treason! The barracks, you say? Thank you," she growled through gritted teeth, leaving the speechless soldiers behind.

The men sat at the table quietly and looked at each other with serious expressions. "I don't think you'll be getting that leave, Jerald!" one of the guards declared, chuckling darkly.

***

It was near midday, and Žaneta had the horse galloping in a full sprint toward Solitude, which was only a few miles away.

At the palace, it had begun to rain. Captain Tobias was talking with Captain Blackner as they walked through the courtyard then into the receiving hall, where Blackner kept pressing Tobias on his time away, demanding details.

"Where did you go fishing? What did you use?" he probed.

Captain Tobias had been caught in a lie by Blackner once before about fishing and had paid for it since, having to share illustrious falsities time and time again. "Niben Bay. I caught some huge salmon and spadetails!" he replied, scrambling for an answer. All he knew about fishing was what he'd gathered from talking to his coworkers.

"Spadetails! That's a rare find up in the Bay. I don't like being shown up—you're gonna need to mark on my map where you were. I bet you didn't bring any back, did you?" Blackner asked with a suspicious smile.

"Already eaten." Tobias smirked.

"Uh-huh." Blackner pursed his lips and narrowed his eyes. "Well, I'm off then. Falkreath bound for the next few weeks. I might just take the family to do some fishing. But just so you know, the men have been working on their archery skills. And their shield work could use some attention… It's sloppy, and they keep leaving openings in the line. Also, to bring you up on current events, King Thian's marriage to Queen Macalla is less than a month away. Do be sure the royal guards stay in practice—they've gone over their detail every Fredas since you've been gone," Blackner finished, shaking Tobias's hand. "Farewell." With that, he left the receiving hall.

Captain Tobias did a brief walk-through of the palace and stopped by the throne room to greet King Thian, where he stated his return to duty. It was business as usual.

Little did he know, Žaneta was flying up the road. She slowed down as she neared the city; the rain had made the cobblestones slick for horseshoes, and she was too close to start being careless.

High cliffs rose up into the mountains on her left, and the view to her right was of a large valley riddled with ponds and streams in front of the distant mountains beyond them. The open sea lay just beneath Solitude, stretching to the north.

She passed a large guard tower on her right that stood at a turnoff toward the docks down the hill. The secondary gatehouse lay just ahead, and Žaneta was sure the Solitude Legion soldiers always dealt with traffic in the area since they were the main garrison in the region as well as the hold's capital. But her heart skipped a beat when she caught sight of an approaching Imperial officer on horseback up ahead. She was heading straight toward the soldier and wondered for a moment if this could be her man. As she subconsciously tightened her grip on her sword, she maintained a steady appearance on the surface— taking in all his features.

He didn't look scared, just surprised at the Khajiit before him.

"Excuse me, are you with the Legion?" she blurted breathlessly.

"Yes. But I'm on leave currently," he said with a tinge of relief.

"What's your name?" she asked casually, holding her breath as she waited for his response.

"Lucas Blackner… Captain Lucas Blackner. What can I help you with?"

"Is Captain Tobias here?"

"Yes. He just relieved me!" He raised an eyebrow, giving her a curious look.

"Enjoy your time off, Captain!" she said quickly before riding past him.

He shrugged and went on his way, briefly looking back at her over his shoulder.

After passing through the secondary gatehouse, she dismounted and tied the horse to the hitching rail off to the side of the main gate. A guard stood post outside the entrance, and based on Captain Blackner's response, Žaneta knew Rodai's courier obviously hadn't made it there yet.

"Good day!" she called as the rain started pouring harder.

"You're joking!" The guard chuckled, looking up at the dark clouds then back at her.

Žaneta ignored him and continued. "Have you seen Captain Tobias?" She forced a smile.

"Recently? No. But I know he's in because Captain Blackner just left."

"Thank you." She entered the city.

She knew she was being redundant but didn't care; she'd question every soldier she met until Tobias was standing in front of her. Since she'd arrived before the courier, she would deliver the message of his betrayal herself.

Once inside, the large open area narrowed into a street boasting storefronts as well as an inn and tavern. Most of the buildings had jettied upper floors, inviting her to stand in front of the inn's entrance under the cover it provided from the rain. Her fur was soaked, and she cupped her hands around her shoulders and upper arms to squeeze some of the water from them before wringing out her hair. The next building down the street had an overhanging roof, so she hurried toward its shelter and looked out at the city. Straight ahead was an open courtyard with a large well at its center. Surrounding it were merchant and vendor tables, but with this weather, it seemed they'd closed early.

Past the courtyard was a huge archway that connected the tower in the center of town to another equally large tower and windmill along the edge of the city walls. On her left, an Imperial soldier was walking down a switchback ramp that led to Castle Dour.

She approached him. "Excuse me! Where are your barracks? I'm looking for Captain Tobias." She had lifted her shield over her head, using it like an umbrella.

"Up the ramp I just came from. Once up top, walk straight through and you'll see our banner. Our barracks are just inside, down the first set of stairs to your right. But the captain's not there."

"Are you sure?" she asked quickly, lowering her brow.

"Yes, I just came from there. He's probably at the palace."

"Who's second-in-command? Under the captain."

"Senior Lieutenant Juergen. What's the meaning of this?" he asked firmly, growing concerned.

"Please take me to him. I'll explain inside!" she insisted.

"Lieutenant Juergen is a she. Follow me." He turned and led her to Castle Dour.

***

Captain Tobias sat by the window, watching the rain while he ate lunch. He came to this tavern often since it was a straight shot from the Blue Palace and mere feet from the Castle Dour courtyard. As he took a bite, a group of soldiers passed by outside, heading toward the palace—and they were accompanied by a large female Khajiit. He almost choked, gawking at the group until they disappeared from view. Utter fear tore into him. The Khajiit he'd glimpsed in Cyrodiil was now amongst his own soldiers, walking with a purpose. He couldn't fathom how she could possibly be here. He rushed out of the tavern in a panic, leaving his food behind.

Scurrying off toward Castle Dour, he passed by a patrolling soldier who stood at attention. "Good afternoon, Captain!" But Tobias offered no recognition and proceeded down the ramp toward the city entrance. He kept looking back over his shoulder but suddenly heard someone call out from in front of him.

"STOP! Tobias, you are wanted for treason!" It was the courier from Helgen, who'd just entered the city and was standing beside a Solitude soldier.

***

At the palace, Lieutenant Juergen had introduced Žaneta to King Thian and discussed the ordeal, showing him her letter from Emperor Septim.

"Let's get to the bottom of this," he said calmly. "Lieutenant, you're in charge until all our questions have been answered. I don't want any—" He was interrupted by a commotion from the receiving hall.

A soldier came running up the staircase into the throne room. "Sire… Captain Tobias… he killed two guards!" he gasped, while the king stared at him. "One of ours and a soldier from Helgen, then he fled!"

King Thian lowered his forehead onto his fist with a look of disgust and frustration.

"Which direction did he go?" Žaneta demanded.

"Through the main gate—south—on the Helgen soldier's white horse!" he said.

Žaneta didn't waste another breath and briskly strode out of the palace. Outside, she ran toward the entrance to the city and came upon the scene reported of the two murdered soldiers. One wore the Solitude wolf banner over his chest plate, while the other wore the Akaviri Dragon. The courier lay dead in his own blood with a large gash in his neck. Žaneta knelt down and picked up his bow, which was lying by his side. Four Solitude guards stood around the scene, and onlookers from the surrounding businesses stared in shock. Without speaking to anyone, she left through the front doors and rushed to her horse, scrambling onto his back.

***

Some time had passed, and the rain was starting to let up farther south as Tobias fled for his life, riding his stolen horse to the point of exhaustion. He tore through the town of Dragon Bridge, only giving a couple of people a brief glimpse of him before he galloped over the bridge then east toward Morthal.

Žaneta, still en route to Dragon Bridge, kept up a break-neck pace as well, glancing at any small trails off the road he could have ducked into. They showed no fresh tracks, so she pressed on, her eyes constantly scanning the area to make sure she didn't miss anything.

Once in Dragon Bridge, she approached one of the soldiers she'd spoken with before. He didn't even wait for her to stop and was already yelling at her and pointing. "East! Toward Morthal!"

Žaneta dug her feet into the horse and snapped the reins to pick up speed as she tore over the bridge. After crossing, she found tracks Tobias had left behind in the mud off the path to the left. She rode hard across the River Hjaal toward Morthal. As her blood pounded in her ears, she couldn't stop thinking of how, beneath the surface of his false reputation, Tobias was such a vile coward. He'd killed his fellow soldiers and anyone who got in his way, and for what? Money? Money wouldn't save anyone from this. Žaneta always thought past mere single acts of violence, focusing on the motivations and lasting effects that outlived the victims. Soldiers died, but what did they leave behind? Families? Children? The hopes of their soon-to-be mourning parents? Every time she experienced someone's death in all this, her children's faces would spring to mind. Good people, dying for a cause they never knew. The fact that she knew her children were being waged over infuriated her. Tobias knew where the kids were. And she was catching up to him.

***

It was a hard ride east from Dragon Bridge, but Tobias wasn't heading to Morthal. He stopped short at the fort along the road, dismounted from his horse, and smacked its rear so it rode off.

The men at the fort looked like paid mercenaries, only loyal to coin. Archers stood on top of the two towers in front, one on each side of the main gate. They both slowly let down their draws once they saw who was approaching, then one turned and yelled to the others inside, "Open up!"

The heavy double doors creaked open then closed behind Tobias. He entered the main tower and descended the stairs that spiraled from top to bottom of the structure. At the lower level, he passed several mercenaries through the large sleeping quarters, then the dining area. Finally, he climbed up a short staircase and into the main office of the fort. He slammed the door behind him and approached an older, nobly dressed man.

"Captain Tobias! You grace Fort Snowhawk with your presence. To what do I owe the pleasure?" the man greeted him.

Tobias nervously pulled off his gloves and disregarded the man's sarcastic attempt at formalities. "Knock off the manners, Torbens. My time with the Legion is over, and my lucrative trade has fallen apart! Now I'm calling in favors!"

"You—you're in trouble with the Legion?! Then what the hell can I do? My kingdom used to be busy with life, but… people have left and moved on!" Torbens stammered, standing from his seat behind the desk.

"I've paid you enough gold to cover my salary a hundred times over so your men could help me operate in places I otherwise couldn't. I've got a Khajiit on my ass that's been nothing short of catastrophic. You and your men need to deal with her if you ever see her, and I'd say she stands about… eh, I don't know… this tall!" he growled, stretching his hand high over his head.

Torbens burst into laughter. "Tobias, you had me going. What… did you fall into a batch of Skooma?"

"I'm serious," Tobias seethed with a murderous glare. "I didn't get a good look at her the first time when she destroyed one of my transports in Cyrodiil. Now she's got the Legion on me—it's why I fled Solitude."

Torbens became deadly serious. "Who is she? And why does she concern you more than the *entire* Imperial Legion?" He leaned forward with both fists on his desk.

"Look, I don't know who she is… but she's after me. The Legion I can disappear from. After a short time and some money spent, I'd be forgotten. But this Khajiit—she wants something. If it was my cargo, well… it's gone. Bargaining isn't my strong point anyway," he replied, sneering.

Torbens glanced down and shook his head then looked back up at Tobias. "Sure it is, Tobias… You're bargaining right now, trying to make me feel like I owe you." Suddenly, he looked over Tobias's shoulder and yelled, "Guard!"

Tobias looked confused for a moment as one of the mercenaries rushed down the hall. "Yes, sir?" the merc asked.

"Rally your men! Tell them to be on the lookout for a 'larger' Khajiit woman or a force of Legion soldiers—whichever comes knocking!" Torbens instructed.

The guard left and whistled to others outside in the hall to get their attention as he gestured to another guard nearby.

Tobias closed the door and turned back to Torbens.

"There. Does that make you feel better?" Torbens asked sarcastically, plopping down in his chair. "Now, you need to think of a plan to find a new home. Somewhere a little more… Legion-less. If they come around here, my men are scattered across the country working, leaving only around twenty to fight. Hardly enough against a brigade of Legionnaires. You need to disappear."

***

Žaneta was on the road, closer to Tobias than she realized. The temperature cooled as she rode higher into the mountains, and she suddenly came across a white horse walking toward her on the path. It was saddled and slowly finding its way back west as it chewed on shrubs and exposed grass along the side of the road. The long red saddle blanket draped from its sides told her it was the courier's stolen horse. *But where is Tobias?*

From there, she decided to slow her horse down to a walk, paying attention to everything around her. A light dusting of snow lay over the area, and she began to see the edge of a stone tower of a fort, then another tower, and another. She might've passed this place if not for seeing the Helgen horse along the road. Looking closer, she caught sight of the awkward gathering of men guarding its walls, standing at the ready. It was staffed by two archers and three times as many men armed with swords and axes. They were carefully scanning the surrounding area, catching sight of anything that approached. She knew they'd already seen her, and she didn't try to hide, knowing this had to be the place. *Don't make it too obvious, fellas!* she thought. She stayed on the road, matching their stares with her serious gaze.

Žaneta stopped the horse at the turnoff to the stronghold and dismounted. Her sword and shield rested against her side, and her commandeered bow was in her left hand. She hung it on her wrist then turned to open the container of broadhead arrows. Grabbing ten, she walked closer to the front of the fort and slowly came to a stop less than thirty yards away.

The silence was deafening as she looked at the men on the towers—and the walkway connecting them—counting them and preparing herself. She laid the arrows on the ground at her feet and set one on her string. As one, the archers drew back their bows, but to Žaneta, it was almost as if it were happening in slow motion. In that instant, she had a flashback to last night… to Paarthurnax.

They'd gone over the words of power he'd shared, and he helped her decipher what the Time Scroll markings had shown her. She gained knowledge of many things with him, many powerful uses of the Thu'um. She remembered his question: "What have you learned?" He'd asked it with pride, appraising her as she stood before him. "Show me!" he'd challenged her.

Snapping back to reality, her eyes were trained on the archers as she shouted, but they couldn't hear the words; all anyone could hear was the crack of thunder as they left her mouth. *"Tiid-Klo-Ul!"*

The archers had just loosed their arrows, but nothing moved. The men armed with melee weapons also seemed frozen in place. The breeze, motions of the men, even their exhaled breaths, simply hung in the air, nearly inanimate… nearly. She'd slowed time, but it was only temporary. She didn't waste a second.

She shot her arrow at the first man to her left, and after it left the bow, it hung still in the air. Kneeling to grab another arrow, she repeated the motion until she'd sent an arrow at every man on the towers and walkway, leaving her two more to use. She picked them up, moving around her arrows that were slowly flying toward the men, then ran and leaped onto the corner where the right tower met the walkway.

Standing on the walkway above the main gate gave her a great view inside the fort. Three men below her, who looked to be running toward the gate, were at a near standstill. Žaneta sent her last arrows at two of them then drew her hand back and sent a firebolt at the third. The arrows and fire were all suspended just in front of where she'd launched them, moving at a snail's pace as time crept forward. She could see one man rounding the left side of the tower, so she jumped down and ran straight toward him, casting a firebolt about a foot from the side of his head as she passed him.

She reached an entire training yard at the back of the fort where multiple mercenaries were scattered about. She ran to one of the archers on a walkway by the back wall and began pulling arrows from his quiver, shooting them at very close range at the last few targets. She could tell the shout's effects were coming to an end.

Noticing two men who had come from the rear tower entrance, she cast a firebolt at the back of the archer's head next to her then jumped down and ran toward them. Žaneta pulled the sword from the first one's scabbard and ran it through his chest just as time began to speed back into motion. The remaining man sprang into action but ran right into her left forearm. Meanwhile, every person outside simultaneously met their demise. The tower archer's arrow he'd shot at Žaneta found dirt, while he and the other mercenaries caught arrows and firebolts in their heads, necks, chests, and backs... all in one loud, precise second.

But the fight wasn't over. Slowing down time couldn't be done repeatedly, and Žaneta would have to rest a moment before using it again. For now, she'd fight as she always had.

The man she'd clotheslined with her forearm tumbled to the ground as if he'd run into a tree branch. Before he knew what had hit him, Žaneta slammed her foot down on his neck. Unslinging her shield, she quickly strapped it on and went inside.

Only a few men were left alive at the fort, and two ran straight for her from under the stairs that led to the office. They had axes and shields at the ready, and off to her left stood another man, unnoticed as he crouched above her on the wide staircase that led up to the top of the tower. Armed with a bow, he readied an arrow as the two men with axes charged through the gate toward her.

Instantly, they regretted it; they were met by a wall of fire streaming from her hand. It stopped suddenly though, when pain from an arrow lanced through her left thigh, forcing her to stop her cast and stumble back. She looked down at it then up to see where it had come from, just in time to see the archer draw back another arrow and release it.

Žaneta swung her shield up toward him, and his arrow crashed into it and shattered. She quickly lowered the shield and shouted directly at the archer, booming out the thunderous words. *"Fus-Ro-Dah!"*

Immediately, he seemed to have met an invisible, explosive force. His body was thrown into the steps behind him, nearly tearing off his limbs in the process. She'd used the same words as Hakon in Bromjunaar, and they made her ears ring as the deafening blast echoed through the halls.

She reached down and broke off the fletch side of the arrow, and terrible pain shot up her leg as the shaft strained her muscle. Holding her breath, she pulled the rest of the arrow out the back of her leg by its broadhead. She glanced around quickly to ensure no more mercenaries were coming as she began healing herself. But above the gateway she'd just incinerated moments before stood a man staring at her from the top of the stairs. He'd come to investigate the noise in his disgraced Imperial armor and watched as light streamed from her wounds. The gashes steadily closed, and she looked up at him.

A deadly cold chill ran down his spine as Tobias ducked back through the hall and sprinted into the office, barring the door hard behind him. He pushed away from it and stumbled toward the other barred door on the opposite side of the room.

"What are you doing?" Torbens asked quickly, approaching the door Tobias had just locked.

"We have to get outta here! Help me lift the beam!" Tobias muttered, struggling with the bar he didn't realize was pinned in place.

"What are you talking about? What's happening out there?" Torbens said in a rush, gawking at Tobias. "This is the back door—that one'll take you right out front! Is it the Legion?" he pressed, standing dangerously close to the door.

"It's *her!*" Tobias screamed, frantically trying to shove the bar up with his shoulder.

Suddenly, the heavy wooden door exploded, and Torbens was torn to pieces along with it. Bits of his body and the door flew across the room as Tobias slid to the ground, staring at the dust and debris in horror.

Žaneta had shouted her way in. She stepped through, over the remnants, then stoically turned to Tobias with tears in her eyes. Her hands were clenched with rage, and her jaw tensed at the sight of him. She'd been chasing this moment for weeks. All of the anger, all of the heartache, all of the loss now sat with this pathetic man. She wanted nothing more than to deliver his sentence, but first, she needed answers.

His hands trembled as he raised them in surrender, and he slowly and clumsily stood with the door at his back. She walked around the desk, dropping her shield to the ground, then grabbed him by his throat and pinned him against the door. She gripped his sword and tore it from its scabbard, tossing it across the room.

Looking into his eyes, she saw a spark of recognition in his gaze. Her children had caught even his attention, and he now understood exactly who she was.

"They're not here!" he gasped, shaking.

Just hearing him speak was more than enough to ignite her fury, and she suddenly snapped. She slapped her left hand over his mouth and squeezed, releasing her claws. They sank into his cheekbones, and his horrible screams filled the halls of the fort, muffled slightly by her palm over his mouth. He twisted and thrashed, trying to shake her off, but she pulled him from the barred door to open it.

She placed her right shoulder under the beam and stood up forcefully. It cracked and lifted, breaking the wood where the pin had held it in place. Then she calmly opened the door, dragging him out by his face while he held on to her wrist, shrieking with pain.

Žaneta believed he'd tell her anything to save himself, but she craved retribution. This raw anger clashed completely with her core beliefs, but she shoved any hesitant feelings to the side. She ignored the notion to show compassion and was desperate to draw this out for as long as she wanted. She *needed* him to feel the pain she'd suffered. *I'll take him up!* she thought wildly, looking to the staircase on her right. Up the stairs they went, and Tobias struggled to stay on his feet. But once they reached the top, she noticed she could only access the roof by ladder. Her hooks were in, and she could lift him—so up they went.

She gave no attention to his cries. All she could think about was how she'd been searching and searching for her children for too long. And here was the man responsible for their suffering; the knowledge left her numb, immune to his pleas. He was still grasping her wrist, which did next to nothing for the pain, and he almost blacked out from it. Rung by rung, she lugged him along like a heavy sack until she reached the top of the ladder. She quickly hit the latch door above her to open it.

High above the ground, Žaneta stood him up. She let go of his face and grabbed his chest plate, pushing him back to the edge of the tower.

Blood poured down his face and drenched the collar of his shirt beneath his armor. He stood on shaking legs, his breathing labored as he winced from the gaping gashes in his face. He loosely held on to her forearm, trying to balance himself on the edge of the building.

"Don't you dare pass out… I want to talk!" she hissed, bringing up her hand and healing him just enough to close his wounds a little. His grip around her arm tightened as he struggled to remain conscious, and he was steadily becoming more aware of just how deadly his situation was.

Žaneta watched the focus return to his eyes, along with the fear. With a look of disgust, she began speaking to him slowly, hatred dripping from every word. "What did you do with them?"

He didn't respond at first and pursed his lips as he looked down at the ground far below.

"You know… a head start won't hurt if the empire is after you. Now—tell me where they are."

Tobias held on tightly to her arm. She could see the desperation in his eyes, and they both knew he had no other choice but to talk. "The client… he's… he's on an estate outside of Riften. They're all there!" he stuttered, panting, his eyes flicking between the ground and her face.

"A name!" she pressed, raising an eyebrow.

"Octon… Octon Black-Briar. East of Riften," he answered, trembling.

She let out a slow sigh and blinked away the emotions threatening to overtake her before speaking. "I wonder how many families you've ruined. How many lives? But I'm sure you were paid well!" she whispered softly.

She pushed him back farther, holding tightly to his armor. He grasped at her arm even more, his eyes widening in panic.

Bringing her right hand up, she healed him completely. "Do you feel better?" she asked with artificial kindness, but her chilling tone gripped him with fear. "Sandrew said he'd heard, 'Get them to the Briar,' from your friends before he died. I couldn't figure out what it meant…" she said, her eyes filling with tears again.

"Who…? Who's Sandrew?" he stammered.

Žaneta held him over the tower's edge. "My husband," she replied through gritted teeth.

She let him go.

Tobias didn't scream; he only let out a strangled gasp as he fell. He smashed into the ground below, surrounded by dead mercenaries littered around the front gate of the fort.

He lay dead with the rest of them, but Žaneta found she didn't feel good or bad about it. She didn't feel anything… just empty.

Chapter Five

Žaneta had never given into darkness before, had never wished the fires of Oblivion on anyone. Tobias had changed all of that. For a moment, she felt a brief wave of guilt wash over her, but it was only out of consideration for her mother and Lady Mara. Looking down at his corpse and the other dead mercenaries, she knew his deeds had earned him a just reward on whatever hellish plane he found for himself. Her time with him was finished.

It was time to meet this Octon Black-Briar and get her children back.

Žaneta left the roof, retrieved her shield, then walked back to Rodai's horse—who'd wandered a little but not far. She climbed on and considered her options, pulling out her map. The best path looked to be the canyon that cut through Labyrinthian—or Bromjunaar, as she'd experienced it—then to Whiterun and south to Helgen before going to Riften. Not hesitating, she began riding east.

***

By midafternoon, she'd passed the turnoff to Morthal and come to the road south, toward Labyrinthian. Heavy snow swirled along the northern path to the city, but the wind stopped it from becoming too deep. The road snaked its way up the mountain until she finally reached stone staircases zigzagging high up its northern face. The architecture was all too familiar as the stone archways came into view. Once she started up the final staircase near the north entrance of the city, the snow and wind had almost stopped completely.

The natural bowl the city sat in, surrounded by mountains, protected it from the wind. An eerie quiet lay over the place as she looked around then stared ahead to the right. Staggered staircases led up to what used to be the Dragon Cult's temple entrance, and she looked up to the platform where people were sacrificed that night, where the dragon had been killed. Suddenly, a bellowing groan echoed around the buildings, and she could tell there were more than one of these unknown creatures nearby.

Žaneta drew her sword and held it backward in her left hand by its ricasso, her eyes flicking toward the various entryways and dark spaces where anything could be hiding. She motioned the horse forward, faster and faster. She was determined to keep her eyes on the prize. *Get to Riften and get your kids. You can't delve into dungeons and fight monsters all day*, she thought to herself.

However, seconds later, a large, furry, white beast ran on all fours from behind the staircase in front of her. It was a Frost Troll, and Žaneta remembered they were known by the Nords to be violent toward everything, aside from each other. The huge beast rushed right at her. She drew back her right hand then sent her firebolt through the center of the animal's chest, creating an enormous hole. It collapsed and slid toward her.

She continued up the stairs to the southern pass, but when she reached the top, another one was nearly upon her. At a split second's glance, she could see the troll's attention was set on the horse. Žaneta intentionally leaned to the left, falling into the chest of the troll with the point of her sword and driving it in hard. The troll had swiped the left shoulder of the horse before it collided with Žaneta, and the horse was knocked off balance and fell hard on its side, where he lay bleeding profusely.

But the Frost Troll wasn't dead. With the sword sticking out of its back, it seized her, sinking its claws into her arms and shoulders. She let out an excruciating cry as the troll's three eyes stared straight into hers, its salivating mouth open wide. For the first time, she was out-clawed and couldn't kick off with her legs since it could mean losing her arms. Desperate, she drew in a quick breath and shouted, *"Yol-Toor!"* into the open mouth of the troll.

The forceful blast of incinerating fire burned nearly all the flesh from its face and blew off the back of its head. The troll stood there a moment, then its grip slackened, and it dropped to the ground.

She tried reaching down for her sword, which was still stuck fast in the troll, but her injuries were too great—she couldn't grip it. Žaneta knew there were probably more around, and she needed to move. Leaving her sword for now, she looked to the horse. "Not again!" she cried, running to its side.

"Shhh… Don't worry, you've done this before," she soothed, listening to his labored breathing.

But these wounds looked far worse than the ones from last time, and he'd already lost a lot of blood. The only thing keeping him alive was the freezing temperature, which slowed the bleeding.

Žaneta dropped to her knees and began her art. The healing coursed through her arms, back, and shoulders, and she focused, bringing her hands closer together. Light streamed from her injuries like sunbeams through the clouds, and the horse's wounds began to close as the healing orb grew larger. Finally, he rolled off his side and rose from the ground like he had just woken up from a sleep.

Relieved, Žaneta leaned forward with her hands on the ground and her head bowed. "Thank you, gods!" She walked back to the dead troll to reclaim her sword then climbed on her horse and rode quickly south through the pass, away from that dreadful place. As soon as she left, that familiar wind returned, picking up as she rode through the canyon. Whether or not Labyrinthian was the best choice for her travels, it saved her from having to circle back through Rorikstead; she needed to cover as much ground as possible with Riften being so far away in the southeastern part of the country.

Once out of the canyon, she looked at her map again. Heading straight south until she reached the road to Whiterun was the simplest path, so she started on it. The lowlands west of Whiterun were blanketed in rich forest and surrounded by mountains, making for a gorgeous view. The towering trees were a welcomed sight, and her ride was dotted with clearings where huge mammoths slowly grazed. Then came the deer—she'd never seen so many—which simply stared at her as she passed.

She hadn't eaten but planned to reach Whiterun before stopping for food. After a short time, she broke through the tree line and came upon the road to the city, just in front of a large watchtower. Some Imperial soldiers watched her exit onto the path, and she gave them a simple wave of hello as they gawked at her. There were only a handful of men tasked with keeping watch at this outpost. And catching a glimpse of such a large Khajiit was probably the only surprise they'd had all day. As late afternoon approached, she quickened her pace.

The storm that was in Solitude earlier had pushed south; the sun was steadily blocked by dark clouds, and the breeze smelled of rain. Heavy clouds to the northwest brought the cooler air—perfect for running the horse—but Žaneta didn't feel like being out in it after dark.

Nearly half an hour had passed, and raindrops were pelting the roof of the Whiterun Stables as the ostler pitchforked hay for the horses. Žaneta trotted up on her horse and dismounted, leading him under shelter to see about boarding for the night. After making arrangements, she proceeded into the city to find herself a room. Before entering, however, she met two of the hold's guards by the front gate.

"Well, you're a different one, aren't you? Did you come in with a caravan?" one asked rudely.

"No, I'm not with a caravan. One of your captains kidnapped my children, and I've traveled to Skyrim to get them back," she said evenly, glaring at him.

"Oh! You're the one here from Cyrodiil? Captain Rodai's messenger was here yesterday." He gulped and shifted uncomfortably. "Sorry for the mix-up. We've just had bad experiences with the Khajiit that've come through… mostly with Skooma or theft."

Žaneta was silent, but her eyes said it all—she didn't have any patience for this nonsense. She changed the subject. "I'm just looking for a room for the night. Will that be a problem here?" she asked, unamused.

"Try the Huntsman's Hearth, straight ahead on your left when you go in," he replied quickly. He hurried to open the door for her.

As she entered, evening was closing in, and the city guards were lighting the street lanterns while the rain began to pour down harder. Whiterun was a small, well-maintained community with a rich history. For Žaneta, this city held more importance than she could possibly explain. What seemed like only yesterday, she'd been here with Felldir, Gormlaith, and Hakon, celebrating their victory over the Blood Dragon. It was surreal as she walked down streets that hadn't existed all those years ago. She would never forget that place, which only shared the mead hall—Jorrvaskr—and the Skyforge with the present city.

She would have liked to see what had changed, but perhaps she would have the chance another time. For now, she wanted to sleep and move on as soon as possible in the morning.

Žaneta climbed up the steps next to a sign that read, "The Huntsman's Hearth" and entered. Behind the counter sat a Bosmer man who looked to be half asleep. As she walked in, he jolted awake and smiled at her, excited to have a customer.

"Welcome! How may I be of service?" he asked, standing.

Bosmer were the Wood Elves originally from Valenwood, just west of Elsweyr. Since their countries were neighbors, Khajiit and Bosmer saw each other often, but he'd never seen one that was so much taller than a Nord. And he was short—even for a Bosmer—only standing about five feet tall.

"I'd like a room for the night…" She smiled down at the man, thinking he had to be shorter than Tai. "And is there anything on the menu?"

"I caught some salmon from the river earlier. I don't have many food options, but I'd be willing to cook you some," he said politely. "They're on ice, and it wouldn't take me long to whip something up for you."

Žaneta was relieved by his offer, not wanting to have to go looking for something at this time of night. "I'll take two of your fish and whatever you have to go along with it! And do you have something to drink besides mead or beer?" She wasn't cheered by the thought of only alcohol.

"Water or wine?" he asked with a smile.

"How about a cup of both?" She placed a small diamond on the counter.

His eyes grew wide; Žaneta knew its value was much more than he'd charge for a room and dinner. "I-I don't have change for that!" he stammered.

"And this is the only use I have for it!" she insisted. "In my travels, I've paid attention to the people who've offered their kindness before payment." She spoke with conviction then turned away and sat down at a small table against the wall.

The innkeeper stood there a moment, analyzing her and considering her story with a shocked gaze. He gently picked up the diamond and went back to his kitchen to get to work. A short time later, he brought her a glass of water and red wine. She gulped down the water without taking a breath then sipped the wine.

While waiting on her food, she thought back to the last time she'd written in her journal. She'd been in the Imperial City and knew there was no way she'd covered everything that had happened. She began writing, trying to catch up.

After a while, she was distracted by the smell of salmon and steamed vegetables with bread and butter. She turned toward the kitchen right as the barkeep came out. She gave him a pleased smile as he placed the plate down along with a small towel and fork. Then he gave her some privacy while she ate, only interrupting a second time to refill her water. After she was full, she finished writing in her journal, leaving plenty of room for her next entry, then approached the clerk.

"Where will I be staying for the evening?" she asked. She was exhausted, and it was starting to show. She stretched out her shoulders then rubbed her hands down her face before resting them on her hips.

"Follow me." He set down the broom he was using, led her upstairs to a large bedroom, and showed her inside. She looked around at the accommodations then turned and thanked him.

"If you need anything, just let me know!" he said kindly, closing the door behind him.

Žaneta lowered her shield to the floor then removed her sword and leaned it against the wall beside the bed. After taking off her satchel, along with her leg and arm plates, she kneeled and prayed, resting her head on her hands.

"Thank you, Lady Mara, for the blessings you've shown me. Help me to be confident and command the respect of others while also being respectful in return. Help me choose wisely and be blessed through the choices I do make. I am sorry for what I'm about to do… but please keep me safe and strengthen my children's spirits. I am coming."

She'd said the same prayer to herself for years, adding the last part due to the circumstances. Now more than ever, she knew she needed all the luck and gods' good graces that could be afforded.

All during dinner, she'd thought about tomorrow, how important a wise plan would be. Should she kill everyone? Or would there be a mix of slaves that could be mistaken for threats? Should she call on the Legion for support? Or would their involvement turn slaves into hostages?

She knew she needed to lay eyes on the estate before determining how to proceed. If she could get her hands on Octon before making a commotion, she'd have the head of the snake. Her mind was racing, but she needed to stop thinking about the "what ifs." One major comfort came with her newfound influence over time. Thanks to that, Žaneta's worry slowly melted away, but not enough to cause arrogance. She couldn't use the shout often since she had to rest her voice in between. And she couldn't truly control tomorrow's outcome, an uncertainty that had nagged at her since she was a child.

Her father had once said, "Failing others is impossible to live with if it occurs when you aren't giving everything!" These children, including her own, were depending on whatever she decided to do. *No mistakes!* she thought.

***

Far away in the dining room of a large house sat a brawny, dark-bearded Nord with a shaved head. His wife was next to him, and they were accompanied by two guards. While eating dinner, they heard the front door open then slam shut, followed by the sound of quick footsteps. The Nord stiffened, waiting to see who was interrupting their dinner, as one of his men entered.

The guard rounded the doorway and approached him, a look of concern etched on his face.

"My lord, our people in Riften have reported that a Legion courier came through telling soldiers to be on the lookout for Tobias and the cart of children. We've not heard from Tobias, and no scouts report having seen him!" the man stated.

The Nord slammed his hand down on the table, and everyone fell silent. He ground his teeth, glaring at the messenger. "Put a man on that cart and tell him to ride as far north as he pleases. Fill it with hay, food—hell… anything! Then ditch it anywhere he sees fit, just far from here. Tell him to say he's a merchant or something if asked, but *get rid of it!*" the Nord barked.

"Yes, Mr. Black-Briar." The guard turned to exit but paused.

"What else?" Octon asked impatiently.

"Yes, uh… one more thing…" he started, turning to Octon. "One of our people from Helgen said the day couriers left the fort… a Khajiit woman had come through with a letter from the empire. Said she was… 'unique.' With two different colored eyes."

Octon looked down at his plate and ran his hand over his head, reflecting on the children he'd seen downstairs. He recalled the "uniqueness" he'd seen in their eyes—an exotic investment that was now proving detrimental to his own home.

"Hire a local—a Khajiit. Tell them the job is as a night watchman. If anyone finds their way around to us, I want to know they're coming!" he ordered, glaring up at the messenger.

"Yes, sir." He nodded and left to carry out his orders.

Octon turned back to his dinner and could see his wife looking at him. She was well aware of his affairs; after all, this was just one facet of several activities the family was involved in.

"I don't want to hear it!" he grumbled, feeling her stare pressing into him as he took a bite. "Nothing we haven't buried before. Just give this time, and it'll all be forgotten about!" he callously proclaimed, brushing it away with a wave of his hand.

***

The next morning, Žaneta rose before dawn after struggling through a sleepless night. She started getting ready, brushing her hair, then weaving it into a Nordic crown braid and leaving her bangs down to frame her face. Then she thought to check something before she left Whiterun. She exited the inn, stepping out into the brisk, cool air, and walked east through the city and up a set of stone stairs that led to a tree in the center of a small courtyard. Straight ahead, up multiple levels of stairs, sat the large home of the jarl—a big, beautiful Nordic longhouse called "Dragonsreach."

But she was here for the establishment on her right, a well-built structure still sitting on the hill where it had been thousands of years ago—Jorrvaskr. It looked almost exactly the same as it had then, except it was obvious the wood had been maintained or replaced. *Amazing! It's still completely intact!* she thought as she walked up the stairs for a closer look. With more time to pay attention to its details on this second visit, she noticed the oblong building looked like an upside-down boat hull, with shields hung around its exterior. No one inside would have any knowledge of her presence there thousands of years ago, so she paid her visit then turned and left back the way she'd come.

Žaneta stood near the stables outside the city and looked over her map, reconfirming the best course would be to the south through Helgen. No one but she currently knew about Octon Black-Briar and the location of the children, so making the Legion aware should be done in case the worst might happen. Also, she had a horse she needed to return to its owner—she wanted to thank Captain Rodai personally for it.

She'd paid the ostler last night for boarding, so she saddled the horse and made ready to leave at dawn without waking anyone. Riding east just south of the city, she passed by a few homes and farms along the road until she came to the White River and turned onto the southern path before crossing it. The Throat of the World was just to her left, and its base was enormous, spanning many miles; few travelers could manage the entire distance in a single day. But the path she was following led up the hillside toward the Jerall Mountains with the river running parallel to it farther below and waterfalls interspersed along the way.

A stone bridge crossed the river up ahead, and the path continued on its eastern bank, leading directly into a small town with a lumber mill by the water. It was only a short ride from Whiterun and sat nestled between steep mountains on its eastern and western sides, which were divided by the White River. The Throat of the World's base stood against the city's eastern wall. Aside from the few townsfolk standing watch on the walkways above the road, the town was mostly still asleep. Žaneta rode through it in under a couple of minutes and continued south toward Helgen.

She came to a fork in the road and recognized where she was—two days ago, she'd taken a left here from Helgen and rode along the banks of Lake Ilinalta. Now, Morndas morning, she had come full circle. She turned left up toward Helgen and into the northern face of the Jerall Mountains.

It was light outside, but the sunrise wouldn't be seen for hours due to the mountains. Captain Rodai was dressing in his quarters and getting prepared for his duties. He left his room and walked to the tower office to look over records. He'd still been waiting for reports from two of his riders regarding Tobias, but their assigned paths were the farthest away—Solitude and Winterhold.

Walking to the office, he saw one of his soldiers leading his horse to the stables. "Sergeant!" he hollered, causing the soldier to stop. "When was Mace returned? And where's his rider?" he asked loudly as he strode briskly toward him.

"So *that's* his name!" Žaneta said. She grinned as she walked to Rodai's side. "I forgot to ask you before I left."

He gestured for the soldier to proceed and gave Žaneta a firm handshake. "So, where's our man?"

Žaneta didn't hesitate. "Dead. At Fort Snowhawk with several mercenaries. He killed a Solitude guard and another… I'm sorry, but I think he was your soldier," she explained reluctantly, bowing her head in condolence.

"Shit." His face fell as he glanced at the ground. "I'll have to tell his wife… All this by one of our own. I'll send men to Solitude to collect Jorvis. Damn shame!" He shook his head.

"I took his bow, Captain, and used some of your arrows from the saddle carrier. But you can get them back if you'd like—they're stuck in some of the men at Fort Snowhawk," she said, breaking his focus from the loss of his soldier. "Also, I wanted to let you know—your horse saved my life… more than once!" Giving him a soft smile.

Captain Rodai chuckled. "He's full of piss and vinegar, that one! Thanks for taking care of him. You should consider investing in a good horse, especially in this country!" he replied, gesturing to the vast terrain.

"Ah yes, I have one—Gus. He's in Cyrodiil. I didn't have time to go back for him while I was chasing after Tobias. The whole situation is sort of… strange. But I know where to find him come this next Morndas!" she said, deciding it best to leave out the mind-blowing details. She got back to the matter at hand. "But another thing I need to discuss is what Tobias told me. The transport carrying the children was taken to a buyer near Riften. Octon Black-Briar… Have you heard of him?"

"You've got to be kidding me! This just became ridiculous." He groaned as he crossed his arms and scowled.

"Why? Who is he?" she asked, narrowing her eyes and leaning closer.

"He owns all the meaderies in the entire southeast and has political ties throughout the region. I don't think we did you any favors spreading the word about Tobias… It probably just alerted him the cart was being looked for. I can't believe this!" He paced back and forth, his hands resting on his hips. "I mean… he'll probably make more this year than the empire does on taxes and trade deals. What would drive someone like him to pull this crap? Are you sure you heard right?"

"Octon Black-Briar, on an estate east of Riften. It was very clear!" she confirmed. She didn't care to try and understand why evil men do evil things—she was just ready to get going. "Keep it quiet for now; I'll go see him by myself—"

"You can't go alone!" Rodai interrupted. "He's got a dozen men up there for his family's security, and if he's spooked, Žaneta, those kids will disappear!"

"That's why I'll go alone! They'll never see me coming. If the Legion is seen looking around, those kids… *my* kids… I'll go alone," she said, remaining calm but struggling to keep the tremor from her voice.

He motioned for her to follow him to the side of the nearest building, keeping his voice down. She squinted at the gesture then glanced back and forth to see if anyone was watching. This sudden switch to secrecy made her wary.

"Žaneta, if you make it to Octon, you'll have to kill him. He'd never see jail for this, and you and your family would be on the run for the rest of your lives," he whispered fiercely.

The statement rang true with her, and it didn't change what she already had planned. She'd decided in her heart, probably from the first day of her journey, that she wasn't going to leave those responsible for her family's suffering alive. She could never have imagined the twists and turns she'd face on this adventure. How could she have? But there was no hiding her intentions. She agreed with Rodai's words, knowing his warning was her family's only way out of this nightmare.

"After this is over, I mean to head south with my children. The other kids were from Vvardenfell and who knows where else, but they'll need to be taken back to the Imperial City so they can find a place for them… or get them home. Captain Matius was doing this for the children there. But I need to visit Octon, and when I'm done… I'm gone," she said seriously, walking back out into the open. "Now, you said, 'up there…' I know his place is east of Riften. Is there anything else you can tell me about it?"

"Not really. It looks like a big home, but it's at the top of a hill by the mountains. Watch the woods around the area—I don't really know how many men he has!" he informed her, his eyes full of concern.

"Then it doesn't sound like he can escape if he's holed up there!" She smirked.

He chuckled and shook his head. "You sound pretty sure of yourself. When are you leaving?"

"Now. What other choice is there? Waiting was forced on me once, and I know where they are now. I'll leave as soon as I get some food and supplies. Where's the smith here?" she asked, glancing around.

Captain Rodai smirked and disregarded the question. He wasn't about to let her pay for anything. "Follow me." He chuckled, leading her to his barrack's armory by way of the pantry.

Standing by shelves and tables of food, he pointed at the fruits and salt-cured meats. "Take what you want. Here… use this." He handed her a burlap sack.

Žaneta placed a couple pounds of dried meat inside, along with fruit and sweet rolls, then walked over to two large drums that were both tapped with spouts. "What's in these?" she asked, looking back at him.

"Water."

She pulled out her drinking bladder—which was bone dry—filled it, then drank a little and filled it some more.

Next, the captain led her to the armory. It was stocked with swords, shields, axes, maces, war hammers, spears, bows, and arrows. She walked straight to a quiver hanging next to several others, all full of broadhead arrows, took one, then grabbed an Imperial bow and looked at Captain Rodai.

"Is that all you want?" He looked surprised.

She shrugged. "Yep."

At first, he wasn't sure if she was serious. "You baffle me. You wear no armor, except for your shield, wrists, and shins… and you leave here—from an Imperial armory—with a picnic bag and a bow."

"What else would you take?"

"More men!" he replied with a hint of sarcasm.

Žaneta shook her head, half smiling. She un-slung her shield and set it down then put on the quiver so she could grab arrows over her right shoulder. Then she picked up her shield and bow, threw the bag of food over her back, and walked out with Rodai.

Outside, Rodai again offered her a handshake, so she stowed the bow under her left arm and took his hand. "If I do not return by next Morndas… ride south and inform the emperor about Octon," she stated gravely, as if saying goodbye.

"Good hunting!" he said, concern creeping through his calm façade.

She shifted her bow into her right hand and headed east on foot—it was time to find this Octon Black-Briar.

Chapter Six

eading through the pass leading to the Rift—a large region of Skyrim's southeast and home to the city of Riften—Žaneta traveled between enormous mountains. The Throat of the World was to her left, while to her south, the Jerall Mountains lined the border to Cyrodiil. The rising sun allowed scattered light to stream between the high rocks of the pass, but the switchbacks and natural sunblock of the cliffs kept the light to a minimum. The wind was frigid through the pass, but Žaneta quickly warmed up as she traveled farther into the lowlands of the Rift, with thick forests surrounding her.

The area was beautiful, filled with trees that matched the colors of autumn even though it was the start of summer. The pines wore their unchanging emerald green, but the other trees had leaves of golden orange that shimmered in the breeze. Along the road, she came across a signpost; pointing back the way she'd come, the sign read "Helgen," with another marked "Whiterun," and pointing east were "Ivarstead" and "Riften."

Žaneta ate some of her dried meat and an apple to settle her hunger then continued her swift pace along the cobblestone road to the east. Nearing the turnoff to Ivarstead, raindrops began falling quicker and quicker until it turned into a downpour. The winding path was an amazing sight, but Žaneta quickly realized the smell of death was nearby.

Ahead lay the corpse of an elk. As she neared it, she could see gashes and bites in its flanks and belly.

"Wolves," she muttered. She wasn't too worried about dealing with the local wildlife but made a mental note to pay attention.

After an hour, another sign on the side of the road showed only one marker pointing east toward Riften. All the other paths would take her farther north into Skyrim, so she knew this was the final stretch. Her adrenaline was pumping at the thought of how near Tai and Mazira were.

The momentary distraction pulled her away from thoughts of wolves and other dangers lying in wait on the road. The rain pelted down on her as she neared the top of the hill. In an instant, an attacker sprung from hiding. The hooded individual jumped from the bushes, but the sound of rustling leaves gave Žaneta enough time to react. She mostly avoided the long dagger by ducking, but it still grazed her left shoulder and cut a hole in the bag of food.

Žaneta turned and threw the bag to the ground; she tossed down her bow and gestured with her hands to welcome the fight. Her attacker crouched into a defensive position.

"Well, come on then!" Žaneta barked. Though empty-handed, she was intimidating.

Her attacker, a Bosmer, examined Žaneta warily and slowly showed her hands as she sheathed her dagger. The young woman was dressed simply in leather pants and a gray fabric tunic with a dark shawl wrap that doubled as a hood. "I'm sorry… my family needs the money!" She spoke quickly, her voice trembling.

Žaneta could see the truth in the hunger in her eyes, and she believed the girl was truly apologetic—but it didn't change the fact that she was hurting innocent people for her gain. "Then try stealing food instead of lives, you fool!" Žaneta hissed. She examined her left shoulder and started healing herself then picked up her bag of food.

"Who are you?" the woman asked, still watching Žaneta with careful eyes.

"No one," she said brusquely. Nevertheless, she took out a small emerald then placed it in the woman's hand. "For your family." She gave her a serious nod then picked up her bow and started back on the road east.

The young woman looked down at the small gemstone, confused, then back up at Žaneta as she rounded a corner on the path, already sprinting away. The woman couldn't believe what had just happened. She attacked this stranger, injured her… and was still shown kindness? She felt a deep curiosity and wanted to know more about this woman. Watching Žaneta speed away up the road, the woman knew she'd never catch her. But she was determined to follow her all the same and took off in pursuit.

***

The rocky formations gave way to mountains on Žaneta's right, and she saw an Imperial-style fort on her left across the Treva River. She wanted to stay out of the Legion's path from this point on unless absolutely necessary, so she decided to stay on the right side of the road, as it was higher in elevation than the fort.

The rain made seeing anything from a distance as difficult as she could've hoped for; this would ideally keep her hidden from scouts and allow for easier passage.

Her children were so close, but she needed to stay fixated on Octon, to remain calm. She was struggling to keep her emotions at bay, so she focused on getting her mind right for a battle that could cost her innocent lives. Slowing her pace briefly to regain control of herself, she pushed her worries away. A major part of her journey had been a mental struggle. She'd battled many enemies and faced the stuff of nightmares, including the Blood Dragon. All enemies she could touch. But in the end, the foe she struggled with the most was her own mind. Doubt, fear, panic... all these emotions would only hold her back. Any hesitation, any stumbling, would be unacceptable. It was imperative that she be calm, strong, and confident when the time came. Thinking again. *No mistakes!*

The thunder crashed through the wilderness, and the sound reminded her of a Thu'um. She could see lightning flash around the hold before every crack of thunder—the storm was getting close.

As the trees thinned along the riverbank, a small isle could be seen in the middle of the river, connected to the land by a strong, well-built stone bridge. It looked more like someone's home or business and was in plain sight. Surely it wasn't Octon's estate... Žaneta hadn't even reached Riften yet. However, with her curiosity growing, she had to give the place a look over. Seeing a high set of rocks on her right, she thought it offered the vantage point she needed to at least observe the property.

Žaneta picked a good spot where she could see over the small trees beside the entrance to the bridge and pulled out her spyglass to survey the island. Men and women were working, with some lifting large containers and moving them inside while others manned the equipment sitting outside. They were brewing mead, and Žaneta thought it could be a business of Octon's. But it obviously wasn't his estate, and she didn't care to waste any more time when she needed to be on her way there—speed was of the essence.

While looking at the property, she suddenly saw the hooded Bosmer woman on the road below, looking back and forth as if searching for something. Žaneta collapsed her spyglass, placed it back into her satchel, then jumped down from the rocks. She followed the woman at a distance and watched, but as the rain began to lighten up, a heavy fog took its place, and seeing clearly became more and more impossible. Žaneta ran to catch up to the woman. "What are you looking for?" she asked loudly, causing her to jump.

The woman spun around and drew her dagger. "By the gods!" She sucked in a deep breath then sheathed it again. "I was looking for you! What are you doing here? People who come to Riften aren't the type who care for others... and they definitely don't give them money. Usually, it's the opposite," she said slowly.

Žaneta scoffed, raising an eyebrow. "Oh, really?" she asked sarcastically.

The woman rubbed the back of her neck. "Yeah, sorry about that..."

Žaneta changed the subject. "Some bastard down here has been stealing kids, and he's responsible for taking mine." She stared at the woman's face, or as much of it as was visible. "Take off your hood," she said calmly.

The Bosmer brought it back, revealing her sandy-blonde, chin-length hair, which she pushed behind one ear. Her amber eyes were a complement to her hair color, and she was young but already had scars—one was on her left cheek. "I'd like to help. Who are you after?" Her eyes gleamed with curiosity.

Žaneta pointed at her with the tip of her bow and shook her head. "I'm not risking anyone else's life on this! Go home."

The Bosmer simply crossed her arms and gestured to the bow. "Well, I bet I'm better with that than you! I know I can help. Who is this person?"

"What's your name?" Žaneta asked softly with a tired expression.

"Talia."

"Well, Talia, go home," she said roughly, walking past her.

Talia turned and rushed to her side, lengthening her stride to keep up. "I'm going to walk around these woods until I find out where you're going!"

"To find Octon Black-Briar," Žaneta barked, resigned.

Talia grabbed her arm to stop her. "Are you joking? That man is so involved around here that no one wants to cross him. It'd cost them their money or their lives—probably both. I know he's into a lot, but you really think—"

"And everyone lets a man like this enjoy air?" she interrupted.

"Yes! Because *they* want to enjoy the air!" Talia replied with a nervous laugh, but Žaneta wasn't amused. "Okay, okay… I get it. But what's your plan?"

"Well, I've never been to the place, but after I've found it, I'll go while it's dark. How well do you see without light?" she asked with a tinge of doubt, raising an eyebrow.

"I don't, but I hear very well," Talia retorted.

"I snuck up on you!" Žaneta pointed out.

"True. But only when you were trying. I heard you the first time, and men in their boots are noisy."

Žaneta paused and thought about her offer. "Do you know where his place is?"

"Yes. It's almost straight east from Riften, with the far side of the property up against the Velothi Mountains," she answered, looking a little anxious.

Žaneta considered the incessant questioning and interest of this Bosmer and thought her help could be of some benefit. But also, if she stumbled around near the estate… she could end up alerting the guards. But this was going to be a problem no matter what Žaneta said—she knew this girl would probably just continue following her. "Okay." She gave her a reluctant, stoic nod. "Lead the way."

Talia smiled, but Žaneta was more concerned for the woman's well-being than her ignorant desire for adventure. The two of them traveled together at a slower pace so Talia could keep up, but it was faster in the long run since Talia knew where they were going.

An hour had passed, and the afternoon was winding down. The fog was thick, and they were only minutes away from Riften.

"Go around the south side of the city—it's more wilderness than the trafficked north gate. Nothing happens there without Octon hearing about it!" Talia instructed.

It was evening when they reached the rocky tree line beyond the south gate of Riften, where only one guard stood posted. They could barely see him through the mist, but he couldn't make out their passing either. With the wildlife that roamed the area at all hours, the guards didn't go chasing after every noise.

Once around the city, Talia led Žaneta along the east road a short distance before pausing and looking around.

"What's wrong?" Žaneta asked.

"Nothing. Hurry, this way… We're losing daylight!" she replied. She took Žaneta off the road and up to the right, where the small mountain they'd traveled alongside offered a good vantage point and trees for cover. She led her to a place that was flat enough to camp for the night.

"Leave your things here and follow me; I'll show you what you've come for," Talia said.

Žaneta set down her bag of food and bow then followed Talia, who motioned for her to venture out a little farther on the rock edge beyond the campsite.

Looking northeast, they were high above the valley's treetops and low-lying fog. "There's his place!" Talia said, glaring at his home and pointing straight at it.

Žaneta pulled out her spyglass and took a closer look. Across the forest-blanketed valley, up in the hills at the base of the mountains, was a small estate. It was too far away for Žaneta to make out anything with certainty. She could only see the roof of a large house and a taller structure behind it. She lowered the scope, and it felt like a huge weight had been lifted. It was the last place to look—she knew her children were there. Looking down and letting out a breath, she was beyond relieved she now knew her destination.

She stepped back over to the flat area and opened her bag, tossing an apple to Talia and grabbing one for herself as well as some of the dried meat. "We'll sleep here then?" she asked.

Talia nodded. "I've stayed here before. It's off the road and away from patrols, but it does get cold at night."

"We can't have any fires… We'd be seen," Žaneta responded, taking a bite of her apple.

"I'll go back to Riften and get us some blankets. It shouldn't take me more than an hour. I've been there enough that nothing would seem out of sorts." She tossed the apple back to Žaneta and returned to the road, jogging toward the city.

The sun was going down, and Žaneta started eating her dried meat while listening to the sounds of the nearby forest as it came alive after dark. There were so many creatures, and most she'd never heard before. She decided to write in her journal and catch up on her pages. If there was anything else she was concerned about besides her children, it was the thought of her story not being told, especially when it came to evil being left unchecked. She thought back to Gunther, remembering his pain after the battle of Bromjunaar. But she'd never forget the gratitude she'd seen in his expression. He took heart in the fact that despite the losses they suffered, some had survived to share their deeds. It struck a nerve now. There were only a couple of people who were aware of her mission, and no one knew the entire story. If she were to die, the idea of being forgotten seemed a terrible fate.

The more she wrote, the more she realized that most, if not all, of the things she'd experienced couldn't be fully expressed through writing. There was a major component always missing that she just couldn't put into the pages—smells. She described the rich pine scent of the trees around her and countless other scenarios where the aromas made the memories come to life. However, she had to end by saying, "Stories don't convey smells."

Time flew by, and she finally finished. But she began worrying about Talia—it had been over an hour. *Had she been stopped and questioned? Could she have reported me to one of Octon's men?* She realized she didn't truly know Talia, but she wanted to give her the benefit of the doubt. Žaneta placed her journal on the bag of food and continued to watch and wait.

Minutes later, she heard someone stumbling up the hill; it was Talia, but she was a bit off course, hiking up a different group of rocks.

"Over here… to your left!" Žaneta whispered loudly, causing Talia to stop and redirect.

"I can't see a damn thing!" she said, chuckling. She was holding a couple of large folded blankets and linen rolls. "Sorry I took a bit. I ate at the tavern then rented a room."

"What…? A room?" Žaneta asked, sure there was more to the story.

"Yeah, all the merchants were closed for the night, so I took linens from a room. But I tipped well!" Talia replied, smiling so widely that Žaneta could see her grin gleaming through the darkness. She laughed.

They covered themselves with the blankets and used the linen rolls as makeshift pillows, settling in for the night. The warmth was comforting.

Tomorrow was a big day, and Talia still had questions. "How old are your kids?" she asked softly.

"They'll be six and ten soon. Both of their birthdays are close together; mine will be coming up in a week or so, actually," Žaneta replied.

"Well, hopefully a happy birthday, then," Talia said. "So, two of them? What are their names?"

"Tai is my oldest. He's gray-patterned, and he has my eyes—both of them do. Mazira is my sweet girl; she looks just like her father, a Redguard," she said, looking up at the sky as patches of heavy fog drifted overhead.

"Really? Where's their father?"

"Dead," Žaneta replied shortly, letting out a slow exhale. Her answer was enough to put an end to Talia's questioning. Žaneta quickly changed the subject. "Get some rest. We have an early day tomorrow." She continued lying there, quietly breathing in the cool air as she stayed awake and thought about the coming morning. She hadn't gone a day without mourning Sandrew, but what she hadn't practiced was talking about it. There was still much to be done, and she wasn't prepared to begin healing yet. First, her children were waiting for her.

***

The area was silent, and nothing seemed to be awake. Hours had passed, and Žaneta had positioned herself against the rocks, looking out over the forest below with Talia asleep in front of her. How had she met someone so determined to help? She did feel a bit guilty for putting the girl at risk. But she wasn't forcing her to stay—on the contrary, Talia had insisted. Žaneta tried not to think about it anymore. However, she knew minds wander when it's late, delving into the "whys" and "whats" that would make her head spin.

Surrounded by the quiet wilderness, her thoughts also drifted to Vvardenfell… to Aryon and Calette. Imagining their faces added to her grief. *Did they make it? Are they safe?* It seemed Red Mountain hadn't erupted, but maybe it would. Aryon's vision had predicted it, and his statement rang clear in her mind: "They're never of what *may* happen, only of what has or will." She remembered looking back at the island from her ship to Cyrodiil, the sound that had come from her home. Even then, she was sure it would be lost, and Captain Matius's testimony led her to understand that it *likely* had been… but to something unnatural. *What could've occurred that caused that fear in his eyes? What is happening on my island?*

She'd uncovered so much evil on her journey. While finding her children was most important to her, trouble was obviously stemming from many lands and causes. She'd learned of dragons and had killed one! And even now, at least one dragon still lived, though the creatures were believed to be gone from the world. Paarthurnax had helped her with her mission, and she would be forever grateful to him for that. She'd also faced the Mythic Dawn in Cyrodiil, seen the demons tormenting the innocent… Their plot still haunted her. And saving the children stuck there, considering the screams heard echoing throughout that hell, brought her a small sense of relief that made her glad she helped where she could. She constantly thanked Lady Mara her children weren't lost in that plane of nightmares. Dwelling on these things, Žaneta still couldn't wrap her mind around how far she'd come. But her focus had always been constant—and now, her children were so close, she could almost see their faces. She tried to relax and noticed light was beginning to creep through the thick fog. It was too dark for others to see, but with her eyes, she knew dawn was coming.

Standing up, she folded her blanket, placed it with her linen roll, then reached over for her bag of food and knotted it closed. Knowing this might very well be her last endeavor in life, she left the journal there to be found. Perhaps someone would tell her story, the adventures of a stranger. If she fell, she didn't want her tale to be lost with her. But if she survived, she would return for it.

Her movement had woken Talia, who stared around in the dark. "What's going on?" she asked, rubbing her eyes and yawning.

"Sunrise is coming—we need to be at Octon's before then," Žaneta said. She sheathed her sword and slung her shield around her other side so it wouldn't clang against her weapon.

"But I can't see anything yet!" Talia replied softly, getting up and pushing her linens into a pile.

"If you can see them, they can see us. We have to be better than that! I'll lead you there, where you'll wait until sunrise, but the fight is going to start before then." Žaneta picked up the bow and quiver. "Here, you carry these." She placed the quiver over Talia's head after removing a few arrows for herself. "Now, let's move." Žaneta started down the rocks slowly to let Talia find her footing.

She could tell Talia's fear was growing as the girl squinted through the darkness while they descended the hill. But Žaneta was impressed with her courage, and Talia steadily calmed as Žaneta led her through the rocks.

***

Another hour passed, and daylight began to steadily creep over the landscape. A black Khajiit sat listening and watching the woods leading up to the Black-Briar estate. He'd been given a cowbell to alert Octon's men if he saw any two-legged threats. Hired no more than a day ago, he thought this would be easy money and probably a waste of time. But he suddenly heard a *snip*, followed by a dull *thud…* then again, and a third time. The fog was too thick to see very far, but something was happening. He leaned forward on the edge of his seat, trying to hear or see anything. He knew there were guards scattered lower in the valley, and as he struggled to identify the source of the sounds, his heart began to race. Then he made out a pair of silhouettes about forty yards in front of him, moving slowly up the hill. In a panic, he took the bell and started hitting it with a rock.

Žaneta and Talia had been found. Žaneta turned and sprinted to the noise, leaving Talia standing there with the bow. The black Khajiit dropped the bell and raised his hands in surrender as she came into view, but she slammed his back against the rocks and picked him up by his throat.

"Please… Ple—se…!" he strained, gasping out the words.

She released him, and he fell to his knees, bracing himself with one hand and holding his throat with the other. "You shit!" she growled through her teeth with tears in her eyes, disgusted to see one of her own working for people like this.

"I'm sorry… they never told me… anything about who was coming. I thought vandals, but you… you look…" he gasped out. He gawked at her. "If I didn't know better, I'd guess you were a Mane!"

"A Mane?! Not interested!" she barked, caught off guard by the comment. *A chosen ruler of Elsweyr? Had her appearance become that obvious to another?* There hadn't been a Mane for over four hundred years. No Khajiit could even recall what one looked like, aside from poor drawings and descriptions in history books, and he didn't know the day of her birth. It wasn't a discussion to be had at the moment. "Those people are keeping my children up there, and you just told them I'm coming. Where are they holding them?" she hissed, pulling him to his feet.

"Children? I haven't been to the house—they just paid me to sit here and keep watch." He rubbed his throat and looked up the hill at the estate.

Lanterns began lighting, signaling to Žaneta and Talia that they'd lost the element of surprise. Any control she had over her emotions dissolved instantly. She ignored the Khajiit and took off toward the house, leaving Talia behind with him. The two of them looked at each other, then Talia began chasing Žaneta, while he—still rubbing his throat—looked down and shook his head, ashamed.

With sword in hand, Žaneta focused on the men who had started sprinting out of the estate—eight of them in total. They were all mercenaries wearing mixed armor, and besides their boots, some still looked dressed for bed. Talia was still out of range as Žaneta drew nearer; the girl was afraid to loose an arrow at this distance in such poor lighting.

Žaneta was tearing up the hill, just a moment away from the men, when Talia stopped and attempted a shot, farther than anything she'd ever tried before. She drew back her arrow and aimed at the man farthest to one side, away from Žaneta. But before she released, there was a loud *crack* in the distance, and Žaneta was gone. Suddenly, all of the men met their deaths at the exact same time. Guards were dismembered, bleeding, or blown aside by what looked like blasts of fire, and the front door had bounced open.

Talia lowered her bow in confusion and scurried up the hill toward them.

Finally, she reached the body littered landscape. She stepped around the ghastly sight cautiously. Body parts were scattered everywhere, but she tried not to look too closely as she neared the house. *What the hell happened here?!*

Moments earlier, Žaneta had announced her arrival with her shout. The men before her saw their fate in the flash of her firebolt. After time had all but stopped for them, she cast a bolt straight into the stare of the first man. Swinging fiercely at two more following him, she claimed their heads. Turning and sweeping across their bodies, she cut through the men like practice mannequins, but tried to end them quickly. She shot another bolt of fire through the remaining two as she passed them on her way to the front door. She kicked it open and flew through to no resistance as time returned to full speed.

In her urgency, she'd only voiced two of the words of power. Though time was slowed, it didn't last as long as she'd hoped. She passed a set of stairs leading down to the basement in the entryway and encountered a guard in the dining room. He challenged her as she walked into the open room then swung his axe, which collided against her shield. Her sword caught his left shoulder and arm—nearly taking it off. He lost his weapon in the process.

She brought the shield back around and hit him straight in the face with the edge, causing him to stagger back as it knocked out several of his teeth and tore his upper lip. Then she spun around and backhanded him with her shield arm, sending him onto his back on the dining room table. Žaneta let her shield fall to the floor and swung it over her head with such force that it sank into his chest.

Yelling ensued from downstairs, immediately pulling her attention back toward the front door, to the descending staircase. Right as she passed through the dining room doorway, she was met by a sword swinging straight at her head from a guard who must've come from the basement. He overshot his aim, and his sword stuck fast in the wood as she ducked beneath it. She came up with her left hand, claws out, and tore across his neck, spraying her and the room with a streak of blood. It spilled onto the floor, and Žaneta stomped through it as she rushed down the stairway.

Downstairs, a guard had turned his attention to the children, trying to keep them from making more noise. "Shut up! Or I'll gut ya!" he spat.

Before he had even finished speaking, Žaneta crept in and struck, holding on to the ricasso and grip of her sword; she drove it through the man and into the beam against the wall, severing whatever ties he had to this world. She took the keys off his belt and the knife from her sword then unlocked the cell some of the children shared.

Žaneta let out a sob at the sight of Tai as she cut him loose. His matted, dirty fur and gaunt cheeks and wrists, along with the filthy clothes he'd been wearing since the day of the attack, spoke volumes about his suffering. "Oh, my love… Where's your sister?" she cried, choking back tears as he threw his arms around her neck.

"A man came in and took her up those stairs!" he said, glancing to his right.

Žaneta froze, blood pounding in her ears. There was no time to waste. "Help them… I'm going to get her!" She gave him the knife and keys. She kissed his forehead and touched hers to his then sprinted up the stairs at the rear of the house.

On the next floor, she saw a woman about to slam a door shut. Žaneta quickly rushed to it and kicked it off its hinges, but Mazira wasn't in there—just Octon's wife and baby.

"Where's Octon?" Žaneta boomed, her gaze as sharp as the blade she'd left downstairs.

"He ran out back with a child!" The woman cowered beside the bed while the baby cried out from its crib.

Žaneta slowly walked closer. "If you ever touch another child, you'll not live to see that one grow!" she said, her voice icy. "Do you hear me?" she yelled. The woman bawled and nodded her head.

Žaneta left the bedroom and went around to the dining room, where the guard lay dead with her shield, then found her exit on the next floor.

Outside, behind the back of the house, Žaneta stood by the rear door. She had no weapons, her shield was inside, and she approached Octon with her hands in plain sight as he backed closer and closer toward the cliff's edge while holding a knife to Mazira's throat.

The innocent child was filthy, her clothes were tattered, and the fear in her lovely eyes made Žaneta's lips quiver. Her vision blurred as her eyes welled with tears, but her focus was fixed on her prize. And with Tai all but rescued inside, Octon was all that stood between her and her family's peace.

"M-Mom!" Mazira whimpered, beginning to sob. Octon pulled her with him by her wrist. Žaneta crept forward slowly. She fought every fiber of her being not to lash out, not to risk Mazira's life.

"You should've never come here! This is only going to end badly for you!" Octon threatened. But fear crept through his calm composure with every step. He held Mazira in front of him like a shield.

"The whole empire knows of you. What do you think will happen next?" Žaneta seethed. She was slightly bluffing, as Captain Rodai was the only one aware of the full story—but Octon didn't have to know that.

"What they know and what they can prove is all in a day's work for me!" he lashed back.

***

Just as Žaneta found Octon and Mazira, Talia came upon the bloody spray coating the ceiling and wall from the dead guard lying near the entryway, with large bloody Khajiit footprints leading down a staircase. Talia followed them and found several children downstairs. They jumped at the sight of her, and a young gray Khajiit boy who was cutting the bindings off another child turned and focused on her. He held his mother's knife poised to strike with misty, exhausted eyes, and—off to her right—a guard hung impaled on the wall by Žaneta's sword. Talia looked at the guard and back at the boy, lowering her bow and raising her right hand. "Tai…? I'm a friend! Where's your mother?" she asked calmly.

Tai started sobbing in relief. "That man took my sister. My mom came in and…" He paused, shuddering out a breath. "She went up after them!"

Talia wanted to stay with the children, but she needed to find Žaneta. "Okay… Stay calm. We'll be back for you all—I promise!" Shocked by all she'd seen, she turned and ran up the back stairs.

On the main floor, she stopped when she heard a baby crying from the bedroom behind her. When she ran inside, she found a Nord woman holding the child. "Please just leave!" the woman cried, trembling at the foot of her bed. "No children, I swear!"

Talia was utterly confused by her words but realized Žaneta must have been here, too. She sprinted back through the dining room, where a dead guard was lying on the table, and finally reached the back of the house. When she exited, she came upon a horrifying scene.

Octon had retreated all the way to the edge of the cliffs. His eyes constantly flicked to the watchtower on his left as he backed out onto a rocky projection with Mazira. But when Žaneta glanced at it, she noticed only the reflection of familiar yellow eyes belonging to the black Khajiit peeking out over the paneled rail to observe her. Her glare met Octon's panicked eyes. If there was some sort of trap he was waiting for, it never came.

"Please… give me back my girl!" Žaneta pleaded with an outstretched hand, stepping closer and closer. She saw his desperation fade, and his shoulders relaxed as his expression turned from worry to acceptance. Žaneta's heart faltered—he'd run out of options.

"I've grown tired of all this!" he grumbled with a hateful snarl, bringing the knife closer to Mazira's jawline.

For that moment, Žaneta's heart stopped. Just like Octon, she'd run out of options, too.

In an instant, an arrow zipped past her head and found its mark in the left side of Octon's chest. In a dizzying second, he dropped the knife and began falling over the edge, pulling Mazira backward. She screamed, her right hand stretched out toward her mother.

Time felt like it had frozen to a stand-still. But it was from the adrenaline pumping through Žaneta's body rather than her words of power.

Žaneta's eyes widened, taking in every detail, from the arrow's fletches that had swept by her hair into Octon, to her teary-eyed daughter pleading for her mother to save her. Before she could take a breath, she sprang into action, her powerful legs showing their full strength as she lunged toward her girl. Her claws dug into the ground as she pushed off. She grabbed Mazira's forearm, and they all began to tumble over the edge together. Žaneta skidded on her chest and dragged her right hand along the rocks, clawing at anything she could snag onto until she finally found an anchor and clung to it.

The sudden jolt of Mazira and Octon's weight made the claws of her left hand shoot out into Mazira's forearm. Mazira's left shoulder was dislocated by the pull of Octon's body, and as Žaneta's claws tore into her right arm, she shrieked.

"I'm sorry!" Žaneta cried through her teeth, wincing as she strained to hold on to her daughter and the edge of the rock with the tips of her claws. But she couldn't move an inch. They hung there for only a brief moment, but the seconds felt like minutes.

Octon turned his stare from the ground far below to Žaneta, then past her. Something else had caught his attention. Another arrow sank into his neck just above his sternum. His eyes rolled back, and his grip loosened as he slid from Mazira's arm and toppled to the rocks below. Žaneta looked up and saw Talia throw the bow to the ground. She grabbed Žaneta's wrist, along with the black Khajiit, and they both heaved the pair to safety.

Žaneta pulled Mazira into her arms and lay there crying and laughing. She let out a long sigh of relief. The emotions she'd shoved away were now finally able to escape, and she didn't hold back. Even so, she couldn't fully express how grateful she was to have her children back. Her daughter in her arms. For a while, she'd felt her soul becoming hard, calloused. But in this moment, it softened. She felt more like herself, like the person she'd been before all of this tragedy and heartache. For the first time since home, she felt peace.

But the poor girl's cries were mixed with happiness and pain. Žaneta gently raised her sobbing daughter to her feet and moved her to safer ground as she knelt to examine her. She reset her shoulder, and Mazira whimpered in pain. Žaneta looked left and saw Tai and some of the other children. They had found their way outside, and Tai was running toward them. Žaneta hugged Mazira and stretched out her arm to pull Tai into her embrace. Tears ran down her face as she smiled and kissed them. Then she pulled back and scanned their faces, memorizing them.

"You're safe now," she whispered. She began healing them all in a sphere of luminescent magic. The group stood silent. Žaneta and her children, the Khajiit, Talia… they were all from different walks of life. But the convergence of their paths had brought hope. With her family reunited, there was a new beginning on the horizon.

The sun had risen on a beautiful day. The view of the landscape had yet to be given the attention it deserved, but with her burden lifted, they could travel wherever home would be… together. The mountainous terrain of Skyrim was majestic and unforgiving, and looking to the Throat of the World, all its people had their reminder when they gazed upon it. A beauty that demanded respect.

High above the land, from within the clouds that covered the mountain's peak, Paarthurnax surfaced and glided on the wind's current. With the sun on the horizon as he circled around, he landed on his mountain, folded his wings, and rested. He'd spent countless hours looking upon his domain from this haven. And despite his wisdom, he could only be patient and prepare others for the fight to come. For now, his secrets were safe… Her secrets were safe… but time has a way of changing things.

Though this should have only been a moment of joy, Žaneta's children had lost their father. The truth of it was nothing she could've said made it any easier as she explained what had happened. Clinging to their mother, they knew what he'd done to prevent this, how he'd sacrificed everything for them. As Žaneta held the two of them in her embrace, she knew she would never let go. They were her entire life. And even though Sandrew was gone, their children were the last pieces of him she had left.

***

Evening came. The black Khajiit walked in front of six children, one of which tagged along beside him and would stop at nothing to fill his ear with conversation. The man had made a friend, and he was all right with that. Talia accompanied three others, who were all snacking on things they'd brought with them in the burlap bag. Žaneta brought up the rear with Mazira on her shoulders, holding Tai's hand as they approached the path into Helgen. After she'd recovered her journal that morning, she and the children had set out for the long journey home, and they'd stop here before heading south.

Žaneta came through the gates last and lowered Mazira to the ground. Soldiers went about their business, oblivious to the events that had transpired. The group walked with Žaneta as she entered the office of the captain's guarded tower, and their appearance distracted him from the papers he poured over on his desk.

"By the Divines! You've only been gone two days!" He stared at the children before him. Two young girls, an Argonian and Orc, two young boys, an Imperial and Dunmer, and a gray Khajiit boy and Redguard girl—the last two looked up at him with their unique eyes. "Care to share the details?" His stare drifted from them to Žaneta's face.

"Directly. But they all need to eat," she replied politely. "Would you be so kind? We can discuss it while they're taken care of."

Captain Rodai half smiled. "Follow me." He gestured to the door behind them then led them to the mess hall. Once inside, he sat them at a table and went to speak with the cook. He brought back a basket of fruit and was followed by the cook, who carried a platter of brisket.

"Dig in, everyone!" He smiled and found a seat close to Žaneta. "What of our man? Negotiations seem to have worked!"

"They worked out just like you said they'd have to," she replied very seriously.

He sat up straighter, and his brow furrowed before he glanced away. "What happened to him? His family? I'll need all the details I can get once his body is recovered." He waited anxiously for her response but kept his tone casual with the present company.

"He threatened the life of my girl with a knife against her throat and is lying dead at the bottom of a cliff behind his estate. These children were all locked in his basement." She briefly glanced at them, then back to the captain. "But his wife and child are fine—left untouched to mourn their loss," she finished coldly with a stare that made even Rodai avert his eyes. "She swore, 'No more children.' I trust you can ensure that from here on. I'll inform the emperor once I return to the city."

His work cut out for him, Rodai wanted to ensure there were no loose ends. "Who are these two?" he asked, turning his stare to the Bosmer and Khajiit.

"I'm Sanza," the Khajiit introduced himself.

"Talia," the girl chimed in.

Rodai squinted. "And how are you two involved?"

"I was hired to watch over the property at night. I was never told anything specific, just to alert the guards if anyone was on the estate," Sanza relayed.

"And I *met* her on the road!" Talia paused. She looked at Žaneta, trusting her to keep her embarrassing secret. "I knew where Octon's estate was and offered to show her. This morning, when we arrived, we got split up. I found Žaneta behind the house confronting Octon while he held the child, like she said."

"And I watched it happen from the guard tower at the back of the property. *Jaji trun di shit!*" Sanza blurted, telling them exactly what he thought of Octon, causing Žaneta to nod in agreement.

"Okay, okay… just in a tongue I understand, please." Rodai shook his head. "Then what happened?"

"He wouldn't be persuaded. Then he caught an arrow… and I caught her," Žaneta stated.

"Well, since I've got all these testimonies and your letter from the emperor himself, as well as the evidence before my eyes…" He paused and looked around at the children. "I think you've made my job easier than anything I've ever done in my career. What do you need from me, my lady?"

Mazira walked up with a piece of fruit and stood quietly beside her mother, who pulled her onto her lap and looked at the captain. "Beds. We will leave Morndas morning." Žaneta smiled softly.

The next day, Talia shook her hand. "Farewell, Žaneta. I hope you find safe travels." Žaneta gave her a respectful nod as Talia continued. "I'm glad we met… even if the circumstances were treacherous at first." She gave her a devious smile before turning and jogging out the eastern gate with a quiver full of arrows and her new bow, back to her family.

Žaneta walked back inside to the children, who were still fast asleep in their bunks, and looked at Tai and Mazira lying next to each other under the same blanket. Her whole life lay in that bed. As if feeling her mother's stare, Mazira began stirring, causing her brother to wake.

She didn't tell the others why they were staying in Helgen for the next few days. She simply told them arrangements had been made and that she would speak with the emperor on Morndas. In fact, on Morndas morning, her past self would be meeting with the Blades for the first time with her sealed letter from Uriel, after having learned about the cart in Bruma the day she was training with Cyrus. She needed to wait to return to Cyrodiil until after that point.

She thought of the meeting with Uriel, the battlemages, and Captain Lex… How he'd told her the Bruma Guards had seen her come down from the mountains. Now she remembered it, having been returned to her time with the Elder Scroll, days before ever meeting any of them. And going back to that land, she wanted to make sure she would've already left when she touched the Mantella stone in Cloud Ruler Temple. Still in awe by the fact, she smirked at the thought of it. Scheduling her days to not run into herself. If a story of influenced time were to be heard by anyone… First, it would be the Blades. When she showed up the same day she'd disappeared, but with the last six children beside her. As impossible as it had once seemed, now she thought back to where she was going to be and planned accordingly.

***

Žaneta walked to the carriage where Captain Rodai stood with Sanza and the children, who were already sitting—clean, happy, and ready to go.

"I'd be honored to join you… if you don't mind. I know the extra hands would serve them well," Sanza offered, looking at the children.

"Do you not have anywhere to be?" she questioned politely, furrowing her brow.

"There's nothing for me in Riften. Taking these little ones back would be a better use of my time."

She gestured to the driver's seat, climbed onto the carriage, then turned to Rodai. "Farewell, Captain."

He raised his hand in a send-off, and they left Helgen behind them.

The morning and afternoon came and went as the carriage trundled down from the Jerall Mountains. Žaneta set foot in Cyrodiil and lowered the children to the ground as they climbed down from the carriage. She took Tai and Mazira by the hands and walked to the clearing where they could see the Imperial City. She looked down at her boy joyfully then at Mazira, who clung to her hand—her sweet girl. At this moment, she could ask for nothing more.

The Imperial City in the distance with its White Gold Tower beckoned to them. Bruma lay just behind them, and since it was Morndas evening, a visit to the Blades was in order. She needed to reunite with Gus.

Staring at the seat of the empire, she watched the four other children run past her as they played happily together, distracted by the beauty of the moment and the future that lay before them. Like them, she planned to seize it with both hands.

Now was her time.

END

ABOUT THE AUTHOR

Adrian L. Zuniga is a Respiratory Therapist, FFL holder, artist, and has been writing fiction and nonfiction since 2006. Along with his stories, he's also written for his specialty in the medical field. He served in the United States Marine Corps and was medically discharged in 1999. After his experience with health problems, he decided to start work in healthcare. He is an active member of his church and his community—supporting charitable causes that promote music education and practice for kids. He resides in Wyoming with his two children.

GALLERY

A Special Thanks to:

Taylor Davis
The Ta'agra Project
Antti Hakosaari
Minttu Hynninen
Madison Darby
Caitlin Reid
Danielle Ozano
James H. Longmore
Lindsey Stirling
Robert Altman

All three stories were written before 2019, and then published in 2020 and at the turn of the New Year. It's been a fantastic journey to have shared, and in such circumstances when their release was uncertain.

I am beyond grateful to everyone who was involved in helping me deliver.

What a journey!

Well done!

www.ingramcontent.com/pod-product-compliance
Lightning Source LLC
Chambersburg PA
CBHW041159300726
48981CB00004B/308